Dead Man Talking

Dead Man Talking

Jonathan Squirrell

The Book Guild Ltd

First published in Great Britain in 2024 by
The Book Guild Ltd
Unit E2 Airfield Business Park,
Harrison Road, Market Harborough,
Leicestershire. LE16 7UL
Tel: 0116 2792299
www.bookguild.co.uk
Email: info@bookguild.co.uk
Twitter: @bookguild

Typeset in 11pt Minion Pro

Printed on FSC accredited paper
Printed and bound in Great Britain by 4edge Limited

ISBN 978 1916668 096

British Library Cataloguing in Publication Data.
A catalogue record for this book is available from the British Library.

A book for only one reader.
To Sophie.
(Not her real name)

Part 1

We Don't Drink Blood

My First Death

There might be a million ways to get blood. Some of them even legit. But take it from someone who knows, to get blood on your hands you need time on your hands, time to plan and time to kill.

Figuratively speaking.

I've got nothing. Just a pocket full of problems. My own personal packet of pain, conveniently screwed up tight into a hip flask. A couple of pounds of death, give or take a gram. And about ten tonnes of guilt, growing every second. Heavier than hell, pressing down and threatening to flatten me out into a slither of myself, like a cartoon cat crushed pancake thin by an anvil. Except Tom could concertina back into shape with a wry look and a comedy chord, and go right back on chasing that mouse. Whereas I'll be flat forever. And as someone who's seen forever, believe me that is not an appealing prospect.

But self-pity is hardly a luxury I have time for right now. Off-kilter internal monologues featuring flat cat similes still less so. I'm in a rush, need a rush. Need a glass of that precious red gold, a goblet of the ol' haemoglobins. Nature's gin-u-wine tonic.

Okay, I know what you're thinking now, but let's get one thing straight right from page one: No. I'm not a vampire. I mean, yes, I rely on blood to sustain my part-human, semi-immortal lifestyle, but that's as far as it goes, alright? To be fair, it's my own fault on this occasion for leading you down the Gothic garden path, splashing out on all the juicy metaphors. But come on, drinking blood? No chance. That's just disgusting. So yeah, I do need blood. But right here, right now, this is not about me. It's about the girl in my pocket.

My earliest memories are of pain. It would be a bad start to my stint as a writer to state that they're indescribable, but... they aren't tangible. I could get into some hippy dippy literary shit and say it was like white fire, burning ice, sharp and stark and brutal. But really, who has the patience to read claptrap like that? I'll give you a comparison instead. Shark attack.

I've felt sandpaper skin shave over my leg, before serrated teeth ate into my flesh to grate on my bone. I've felt panic fill my waterlogged lungs and stifle my screams, tugged down through a pink cloud of my own blood. That's pain. That's fear. That's the worst I've lived through. But it's not the worst I remember.

When I was a child I lived in a hospital bed. That's a memory so sore it still makes me sick, and if I'm not careful I can travel back quite vividly even now.

I feel the stuffiness and taste that stale sterile smell that sticks in the throat. Plumbing and wires surround me, tangled together. I'm plugged into a computer which tells me I'm alive by chirruping intermittently. Interminably. I'm not just in the bed, I inhabit it. We survive together like sick symbionts. Half-boy, half-bed. Neither much to speak of without the other. And all I know is pain, all I am is hurt.

My only window into the world is my mum. She sits beside me, trying to drip-feed me fluid from a Styrofoam cup. It's radioactively green and tooth-achingly sweet, clearly hiding something. I don't want it, but I try to sip. To please her. She sings to me. Her voice is the only softness in a world of sharp edges. Sharp needles under my skin. Sharp tubes invading my throat. Sharp looks, sharp pain. I squeeze my eyelids tight and think of nothing but her song.

Of course, these memories are old. And it's a fine line between old memories and making stuff up. I mean, I make no pretence it all happened exactly like this. I'm writing a book here. You've got to give me some artistic licence. Sometimes it's really just about picking the words that feel right, on the page.

I took a class, actually. Creative writing. Can you tell? Feedback was I'm self-indulgent, but that's just a character flaw in general. It's hard not to be when you're basically invincible. Still, I picked up a bit. The odd tip. Start with something dramatic. Pose a question. Reel 'em in. Mess with chronology. They're all just tricks of the trade, thumbs on the scale, but every little helps when you're trying to lie your way to some essential, deeper truth. But that's exaggeration, more trickery. Like I say, it happened. Shit happened. Maybe not quite like this, but close enough.

Now where was I? Ah, of course. Hospital.

I sometimes wonder if things would have been different if I hadn't of got sick as a kid. I suppose you could say that about anything. That's how the fates of nations rise and fall, isn't it? What if Typhoid Mary hadn't of had typhoid? What if King Tut had never met a mosquito? What if George III hadn't thought he was a tree? I guess we'll never know.

What happened when I was seven might still have happened, but then again, maybe not, because maybe we'd never have moved. We'd never have had to.

So I might even have lived through my whole childhood. Imagine that.

One thing that does seem fairly certain, I wouldn't have spent my toddler years on drugs. Might even have got some actual toddling done, instead of lying around getting pumped full of poison.

Stuck to a bed, glued with sweat and pinned back by lethargy. Toxic medicine chasing damaged cells through my bloodstream in an internal blitzkrieg of collateral damage, breaking me down until illness defined me and became all I owned, left me nought but skin and bone.

Half the time I didn't know what was real. Were those leprous harlequins and jugglers dancing in my nightmares, or was it just the peeling wallpaper of paediatrics? Was the corner of the room where my dad always sat really steeped in shadow, or could my eyes just not focus that far? I didn't know then and I know less now, looking through a lens dimmed by time and distorted by an overstated writing style.

To be fair to my brain I'm thinking back some forty years here. And I haven't always been that kind to my mind. Maybe there were some drugs I shouldn't have taken. I don't want to get into it now, but if I occasionally played the hedonist was that really so bad? I was Peter Pan crossed with Superman, and with a past I actively wanted to forget. There was always going to be debauchery. Maybe I should have joined the Foreign Legion, I don't know.

Anyway, it's left me with a memory with more holes than a porcupine's pac-a-mac, and, just possibly, a wild propensity for hyperbole.

I'm trying my best, though.

Like I say, my mum was my rock. My warm, tender rock. That room became a home for both of us, and she tried to make it feel like one. Pictures tacked to the wall, finger-painted by other, luckier children. Soft toys to tuck me in, imaginatively christened Dog and Cat. It was imaginative because they were both bears. Nah, I'm kidding, they were a dog and a cat. Cassette tapes of stories and rhymes, and, when she thought I was asleep, the soundtrack from *Fame*. A hundred other touches and a thousand thoughtful gestures. All of her care, her love. All of her. God, looking back on it now I feel like she had it harder than me. I mean, I was only dying. She was watching me do it. Plus, you know, at least I actually had a bed, and slept, however erratically. Could be my disconnected recollection, but I'd swear she never even closed her eyes.

Could also be that all that impacted on my dad. Seeing me, seeing what I did to her. He had to watch it too, and all the time knowing what he knew. He must have thought, and surely more than once, of just picking me up and carrying me away. Ending it, and seeing if I could begin again. I could begrudge it now, that he never did. All that he put me through, all that he put my mum through. All that could have been avoided. I could be looking back at him now without these thorn-tinted spectacles, thinking about two rocks, instead of one rock and one shadow. Because really my impression of that room is just that, impressionism. An artist's draft laid on thick.

But he never acted. And, just maybe, now I see why.

Because since it's come right down to it, I'm reduced to this. A creature of the night.

My phone is flashing with a message. It doesn't take a mind-reader to know what it will say. More of the same. *Where? Why? What the hell?* Nothing I can give an answer to. I ignore it and keep moving, as if physical momentum might somehow give some impetus to this. But what I really need is a clue what to do. All I can do in lieu is keep walking, except when I'm half-running, hoping something presents itself. I don't know what I expect. There's nothing here. I'm in the elderly part of town, where ye olde shoppes seem to grow naturally out of the ground, like weeds. Cobbles become raggedy walls which become ornate ebony window frames which become bent wooden beams which become layers of roof tiles garnished with guano by generations of seagulls. By day they're made for sunny picture postcards, by moonlight they lurk, deserted by tourists and open only to their ghosts. I'm the only one awake. The streets are empty, oppressive dark folding the town in a mantle of concealed sights and stifled sounds. Buildings huddle and shape-shift, black amidst the twisting wisps of coastal mist. Windows shut tight, like sleeping eyes, hide their secrets safe inside.

It would seem like the perfect time for murder. But the kicker is, I can't see anyone. Actually, rewind. Let's just examine that. Murder. That's my plan. I'm going to cut someone and take their blood. Although I only really need about a jam jar's worth, so best-case scenario may be I get away with GBH. Or ABH. Who knows? Who cares, the acronym police? Well, and the actual police, but that's a worry for another time.

Somehow, this admission calms me. Maybe it's the knowledge that I have no other choice. I slow down. I close my eyes. I breathe, counting the air in for five seconds, counting it out again. I literally stop and think. What do I need? One, something that bleeds. But not just anything. A living, breathing human. No other attributes on their part required. Just humanity. Unfortunately that rules me out. Two, something sharp. I'm going to need to cut them. Deep. You can't draw a pint from a scratch. Three, something to drain the blood into. A flask would be best. A beer glass would do at a pinch. Four, the balls to actually carry this through. It's that or quit now. Go back to being alone. One way or another, death comes calling tonight. One way or another, everything changes. I kill, or my inaction does. What can I live with? What can I live without?

I seriously miss when I had a minion to take care of these little problems for me.

My dad was a different beast, did his own dirty work, always had a full jar around in case of emergencies. But he still needed someone to help out with the actual process. There are limits to what you can do by yourself, after all. Every witch needs a black cat, every mad doctor needs an Igor. For years I had Vlad. And my dad, well, my dad had my mum.

I never found any of this out from him of course. Never got anything from him after I was seven. Never got a whole lot before that either, save for genetically. I got his slight, slightly shifty, good-in-a-good-light good looks; his sardonic sneer that's supposed to be a smile. I got his propensity to lose hair after thirty, his sensitivity to certain types of pollen. Oh, and his ability to come back from the dead. I'm always forgetting that one.

Really, I suppose the time for recrimination has probably passed. Particularly given, as we now know, the apple really could hardly have dropped closer to the tree. But I obviously still enjoy the bitterness, so what the hell? Maybe if he'd told my mum earlier that his disorder was hereditary, things would be different. If he'd spared us both the suffering, spared us the sorrow. Just spared us really, full stop.

I don't really know the ins and outs of it all, I suppose. I mean, come on, I was four. But even I can put two and two together. He can't have told her before I was born, and it can't have been while I lay in that bed, breathing life through a tube like an astronaut strung out from his starship. If she'd known, there's no way she'd have let that happen. Is there? No. It can only have been after it was too late. After the doctor told them I was going to die. Or after I was dead.

I don't know. All I know is he must have told her eventually. And when you're dying, slowly, when increments of your existence are peeling away, exposing you day by day to harsh new realities of nausea, distress, and, quite frankly, tedium, well, eventually is just too damn long to wait.

So you'll forgive me if I hold on to the bitterness.

Unless…

Unless he told her it doesn't always work?

Whitby. Stupid to be here. Stupid to have come back. If you're supposed to be dead somewhere, then don't go there, it's a simple rule and should be easy to stick to. The world's a big enough place, after all. So why am I here? I know the answer all too well, if only I'd care to admit it. I'm here because I don't want to do this myself. I can't do it myself. I need him. I need him to guide me through the night. Jesus, what is it with me and father figures? I honestly have so many daddy issues, it's a miracle I never ended up becoming a stripper.

Pause to sympathise with all the unfortunate hen parties who never got to experience that.

The truth is, I've been on automatic pilot, and all this soliloquising on knives and cuts and murder has simply been so much unreliable narration. Although if you believe that you'll believe anything. However, whether through denial, or simple panic and confusion, my internal satnav has led me to the wrong side of the tracks. He doesn't live here anymore.

I shake myself back to my senses and start to move again. Quickly now, and with purpose. Jog-trotting back to the bridge. Beneath me the water is blue-black with shadows, lapping around the marina and slapping the sleeping hulls of moored-up trawlers. Timbers creak, and distant, pencil-thin masts draw sketchy arcs in silhouette across the sky. The waterfront is pinpricked with sporadic blisters of light in red, white, gold. But the town still slumbers. Even the ubiquitous seagulls have gone to roost, leaving the sky wide-open and empty. I doubt they are anybody's favourite feathered friends. Flying rats, some call them. But when not botching words, I do like watching birds, and I miss them. Now the only movement comes from real rats, scuttering through stinking low-tide mud.

As I hit the west side and angle left towards the pier a stumbling drunk reels up between me and the corner and his sudden angry shout startles me sideways. He staggers against the door of the *Three Jolly Sailors*, waving an empty bottle from one paw and yowling. It's long past kicking-out time and however loudly he knocks and swears sour-nothings up at the pub no one is going to let him in. He turns to me, expression belligerent, bleary and bloated. You think being caught between a mama bear and her cubs is bad, try being faced with a pissed-up scumbag fresh out of booze. Tension knots in my guts. Fear plays her shivering tune, using my spine as a xylophone and bewitching the hairs on my neck. But it's not normal late-night fear. It's not what he might do to me. It's what I could do to him.

What should we do with a drunken sailor? He's got to be six-foot plus in his steel-toe boots and must outweigh three of me. He is hammered, though. He wouldn't even see me coming. I can picture it in my head, racing across the road, hop, skip and jump, palm under his chin, slamming his skull against the brick wall behind him. I can hear the hollow pool-ball clunk of his nut cracking on the masonry. Feel the fat waste-of-life go limp against me. So close to that dark little snicket too. A bit of exertion, a bit of adrenaline, I could drag him down there. Then he's all mine. He's even brought the weapon with him. It's almost too convenient. Smash the top off that bottle, should give me a nice cutting edge and a handy receptacle. A two-for-one deal. Bending down by his wilted bulk, my fingers feeling for the throb of pulse in his neck…

I'm halfway across the road and my heart rate is off the chart. He's swaying, staring at me, red-rimmed eyes struggling to focus. I can't believe I'm going to do this, I'm going to do this, I'm going. I shear away, all but running, careering back into the railings set there to stop drunks and idiots from cockling into the harbour. He's shouting something but I don't stop or look back. I'm really running now. Hip flask bouncing, reassuringly heavy in my pocket. I know where I'm going this time, as if I didn't know all along.

I'm going to find my Vlad.

I'm blocking out the genetics thing for now. Sometimes you've just got to lock in on hope. Maybe that's where my dad slipped up. Not enough hope. He might have gazed down on me in my hospital room, as I lay in that grave of a bed, tucked up with a capital F, my blue eyes, my mum's blue eyes, weakly blinking up into his teak-brown stare. Did he simply believe there was too much of her in me, not enough of him? Did he really just think it wouldn't work? Christ. That's almost a charitable thought. Maybe this novel-writing lark is therapeutic. I could turn up all sorts of repressed memories here. Better keep an eye on that.

So yeah, maybe she'd always known too. Maybe she'd sponsored him for years and knew every in and out. Maybe even as she leant down to kiss me, the faintest of touches, lips barely breaking the sheen of fever on my forehead, maybe she knew then they might have the power to take it all away.

But I don't buy it.

I'm sticking with my theory, the one that's served me well enough through four embittered decades. That he waited until the last pathetic life-supporting beep had flat-lined, and then he told her. Spilled it in a splurge of catharsis and well-deserved self-loathing. I picture him purging, letting it all out, right there in the room. Me, between them, leaden still and cold. Her incredulous, not wanting to hear, not daring to believe. Why would she? How could she? I mean, what would you do if your partner told you they weren't entirely human? Not you specifically. Well, yes, I suppose. You specifically. Might be something you need to consider.

I wonder, did he tell her how it's done? The nuts and bolts, the ash and blood? The double, double toil and trouble? Did he let on who his sponsor had been, describe the hot mess it always makes? Did he talk about before? The white light, teasing, candle-like, behind you in the dark, widening, flowering until the air catches into cold fire and you disappear, swallowed whole into the flame, and you get that microscopic moment of knowing everything, being everything – the breath of the gods and the foam on the sea – before you're nothing, and you forget. Did he tell her all that? I hope if he did he can describe it better than I can.

Or did he just say, 'When I die, and am cremated, an accomplice (which my kind call a sponsor) pours fresh human blood on my ashes, and I rise again'?

Yeah, maybe he just said that.

I sort of imagine they decided together whether to try. To find out whether being undead is a dominant or recessive gene. I suppose maybe she thought there wasn't much to lose. Save maybe a soul.

She became his sponsor at some point, so perhaps that was her first time. It might have been her blood. She might have mixed it, and watched, and waited. Boil thy first i' the charmed pot, so to speak.

Basically though, I haven't a clue. I mean, I wouldn't, would I? I was dead. I guess there's a slight chance he never said anything. Waited until after the cremation, waited for his opportunity, held fire until she was blind with tears and exhausted grief then took his chance. Decanted the ashes of his firstborn into a hip flask and just sodded off. Left her lost, confused, alone and broken-hearted.

Hard to believe, though. After all, what sort of absolute bastard would be capable of that?

Lies, Damned Lies, and Sadistics

We didn't have to skip town every time my dad died. Just when he did something stupid.

I suppose he never saw the need for self-preservation.

My dad, and I'm going to have to try pretty hard not to resort to expletives here, treated people like shit. Sorry. Sorry, I'll try harder. Like worms. He treated people like worms. Not even like he was the early bird though. More like he was the fisherman. Or just the hook.

It was the same with anyone he encountered. I don't know if he was past caring, or if he'd never had an empathetic bone in his body to begin with. Maybe he was just a shit.

It led to trouble, at home, at whatever was passing for work. That was never ideal. Not really, not when work generally meant mixing with undesirables.

How, he used to moan, was he supposed to earn

an honest crust? He'd left school at twelve, and again at fifteen, both times with no qualifications. He had no trade, no training. At least, not in anything above board. Or even level with the board. What's left? Sub board, innit?

That's the kind of crook he was. Inferior, lesser, lower.

I imagine some people make a good livelihood out of larceny. Set up in comfortable accommodation on the wrong side of the tracks. Drive a nice car. Treat the kids. I'm not saying I recommend it, or condone it. I don't even know if I'd have preferred him to have been good at it. I can't really imagine me as the prodigal son in a mafia family. Don't think I've ever made an offer that couldn't be refused.

My dad never made a living anyway. He wasn't the type. He was more about dying.

Always ended up beaten down by life, beaten up by the wrong crowd. Literally, on some occasions. Like this time I'm telling you about. There had been a falling out, best guess, over the cut. A cross or a double cross, I don't even know. He'd wanted his share, or more than was fair. He'd have wound them up, pissed them off, ground their nerves. He did it to everyone.

They all but killed him.

Left him black and blue, and mostly red. Left him for dead.

He came home; it was late. I'd been asleep.

It was just stifled sounds at first. Crying. Groaning. Him. Mum. Both of them.

I got up for water. The hallway, moonlit through uncurtained windows, stark and cold. Naked floorboards before it was trendy. No family photos on the walls. No paint on them, come to that.

There was blood in the bathroom sink. Red handprints smeared on the door.

I should have stayed upstairs.

Something drew me down. The muffled sound of a scuffle. The scent of heat rising up through the floor. It smelt bitter. Recrimination, criminalisation, caramelised realisation. The reek of burning bridges.

The smell of hell.

In the hall the front door stood unbolted. It would have been so easy to leave.

Further down, the stairs to the basement. Rough and splintered, rusted nails, spiders big as your fist. No place for bare feet. No place for anyone that night.

He had it contained in the cellar. A beaten old oil drum he must have dragged in for the purpose. Subtext: he'd had this planned. Flames spat and sparked, sprayed his face with heat and harsh light. Madness blazed. To be fair, his features didn't need a fire's help for that.

I froze against the banister, insides chewed, eyes glued.

She was weeping. That's a shocking word, isn't it? Shockingly bad. Melodramatic hyperbole beyond acceptable usage. I'm not changing it, though. I want you to feel the shock. Crying doesn't cut it. Tears don't tell the story. She wept.

'I won't bring you back.'

She would though. She would have to.

He spelt it out for her. Where would she go without him? What would she do? How would she explain what had happened?

There would be a body in her basement. A man who technically didn't exist, beaten dead and burnt. She needed him. He needed her. He loved her. He said. Begged her. Pleaded. They were tied together. We were.

That was key, we. The submission was in her slumping shoulders.

We were tied together. All three of us.

I wasn't just watching.

This was my family.

My deeply damned and unstable family.

I walked down and held my mother's hand.

His eye was split, jagged black scabbing stuck his brow in a stricken scowl. His lips puffed purple and his nose sat thick, slack and flat. That was about the best of it. The other bits I can't describe without wanting to vomit.

He slit his own throat and self-immolated.

The next day, he went back to his business associates. He never got tired of telling that part of the tale. Which was a pain in the arse, because, by its secretive nature it had only one audience, and that was me. That's my dad for you. He never read me *The Very Hungry Caterpillar*. Never dandled me from his knee and took me to Narnia. But he told me a thousand times how he got his own back on some scum who pushed him around one time.

Result being, I can still picture that room.

I never went there, not that exact location. Been in a few dark places. But not that particular one.

Picture a gangsters' lair without the glamour, a clammy den for clumsy denizens. A lousy warehouse of goods gone bad. Rotting, grotty, a petty little thugs' space. Ill-lit, ill kempt. Ill met by any light.

You could ask why I need to picture it at all. True, I generally don't have a lot on, so I have a fair bit of time for quiet contemplation, but why waste it sketching outlines in my head, embellishing hand-me-down fantasies from a dad I supposedly have no time for? Couldn't stand the sight of him when we shared a house and hearth, so why invent ways to keep him around now? Answers on a postcard.

Picture a cold and dreadful place.

But we're getting away from the point. My dad walked in.

Strolled in, swaggered in.

They were seated around a table. Less a table than a broken old door, dragged through dust and balanced on bricks. There to hold fag ends and lager dregs. Crisp packets and discarded poker hands.

And the money, stacked neatly into piles, one for each of them, less my dad. My dad, whose blood still specked the top layer of notes, dried hard and black. Like clubs on a playing card.

And now he was back, the reanimated corpse of the big bad from a hundred low-budget slasher flicks.

The first surprise must have been that he walked in at all. That he dared to walk in, sure, but more that he was capable of it, strutting in on legs that had been hobbled with crowbars only hours before.

'The look on their faces!' He used to smile as he relayed it. A corrupt little smirk, undermined by being skin deep.

No doubt their daze were numbered, ten out of ten on the rictus scale, warped in astonishment. His own face the cause, of course. Not the way they'd left it, stoved-in, flayed and misshapen. If he had a face left at all, it should still have been under wraps, swaddled up and shielded from sight.

Yet here it was, back again. With not so much as a tissued-shaving cut. Casual, smiling even. Showing a full set of unbroken teeth, the same incisors they had left embedded in bats, or scattered, shattered across the floor. Winking too, with an eye that had been blacked, hot and burst and broken, now clear and cold.

'Looked like they'd seen a ghost!' Hyena-maw twisting, jackal-eyes glistering.

The way he told it, they sat like statues and he passed among them. Back from the grave, like that bloke with the beard and long robes. What was his name? Gandalf. As if under his spell they skulked, hunched motionless, gawking.

Taking advantage of their shock and awe, he stole between their petrified glances and stole, in the other sense of the word, what he felt he was owed.

Walked out with it all, right under their noses.

As I say, that's how he told it. But this is a guy who lived off the blood of others, so why take his word for anything?

Maybe he crept in, window for a cat-flap, crapping himself every second in case he made a sound and they caught him. He could have found them gone and just got lucky. Or he could have killed them. For all I know he was capable of that.

Could have cracked the safe or cracked some skulls. Don't know. Don't want to know. I'm sure he had his reasons for telling it, selling it, like he did. Projecting an image of himself, hoping to impress me. Can't even rule out that it was just the truth. It doesn't really matter. He walked away with the loot. Had the last laugh.

That's what really sticks, I think.

He laughed when he talked about it.

I've said some horrible things. Done some too, come to that. Uncalled for, unconscionable. Unforgivable, even.

But I never fucking laughed about them.

He thought it was funny. We didn't. My mum and me. We remembered the night time, his face and the fire. Panic and pain. His blood, his body. The stench, the sickness. His ashes, her blood. His body, back. No end to the pain.

My dad laughed.

And we all had to move house again.

Not sure why they chose the town. It would've been easier to disappear if we'd gone somewhere bigger, busier. It's amazing what I don't know, when I stop to think about stuff like this.

Or not. Do people normally know why others do what they do? Even the closest of others? Mothers? God, do people normally know why they do what they do themselves? Why are you where you are? Who knows? Not me.

Either way, we went to Whitby.

One thing I'll say for it, if it was a hiding place: it's nowhere. Not to disparage, but it's a speck on the map. On a detailed map. Nothing wrong with that. Some of the best places in the world are invisible on your average globe. Size isn't everything.

Nelson's Column might just jut up higher than Captain Cook's statue, but London's pigeons are no happier than

Whitby's seagulls with their target. Sydney Opera House may be more ostentatious than the Spa Pavilion, but is that Aussie bastion of braggadocio prioritising talk over trousers? The Yorkshire coast links might not quite be St Andrews, but the salt air smells the same. The Turnball Ground ain't the Bernabeu… I don't know where I'm going with that one.

The Eiffel Tower? It's a glorified pylon, isn't it? And don't even get me started on that wonky effort in Pisa. What you need is a good, solid whalebone arch.

Whitby might be small, but it isn't insignificant. Who needs skyscrapers when you have higgledy-piggledy hotch-potches of haphazard cottages, rambling up hillsides in tipsy rows? Who needs high-rises when you have Gothic ruins, black rocks of withering mystery, whispering history?

Who needs an inferiority complex when you have that magical amalgamation of moor and sea and sky? Why should a place have a chip on its shoulder, when it does such good chips, and, for that matter, plaice?

I moved there when I was sixteen. About two years before the age when half the kids want to leave. It's hard to lay down roots, when everyone else is plotting to pull up trees.

How do you settle to anything, when there's so much flux around you? It's a migratory town, in many ways. Look at Captain Cook, who launched himself on voyages of discovery, boldly going, strange new worlds and all that. Bram Stoker stayed for his hols, tapped out a parasitic myth. Fair to say, I wasn't set to emulate them, plant a flag in a future penal colony, or pen a pulp thriller. But

I'd like to have done something. I couldn't even find my feet. It's rough learning to stand still, when every other head is spinning. Not saying everyone I met was obsessed with exams, university, and the call of the big, wide world, but there was a general sense there was more out there, somewhere.

Of course, it was doubly difficult because I didn't technically exist.

Between my deaths and my dad's, I'd lived a gypsy childhood. Been to more schools than you could count. Unless you'd been properly taught, I suppose. Even when there'd been no particular need to move, we'd bounced about. I ended up with identities stacked to match your average international superspy.

As I said, my dad mixed with the out-crowd, the butchers, the breakers and candlestick-to-the-face mischief makers. Also with the thieves and the forgers. I had a lot of passports, lot of birth certificates. A lot of names.

Some I couldn't use, the ones I'd died with, the one I was born with, the ones associated with any of the more notorious things he'd done. But some held up to scrutiny, in the age before digital records and internet searches, held up well enough for me to go to school.

Trouble was, the only ones available had nothing attached, no record of GCSE glory, or any school story at all, come to that. I'd inherited lying from the master, along with some other nasty traits, so I wriggled in. But I had to start at the bottom. Or at least, I had to be fourteen again.

Perhaps it's churlish to complain. How many people never get a first chance? Let alone a third, fourth, fifth, or whatever I was on. Would it have killed me to knuckle down? Poor choice of phrase. If one thing never mattered to me, it was being killed occasionally. It might not have been the end of the world though, to have tried.

I didn't.

I could lay out all the excuses, line them up like dominoes, stack them like a house of cards. But in the end I'd just be playing games. I could say I was sick of starting over, or that I couldn't face the same lessons I'd already lazily half-learned. I could say it was weird being the oldest in class, never being able to let on, let anyone in or let anything out. I could say I lost track of the point, misplaced the plot. Couldn't stay motivated to get qualifications I might simply lose again, next time life went amiss.

Maybe trying was just never my style.

There was no crash though, no literal burning. There was just enough incentive in not drawing attention to myself to keep turning up. We didn't need any trouble, any unnecessary brushes with authority.

So I kept my nose clean, took my medicine, took my tests. Wrote a few papers, wrote the book on scraping by. Did just enough to toe the line. Sure, some educators are affronted by apathy, but most just don't have the time. Too busy nurturing the cream of the crop, or whipping along the detritus at the bottom. No time to worry much about monitoring the mulch in the middle.

Being only marginally below average can go a long way, if your only ambition is not to be noticed.

As this chapter potters to a close in a post-pyrotechnical petering out, I feel no need to strive to change the tone. No need for any abstract, invented cliff-hanger to invert expectations and reignite the pace. No demented *Demeter* need wreck upon the shores of my story. Instead I just accept it is apt.

Life had slackened, and entered calmer waters.

Becoming Familiar

He was powder-blue and cherubic. Round-headed, wide-eyed. Even the widow's peak and pointy ears were a cutesy version of creepy. Dressed in evening wear and a crimson cape, his arms splayed wide. Was he about to take off, or did he want a hug? His fangs were two white triangles, either side of a Cheshire Cat smile. This was the friendly face of demonic blood-sucking – which made the slogan underneath, "We don't serve vampires", seem somewhat mean-spirited. I didn't take it personally.

The mongrel-eared sign was thumb-tacked between another pair of stained classics, letting me know you didn't have to be mad to work here, and that Tipping was not a city in China. Even twenty years ago, these were not young jokes.

Perhaps the idea was you drank more, 'til they were so blurry you couldn't read them.

I didn't really need that excuse.

Cherchez la femme, as they say in Greece, during French lessons. I was twenty-two and peering into a half-empty glass. Obviously there was a woman at the bottom of it. It's an angsty sort of stretch, isn't it? Post-adolescent but still unformed, uninformed. The time in your life when you're dealing with the most flux and change. Breaking up and breaking down.

Like any sensible boy getting over a girl, I was getting insensible. Stick something maudlin on the jukebox, order a drink. Repeat. Works a charm.

One thing you might expect though, at that age, is a few mates. Standing around, standing a round. Arms around shoulders, too-soon jokes, good-natured hair ruffling. Does that sound right? I don't really know how it works. I never had any friends.

I was alone, drinking by myself in a sad, mid-life crisis-y way. Can you have a mid-life crisis that young? Maybe, if you're only going to live another two decades. Now there's food for forties.

Weird thing is, I honestly wasn't actually that bothered about the girl. I can't even remember her name. I can, it was Carol, but I'm trying to make a point. She was a tomato, I was a potato, or however the song goes, and it was me that called the whole thing off. Admittedly I did it in that bastard passive-aggressive male way, of just being such an arse that she dumped me, but still. In a roundabout, spaghetti-junction sort of way, I was kind of being kind.

She was nice, Carol. I just didn't care enough. We could have hung out, kept it casual, but even then, there would have been lies. Stories about a made-up past. Effort. I didn't want to run the risk of her thinking I was the one, when I wasn't anyone.

It feels like there could be a lot more backstory to this. Who said what, who wouldn't do which and why. Wheres, whens, hows. But I've heard that a good expository segment should be petite and to the point, and I've just spent a page yacking on about nowt.

So long story short: I was sitting in a pub, feeling sad.

I'd just wandered in on a whim. Should have been in some flash bar, all alcopops and MTV. Instead, I was in the place where the old men go, fishermen and forgotten men, all stout and bitter, even when drinking mild. Beer guts and former glories, balding and spreading. Smogging the ceiling yellow with their exhalations, surrounding themselves with the things that men like. Maps and pictures of ships. Mahogany and other inanimates. And those hilarious posters, which is where we came in.

I came in. By myself.

With no boisterous circle of friends to attach to, I stuck by the bar. The first pints were self-conscious. This was back in the nineties, remember. Pony express days. No mobile computer in your pocket to pass the time. If you wanted to pretend the person you were meeting was late, make a fake call to check up on them, you'd have to pay ten pence to use the phone behind the bar. More trouble than it was worth. If you were on your own you had to lump it.

As if to accentuate the fact, a family group trailed in

together. Mum, dad, son, daughter and, you'd be forgiven for assuming, embarrassing uncle. It was obvious pretty quickly though that he fitted in even less than that. He was round in a world of squares.

His fingers, as well as hosting at least one ring apiece, were thick and white with nails lacquered black. A silver spun spider was pinned to one lapel, and a skull grinned from a single earring. Eyes, old and yellow as papyrus scrolls, looked out from crow-footed caves. A neat trim of cobweb beard curled down his chin, blending under his neck with a forgotten squirt of shaving foam. He wore a woven waistcoat and his clothes were heavy, velvet and leather. And black. Everything black. From the toe of his boot to the top of his hat, which, by the way, was a top hat.

In short, he was a Goth. And while I shouldn't speak for other members of the undead fraternity, I'm going to anyway: can you imagine anything more annoying to a vampire than a fucking Goth?

You play them back in your mind, these key incidents, and it's easy to see what you never saw at the time. Like when, just to say, for example, off the top of my head, I met Vladamir Precua. I know I was off my head, but it really didn't seem that big of a deal. If you'd have told me then that this would be the start of the most important relationship I'd have this side of thirty-five, I don't know what I would have done. Probably killed myself. Of course, I did that anyway. So maybe nothing matters.

Enough philosophy. Back to chronology.

The party seated themselves sheepishly around a table, while the goateed old Goth made his way to the bar.

'Greetings, quartermaster!' he chirruped, smiling broadly.

'Evening, Vlad,' the barman nodded, looking up from his task of smearing dregs from one end of the counter to the other. 'Quiet night?'

'Numerically, yes,' Vlad replied, with a wink. 'Six on the tour and we're left with but four. Hopefully a few drinkies will make it all worthwhile.'

Turned out, if I may be forgiven a little exposition, that Vlad turned a trade as a tour guide of sorts, running a vampire-themed version of the successful Ghost Walk model. Certain nights a week he'd round up a flock of tourists, the bored and the gullible, and lead them around the town to see the sights, emphasising any links to Stoker, Dracula, or the pointy-toothed fraternity in general. And by standing agreement, the tour always ended in this pub. Hopefully they bought a few drinks, and their erstwhile chaperon received some modest cut.

Bejewelled fingers beat a tattoo across the wood as he waited for the barman to pour his order. Four pints the worse for wear, I felt those polished nails scrape along my nerves like a chalkboard. When he glanced up and our eyes met I ignored the overture of his smile, and he turned back to bother the barman.

'I do wish you'd take down that picture,' he sighed theatrically, nodding at the baby-blue cartoon pin-up on the wall.

'Why's that then, Vlad?' asked his captive audience, favouring me with a "not-this-again" roll of the eyes. As if

I gave a flying piece of fudge.

'It's just not a very accurate depiction of a real vampire, is it?'

I snorted so hard that beer came out of my nose. Surprisingly, eye-wateringly, painful. When I'd finished spluttering, snotting and wiping my eyes the first thing I saw was him staring at me. The severity of his expression set me off giggling again, childish and silly-shrill. Shaking his head, he made a point of turning away.

Away, back to people who, inexplicably, paid to hear him chat that shit.

The evening grew old. The pub crowd thickened through ones and twos. A former trawlerman in oilskins, wild and weather-beaten albeit he'd not been about a boat in above a score o' years. A married couple, him in jeans and a rugby shirt, her in fake platinum jewellery and matching hair. The disparate and the desperate. The eclectic clientele of the small-town pub.

At a certain fuzzy point I left my stool for a slash, stumbling back to find it filled. Some buxom ballbreaker beckoned me to her knee, to a maelstrom of laughter from the wings. A covey of gossips looked on, lascivious eyes and lavish appetites, no older than I am now, but ancient nonetheless. I've aged alright, I suppose. Something in the regeneration process, perhaps. At that time though I wouldn't have fitted the pick-up-behind-bars type, didn't have the wolfish smile and dangerous eyes. Never had the Lost Boy looks. Certainly wouldn't have got a part in *Twilight*, had such a thing been conceived of.

She was piss-taking then, and I backed away. It could have been a sign to call it a night, that and the fact I was seeing double. I decided to start seeing doubles instead, ordered bourbon and scouted around for a new perch. It was standing room only, but I found a nice place to lean. Only conceivable downside was being back in earshot of the Gothic vampire expert.

He was still the centre of attention, holding court to his family of fans. They were… they were normal. So boring I'm finding the thought of describing them too tedious. Can only imagine what it would be like to read. Whole paragraphs on anoraks. Let's skip on.

'And so, in answer to your question, young lady,' the Goth was proclaiming, 'I would indeed say the creatures of Anne Rice's *Chronicles* are as valid as any other vampire, it is simply my personal preference to regard the Count above Louis and Lestat.'

You're probably thinking, nobody talks like that. You're right, obviously. Unless you've ever met Vlad, then you'll know you're wrong. The beige anoraks were rapt.

'And the same with, what, *Salem's Lot*?' asked the father.

'Indeed,' Vlad agreed. 'King, of course, pays great homage to Stoker in that novel. But I would say the same applies, and to anyone else you care to think of.'

Further suggestions came from the floor.

'Blade?'

'The ones from *Buffy*?'

'Count Duckula?' I chipped in from the side, earning myself a withering look.

33

'Just as valid, yes,' Vlad went on quickly, 'though of course one must allow for personal opinion. Call me old-fashioned, I happen to like my vampires in capes and coffins.'

'Why?' I interrupted loudly, and, I'm willing to admit with a healthy amount of hindsight, rudely.

'It's a fair question,' the mother smiled. I may have imagined it, but she seemed to smirk and try to catch my eye. Let's be honest, I definitely imagined it.

Or did I?

Vlad writhed in irritation.

'Well,' he wriggled. 'Firstly, I happen to rate *Dracula* over, to take a recent example, *From Dusk till Dawn*. I rather believe it to be superior on aesthetic grounds. But I'm not such a vampire fascist as to suggest that this is the only opinion worth having. Myths can be altered. I don't hold that lore is sacrosanct, that everything that has gone before must be acknowledged, or that nothing new can be invented.'

'I'm not really sure I follow?' the father's brow crinkled like a certain cut of crisp.

'Take elves,' Vlad proposed, 'or fairies. My idea of an elf, well, it's not my idea at all, it's Tolkien's. When I think of an elf I think of the beautiful folk, all tall and lordly. But they aren't the only elves, or even the original ones. Are those from Grimm less convincing? Shakespeare? Enid Blyton? Or what of Christmas elves? Is a toymaker from Santa's workshop less legitimate than Elrond? After all, I've never seen an elf. Who am I to criticise the visions of others?'

'Vampires can be whatever we want them to be?'

'Well, I still believe they have to be… how can I put this? Probable.'

'And you don't think some of them are?'

'The new-fangled ones? No, I don't find them feasible.'

Personally, I didn't find a man wearing a velvet cape and carrying a silver-topped cane *in real life* all that feasible, but I managed to hold my tongue.

'Feasible?' queried the father. 'What exactly do you mean?'

Vlad gave a dry cough, finished his drink, looked mournfully into his glass and rattled the melting, lonely ice.

'Feasible,' he mulled. 'Probable: by that I mean could they exist? Would they be likely to exist? Would they behave as they do if they did exist? The real problem though, and I take into account this is a matter of taste, in terms of Tarantino, the vampires are simply too gory. They have no class.'

'Oh my god, what an absolute crock of crazy,' some idiot blurted. Turned out, after a quick scan around the room, to have been me.

'No class,' repeated Vlad, deliberately.

Five minutes later, his fan club were filing through the door. Possibly it was just getting late, possibly my bad behaviour had driven them to it. Fair to say we'll never know for sure. Vlad's eyes lingered morosely on the exit. He beckoned to me.

'Come on. At the very least, you owe me a drink.'

'You think?'

'I know. They literally just said they were leaving because of your bad behaviour.'

I may have argued, not having known him well enough at that point to know it could never be worth the effort.

'They were the perfect clients,' he elaborated, groaning with amateur dramatic yearning. 'Dad was a Quentin Tarantino fan, loved *From Dusk till Dawn*. Girl was a teenage idoliter, adored *Interview with the Vampire*, and the boy,' the old Goth mewled wistfully, 'old-school Dracula. A lad after my own heart.'

'So?'

'A whole family of vampire obsessives! How often do you think I get that? They'd have listened to me talk about the undead all night.'

'The mum was the only one actually interested in anything immortal,' I muttered, thinking back to that smirk.

'How so?'

'You wouldn't believe me if I told you.'

'Buy me that drink, let's find out.'

'Never going to happen.'

I straightened up to leave.

Ten minutes later, I somehow found myself still there.

'I can't believe people pay you to talk about made-up stuff.'

Vlad spluttered on the drink I'd bought him. 'Made-up stuff? Dear boy, we are talking about vampires! Not ghosts.'

'Made-up stuff. You literally just said new myths can be created, old lore isn't sacrosanct. You can make stuff up.'

'I said no such thing. I deny it strenuously.'

Of course, if you look back a page or two, you'll see that

I recollected that almost precisely. Perhaps too precisely, for a sailor two point nine sheets to the wind.

A brief pause then, or interlude, for a note on dialogue in memoir: obviously not everybody said exactly what I'm saying they said. Even me. Take the words as a flavour. This is more a tang of how the conversation tasted than an exact replica. Clearly in real life there're more uh's and ah's and "I turned round and said" and "she turned round and said", and, quite frankly, bad prose. Just believe that the spirit of the exchange is accurate, and we'll all be happy.

'I deny it strenuously,' Vlad went on. 'One can't wing it with vampires.'

'You said, whatshisname, Tarantino, was allowed to make stuff up about them.'

Vlad shuddered at the memory. 'I take it back.'

'People aren't allowed to make up new vampire stories?'

'Of course they are, as long as they follow the old rules.'

'So all that stuff about elves was… what?'

'Nonsense. Everyone knows that elves don't exist anyway.'

'Load of old cobblers,' I agreed. 'That was a shoemaker joke,' I elaborated, after the original remark was allowed to dangle without a response. Vlad shrugged.

'That's where you draw the line? Vampires exist but elves don't.'

'Well, I wouldn't like to say for certain. It can't easily be confirmed or denied. I'm an elf agnostic, if you like.'

'Fair enough,' I shlurred thoughtfully. 'But vampires?'

'I'm a believer.'

'But they can't be easily confirmed or denied?'

'Not as such. It's a matter of faith, you understand.' The Goth stared seriously out from under his top hat.

'And in your faith, we – they – sleep in crypts and coffins?'

'Well,' he said, eyeing me carefully as he gave the question some thought, 'why not?'

'Just a bit silly, isn't it?'

He tutted.

'What about garlic then?' I persisted. 'I mean, do you think France is empty of vampires, for example?'

'It's plausible. Why shouldn't some substances, which are commonplace to us, be poison to them? They are different beings, after all.'

'Religious iconography? Crosses? Holy water?'

'Ah, now there you ask an interesting question.' Vlad paused, to ponder. 'Myself, I think it unlikely. But that's merely because I don't believe in God. Heaven, hell. Angels and demons.'

'You have a very idiosyncratic belief system, if you don't mind me saying so.'

'For the religious believer, vampires, as creatures of the night, must necessarily seem evil. Devilish, ungodly. It would make sense that they would be repelled by the sign of the cross.' Vlad demonstrated a cross with two fingers, in case I might be too stupid to know what one was. I showed him two fingers of my own.

'Really, it's a matter of which myths and magic you believe in,' he went on, ignoring me. 'And as I don't believe in the Father, Son, or Holy Ghost, I can't believe in vampires that would be bothered about them either.'

'So you pick and choose which parts you like best.'

'Not exactly. You pick and choose which parts you *believe in*.'

'You aren't really a vampire fundamentalist then?'

'Not at all. I'm very New Age.' He laughed. It was infectious, and I caught it. Maybe it was the loneliness, but I wasn't actually hating talking with him.

'What would your vampire look like then?'

Vlad sat back on his stool, spread his arms, and framed himself.

'Like you?'

'Why not like me?'

'I don't know,' I sniggered. 'It just never occurred to me.'

'I'm not being egotistical,' he clarified. 'I'm not suggesting I physically resemble a vampire.'

'I didn't realise there was anything egotistical about wanting to look dead.'

'Undead,' Vlad corrected automatically. 'And as usual, you don't appear to know what you are talking about. But I'll let it pass, for another drink.'

'Of course, my eyes aren't overly vampiric,' he mused as I returned from the bar, the last-orders bell ringing in my ears. 'And my nose could be sharper.'

'Let's get this straight,' I interrupted. 'You think that if vampires exist, they look like middle-aged Goths?' He rocked back as if slapped, and even if the pain was clearly simulated, I regretted the discourtesy. It didn't stop me plunging in deeper.

'It'd be crazy. Mysterious bloodless corpses keep turning up, holes all over their necks. Who do you think is going to get blamed? Average Joe in jeans and a T-shirt, or the Christopher Lee lookalike with red eyes and a coffin in his basement?'

'I'm flattered,' said Vlad, 'though I don't have a coffin in my basement. It's in the living room. I use it as an occasional table.'

'I'm just saying,' I just said, 'it would be a pretty weak disguise. Sure, for someone who isn't a vampire but wants to look like one, white foundation and crimson lipstick is probably the way to go. But for your actual vampire, wouldn't a blonde wig and some fake tan work better?'

Silence.

'I'm right, aren't I?'

He was looking at me.

'Hey. I'm right, right?'

Really looking. For the first time I noticed the curiosity steaming off him. You could practically see it, like an iridescent wave of heat. You could smell it, and the stench alone would have killed a decent-sized cat.

The throng seemed to fade away into a fog, leaving only him and me. He took a breath.

'How long have you been a vampire?' he asked, out of the black.

I felt myself turn pale.

Look Who's Stalking

It was a dark and stormy night. The wind was whistling through the trees. It was whistling the score from *The Rocky Horror Picture Show*. Or that was just in my head. Because I was being stalked by a monster.

Obviously there's a certain amount of irony here.

Being a being who acquires the blood of others, often with differing levels of consent, I'd be more one of life's stalkers than stalkees, you might think. In general, I've managed to avoid the whole sinister sort of hunting people down dark alleyways thing. For the most part.

If you just took a snapshot though, froze my life for a second, knowing what you know... and if the instant you chanced upon happened to be two men secluded in a backstreet; if this was the dead of night, and if the full white moon chose that moment to crawl from behind a shred of cloud; if a shadow was cast down the cobbles to silhouette the first figure, long and freakish, splaying shadow-puppet fingers like swinging hooks on arched brick walls; and if the other startled back, struck by a chord, jarring, stumbling, silent-screaming…

Well, which one would you guess was me?

It's that thing though, isn't it? Who are the real monsters? Is it the creatures, bolt-scarred and stitched-up, all sore thumbs and left feet, outsized, ostracised, and shambling with torn-out hearts? Or is it their creators? Frankenstein or the monster? Jekyll or Hyde? Goldilocks or the Three Bears? Who should we really be afraid of?

Vlad was a sheep in big bad wolf's clothing, projecting an image to scare grandmothers. I might not often wear a little red riding hood, blue is more my colour, but I know something about lost innocence.

So who should have been scared of who?

Only fair to say at this point that Vlad never followed me down any alley, dark or otherwise. We never had that moment where he cropped up like a jack-in-the-box, clown-faced and leering, Hammer-horroring his way through the bumper book of scary movie clichés. It just felt like that.

He did follow me, though. Inconspicuous as a six-foot crow.

I'd leave the house and he'd be there. He followed me home that first night, so he knew where I lived. We had a running argument most of the way. Walking argument. Staggering?

'It didn't mean anything,' I chucked back, over my shoulder.

'Have you ever heard of a Freudian slip?'

I was more worried about literal trips after too many sips. Cobbles and beer hobbled my gait, troubled my escape.

'You came to me,' he called.

'You sought me out.'

'I think you wanted it.'

I swam around to face him, right up in his space. Confrontation has never been my instinct but there must be a little animal in all of us and it isn't always cute and fluffy. We were down on Sandgate by this time, a tight and tapered lane. Darkling shop windows sold only our reflections, and even the sky felt low and close, a dam near to bursting.

'So what? What, old man? What do you think? What am I? One of your precious vampires? You wanna put me on your tour? You want me to *turn* you? What?'

'I just want to talk.'

I didn't.

He thought he had me, back there in the pub.

'So how long have you been a vampire?'

'What?'

'You said my clients never showed any interest in the actual undead, clearing meaning yourself.'

I simultaneously sobered up and span out of control. It's a bit like, I don't know, what's some dumb, cuddly animal? Like a teddy bear, but real? Like a panda. It's like I was talking to a panda, and there's me, being all clever and condescending. "Hey, panda, why's everything so black and white with you?" thinking he's totally bamboozled. Then he comes out with all this.

'Then later you said "we", talking about coffins. You corrected yourself, but you said it.'

And I grasped it. He wasn't a panda. He was a raccoon. Similar colour scheme, just way more behind the eyes. And suddenly I was the one with fluff between the ears.

'I don't know what you mean.' The bar had all but emptied by this time. Patrons like driftwood, drawn out by the late tide, coasting back wherever they came from, doomed to return soon enough. Only the lingering and malingering remained.

'I'm a good listener,' said Vlad, mugging a smug smile. 'I hear a lot.'

'Maybe you hear what you want to hear?'

He shrugged. Smug shrug, somehow. I had to backtrack.

'You've been watching me drink all night. What's your theory? Blood in the beer?'

He stared back, unblinking.

'Yeah,' feigning a smirk so hard my face locked. 'Doesn't fit your philosophy, does it?'

'I wouldn't presume to suppose I'm right about everything.'

'You're right about nothing!' I derided, doubling down, swilling the sauce of insouciance.

'You're certain about that?' The Goth looked up with guileless eyes, dryly savouring his manoeuvre.

'Yep.'

'How can you be?'

Struck, stuck stock still, as another slip sank through the fuzz. Short-sighted, in a hole, digging on down. At risk of overextending the animal metaphor, I was now a mole.

I may have missed a few zoology lessons, but I'm going to go ahead and assume raccoons eat moles for breakfast. Or for a midnight snack.

The clock struck twelve.

After that, he wouldn't leave me alone. I had my very own dark shadow. I went to different pubs, but somehow he'd be there. I walked on the beach, he'd be there with his dog. In the park he'd be feeding the ducks. Exhuming bodies in the graveyard, he'd be tending the flowerbeds. As with the alleyway, not all of these events occurred. It's just a bit of colour. I don't even think he had a dog.

Eventually, it came to a head.

For the sake of narrative drive I'd like to say we were up on Abbey Plain, beneath the ruins, in a thunderstorm. We weren't, we were outside a chippie down Pier Road, nestled amid the trinket shacks and tourist traps, threatened only by a sea fret, and belligerent seagulls.

I'd gone in for a battered sausage, and when I came out he was there. Lurking, wreathed in pipe smoke, and what he took for mystery.

Somehow that doesn't seem dramatic enough, though. Let's go with the storm. Thunder, fat drops of rain, lightning. Tipsy grave stones and jagged crumbles of Gothic debris, each broken tower a dark shark's tooth steeped in decay. Why the hell not, eh?

Silence reigned as it rained silently. We glared, eye-to-red-eye through straits of water. Hair stuck to scalps, slicked back, black. Cheeks streamed as though through icy tears. Coruscating forks struck the scene in blazing madness.

Or, if you prefer realism, I took a bite of sausage and tried to ignore him.

'We meet again.' He beamed, beguiling.

'Why are you here?' I spat, unsmiling.

He shook his pipe with a chuckle, exuding his showman's confidence. 'Coincidence.'

'Lot of that about lately.' Thunder clapped. I smiled. I'll take a round of applause from anyone.

He grinned back, rolling and portly. 'We do seem to have some common interests.'

'I was taking the piss.'

He arched a brow, an archer's bow, fired off a wink. 'Were you though? Or were we connecting?'

I pulled a face. It was happening again, like back in the pub. He got to me. He had that extrovert power. Friendliness. Showing an interest. Notions and emotions I'd never courted or cultivated. He could get inside my head, and I'm not talking about perception. Not really. More like he knew how to twist my façade and physically force a smile.

Shaking him off I shouted through the storm, 'What do you want?'

'All right.' He faced me, leering, Lear-mad in the tempest. 'How about I give you a straight answer, then you give me one?'

I nodded. I could always lie.

He took a moment, arranging his gale-gusted thoughts. 'You came to me in the pub.' He held up a hand, forestalling an objection I'd never planned on making. 'You intruded on my conversation. Now on the face of it, you're "taking the piss". You're just a jerk who hates what I like. Yes?'

I waved him on.

'But then: why do you hate it? It must mean something to you, it must matter. You're so sure I'm wrong, about everything. Why does it matter to you?'

He took a breath. 'You're the expert. But in something you hate? Why? Because it's part of you. It's in you. Because you are a vampire. You must be.'

'You're mad.'

'At the very least you know this is real. And now I have to know what you know. Even if it—'

'Even if it kills you?' I deadpanned back, jagged bolts of electrical embellishment charging the remark with a frisson of open-air theatre. Either that, or I picked a bit of pig gristle out of my teeth.

A sick smile broke over his face. 'I think that would be an awfully big adventure.'

Why, in the frigid light of day, did I bring him home? Well, there was nowhere else. This was midweek Whitby, not some la-de-dah metropolitan hotspot with late licenced locations. No discotheque or speakeasy catered to the whims of the night owls. You might get a lock-in if you knew a landlord, but for the drifters, the wasters, the insomniacs and the run-of-the-mill creatures of darkness it was home by eleven with a bag of chips, to search the premises for hidden units of booze.

Unless what my rhetorical question really asks is: why did I bring him anywhere? That one is a bit thornier.

The easy answer is, he was on to me. My drunken tongue, Freudian or otherwise, had aligned me with his blood-fiend heroes. Ironically enough, a group I'm

47

normally desperate to disassociate myself from, on the grounds that: one, they don't exist; and two, even if they did I'm nothing like them. So, I sort of had to tell him something. Throw him off the scent.

Only other option would have been to silence him. Which can be uncomfortable. I'm not big on the whole concrete-boots, food-for-the-fishies thing. It sounds like horribly hard work, and I'm fundamentally lazy. Flippancy aside, go try hiding a body. Physically, or from your conscience. Better yet, don't. Just take my word for it. It's hard, and it hurts.

Scent-throwing clearly the way to go.

There's an even more obvious answer though, if we're going psyche-spelunking. I brought Vlad home because I was lonely.

Not gonna lie, like most guys in their early twenties, I'd had the odd fantasy of meeting a mysterious stranger in a bar and spending the night with them. No judgement on anyone else's idea of fun, but in none of these imagined encounters had the dream been about a round-middled, middle-aged Goth bloke. Still, adopt, adapt and improve, eh?

I left him while I went for a bottle, and when I got back he was just standing, with his soul coming out of his eyes. The mundanity of it must have gutted him. Just another humdrum human kitchen, bills behind the clock and cereal boxes on the counter, net curtains in the window and washing-up in the sink.

I genuinely felt for him. He might have waited his whole life for this, to be there, in the lair. A guest in the creature's den. And he got nothing. No waning wax candle or red velvet drape, no seeping stone walls or coat hooks for capes. Not so much as bat droppings on the linoleum.

Home-sweet-home crochet and a portrait of a dog.

We sat either side of the laminate-coated table and I poured cheap gin into non-matching mugs. Liquor might not have been the smartest idea to shift the discourse and suspend his superstitious suspicions. My head would have been far better clear. Disarming idiocy was plan B.

'You owe me a straight answer,' he began.

'What was the straight question?'

He rolled his eyes. 'Who are you?' A pert pause. 'Or what?'

I returned the eye roll. We were basically playing eye bowls.

'This again?'

He watched me in silence, waiting me out.

'Okay, but look. I think we're still on you. What did you actually tell me? Nothing. Nothing real about yourself.'

'And if I tell you?'

I hunched back, non-committal.

'I tell you my story, and you tell me yours? Do we have an accord?'

'Do we have a fucking accord? Who talks like that, Long John Silver?' I may have actually laughed out loud. 'Okay, Captain Flint. We have an accord. But I want the real you.' I flicked a gesticulation in his direction, taking in the hat, the cloak, the make-up. 'None of this.'

'What makes you think this isn't me?'

'Because it isn't anyone.'

A snort. 'New in town? There are plenty like me. Pale imitations, anyway.'

'It's a game though, isn't it? Dressing up, disguise. Camouflage.'

A flamboyant self-gesture. 'You think this is meant to go unnoticed?'

'A suit of armour then. It doesn't matter. Who are you really?'

Vlad ran manicured fingers through a groomed beard and, like a knight-errant, thought for his cause.

'My family, we never really connected. They were stringent conformists. I wanted to walk a different path.'

He sat his hat on the table in front of him, and his thick dye-black hair framed a face that, despite predator-parasite impersonator aspirations, appeared avuncular and benign.

'My father owned a small gift emporium. He worked seven days a week, from the day he left school almost to the day he left this mortal coil. He was regular as clockwork and found it hard to accommodate anyone who wasn't. My mother cooked the same meal on the same night of the week for their entire marriage. I still feel strangely severed from her if I don't eat fish fingers on a Thursday.'

His head shook slowly. The mug in his paw mimicked the movement.

'They never said it, but I disappointed them. I didn't care for the family business and they took it to mean I didn't care for them.'

I kept quiet. My eyes on his trembling hands. Outside it had started to rain, or it kept on raining, if I remember to stick to that storm story. Water rattled along the guttering above us, and I had to listen harder as Vlad's voice sank to a whisper.

'My mother died when I was sixteen. Cancer. She was a Christian, a social one anyway. She liked the community of church, the singing and the flowers. Her death was the final nail in any conventional faith I ever felt.'

Perhaps there was more to the black apparel than showing off. His full face hung low.

'The only part of herself she left behind was me. I stayed with my father because of that. I could tell he hated seeing her that way, in my face, my gestures. But he couldn't live without it either.'

Vlad held his hand in front of his face, inspected his painted nails. Demonstrating a gesture. He paused for a long time. I let him. There was only the rain, and the house, moving as buildings do at night. The creaks and groans that encourage folks to believe in ghosts.

'My father took to taking Sunday off,' Vlad began again at last. 'His recreation was talking to her headstone. Laying flowers. On the third anniversary of her death, they found him dead on her grave. It was a cold day; he drifted away. It must have been peaceful, people said. The post-mortem exposed advanced prostate cancer.'

He coughed, hacked into a handkerchief, and his voice, which had constricted, tightened and clipped, regained a measure of its former informality.

'I inherited the business, the house. Everything he'd accumulated in his safe, consistent life. Sold the lot. I wanted to travel.' He sighed. 'But I never got far.

'The plan was one crazy year. See the world. Pyramids, Uluru, Notre-Dame. Antarctica. I always thought I was an adventurer. Now I had the chance. My life was in my hands, nothing to restrain me but my imagination. I hesitated.'

His mug rang hollow on the table. Another empty vessel. I reached across to fill it.

'It wasn't fear. I like to think it wasn't fear. Not of travel, experience, the strange, the new, the unforeseen.

'It was my father. His ghost inside me. The pull of security. The knowledge I could live, quite securely, for quite some time, if I didn't act rashly.'

We sat together, apart. The portly Goth and the gin-soaked boy. The fox and the hound, whichever way around you want to run with that. I'd made a mistake, it was too late to stop him now. We'd passed some intimate hump, if you'll forgive the clumsy turn of phrase, and were racing onward, downward, sinking fast, into uncharted territories, still waters, running deep.

I was remembering things I'd never known. What it was like to be close.

I was missing whatever he was rambling on about.

'What if I started my own business? I thought. That could be an adventure too, in its own way. What if I did something I loved, and so never needed to work a day in my life?

'I knew the town. I knew the history. The legends and the myths. I'd always been proficient at playing a part. I started doing this, guiding tours. I love the people. Love how they behave on holiday, away from reality and willing to imagine. I love making them laugh, making them jump.

'And I love listening to them, taking their own tales.'

His eyes seemed to gleam. You think that's just an expression, until you see it happen. I'm not going to hold myself up as some expert in truth, but that was the real Vlad, right then, right there.

'Business never boomed,' he went on, 'never needed to. I'm comfortable enough. Any little extra is a bonus. I'm happy.'

He stopped. Stared into his drink. I stirred myself, realising a response might be required.

'But you never saw the world?'

'I never saw the world.'

He helped himself to more gin. My mother's. My ruin. I hadn't planned on drinking much. I wanted to stay in control. For him to be further oiled than me, to shift that panda dynamic back. Also, I've always hated gin.

'Your turn.'

I dug a knuckle into my eye, tried to massage an ache out of my head. He'd won, worn me down.

'I still don't exactly know what you want.'

He looked at me. I mean really looked. 'I want to know who you are.'

'I don't think you do.' I laughed a dead laugh. 'I think you want to hear that I was born in 1431 and I turn into a bat on full moons.'

'Vampires don't turn into bats on full moo—'

'You have no fucking clue what vampires do.' I wasn't even angry. Just tired.

'But you do. You have more than a clue. Yes?'

I gave up on controlling the headache. It was like trying to hold back gravity in an orchard. The apples were falling like rain, pummelling my brain.

'I don't, not really. They could be out there, partying it up in Transylvania for all I know, listening to trance and dancing with wolves, or whatever it is you like to imagine them doing.'

'But—'

'But what? I'm not a vampire. They might exist. Personally I highly doubt it. Like I doubt, I don't know, elves and ghosts and gods.' I paused and gave a half-hearted, quarter-hearted, smile. 'Although I did see a mummy once, in the serious burns unit at Scarborough Hospital.'

'You won't take this seriously.'

'How can I? You're a grown man in a Halloween costume.'

Vlad performed a world-class impersonation of a kicked puppy. 'If you had searched for something, for your whole life. If you'd dreamed of a moment, if you had, and then if everything you'd sought for came within your grasp—'

I stopped him again. 'Why can't you get it? This isn't everything you sought for. I'm not what you think.'

'Please, tell me? Just. Please?'

I don't know what it was. Maybe the puppy dog eyes.

I gave up, and just told him.

Interview Without a Vampire.

'I might be immortal, or sort of. I don't really know. I'm sustained by human blood. If that's the right word. It keeps me going.'

I strangled a laugh. There had been no humour in it anyway.

'That's where the confusion comes in, I guess. But really, I'm not a vampire.'

The first ray of a grey dawn crept down, yellowed the room to a lighter shade, and lit the pattern of the net curtain across the table between us. I didn't turn to dust, which I felt underscored my point quite nicely.

'I dunno what else you need to know? I'm not scared of crosses. I quite like a bit of garlic. Makes a bolognese really zing, you know?'

Vlad frowned.

'What else?' I ticked the points off on my fingers. 'I have a reflection, I can cross water. I've never slept in a

55

coffin. I'm not mates with any wolves, can't turn into a bat.' I paused, for comic effect. 'Although come to think of it, I've never really tried.'

We faced each other, quarter empty bottle between us. Quarter full, Vlad might have called it. If he hadn't known I was about to bleed his dreams dry and leave them, empty husks to crumble to dust and drift away with the morning drafts.

I'm exaggerating, of course. It would take more than the truth, more than facts, to make Vlad reappraise his view of the world. Or the underworld.

'How do you get the blood?' he asked, his fingers tracing an unconscious path through his beard, down and across his neck.

'Well, I've never bitten anyone, if that's what you're thinking.'

'I wasn't thinking that.' He put his hand back on the table.

'I don't actually drink it.'

'You don't?'

Who else but Vlad Precua could have been disappointed to hear that?

'Maybe I need to start at the beginning,' I sighed.

It could have been fun. Should have been a riot. Taking down a vampire aficionado, particularly the all-singing, all-trancing type like Vlad. One who had read all the books and bought all the T-shirts. Who dressed as he dressed, and spoke as he spoke, like a refugee from tea with the Shelleys. But somehow, it just made me sad.

I told him I was mortal, I told him I could die. Die in any number of ways. No need for a stake through the heart. Although rest assured, that would do the trick. I set about debunking the myths, the ones I could remember.

I admitted I could sunburn, although I'm not particularly pale or susceptible. I'd be safe enough with the mad dogs and Englishmen. Pasty Vlad would have more trouble there. I stood up and drew the curtain fully back, opened the window and waved in the pale sunlight. He looked on through red-rimmed eyes.

'I don't know how hot it would have to be, before I disintegrated.'

He failed to laugh.

'But long-term exposure would hurt me as much as anyone, I suppose.'

I thought about his parents, and the creeping malignance of cancer. Perhaps his interest in eternal life was not so strange.

'There's no biting,' I felt compelled to spell out, 'no drinking. It'd be disgusting, and it wouldn't do me any good. And it wouldn't...' it was weirdly hard to put into words, '... there wouldn't be any, you know, turning.'

'You can't – you don't – transmit your powers?'

'Jesus. I wouldn't call them powers.' Although I stopped, and thought: why wouldn't I? 'No, I can't. Far as I know.'

'As far as you know?'

'Well, it's not like there's an instruction manual or anything.'

'What about a blood transfusion or something?'

I scratched my head, which is what people do when they're thinking, right?

'I don't know. I'm not a doctor. You'd have to try it. What would happen?' I mused. 'Not much, probably.'

He nodded slowly. 'So, if you can't turn others… how did you… when did you.?'

I looked away. 'It's in the genes.' I drew the line at talking more about that.

He was weirdly calm, looking back. He'd told me he believed in the unnatural, really believed. I suppose I never really believed him. But as I laid out the facts of an undead existence, he was nowhere near as shocked as he should have been. Which, when you think about it, just proves how mad he was.

'Your blood,' he kept at me, 'is normal?'

'The blood, my blood, if that's not a contradiction, seems to come from – well – from the victim. I think so, anyway. My blood type changes with each reawakening.'

'Reawakening?'

'I can die.'

Can die, do die. Have died.

'But?'

I shrugged. 'I can come back.'

More accurately, I told him, could be brought back. I tried to sketch over the details. I wasn't in the mood to do specifics. It's hardly polite breakfast-time conversation, after all. But I told him about burning the corpse, and mixing ashes with human blood.

He had questions, of course.

'It has to be human blood?'

'That's what I've always been told.'

'It wouldn't work with anything else? A chicken or something?'

'Not unless you want to end up with some next-level Doctor Moreau shit.' I tried to give a watery smile, but it drowned. 'Chicken man.'

For the first time he actually looked surprised. His face was pale enough anyway, I don't know if it was make-up or what, but he managed to turn whiter.

'I'm kidding, I'm not that weird.'

I'm not normal though.

I told him how each regeneration cures me, repairs whatever fouled up and let me die. From an aortic aneurysm to zygomycosis, it makes no difference. I come back new, but the same as before.

'The same as before?'

I told him I age. I'm not frozen in time, forever young with alabaster skin and dark wisdom confined to ancient eyes. I told him that when I died age four, I came back age four, looking the same. On the outside. Inside less eaten up with tumours.

'I aged normally from four to seven. I died when I was seven, I came back seven. If I die tomorrow, I'll come back twenty-two.' I finished my drink. 'If I come back.'

'If?'

I sniffed, ignored him, and carried on. 'If I live to be a hundred, I'll look a hundred years old. And I won't live forever.'

'Why not?'

'Because why the hell would anyone want to?'

The gin was gone. I put the kettle on, and kept talking. I can't say I exactly found catharsis, but, in so deep, there didn't seem much point in stopping. While I made tea I explained about the expediency. How memories and muscles seem to suffer if I'm ashes for more than a week.

'The sooner you do it, the better the regeneration, in my experience.'

Vlad stirred in three spoons of sugar. 'It appears you're somewhat indestructible?'

'Not quite,' I raised a rueful eyebrow, 'but destroying me is pretty futile. As long as I've got someone to bring me back. Hard to pour blood on your own ashes.'

'Yes, I can see that,' he murmured.

'I need a sponsor, a friend basically. Someone not too squeamish.'

He was looking at me, keen and close. His eyes full of something hard to read. Puzzlement, curiosity. Something else. I endured a full fifteen seconds of his stare before I realised what I'd actually said.

'I wasn't asking,' I burst out. 'I didn't mean you.'

'No!' he cried. 'No,' he said, more thoughtfully. 'No.'

'My mum normally does it for me,' I said, embarrassed.

'Your mother's house?' asked Vlad, glancing around at the room again, seeming to see the clock, the curtains, the crochet, with fresh eyes. It would be easy to understate, but he was curious in every sense of the word. Forever fascinated by everything. He didn't just want to know about vampires. He wanted to know about people, too.

'Mum and Dad's, I guess. My dad hasn't been around for a while.' I tried to emphasise the full stop. To say it in a way that would close him down. He seemed to take the hint.

'Is your mother at home?' Possibly it occurred to him his presence might seem a little strange. Like if she came downstairs for a bowl of muesli, and found a random man in eyeliner seated at her kitchen table.

'She works nights,' I checked my watch, 'at the hospital.'

He was interested in that too, but I didn't know a lot about it. She was a porter or something, stocking and stacking, industrial cleaning. Mopping up blood. Pretty much what she did at home. She started those kinds of jobs when I was a kid. All that time spent in clinics and waiting rooms while I was sick, all the sympathy she received from staff. Maybe she felt she wanted to give something back.

I didn't ever ask her, of course. Because I still was a kid, really, still acting like one. As if that's any kind of excuse for being such a selfish little shit. Never missed an opportunity to ignore or undermine her, the one parent who actually cared for me. It twists me inside how badly I behaved. I loved her so much when I was small. Not that I think I ever stopped. I just think I stopped knowing I had to show it.

Maybe that's harsh. What twenty-two-year-old wants to live with his mum? I needed to get out.

'I need to get out,' I groaned.

Vlad took it I meant out of the kitchen. He proposed breakfast, his shout. I was slightly suspicious, as if he still didn't really believe I ate human food, and was planning a test. But it made sense to get him out of the house. Plus I quite fancied a fry-up.

We found ourselves back down Pier Road, heading for a café, blinking in what passed for the light, breathing through a miasma of salt and shellfish.

'You must admit,' Vlad twirled his goatee, 'it's uncanny. Of all the places a vampire could turn up—' He gave an exaggerated wave, taking in our view of the town: the harbour, the beach and the cliff beyond, the hundred-and-ninety-nine steps clambering untidily to the summit, and the castle-like outline of St Mary's church, rising up to glower with the skudding clouds.

'Not a vampire,' I corrected, automatically. Vlad often behaved as though afflicted by some wilful amnesia. He never really let himself accept he was wrong.

He smirked, 'No, but shall we say non-human?'

'Charming.'

It was amazing, really, how quickly we found our feet with regards to bickering.

'You take my point, though? This town, with its history of myth and vampirism, could it somehow have drawn you here?'

In front of us a great grey gull dropped on sail-wide wings to the pavement. Fat and moody it pecked in anger through the plastic of a discarded chip carton. When our approach did nothing to bother it away, we parted to skirt around.

'I think I just came here because my mum did. And I sure as hell don't feel any compulsion to stay.'

'No? What's wrong with here?'

'Nothing you never thought yourself,' I semi-smiled. 'What did you say you wanted to do when you were my age? See the world.'

He barked a joyful guffaw. 'Any part in particular? Or are your dreams as ill formed as mine were?'

Dreams. He was dead right there. Fantasises had sustained me, through bad times and worse. When you move about a lot, the only consistent space is inside your head. When your present is unpleasant, your future is your escape. I was never much of a reader, but I picked up those old travel books as if they were holy texts. Jack Kerouac. Paul Theroux. Freya Stark. Lemuel Gulliver. I wanted to wander, to wonder. To live life, get high in Amsterdam, roam through Rome, make up terrible puns in the Punjab.

If anything drew me to Whitby, and I'm in no way admitting that it did, it would have been the ships, the sailing away. Breaking away.

But Vlad was right. Painful to say. They were dreams, and as ill formed as his. Even when I was old enough to go, I couldn't. I couldn't leave my mum. I could try and be cute and say that was because she needed me. But you know that would be a lie. It was because I needed her. In case I died again.

You can say that's crazy. A fit, healthy twenty-two-year-old worrying about death. A fit, healthy twenty-two-year-old capable of reincarnation at that.

Well, think what you want. But until you've died a couple of times yourself you can leave off judging me about it.

I didn't want to leave, because if I died by myself there'd be no coming back.

But I didn't tell Vlad that.

'I can't leave my mum. She needs me.'

Seabirds wheeled overhead, calling mournful lamentations.

'You're never going to see the world?'

'I'm never going to see the world.'

We went into the café and had cholesterol on fried bread. Six months later we were in Romania together.

Chapter Six (six, six)

Like any couple, we had our arguments. That is a deeply depressing sentence, and sentiment. The admission that Vlad and I were, to some intents and various purposes, a couple. A couple of kooks, a couple of swells. The unoriginal odd couple.

Sexless, feckless, one wrecked, one reckless. You could have written a song about us.

But it probably would have struggled to chart.

I've never been much of an arguer. Someone said I was once, but I soon persuaded them otherwise. Seriously though, I'm not one of those contentious quarrellers who thrive on debate. I don't enjoy politics, or family games of Monopoly.

Vlad, on the other hand, could start an argument on an empty moon. He hardly needed to breathe.

We'd still probably have been alright, with a bit of space. Trouble was, travelling didn't give us that in spades. Vlad could be considered good company in carefully diluted doses. He was a decent enough stick in his own stupid, annoying way. But by the time we'd been on the road six months or so, I was ready to beat the bastard to death with my battered copy of Kerouac.

The fundamental problem was our expectations were mismatched. Mine were fun and his were mental. Although I suppose it's all a matter of perception.

We both wanted to travel the world. Or thought we did. Different travel, though. Or just a different world. I wanted hedonism. Hippie trails and hookah pipes, Hare Krishna and hitch-hiking. Voyages of self-discovery in VW vans, guided by bearded guys in tie-dye moo-moos, stargazing with girls named Moonshine and Harmony. I suppose what I wanted was history. Or more likely, mythology. I wanted what I'd read about in my bedroom, under the covers with Theroux and a fantasy.

Vlad might have wanted something similar, once. Thirty years before. He might even have gone, in an alternate reality, on the Grand Tour. Given himself a different silly pseudonym, swapped one mask for another. Become a Buddhist in Tibet. Worn orange instead of black.

By the time our paths crossed, his interests had moved on. He wanted to hunt vampires.

'You know they don't exist, right?'

'You exist.'

'We've been over this. I'm not a vampire.'

'But you're something. And whatever you are, your

ancestry may have influenced mythos and folklore. Don't you want to know more?'

'Not really.'

And I didn't, at the time. But our schemes, equally unrealistic dreams, at least led us in similar directions. Into Europe, and the East.

With about as much chance as each other of finding what we were looking for.

By the time we reached the Black Sea we had trekked through a gamut of colourful moods. Journeys by nature are tense and taxing. Trains strain and drain. The unknown exhausts.

Prone to introspection and reflection, I have always been disposed to sullen silence. That rubbed Vlad up one way, and his constant gregarious patter rubbed me up the other.

By July, hot and dry, hot and bothered, hot and dirty, we found ourselves lost. Not so much geographically, although we'd never really known where we were with any degree of certainty, but, god, how can I put this non-pretentiously? Spiritually. Philosophically. We were out of patience, out of sorts. Out of money.

In a tavern garden, sun-browned and moodily shaded, we reached the end of the line.

Rough shod on rough seats, we sat, shoulders backpack sore and stooping. Vlad beneath a wide black brim, cultivated his best Van Helsing look. He drank red wine, sun warm and russet. His book lay open in front of him, leather bound and full of lore, and I was studiously ignored.

Full disclosure, it might have been a different garden, different land. Romania, Croatia, Greece and Cyprus. All had merged together. Their scents of citrus, olive, resin and lemon. Pines and palms, green scorched brown, rocky outcrops under unrelenting skies. And the water, that palette of blue, making you want to pick up a brush and try to capture it, even if you had never painted more than a wall in your life. Countries and countryside, people and places, all perfect, each special to someone. All blend into one for the nomad.

Every bar, each row of bottles, every paved courtyard and twist of vine became the same. Even the walnut skin on the old men's faces, their eyes like currants, buried deep, their chat and the click of their tongues, language and laughter, began to blur.

And always the sun, that painter's light, the shadow and the crawling lizards.

Vlad was leafing through his book, blue-tinted lenses flipped down over his reading glasses. I was scribbling in a notepad, or more often, not scribbling. Roughing out impressions for a travel book of my own. One I guessed I'd never write.

Nothing but grunts for an hour, until he broke the silence.

'Here's an interesting case from 1732: the staking of Arnold Paole.'

I was on the point of stifling a yawn, before I realised that would be wasteful and counterproductive. I exaggerated it instead. Vlad didn't care.

'Paole was serving his country in Greece, but

following a string of disturbing occurrences he resigned his commission and returned home to Serbia.'

By mistake, I bit. 'Disturbing occurrences?'

Vlad let me have it with a knowing, sideways look.

'Interested all of a sudden?'

It had been a feature, a swollen lump on the face of our trip. From the very start, he fought to interest me.

On the first train out of Yorkshire, hope still shining out of his eyes, he read to me from that bloody book.

'"For, let me tell you, he is known everywhere that men have been. In old Greece, in old Rome: he flourish in Germany all over, in France, in India, even in the Chersonese."'

'What's that supposed to mean, then?'

'That vampires have always existed, and in every culture. How could that be possible, if there were no basis to it?'

'So?'

'Maybe you're the basis?'

But deep down that thought never really satisfied him. He still wanted me to be something I wasn't. Something more akin to the monsters of literature. He kept trying to catch me out. Sneaking garlic into my supper in an Austrian pension, flicking Holy Water at me from a font in a church outside Dresden. Looking disappointed when I didn't go up in smoke.

By the time we made it to Romania, long, slow months later, his tome was blanched and dog-eared, his mien dulled, deadened by the lack of romance in my soul. Or so he said.

'I'm not *interested*,' I picked at the label on my beer bottle, 'but you're probably going to tell me anyway.'

He gave a false little one-note chuckle, which gave me an instant, albeit fleeting fit of rage. I don't know anymore, whether we deliberately pushed one another's buttons, or if we just stopped trying not to. That chuckle though, it could have driven me to murder. I dragged a hand through a fortnight of stubble, scratched around to the prickly heat at my neck. Hurt myself to control the pain of hearing that chuckle.

'I'll tell you then?' he smirked at my wince.

I looked away, across to the bar.

'He married the daughter of a neighbouring farmer.'

'What's disturbing about that?' Bitten again, begetting the chuckle. There are layers of hell reserved for that chuckler.

'That isn't the disturbing experience. That came when he got back home.'

'And then they lived happily ever after?'

Vlad raised his glass, all for effect, so he could glare at me disapprovingly over the rim, and return it to the table with his lips barely moist.

'No. His experiences had left him melancholic. He worried his wife with his fears of meeting an early death.'

I nodded. 'These experiences would be the disturbing occurrences, yes?'

Vlad nodded. 'Apparently while in Greece, Paole was visited by an undead being.'

'Sounds like someone overdid the ouzo.'

I suppose comments like that were my equivalent of

the chuckle. They never really got a rise out of him though. Just a sigh and a silent headshake.

'You know, for an actual undead being, you can be remarkably cynical about the existence of others.'

'I'm sorry, I'm sorry. Go on, what did he do? Ward it off with a particularly garlicky tzatziki dip?'

Just because I never got a reaction, doesn't mean I knew how to stop.

'He sought it out and burned the corpse.'

'Well, you would, wouldn't you?'

'I'm just relaying the facts.'

'Sure. *Facts.*'

He made a little play that he was upset. Showed me the nearest thing in town to a cold shoulder. Disappeared back behind his book. I swear I even heard him sniffle.

I smiled, watched a flit of grey-and-yellow songbirds dart in and out between the thorns of an olive tree. Enjoyed the brief peace.

They always sent the pretty ones to us. Swarthy guys were reserved to serve the ladies of a certain age, congregating in a corner beneath what passed for shade.

She wore white, bright against golden skin, hair in rich waves fashioned to complement the flower at her ear. Eyes you wanted to disappear into. Silver cross at her breast.

'Worth turning to dust for,' I muttered.

Who says I had no romance?

She brought us a gift, a bowl of salt disguised as bar-snack nuts. The moment you touched a handful to your mouth, you had to order another beer, whether you could afford it or not. I ordered two.

She left with a smile so sweet she made my chest hurt. Left me for some drunken stags who tried to grab her arse. Left me feeling alone, and longing to be human.

My turn to sigh. I pushed Vlad's glass until it nudged his hand.

'Go on then, what happened next?'

He'd been waiting.

'Paole died in an accident.'

Involuntarily, I looked up. Accidental death was more my speed than Vlad's usual factoids.

'He was buried in the town cemetery.'

Facetiousness rose to the tip of my tongue, was swallowed back. For once I actually wanted him to go on.

Vlad needed no encouragement. 'In the weeks that followed, there were reports among the townsfolk, stories of Paole walking abroad.'

For the first time, probably the first time since that first train, I looked at him properly. Saw past the joke, the elderly Englishman abroad, too-short linen trousers exposing bone-skinny ankles. I looked below the ridiculous hat, through the over-earnest expression and self-importance and saw the man, taking an interest. Maybe even trying to help.

Perhaps because he in turn had finally found something, gone beyond the mountain-pass castle hideaways, away from lupine guards, ruby-lipped succubae and screams in the night. Turned away from the glamour and the drama, and found something real, normal, down to earth. My earth, at least. My normal.

I'd heard a thousand vampire stories. Nine-hundred-

and-ninety-nine of them from Vlad. Nothing I could relate to. Maybe Arnold was the man.

An accident. Not bitten, not caught, or turned. Falling, sickness. Dying, and yet walking, not floating, not bat-winged or fanged. Just a bloke, in his village, wishing he could still be himself.

Not undead, with the creepy connotations. Just dead but not dead. That was me.

For the first time it occurred to me, Vlad might have been right. Or at least, if I couldn't quite admit that, perhaps not wholly wrong. My kind might be the root of the myths. At least some of them.

'They saw him?' I twiddled my beer, spilled a dribble on the table between us.

'Some even claimed he had visited their homes.'

Dabbling my finger on the table, I doodled in fizzy puddles.

'Then what?'

He read for a moment. 'Time passed. Those who maintained the rumours began to meet with mysterious deaths.'

'Fuck.' I sank, sucked down like a lead-lined *Titanic*. We were back to mystery. Back to mysticism.

'What now?' he snapped. Not really interested, not really caring. I waved him on.

'A group met to exhume the corpse: two doctors, two soldiers and a priest.'

His words wafted away, no need for a breeze to carry them.

'They found the body fresh, the lips coated with blood.'

I glanced up at him. His glasses had slid down his

73

nose. He didn't need them for his book anyway. Another affectation. Our eyes met as he read without looking at the page.

'They drove a stake through the body, Paole cried out in pain, and fresh blood poured from the wound.'

I stood up, without another word, and walked away.

He found me by the water.

A pier, white metal balustrade, bolts crusting with orange rust, railings casting long trails of spindly shadow down crazy paving. Weathering, barnacles. Seaweed climbing the sea wall like plaque up a tooth, black rock jutting in a jetty, a scar across the harbour. Waves turning to cream: frothing, lapping, coating.

'The mermaids become the sea foam when they die. They have no souls, you see.'

He was behind me. The sun was on my face. I didn't care.

'Hans Christian Andersen.'

At the horizon, wherever that was, the sky was almost yellow. By gradual gradients, so subtle you could never make them out alone, it turned to blue.

'But then, mermaids don't exist either, do they?' He came and leant beside me, sharing the view.

'That sky is a miracle.' I pushed my shades up onto my forehead, to look with my own eyes. 'Nature is a miracle.'

He didn't ask me to explain, and we just stood, side by side contemplating this world, this life. The sky alone is replete enough with wonder, why go searching for more?

'I like it here,' he said at last. It was probably all of three minutes since he'd spoken. For Vlad, that counted as an extended period of introspection. 'It reminds me of home.'

'Never had a home.' Looking out into the world, that felt heart-aching to admit. You could claim, belonging nowhere, to belong everywhere. But you would know inside that you were kidding yourself.

Vlad sniffed. His hand crept out to hover around my back, considering a pat, perhaps even a hug, before evidently deciding against it. I don't know who would have been more embarrassed. It was all slightly sweetly sad. Both of us with bits missing, neither with any spare parts.

'Do you remember Transylvania?' I asked.

Of course he remembered Transylvania. For him, it was the realisation of a lifelong dream. You might find it a strange dream, to hanker to be Harker, treading the pathways of the damned, actively hoping for dank, for dark, for dungeons. For bats in the belfry. Less a dream perhaps than a nightmare, a hypnotic trance. For a feeling within him had been induced, seduced. He had a longing.

Whitby might style itself the cradle of Dracula, but the Count was no more than a tourist. His homeland was one of deeper valleys, channelled through mountains, Carpathian peaks bold and craggy, climbing up to meet the yellow moon and block it out. Jagged foothills growing into turrets, boulders becoming bartizans and battlements, castles emerging out of rock. Pine clambering, evergreen spikes puncturing frosty forests, cold lurking places for wolves and worse. Fog, shrouding vapours, a hazy pall, thick and copious, demanding the extra synonyms, scorning to be merely called mist.

A place that did not exist.

That is, it does, in the sense of there being an actual Romanian region of that name. It even has forested mountains. And they have a cold beauty. But they are not scary, no more so than any other large geographical feature. Awe may be inspired, you might be frightened by a sense of your smallness in the universe, or just by the prospect of a precipitous drop. But there is no creeping sense of supernatural dread. At least, there was not for me. And sadly not for Vlad.

Vlad, doyen of his Whitby Goth community, curator of the myth, had wanted only what he had read of in Stoker. He went looking for something with teeth. Should have known better than to believe something he read in a book, really.

We found Bran Castle, the Habsburgian holding, high and haughty on its perch, reached via a winding path hacked through hard rock. It had its history, Teutonic titans, Turks, even Tepes. And it did not hide its connection to our friend Dracula. But it did not move Vlad.

Perhaps we should have gone in winter.

'What's wrong?'

'It's all wrong.'

He was unusually grumpy in the heat, his hat an ostentatious fly-swat amid a plague of midges.

It seemed epic enough to me, though I'd been happier in the vales, among the small villages, where beer and accommodation were cheap and cold. I was never averse to a bit of sight-spotting.

'Let's just go, okay?'

'Why?' I shrugged. I didn't really mind.

'It's not what I wanted.'

'Do you remember Transylvania?'

His face rolled back the decades, showed me his past as a rueful schoolboy.

'Books don't always get it right.'

'Stoker never even went there, you know,' he smiled sadly.

'We're both mad, aren't we?' I laughed, looking across at him, next to me, beside himself. 'Both chasing something we read about, but it's...' I trailed away, words empty.

Words. Harder to use than we think, when we're talking, anyway. Give me a library, and a literary encyclopaedia, and I'll make you understand me. Or I'll overcomplicate things and confuse you. Our conversation took place in real life, not in the pages of a thesaurus. But it's more fun to write it down this way.

'It's ethereal,' he whispered, hushed like the shushing waves.

I laughed again, louder, wilder. 'No. No, that's not what I was going to say. Not at all. Not even close. It's not ethereal, it's not...' I grasped for the language, '... ephemeral, it's not hard to grasp. It's just bloody mad. We're as bad as each other. I read Theroux and Kerouac and thought that was what life could be like. I thought I was going to experience everything. I thought I was going to inter-rail through youth hostels with Sal and Moriarty. God, it gets madder the more I say it. Half of that isn't even the right continent. I might as well have read Marco Polo and used it as a map of Argentina.' I flailed for my meaning. 'I was deluded,

Vlad. I came out here searching for something that's gone, or maybe it was never here, maybe it only ever lived in a writer's mind. Like if you only knew Vegas from Hunter S. Thompson, then you went there sober and it wasn't what you had in mind. You know?'

'You're saying I can never find the real Dracula's castle.'

'Yes. No. More than that. None of what you want. It can never be what you expect, what you hope. I'm talking about me, Vlad. Me and you. I'm not what you want me to be. This was a mistake. You're not William S. Burroughs and I'm not Nosferatu.'

I looked at him, since I'm channelling high-brow literary inspiration for this segment, with a *hard stare* straight from Michael Bond.

'Do you see?'

He looked away, into the ether.

'I thought you had it for a moment, back in the tavern. I thought you'd let go of the legends. But it was just another story. Things get a little bit gory, contagion, bat crap. Bedtime tales to frighten the kids.' The breeze was in my eyes, salt and spray, reddening and blotching.

'I suppose I just hoped,' he started, slowly, seriously. 'You can laugh at me, laugh at the ghost walker, reading horror stories and believing them. But it's no sillier than the cynicism of science. We used to be afraid of the dark. We lit a fire and now we pretend there's nothing hiding there, beyond the tiny circle of light we've created. We used to write "*here be dragons*" on the blank spaces of our charts, now we kid ourselves we've filled in the edges of the map.'

He held tight to the rail. He wouldn't let go.

'I believed there was more. Always. Truth behind the campfire songs. Could we really have invented these monsters, with no foundation? I believed. I took it on faith. I had to. But then you opened a door.'

He looked at me, like a drivelling Renfield at his master, like a drooling Dr Gonzo at a mind-expanding mushroom, like a dribbling Paddington, at a marmalade sandwich.

'I'm not what you want me to be though, I can't be what you want me to be.'

'And yet you are all there is.'

'Vlad—'

'There's no gypsy caravan for me, no caravan of love for you. Let's agree, but that's not to say we can't give each other what we need.'

'Don't make this weird, mate.' I hardly ever call anyone mate. It was jocularity at its most affected.

'You want…' He gave a shifty glance about. We were alone. 'You want to revel in your *immortality*.' He laid the emphasis on thick in a stage whisper louder than his normal voice, 'You can do it all. Take the drugs, run with the wolves. Risk it all on one turn of pitch and toss. You have the licence to live dangerously. Hedonist, epicurean, degenerate, rake. You can live in an ivory tower, or leap from one.'

He was right. I could. If I had a safety net. He knew it too.

'And what do you get?'

'I observe your world.' The sun was lower now, the sky redder. He stared into the umber gloaming. 'It's as close as I can get to being part of it.'

'Supernatural by proxy.'

That look again, madman, addict, hungry bear. 'It's the only path left. For either of us.'

Out of the literary lexicon for the finale, back to veracity:

'And you're willing to do it?'

'I want to do it.'

'You want to?'

'I need to.'

Chills.

'I need to see it. I need to watch it happen.'

'You don't know what you're saying.' I pushed back, away from the edge.

'We've come this far. You have to show me.'

'You don't know what you're asking.'

'I think I do.'

'You're asking me to die. For what, your enjoyment?'

He spread his arms, attempted a guileless smile. 'No, for yours.'

'This isn't going to work.'

'What?'

'This.'

'Don't be stupid.'

I began to walk away.

'Don't do something you'll regret.' Undertones, by the water, by the undertow. A threat to drag me back, drag me down.

'That's the only sensible thing you've said all day.'

I left him, by sea.

Midnight.

Well, it probably wasn't, but, you know, drama.

There's a certain double-standard there, I suppose. Laying on the theatre with a shovel, after accusing Vlad of living for the spectacle.

I am actually trying to write a book though. Vlad was just some nut-job intent on turning me into a fairy-tale bloodsucker in order to justify his own bizarre lifestyle choices.

So, apples and blood oranges, really.

Where were we? Ah yes. Midnight. The dead of night. The witching hour. A strange room. Strange as in unfamiliar. Strange also as in, well, strange.

Back at the bedsit. Checked in alone. No sign of Vlad since sunset. Not caring. Too tired. Too dead inside. Hot with drink, shivering under sweat-damp covers. Sleep at the centre of a labyrinth, impossible to find. Mind occupied with the unseen, unseeable.

From my pit, I sensed it all.

A wind in the eaves, creaks and whistles. The place was old, the bed, the wood, nooks and knotholes, mothballs in cupboards with doors that didn't close, swinging, unhinged, crying out for grease or oil. Noisy enough to drown out the ghosts, ghosts of drowning this close to the sea. The sea, somewhere close, the smell of it, the sound, pound, pound. All around, things that go bump in the night.

Not every bump can be accounted for.

Deep, slow, careful breaths.

Not mine.

It's horrifying. The gradual realisation that something is in your room with you. Something more than the spiders, and the cockroach you saw in the sink. Something more frightening. Maybe more frightening than you.

More frightening than me, more to the point. And I'm an indestructible monster sustained by human blood.

Moving slowly, sloth slow, tortoise cautious, inch by incremental inch, I stretched out a hand towards the bedside lamp. My fingers feathered the drawstring, touching, knocking it, swaying it away, out of my grasp. Seconds slithered by as I tried to fumble, simultaneously pretending still to slumber. Sound asleep, no sound. I grabbed the string and drew.

In the instant before the bulb popped I saw him there above me, close enough to touch. In his bandaged left hand, a trembling glass of blood, in his right – no time to look – on instinct alone my own arm whipped across between us, as the knife swept down.

Part 2

We Don't Freeze in Time

Headspace

Do you remember chapter one? I started with a sort of framing device. Me, in Whitby, mulling over life, giving a bit of the old backstory and semi-searching for Vlad. In the present tense of all things.

Reason I ask is, if nobody remembers, I could perhaps quietly disassociate myself, walk away, and speak of it nevermore…

But obviously it made too big of an impression? Okay, well, if you're sure.

Here we go again.

Whitby, after sunset. Jet black. In a town where that means something.

Not everyone is fond of the darkness. Those who aren't monsters, I mean. That's not a crack at the undead. I could give you a hundred-and-one examples of this particular creature of the shadows chilling in the sunshine, sipping a poolside smoothie.

It's not the condition that has drawn me to the night, it's bad choices. That's what makes a monster, in the end, isn't it? The way we forge our path. Like Fagin, or any one of forty thieves. Cut-purse, cut-throat or disaster capitalist; like any villain, like anyone with a past: I like the shadows because they hide me.

Creeps like to creep, who knew?

Up on the cliff top, there is precious little moonshine to lead me. The satellite itself is a slither of toenail clipping, the lamp posts are asleep. Yet even outside the light, there's a sense of presence here. The sea. The crags, the beach and the ocean. Force and age and might. A power out there somewhere, as deep as space, as old as stars.

Unseen waves beat at the sea wall, rhythmic claps of wash and spray, the rush of the tide rasps and rustles. A bite of breeze teases my T-shirt and slaps the cotton against my chest. Ruffles my hair. Whips up memories.

Memory is like a kite string, it sometimes seems. The kite is life, born aloft on tumultuous whips and weathers, drifting immune to wants and wishes. And the string streams out below.

Short and taut at first, like this sentence. But increasingly lengthening, buffeted, bewildering; bold or belligerent or both, winding out in chaotic reels, out of control, ill thought out, alluding much yet eluding grasp and meaning… much like this sentence, in fact. The problem is where does it end? Who is holding the string and trying to make sense of it all? Perhaps I have it backward, perhaps the kite is birth, beginnings, and it is the liver of life who is grounded, staring up at the past as it bobs above, dancing and distant and difficult to distinguish.

Imagine then, that you have two kites to keep track of. Three, or four, five, six, seven. Imagine how memory must appear to me.

The point, if I dare to dream that there is one, is that some parts of my story are clearer than others, some more colourful. Perspective is a surprisingly fluid concept. Distance is relative. Close up can be a blur.

Memories don't tend to come out in a logical order, so don't expect chronology. I know that at some point I'll need to tell you about what happened after Vlad murdered me. But not yet. I'll get to it. I'll bare all, if you can bear it, but you'll have to bear with me.

For now, I'm just letting the wind take me.

A kite might not be the best analogy, or the most apropos. I don't know. I wanted one about the tide really, or the river, so I could have segued nicely back into my actual geographical location, high above the harbour and the Esk.

A river should have worked. Winding, wending, inexorable. Somehow I couldn't find the words.

Still, even if not utterly apt, the string theory is hardly outright inept. Whitby, I would say, has as much sky and squall as anywhere.

I'm too deep in it now, anyway…

… Sometimes the twines intertwine in curious and unexpected ways. Like how the first time I met Vlad is knotted and tangled with the last time we spoke. Both meeting and parting occurred in the same pub.

That might explain why my legs had been heading there, independent of my head, before I recollected, and changed course, heading up to the cliff top.

Reading that back, it sounds slightly like I have a disembodied head. Not the case. Whatever other inhuman traits I possess, you're unlikely to catch me cantering around Sleepy Hollow. It was merely a remark on muscle memory. My feet followed a well-trodden path, taking me where they assumed I needed to go, while my brain was otherwise engaged. Can you wind out my metaphor to explain that?

Let's not worry about it, let's get back to the pub.

One of the first things I did when I found myself back in Yorkshire was to look him up. Just in the phone book, you know. I wasn't sure I actually wanted to find him, still less meet him. I kidded myself I just needed to know if a chance encounter was on the cards.

And he'd come home to roost. Of course he had. Maybe because lodestones run through the souls of our towns, or because certain spots exist at the centre of spiritual whirlpools and emotional vortexes. But probably not. More likely he just wanted to retire somewhere he was accustomed to. For years he had been a familiar in strange lands. Perhaps in the end there was no place like home.

His name had been in the book, with an address back in the old town. And so, one day, inevitably, curiosity got tired of dispatching cats and drew me around his old haunts.

The pub still stood, semi-detached from reality on the harbour shore. It hadn't changed much over the years. Same veins of dry varnish running ridges over oak-effect tabletops. Same knotholes in the beams, same not-beaming looks on the local faces. Same maroon walls and marine-theme decor, ships in bottles, barometers, old rope. Same low lights streaming from faux gas lamps. Same old Vlad. Except older.

He was even seated in the same corner, if memory served. Although it doesn't serve, does it? We've already established that. It dallies and it dances, dashes and darts. You may try to reign it in, fight the kite all you like, but you'll never truly control it. So maybe it's just dramatic licence, but in my mind he seemed to occupy the same space as before.

'The prodigal son!' he intoned, managing to remind me in a mere three words why I hadn't seen him in years. Not so much the words, I suppose, as the tone. What lay between the lines. Between us.

Obviously I'm not one to hold a grudge, otherwise I'd never have stuck with him even after he tried to go all Van Helsing and stake me. But it would be pointless to pretend he's not one of the most annoying, cloying people in the world.

We took a moment to take each other in. I was fit and healthy then, off the bad stuff. Looking alright. Tanned. Happy. Vlad managed to appear disappointed.

He looked ill.

'Good to see you,' I attempted a smile. I'd call it watery, but water might get offended.

'Of course it is,' he blared. 'And abnormally well timed. We were just discussing our favourite *leaches.*' He gestured to his companion, a girl in a white shirt, with a white face. A make-up cake designed to make her seem older, though having the opposite effect.

'This little lady is a Poppy Brite fan, she swears by *Lost Souls,*' Vlad explained, 'but I'm educating her!' He beamed at his fortune, a chance to show off his expertise.

'I'm just collecting glasses.' She shot me a pleading look. Her white towel thrown over one arm.

Like an elderly tiger, too lame and blind to catch a meal, he'd clearly fallen to carrion. Without his tours, his little pockets of influence, he was reduced to cornering hired help.

Regret tapped me on the shoulder, nodded towards the door. Told me I shouldn't have come. Why had I come? Did I still feel the need to explain myself?

I figured I should at least save the girl before I left.

'Don't let Vlad bore you,' I smiled at her. 'He wouldn't know a vampire if it bit him on the arse.'

'Ha!' Vlad jabbed at me, pointedly. 'Don't ask this one about *real* vampires. He's not at all to be trusted on the issue. Or on others.'

At least some of us were aware the conversation had strayed into awkward territory. The girl shuffled sheepishly, edging back towards the safety of the counter.

'You don't have to go,' Vlad wheedled, trying to herd her back with his cane. 'I may have exaggerated my acquaintance's ignorance.'

That was about as close as the old bugger could get to offering me a compliment.

'And I might have been hard on *Lost Souls*,' he murmured, slipping out of the present. 'There is room for more than one interpretation.'

Soaring up, I stared down on the scene like a spectator. I hadn't turned into a bat or anything. I'm speaking figuratively. It was just an odd little out-of-body experience, travelling out of myself and, I don't know, dreaming a waking dream. Reliving a touch of déjà vu.

History is doomed to repeat itself, or so I've heard. Then again, I've also heard that history is doomed to repeat itself. And that history is bunk. It's difficult to know what to believe. All I have to rely on is my own broken record, and that tells me the kite string can tie together so tightly you sometimes can't tell whether the strand in your hand is the one you were looking at earlier, or simply something remarkably in sync and similar.

Truth is, all nights, like all of us, grow older, age and slowly die. Some nights, like only some of us, are doomed to come back again.

'It's just to me, Brite's creatures are a little… uncouth.'

It was almost comforting, this spiel, after all the water under our shared bridges, running water, crossed together. Except now he knew he was wrong. He'd gone from peddling myths, to actively flogging out-of-date pork pies.

The glass collector looked up at me, kohl-eyed, so young. She did not seem convinced. My guess is it takes a lot more than a rival practice's preacher to shake real faith. Vlad's own devotion had certainly survived stronger tests.

He finished his drink.

'I should go,' she said, taking her opportunity, and his glass.

We were left.

A beat of silence.

'What's the story then?' he slurred, too loud. 'Back for blood?'

'I don't do that anymore.'

'What's the matter? Am I not your *type*?' A joyless giggle from North Yorkshire's Oscar Wilde.

'You know that isn't it.'

He took a drink. Literally took it, I'd bought it for myself.

'Good to see you're managing to steal a living.' I showed a phoney grin.

He returned it. The look, not the drink.

It was almost frightening how quickly we slipped back into our old roles. Obnoxious pettiness, snarky remarks. Each trying not to show it when the other burrowed under the skin. But there was a delicate sea change. A harder edge.

We were alone. Alone in a room full of people. I was going to write *alone in a room full of strangers*, which I thought sounded quite poetic, but it would have been an outrageous lie. Vlad was Whitby born and raised, on nodding terms at least with most folk, and half the time the talk of the town. There was only one real stranger present, reborn and hell-raised. And no prizes for guessing who that was.

Still, the odd gruff greeting, glance, metaphorical hat-tip aside, we were alone.

He finished my drink. It was one too many, tipsy over that hard edge, he turned his on-stage persona off, quickly went dark.

'Still with *her* then?'

'Yes.'

Vlad snorted. 'I guess she does your dirty work now.'

'Stopped the dirty work. I told you.'

'I thought it was a phase you were going through.'

In writing class they always say "show, don't tell." I do my best. He took a long swill of bitter.

Those nodding dogs you get in the back of cars, he looked like one of them. Some black breed with ungainly jowls and sorrowful-soul eyes, head in constant motion, just gentle rocks. Except not nodding, but shaking. Silent, back and forth, over and over.

I wasn't bothered. I let the silence draw on.

'You're really going through with it?' he muttered through the curl of his lip at last. 'You're just going to die?'

'S'pose so,' a verbal shrug, 'eventually.'

'I can't believe it.'

My turn to stay silent.

'You're a vampire.'

'No.'

'The closest thing there is to one,' his eyes bloated, 'and you would throw away immortality? Give up everlasting life?'

I took a quick scope over my shoulder. I was the sober one this time; the reckless, wrecking-ball language was his. The locals drank on, oblivious to oblivion.

Vlad pinned me with loaded eyes. It occurred to me that perhaps I hadn't always treated him well. Was it my responsibility though, the path he'd chosen? I hadn't dug him up, carried him away, cast him aside. My curse had given him an opportunity. Opportunity of a lifetime. Opening a door for someone doesn't oblige them to go through it.

Still, he'd given up a lot. Or put it on hold. A home, friends. Attachments I never understood at the time. And here I was, chucking it back in his face.

'I've seen what I'm giving up.' An apparition of diaphanous fragility, stretched skin and horror swam behind my eyes. I quickly blinked it away.

'And?'

'It isn't life.'

His head sank, chin to chest.

'Then this really is goodbye.'

He was right. It was. Goodbye, a matter of metres from our first hello.

It was two weeks later, I think, that he suffered his cerebrovascular accident.

In a stroke the night sky above the cliff top grew darker. No twinkle of star or satellite, no light at all through the cumulonimbus. It didn't seem possible, though of course it is. Droplets of water can overpower a ball of burning gas, twenty kilometres in diameter, if the optics are right. Life, like art, like a novel, can always get darker. I took out my phone to show me the way. Immediately wished I hadn't. Those messages still glowed. Little envelopes of doom, packaging the end of the world. My finger clicked one of its own accord. I tried to look away.

I know you've got her.

94

Why have you done this?

Is there such a thing as ill-illiteracy? Not being able to not read?

Don't come back.

Don't ever speak to me again.

Dead to someone else, then.

The moon rose, or the fog parted. Either way, a chance to put the phone away. A chink of light. A little beauty. The sky's a time machine at any time. You're seeing things that moved on light years ago. You'll never see a sight twice, and yet, it's the same old heaven it's always been.

I thought of the view Vlad and I shared, the day he killed me. The sun setting into the Black Sea. We were dead to each other, now. But he'd understand. We could both be reanimated, this time.

Above me now was a dimmer glory, a midnight canvas. But beauty doesn't have to be obvious, rainbows and stars, sunbeams and so forth. There are unsung shimmerings too. Clouds, wandering, waving like daffodils, golden in their bliss of solitude, until you see they really do have silver linings.

Go and look if you don't believe me. Your book can wait.

Did you go? Probably not. Check though, next time you're out. Make time to look up. See the sun, or moon, or both. It's a quirk of *Twilight Zone*-level strangeness, isn't it, that these two circles in the sky, one smaller, closer, the other larger but further away, should appear the same size to us. No wonder the ancients invented gods to explain it.

It's almost enough to make you believe. Although I don't know what in. Lunar deities and solar powers. Nothing you've dreamt of in your philosophy. Though stranger things exist.

So we end where we began, with perspective. Or maybe it comes down to focus, and my kite string, tugged and rolled by flight and flurry.

Picture now the part closest to the kite, the length adorned with twists of coloured ribbon. So high, remote. Feel how your gaze is drawn. The eye follows, entranced. The kite swoops, the ribbons fall and flutter, closer to your face until they're all that you can see.

I've lived a whole life – lives – been cursed to abide in interesting times, wandered from Timbuctoo to Kathmandu. Partied with puppets, paupers, pirates, poets, pawns, and, if that Nigerian bloke I met on the internet is to be trusted, kings. I've swum with sharks. I've fallen in love.

But right now Vlad is all that I can see. And I know I need yet another, still more final, goodbye.

Because only he can save us.

Headaches

It's the worst of both worlds. Like if you've ever been drunk and hungover at the same time. Unable to control your own headspace, spaced out and sluggish, yet already exposed to the encroaching creep of throbbing pains. Fighting a headache that doesn't just pound; it kicks, bites, scratches and pulls hair. Pulls teeth.

Stomach knitted, knotted, not capable now of keeping anything down or anything in. Bowels looser than an England bowler's first over of the day. Does anyone get cricket analogies these days? Screw 'em, it's my book. I'll include an anthropomorphised insectoid conscience in a top hat and tails if I want.

But I'm not in the mood for levity.

I want to talk about morning afters. Or month afters.

Talk about being sick. Aching. Broken.

The comedown. Blurry, bleary, blotched vision and

botched decisions, too much of a bad thing. Scraping yourself up off life's sticky carpet, mothballed mouth and missing memories. Withered and withdrawn.

Same as any come down. Everyone knows about the lows.

The dirty little secret is the highs aren't that hot either, after a while. Comes a time when you'd rather keep your head, when floating on the ether loses its appeal. When you don't want to reach out to touch the sky, and risk losing yourself in the process.

Death could be the ultimate high. I'm not suggesting you jump off a tall building and try. I'm not writing a suicide manifesto here. Heaven, if it does exist, is fleeting, and not worth dying for. But when the time comes, you'll see. Until then, I can't really describe what's on the other side, except it's beyond dreams and imagination, let alone understanding. It's above the senses.

If there are clouds I've never felt their caress, if angels play I've never caught their song. There may be light, or it may be too bright to see. But it's golden. Or would be, if colour even existed. You see, it's futile to describe. It's just a feeling. It's peace, and knowledge, and sweet release.

And then, you wake up.

At least, I do. You probably wouldn't.

I wake up.

Drunk and hungover.

When people say "I feel like death", I think they mean they feel like this.

I woke up.

Same room. Cobwebs a thread thicker, dust shed a

shred deeper. Window shut and shuttered, air stale and hanging. Bedclothes tangled, tainted, sweat stained, bloodstained and overall unpleasant. Situation: normal.

I rolled over, testing out the old sinews, the new blood. It didn't really feel any different, never does.

Vlad's round face, white, like the man in the moon, loomed.

'Holy fuck.' Softly, whispering, slowly. Each syllable given space to breathe.

'I cannot believe that.' I. Cannot. Believe. That.

The whole thing seemed to have broken his ability to talk.

'I wish you could have believed it,' I spat. 'Then you wouldn't have to have bloody done it.'

Naked, unstable, I crawled out of bed. He backed away.

'Don't be shy now,' I muttered. 'I know you've seen me look worse.'

His eyes were searching for the wound, or a scar. Tipping my neck back, I let him see the unbroken flesh. Untouched by blade or blemish.

His brain was ticking over behind blanched eyes, suitably shaken and stirred. Probably for the only time in all the years I knew him, he had nothing to say. I threw him a metaphorical bone.

'Stick the kettle on. I could murder a brew.'

I sipped from a bottle of water. There hadn't been any teabags in the room. Or a kettle. We were down in a dumpy kitchen-cellar. Unsteady cupboards, empty. Rat traps. A smell of damp.

I wondered how he had coped with the hours while

I'd been under. What he had done. Not that it mattered much. There was still me, still Vlad. Only, now we shared a blood group, and he had a degree of knowledge from the University of Death, the real school of hard shocks. I sure didn't know anything more, in fact I remembered less. Sickness sucks the substance out of your senses.

There was no table, and the only chair had fewer legs than it ought. We leant against opposite slabs of crumbed and cracked ceramic counter.

Vlad unsteadily tipped a pot and poured a greenish tea-stream, pulling a face. The petty tribulations of the Englishman abroad.

'So, what now?'

'Well, you could stab me in the face? Oh, no, wait. We've done that.'

He grinned, but only with his mouth. Otherwise, chagrined. His eyes betrayed him, deeper than his thespian mask they laid bare the abyss he had witnessed. His hand shook and his spoon rattled hard in his cup.

'Yes.' He looked down. His fingers left the tell-tale teacup, and twisted fidgeting revolutions with his rings. A little black skull span around below his knuckle, empty sockets on me, then on the spattered worktop, then back to me. His own eyes followed, flicked up, almost ashamed to meet mine.

I'm no great reader of men. At best I'd be at a sort of board-book level, two words to a page, and pictures of farm animals. But it seemed to me he was scared. That seemed fair enough.

His gaze stayed averted, but silence oppressed him.

He stuttered, 'You know, this isn't easy for me either.'

'Yes, Vlad. You're the victim here.'

I meant to be cynical, to be cruel. But I suppose he was, in a way. Not a victim of mine, but of himself.

Later, back in the room – we had nowhere else to go – I tried to sleep. No matter how tightly I closed my eyes, winks never numbered near forty. I folded myself in a cloak of my own thoughts, and tried to ignore the world. Most of all Vlad, nesting in a chair in the corner.

Brooding, wrapped in a cloak of his own, a literal one in his case, he watched for a while. Then, finding no entertainment in my failed attempts to sleep, he bulldozed them. Unbidden, he began to unburden.

He was cornered, he insisted.

He had no choice. Like the apocryphal cat, curiosity was his nemesis. Except it didn't kill him, it killed me.

'I was happy enough, you know, in my old life. You may mock, you always do, but it was my existence, and it suited me.'

He treated the nearby wall to a faraway stare, full of dole, holding the long-dry paint in contemplation. One second, two, three, before a shifty eye flicked back to me, to see if I was buying it. I was not.

'I had a hometown, a home. A local pub. I had habits. I had people, friends. I had a job. Oh, I know nobody would call it a serious career, but I had a living. I had a life. You can't understand any of that, because you've never had anything.'

If looks could kill, I would have put a stake through his heart. He seemed to notice, and balked. That felt like progress. He never would have given a withered fig for my feelings before. I wondered if this new, fearful Vlad might be more compliant.

'It's not an excuse,' he lied, derailing my thought train like a tree trunk on the tracks. 'If you knew what it meant to be torn away, you would see.'

I took my own turn to give the wall a thousand-yard stare. Vlad trundled on.

'I left it all behind, for you, for what you said you were.'

'For what I am. Don't tell me you still need proof?' I fingered my windpipe, tracking the line where a jagged scar should have zigzagged.

He shook his head and wouldn't look, remaining dwindled in his seat. I picked myself up and found my way to the window, drawing back a dirty blind to look at nothing. The weather had closed in around us, an unseasonable winding sheet of colourless drizzle.

I could feel him watching me, now that he could stare safely at my back.

'Will you at least accept that I was entitled to some evidence, beyond your word?'

My thoughts on who was entitled remained unspoken, my eyes on the lofted clouds where his head belonged.

'Everything I left behind,' he lamented, 'I left upon a word. Everything I needed to know, you had the power to show me. There was no other way.'

'A normal person would say sorry.'

A normal person. Neither of us fitted that category terribly well any more.

I could have ditched him there. Perhaps. He followed me. I could have stopped him. Chose not to.

We left by rail, chasing a rumour of cheap delights, and flights out of Turkey. The journey was a sick, dull blur. The brown gloom that had fallen persisted, misted the route and the windowpanes. Off the beaten tracks unmissable views raced by, faint and bleached and wasted. I concocted a resting position on a single hard seat, cramped and foetal, head and back at wrong angles. My stomach still swam, awash and wobbling. My body pulsed hot and cold. Recovery seemed to be taking longer than before. Vlad rested opposite me, detached.

Only as we crossed the peninsula into Istanbul did he deliver my isthmus present.

'Would it make you happy, to hear me say I shouldn't have done it?'

It was evening. The overcast city was creeping up around us. The sky was closed from my line of sight. I saw no cloudscape, only building shadows. A medley of squared-off structures bled by, off-white, off-cream and ochre. Rows of dark, blank windows staring inward. We slowed, grinding past ground floors. Upper levels, inspired spires, minarets, domes and lights might have existed, higher, unknowable in invisible heavens.

'Only one way to find out.' Ungenerous perhaps, but I was tired, aching. Inside and out.

Vlad spread his hands out wide. His cape, a stretching wingspan, cast him in sinister silhouette and ruined any show of supplication. Which may have been a contributing factor as he issued possibly the worst apology in the history of man unkind:

'Fine,' eyes all but rolling, 'I shouldn't have killed you.'

Heads turned. Empty seats around us had provided

relative isolation. If not alone, we had been alone enough to talk across a table. When Vlad picked his moment to speak up, faces peeked across, questioning with looks. I returned a couple, plying perplexity into my features, suggesting I hadn't quite heard him right either. I was not the actor Vlad was. But when no further drama occurred, the heads turned away.

'Tell the world, why don't you?' I muttered.

The train, slow before, wheeled and crawled as we approached a diversion.

Diversion.

There isn't, as far as I'm aware, any illuminati of the immortal. No shrouded secret society of the sub-human convenes in shadowy corners to safeguard the continued clandestine concealment of our kind. Then again, perhaps no self-respecting society would want no-marks such as myself as a member. It could be that I just never found out about them.

They may be out there, masked, hooded, hunting down the careless and the indiscreet, withdrawing immortality, stilling loose tongues forever…

Or they may not.

Either way, it's always struck me as sensible not to say too much. I suppose I had that drummed into me anyway, aged seven, when my mum and dad sat me down, shortly after having brought me back to life for the second time.

Mum's lip was a trembling smile. She stroked my hair. Leaning in, I felt her warmth. My dad slumped opposite, legs splayed, gawking.

'What's the last thing you remember, sweetheart?' Mum, anxiously.

I shook my head. My throat quivered too, involuntarily. Swallowing down sick. Too young then to know how a hangover felt, I suffered the symptoms all the same.

'I don't know.'

'He won't remember.' My dad, bluntly. 'Coming back messes with your head, he probably feels worse than he looks.'

What had really messed with my head was that they'd just told me I'd been dead. But the coming back experience certainly hadn't helped. Mum rubbed my back.

'Here's the thing, baby,' she started, softly, 'we're going to have to move away. What happened to you, it wasn't your fault.'

My dad's face stood passive. Mum kept gamely on.

'But we can't stay here. Too many people know. Too many people saw.'

My socks weren't all that interesting. But I stared at them, hard.

'It isn't… it isn't normal what you can do.' She stuttered on that, and corrected herself.

'You're special, you're my special boy. Our special little boy.'

I still didn't look at her. I didn't need to. Her sympathy would be shining and vivid.

'We just think it's best – your dad and me – think it's best if we all go away for a bit, somewhere nobody knows us. Start again. So people don't…' She searched for the words, looked around, looked to my dad. He was no use. 'So people don't judge you.'

That didn't mean a lot to me. Judgement wasn't a concept on my radar. People, as a nebulous mass, didn't compute. All I heard was worry, and change. No seven-year-old has a heap of control, and you wouldn't wish it on them either. The lack of it was still scary though. The thought of losing everything I knew, through fault I had to own, however much they, or at least she, tried to reassure me.

'It'll be okay,' she whispered, patting, petting. 'It'll all be okay.'

Of course it wouldn't. Even hunched there in that room the early vapours of guilt crept down on me. My first and final safe space, the last homely house, was disintegrating in front of my eyes. I should have taken it all in, snapped a mental picture, instead of counting my toes. I'm sure there was wallpaper, ornaments, portraits. I can't remember.

With a tetchy huff my dad rolled out of the room.

'Don't worry, love, he's not angry with you.'

She might have been right about that. He had no call to be, anyway. Not without winning some kind of hypocrisy award. Some kind of trophy with two faces. The fact remained though that we were jolted out of our little comfort zone, our illusory Elysium. The world was altering. My actions had altered it.

'You just need to be more careful, baby.' Her only face was genuine, and concerned. That didn't stop her words worming their way inside me.

'This has to be our secret now, okay?'

She didn't make me promise. But in my heart I already had.

In short, silence became me. I didn't need any secret society to keep me in check, I didn't need society in general. Just a family. Just a mother, actually. Just loyalty. I didn't want to make her life any worse than it already was.

My dad did enough to harm her, dragging her around. Lying. I thought the best I could do was give her a quiet life.

I took to not talking. Not making friends, or connections at all. It was easier that way. Silence kept itself.

Keeping mum kept mum safe. It kept me safe too, from the covert organisation who may or may not be policing the undead, but more pressingly, more realistically, from local authorities, psychiatrists, psychologists, police officers, medical experimenters, curio collectors and, in particular, amateur vampire hunters.

Because crazy as it seems, they definitely do exist.

End of Diversion.

The train slid into Sirkeci gari. Wind and heat, bricks, ash, arches, fug and oil. People meeting, parting, kissing, waving. Brakes yelping, announcements garbling. Greasy pigeons scrapping for litter. Really it could have been any station, anywhere. King's Cross, Penn or Gare du Nord. It just had more Turks.

Vlad was still testifying on his own behalf.

'I simply want you to understand it from my perspective.'

Hefting our bags off the train, we emerged into an oppressive heat that belied the dusk and cloud beyond. Vlad, trolley case on wheels, queued politely for an opportunity to leave the platform. Shouldering my backpack, I was half inclined again to abandon him there.

'I had built a life around vampires being real.' People milled around us; he clearly didn't care. His eyes bulged and dampened, on the edge.

'The opportunity came to peak behind the curtain. Was I wrong?'

He found his answer on my face, and winced in irritation.

'In deed then, if not in thought. Perhaps I went too far. But you pushed me. You must see it?'

'Where is this going, Vlad?'

His mouth opened, closed, fished for words. Watching him, I began to see I'd misread him after all. It wasn't fear that was fuelling him, but fanaticism.

With supernatural recovery powers of his own, he had bounced back from his act with remarkable equanimity. Most people, having murdered someone and then witnessed their resurrection, would probably require a lifetime of therapy. Vlad, I can only suppose, had been so mad to begin with he'd somehow got away with it.

Perhaps that's a little blasé. Who would have thought it though, really – the person best equipped to deal with the absurdity of reality turned out to be the guy who most believed in fantasy?

I don't know, maybe it makes a sick kind of sense.

Thoughts were bubbling up in Vlad's gut, I could see him bodily working to get them past the new and unknown bottleneck that blockaded them. There was still uncertainty. Not from fear of me though, I saw, but from fear of missing out. He all but frothed, pathologically unsuited to struggling with speech.

Eventually, words came.

'It proved my little theory though, did it not?'

The station roared around us, rushing in my ears. It felt unreal, as though I'd been superimposed onto somebody else's scene.

'What theory?' I tasted my teeth with my tongue. Searching for certainty.

'That you can do anything you like. No risk. No comeuppance.'

'It's not *no* comeuppance,' I muttered, mind on my guts.

He looked at me, lit red by the lights around us. 'Consider it,' he said.

I did, for about a second. And then I told him I was going home.

Hedonism

And I did go home. It just took five years.

Queue *Odyssey* montage.

Hellenic Islands, Simi, Samos. White sails, boats and bodies. Empty cerulean skies, clear jade seas. Dirty consciences.

Embracing gluttony. Pigging out.

Piquant tangs, pipped olives, pitta, feta. Greek goddesses, peeked tastes, olive skins, pert flirts. A fog of ouzo, cloudy glasses in smoky bars hazing judgement and hastening enchantment, collapsing into Calypso's arms and merging nymph and mortal in a shaky heedless head.

Moving on, a whirlpool on your page swirling one set of images aside to draw you into another. One face becoming six, and laughter turning cruel. Blown by fate and fell wind, ever crossing the course of another seductive siren, prey to any beck or call.

Supplemental substances: some strong, some subtle; stolen, smuggled; smoked, sniffed, shared; soporifics suppressing, stimulants surprising; sending me speeding, hooked around a trapeze through the burning ring of my mind's eye, upside down along a tightrope; eased through soma slowly down to the circus floor to lie and ponder Circe's flaw, to gaze amazed at pink elephants on parade, recycling metaphors and uni-cycling onto distant shores.

Vlad, a one-eyed monster in the true, metaphorical sense, remaining giant, controlling, and blind as one who will not see.

In short there was magic and mayhem, monsters and miracles. There were moments of madness caught between a rock and a worse fate. There was even a descent into hell, but I'll save that for the chapter finale, for dramatic effect.

'Consider it.'

Back on the Bosporus, Vlad made his case. Why not live *la vida loca*, if consequences were so minimal as to be immaterial?

From behind cheap shades my eyes strayed out over the horizon. The water was sea-green and serene. I let it soothe my stripped-back senses.

Another day, a fresh body of saltwater, a degree of latitude down, and a different perspective. Rehydration for the soul.

I took a taste from a glass of tonic. The body craved its share.

We were in a café overlooking the water. Reflecting.

I might have argued. There are always consequences to reckless quests, if we pay attention to portents from the past. Take Icarus; the boy who cried wolf; my mate Ali.

Not all great examples. In fact, Icarus is a rubbish one. What's more likely to have severe consequences than homemade flight apparatus? I guess what I'm getting at is the willingness of people to take rash risks, lulled by a misguided trust in safety. But, as Vlad could have countered, even surfing sunbeams on waxwork wings would have been alright for me, so long as someone was willing to fish me out of the drink after the inevitable.

Dorian Gray might be a better case study. Now there was a man who could do whatever he wanted. And he knew it. He started off okay too. Nice lad, only out to enjoy a bit of truth and beauty. Would just have settled down with Sybil and raised a little clutch of Vain-Grays, if it hadn't been for the malign sway of an avuncular corrupter. A debonair devil in a frock coat, a poisonous charmer who read about decadence in a book, and thought it might be fun to try, by deputation.

Now why does that sound familiar?

I don't actually think Vlad would mind the comparison. There's only one degree of separation between Dracula and Lord Henry after all: Bela Lugosi played them both in movies. Relatively sure that would meet with the old Precua seal of approval. Then again, Lugosi also played Orizon the magician, a mystical mind-reading fakir in a film called *50 Million Frenchmen*, so maybe he doesn't really prove anything.

Regardless, I had a metaphorical painting in my attic. Actually, the attic was metaphorical too, because I didn't have a house. But if anything that just accentuated the truth, that I could afford to cut loose, and get lost.

Enlightenment, experience, aesthetic, I don't know that I wanted to go looking for any of that. But for the first time in my life it occurred to me I could make the most of being able to die.

So, yeah. Vlad was my Wootton.

Just without the *bon mots*.

'Honestly, you act like being unable to die is a bad thing. Dear boy, if there's one thing worse than being immortal, it is not being immortal.'

He lowered a bushy eyebrow and hitched up his lip, arranging his face into a working model of a winking beam. A studied performance, undermined by trembling hands.

Beyond his façade the world moved on. Waves crested silver, even viewed through dark lenses. Shimmering, otherworldly. Apt, perhaps, for the sea is an alien space. A deep place to hold the stare, to bewitch and to scare. A snare with a myriad of fair faces.

I thought anew about the souls of mermaids, lathering the breakers. Their living sisters, living in legend at least, calling, baiting, alluring, luring in men – it's always men – the lost, the desolate and the irresolute, the adventurous adventurers, willing to dive overboard to better hear a song. Who would choose that? Only one with nothing to lose. Or to whom losing everything meant nothing.

Watching the rollers spatter and reel, temptation rose to slide beneath the whipped-up surface chaos. To feel the slippery draw of the depths, to kiss goodbye to wants and cares.

Sitting there, drinking in the Sea of Marmara, I fished for the right thing to say. To encapsulate the concept of shaking off the old ways, shunning the cautious, human-half-of-me approach to the world, and beginning a bolder stage. Travelling was one thing, but I had still never lived a day not previously experienced by any number of trust-funded gap-year types. Perhaps Vlad, of all people, was right. I could do more, be more. Live more. Embrace the mermaids.

On the other hand, I clearly couldn't let him know I agreed with him. He'd become insufferable.

Which was a strange thought to have about somebody who had killed me once already.

In the end, I simply settled for accepting it – his offer, my lot – without quite bringing myself to say so.

So, it wasn't quite that simple. Life rarely is, but I'm not publishing my diary here. There's no plan to account for every week. If you get a gist, I've done my job.

The Homeric hyperbole at the head of this chapter was to that same purpose, impressionism, presenting an essence. For more pragmatic readers, attached to the details, I'll scale it back: in the real world, we turned west, island-hopped through Greece, and wandered on, aimless as clods. Meanwhile I meandered on a parallel journey into an underworld of wine, women and stronger vices, only to learn that having a Dionysian cup spilleth over was not necessarily my mug of tea.

I'm not particularly square, not markedly hypocritical. This isn't the pot calling the weed green. No point whitewashing over the white powder years. No need either to glorify them. Walking down the high street only last week I passed a man older than me, older than my lives put together. He wasn't a walking cliché, no dapple-grey ponytail or donkey jacket. The only clue to his lifestyle choice was the green tee spread over his paunch, adorned with a cannabis leaf motif. Somehow it made me feel sorry for him, and glad that I'd left all that behind.

Drugs were just never my baggy.

So why, for five years, *five*, why did I try? Why did I live as someone I wasn't, popping pills and running risks all on the off chance something would go wrong, and I'd meet some terrible disaster, just so Vlad could treat it as a triumph when he saved me?

Only because you have to belong somewhere. Or with someone. If home is where you hang your heart.

That makes Vlad somebody, doesn't it? Oh God.

Oh, there were other someones. But like I said, this isn't a confessional. I'm not looking to come that clean. So I've edited. I've cut them out. Not chapters full. There weren't that many. I'm not the sexy-seductive sort. The vampires who make a killing are usually the pale and interesting types, or the ones skilled in hypnosis. I couldn't entrance a plant. But yes, there were two or three. Maybe even a meaningful one. Someone who had loved and was lost, a girl with scars, the girl with the saddest blue eyes I have ever seen. Sadder than my mother's.

Susan didn't look like my mum. This isn't an Oedipus thing, I'm not that complex. But there haven't been many important people, not many women, so maybe comparisons are justified.

I found her in the shade of a parasol, in a water park in Faliraki. I'd gone in pursuit of the kind of adrenaline rushes Vlad said I should be searching for. Sort of. I don't suppose I could have died, but some of those slides are pretty radical half-pipes. Anyway, I found something else.

My mum's honeyed tresses, some elusive quality in her profile... but honestly, it wasn't that. It wasn't anything to do with how she looked. In fact, did you ever watch those movies, where the girl lets down her hair, and takes off her glasses, and the boy realises she was beautiful all along? This was the opposite of that. Sun-lounging, just about in a bikini, frankly, wet, she wasn't your average wallflower. It was hot, the day I mean. Savagely hot, so hot that putting a naked foot down risked blisters, and our meet-cute was her mocking my use of a Muppets towel as a turban, and me explaining that this was only to distract from my Inspector Gadget swim shorts.

No, it wasn't that she didn't suit a bathing suit, only it's hard, when you've just barely met, to know where to look.

Somehow, surely against her better judgement, she saw me again that night. Hair behind a beaded headband, eye make-up by Chlorine, she exuded the expression of a girl who didn't have to care.

Hunkered down in a hotel bar, surrounded by plastic potted plants and sun-sore Scandinavians, we tried that whole get-to-know-you thing.

She was a holiday rep, professionally jolly by day, dry as sand when off the clock. Dry in a sly way, a catch-your-eye way. Not that there was anything else competing for my contemplation. Theatrical South American soccer on a big-screen telly. A Swedish businessman, tie around his bald head, beet-red, beat-boxing to Europop pulses from an incongruous, intruding sound system. No, it was only her.

'What about you? What do you do?' she asked. For obvious reasons I've always found the question insufferable, so I've got two hundred answers I can reel right off, none of them true, all of them either plausible or entertaining.

It doesn't really help, of course, to let the lies slip out so naturally. How do you let the right one in, without telling them who you are?

'Oh, you know, modelling, mostly,' because if you're going to fib, fib hard, right? I flexed what amounted to a bicep.

Susan cupped an ear, feigning misapprehension beneath the bass.

'Modelling, really?' she twinkled. 'Mostly playdough, I imagine?'

Her lips twitched towards a smirk, eyes flicked all over me. On the table between us her fingers danced to the rhythm of the disco.

'What are you saying?' I knew she was teasing. I was in shape, if not exactly man-scaped. Not, I imagined, her usual type. No lothario with a jaw like a stubbled lantern, muscles ripped and rippling. My guess is I seemed safe. No excess mass, but no ego either. No glut of smarmy charm. She'd been broken before, and she didn't find me dangerous.

The tête-à-tête toddled along.

'What brings you to Greece?' she asked. 'Business or pleasure?'

'Bit of both.'

'Scouting potential modelling locations?' She couldn't quite supress a laugh as she said it, and I let myself grin.

'Bit of that, yeah, but otherwise, you know, the usual. Travelling. Finding myself. Seeing the world.' I gave what I hoped was a self-depreciating smile.

'Oh? And have you seen anything you liked?' She touched a finger to her cheek, brought away an eyelash and blew it away on a breath.

I was beginning to really like her.

'I like you too,' she whispered, tender and rose-petal delicate. Not that night, another. Later, alone, hidden even from the moonlight. Voices hushed and husky, rising only above the soundtrack of the dusk. A rush of distant waves. Softly sighing, head on my shoulder, as dying embers smoked and smouldered. A lullaby of loss and wine, a lonely tale I never told her. A secret soul I never sold her.

Her eyes still sad.

I'm rushing now, I know. Though I'll pretend I'm still making literary revisions. Pacing my story. In truth it's just what I do: abridge over troubled waters.

Still, here we are. I am what I am. No use crying over chopped onions, and the story must go on, even if only into a deeper circle of the inferno: that finale I promised you.

She left. That wasn't hell in itself. That was just misdirection. My real hell was much more classical. Besides, everyone leaves, sooner or later. Susan left sooner. That's all.

She left me with Vlad. I always had Vlad, my special relationship. Surrogate and fosterer, family and familiar, tightrope and safety net all rolled into one roly-poly Halloween-wrapped package.

I told him about it. Showed him my demons. He always wanted to know everything. Every experience, how it felt, how it stung.

Because he was a leech. Latching on with anaesthetic slather in the form of listening, caring. A bloodsucker feeding on my life. And the juice of a story is pain. That's what he wanted to draw out. I'm not even sure he'd recognise that as an insult, though. Perhaps it isn't, if the care is real. Letting it all go could be cathartic. A leech is a doctor too, after all. Balancing the humours, as if too much blood is a sickness.

But I don't mean to be even that kind. I mean to be mean. What I want to call him is a greedy parasite. Sending me in search of hurt so that he could taste it later.

Let's face it, I want to call him a vampire.

He drew me out.

We were probably somewhere generic, in a corner of a foreign field, but you'll get a better idea of how it unfolded if you picture it metaphorically. The pair of us in some dank dungeon, dim enough to muffle screams. The odour of dead tallow hanging in the darkness long after the last candle had been consumed. The stench of rat dung strong enough to taste. Me, chained into some medieval contraption of cogs and cruel wheels. Vlad hanging upside down from the ceiling, visible only by his glowing bloody eyes.

Me telling him about a break-up.

'She left you in front of an altar, essentially?'

Even this wasn't hell, by the way, we're not there yet.

'No,' I winced. 'Outside.'

Perched on a drystone cairn, in fact, outside a chapel. A little white briquette of a building, more moulded than made. Desultory and deserted, lonely in an arid land.

'It's not you,' she started to say, collected herself before the old chestnut split. I didn't make her tell me what else it might have been. If it wasn't me yet, it would have been soon enough.

She had a backstory, a history to share, to avoid being doomed to repeat. Sharing is a two-way street. I never hinted I could give anything in return. She noticed, and she backed away.

Leaning forward, I worked not to let her wash over me. Willing myself to take it, drink her in and feel every moment. Her voice cracked. As if startled, a goldfinch tore from a gorse of thorns. With a flicker of tinsel gilt beneath the wing, it took flight and flittered in spirals up to the chapel spire, glimmered, and was gone, invisible in the sun.

And there was the descent.

Odysseus met his mum in Hades. I simply saw mine in a daydream. The result was the same. I was still left with a ghost.

The bird was the sign. I was going back to church.

Of Wax and Wings

We never went to church. I set foot occasionally, through school, to carry a Christingle or suchlike. But with my family, never. That's perhaps not surprising; what use did we have for an afterlife?

So I knew something was up, when we crossed between the wide wooden doors and into the ill-lit arena of pews and sweeping arches. Emptiness enclosed us, the vacuum accentuated by airy, arcing interiors, echoing away into distant heights and angles.

It was just the two of us, Mum and me. I recall struggling to imagine what the place might feel like full. Even if every row were occupied there would still have been space above. Cubic fathoms of spare air, towering still and stale, prey to no current or mumble of prayer.

A fault in my own faith and understanding, you're welcome to believe. But I felt no energy there.

We stepped in and stopped, a shadowy blush of embarrassment descending upon us, a weight from above. The very innards of the building folded down in an accusatory glare, non-attenders, interlopers, unbelievers. We felt it, I'm sure. Which in itself does suggest some power, now I think about it. Though why anyone would want to worship it, I wouldn't care to venture.

Mum looked about. I hadn't been told why we were there, and she seemed not sure in herself. My eyes followed hers in slow circumnavigation, apse to altar, nave gazing. Alighting on candles, she led me down a pew towards them. My fingers traced shreds of faded, mothy-green upholstery, punctuated by bibles. A phantom sense of touch wondered how it would feel to open a book, sift through wisps of skin-thin pages and trace the words inscribed. Mum called me on, the moment passed, and I followed her.

The candles, tea lights, stood in trays on trestle tables. Few enough to tally without losing count, they made an uninspiring sight. Little luminescence and less transcendence. A handful were lit, but of those most mustered little more than a half-hearted flicker. More were smoking, or else guttered and spent.

'Find a new one,' Mum said. Her speech missed its usual music, falling hushed and dull from her lips. 'One that hasn't been lit.'

We picked among the glimmers and stubs until we found a fresh wick. I pointed, and she reached across to take it.

Placing it down she unfolded two photographs. The first was an old print, colour, but of a kind you can't help remembering in sepia. It showed a middle-aged lady, straight hair, fair or greying, indistinct crinkling eyes, mouth parted in a smile. She was dressed smartly out of mode, in plaid and wool. I estimated 1970s, with no great working knowledge of female sartorial styles, beyond a ghost and a memory.

Mum's fingers lingered, smoothed out creases with caresses.

The second picture looked clipped from a magazine. It was a goldfinch. Not that I knew that at the time. Then my familiarity with plumage roughly equalled squat. Same as female fashion trends. Then I merely noted, vaguely, a garden bird.

'It was her favourite,' Mum said. 'Her name was Ava, and she always loved birds.'

Her voice clove, words wavering, circling, falling broken. I wanted to touch her, comfort her, to find words or ways of my own to mend her. But I was an awkward adolescent. I stood abashed.

'You won't remember your grandma.' It was a bald statement. Blank, and true. When I think about grandparents, if I think about them at all, it is storybook stuff. Grandads are whistling old gardeners, snowy tonsured hair and half-moon spectacles, proffering boiled sweets and yarns from the good old days. Grandmas are all gummy smiles and rosy cheeks, chopping ruddy apples for crumble and sauce, balling wool and knitting, petting kittens and patting curls. They probably live in cottages, take jolly holidays by caravan, walk with sticks and wince with arthritic joints.

In short, I know sweet nothing. I've had no personal frame of reference, and little enough knowledge of how a real family might work to bother inventing one.

My grandma, Mum's mum, died when I was a teenager. That didn't register with me as an event. I didn't know her, because as far as she was concerned, I'd been dead myself for a decade already. There's a little home truth, for those still supposing there is some glamour in immortality.

A lady, who I cannot describe and do not recall meeting, lived the final years of her life mourning my loss. She maybe had her own illusions of how our relationship should have been. They might even have been as corny as mine. Family trips, ice creams, rock pools, buckets and spades. Or she could have been a cool gran who rollerbladed and bred snakes, or whatever cool people do. Either way, I missed out on her, even if I can't so much say that I missed her.

It was for Mum's sake, not my own, that I felt sadness in that church.

Nobody else had left mementos, at least, none was in evidence. Mum glanced around, furtively concerned she might be pounced upon by a lurking priest. Dragged in to confess if she got it wrong. After a second or two she shook it off. With a long, convulsing sigh she placed both pictures side by side on the table and weighted them down with the unlit candle.

Neither of us had a light. Mum was never a smoker, and I hadn't yet got into playing with fire. After another uncertain pause she used somebody else's candle to light ours. I'm still not sure if that was appropriate etiquette or wildly not: the passing of a torch, or the misappropriation of an eternal flame? Perhaps somebody from the clergy or Christian community could get in touch to let me know? No rush, I'm no more than mildly curious.

Ava's light blinked into being. White, orange – amber, salamander – hot blue at the stem. Nothing dances like candlelight, flittering, flattering, stretching and falling, mesmeric movements in even the stillest surrounds. We watched, and after a while Mum reached down and wove her fingers in with mine. The gilded glow cast a halo onto Grandma's photograph, lit her hair the colour of my mother's, and I saw her there, in the features looking back. The goldfinch beamed radiant too, and that was the picture Mum leaned down to touch, with the last loving draw of her fingers before we said goodbye.

'Thank you, my love,' said Mum. 'Thank you for coming with me today. Thank you, Jay.'

She hadn't called me Jay in years. It was the name I was born with. The name Grandma would have known me by, when I died. And, because she never knew me after that, the name she must have used for me right up until she passed on.

I've had an interesting relationship with names. Jay is one I never forget. They called me Joseph next, though whether there was any biblical connotation is doubtful. Lazarus might have been more appropriate.

Following the Oxfordshire incident I was actively consulted, and became Steve. My parents maybe wanted me to feel involved – they might have seen it as a way of giving back some control to a boy who felt that he had lost everything. I picked the name after an Oxford United footballer. It wasn't my first choice. I really wanted Han (Solo) or Pentecost. Again, nothing religious, but because it was the name of the mouse from the W. J. Corbett novel.

I'm not sure what my connection was with mice back then. Reepicheep was another favourite, although I don't think I'd have requested to be called that. It certainly would have been less appropriate, as he actually made it to the other side.

Anyway, I was gently steered in the direction of Steve. We took Fox as a surname, as a compromise, inspired by Fantastic Mr. So I suppose it wasn't just mice I liked. It was woodland creatures in general. And footballers and space pirates, obviously.

There is a certain sense in not standing out, I get that. Unfortunately logic and I have often made untidy bedfellows. It hasn't mattered often. I've never had to try too hard to blend in. I'm not naturally flashy, I dress down and don't shout out. Vladamir Precua, the obsidian peacock, is almost my opposite.

Except with names. There I have been his equal in perversity. I might never have used an anagram, but I have always enjoyed words, and the opportunity to exercise autonomy and get creative.

Russell Scrunch I took from a poem about autumn leaves. Peter Pun was an obvious enough play. In personality if not immortality I've often felt a bit like the boy who never grew up.

Names, names, names. Some I lived with for a while, and was sorry to lose. Sam I abandoned before I really needed to. Kit fitted like a mitten, Ricky was prickly and uncomfortable. I've been as faithful as a Doug, and I've vacillated between Tom, Dick and Harry like a weathervane.

Certainly I've had favourites, but never an emotional attachment. None have I considered to be unequivocally "my name". The nearest would have to be the first. Somehow that seems like the least invented.

Standing, holding hands, watching candles, none of that flashed through my mind. None of it dully crawled. I was still only into my early appellations, and but dimly aware of a future which could half-fill a phone book. But being called Jay was a big deal. It showed me something in my mum, a wound behind a mask.

She put her arm around me, and I could feel the shudders in her breath. Awkward, crab-like, we squeezed back down between the pews, out again into the real light.

Mum kept hold of me as we walked back home, tattling with a brittle voice on brighter notes, until by the time we had stopped to get ice cream she was reassuringly normal. Grandma was never mentioned again.

What I took away with me was the goldfinch.

Since then, any time that I've spent in an English country garden, hedgerow, woodland or park I've kept a weather eye open for gold on the wing. An ear open for the song.

I like the way they sound, peeping a litany of joyful chimes, happiness growing when in a group or on the wing.

I like the way they look. The sharp blazes are the most obvious eye-catchers. The flashy yellow strip in the centre of each wing, the spectacle of the raspberry-red mask highlighting black goggles and a spike of white beak.

But the most beautiful colour to me is the soft, natural beige plumage of the back and body. Possibly it's all in the contrast; perhaps the gentle, understated fawn would seem dull without the power of bolder down to compare. What can I say? I like the light.

They are sweet little chaps too, it isn't all about the feathers. They're an impeccable shape and size. That's pure perception, of course. An ostrich fan would say two-and-a-half metres of shaggy beanbag body and brown broom-handle neck is the picture of avian perfection. And I wouldn't argue.

It would be boring if everyone felt the same.

Finches are my preference, I don't have to share them.

I like the way they move. On foot, scuttling. On the wing, flittering, weaving, in and around, over and under, fleet and full of quivering life. A tiny heart beating, powering blurring wings.

They catch something in me. A thought of a feeling. But really, deep down, I suppose I like them because of the lineage. Because they hold me to a woman I barely met and don't remember.

Sometimes if I watch a while, I come to wondering what she loved about them. Maybe the obvious, maybe the gold. It wouldn't surprise me, and it wouldn't matter. Although I might prefer it if she had her own sentimental reasons. That would be pretty cool.

If I allow myself free reign to gallop into a world of pure imagination, I could fancy another family connection, conceive perhaps that she loved them because her grandfather did. Dream of a deepening into the past, a line of us, ambling through generations, linked by nothing more than loving to observe a bird we heard our forebears were fond of.

But probably she just thought they were cute.

The Nave of Hearts

"A coward dies a thousand deaths" – who wrote that? Shakespeare probably, or some other nervous soldier. I can probably empathise with it more than most, but really I've just stuck it there because I love a good quote.

"Come up with a catchy slice of wisdom, and your name will live forever." Can't remember who said that either. Point is, the words that last, the clichés and the truisms live on because they resonate. There's a commonality to the human experience, which even as a semi-outsider I've started to notice. The more I live, the more lives I lead and leave behind, the fewer exceptions I find to the rules.

I know not everybody can do what I do, and I'd be beyond arrogant to believe I can do all that others might. There could be anything out there.

If I can come back from death's backyard, who would I be to doubt the impossible? There may be leagues of extraordinary gentlemen. Half of fiction could be based on fact. A real-world Dr Dolittle could be having chit-chats with kitty cats. The Invisible Man might be sleeping in your bed. Magic may be more than sleight of hand.

Thing is though, while not everyone takes the same portion from this giant stew of life, we do all share from the same big pot. And as some ingredients are more common, the bitter ones, there's one mouthful that everyone has to choke down.

We're talking about death. Surprise, surprise. Although for once, not one of mine.

Everyone, everyone who lives any time at all, will lose someone. And anyone who loves with even half a heart will feel it.

Which leads me back to clichés. Tired thoughts, doomed to live forever: death, the great leveller. Death comes to us all.

But it comes harder to those left behind.

Grief, not passing, is the real curse of the living. Have all the faith you like in other worlds, other words, believe it's an awakening, or an awfully big adventure if that comforts you. Ruminate on your own mortality and laugh that death is but a stake in the game; muse that a full life prepares you and prevents all fear. Go ahead and believe yourself immortal, if you wish, ready yourself to enter an eternal kingdom. Tell yourself all the lies you need, and whisper them to others, if they meet their turn before you.

You'll still end up, at some point on your journey, staring into a hole. A grave, a pit. A six-foot drop dwarfed by the chasm that has opened inside you. You'll have to deal with filling that quarry.

What would I know about it? You've every right to ask. Well, I suppose I'm trying to tell you now.

My problem here is I've always existed on a superficial plane. That might be connected to my condition. I don't want to harp on, you know it by now, how I gathered no moss. Never stuck around long enough for a one-night stand. It's hard to make friends when you're immortal.

Or maybe that's the easy excuse. Maybe I'm just naturally shallow as a puddle.

Nature, nurture. I'm no truth searcher. And it doesn't really matter to the facts. I'm not good with subterranean levels, not in real life, not, it turns out, when I'm writing about it.

The tutor at my writing class has been giving me feedback, and I have to believe she knows what she's talking about, because she has the been-there done-that look, she's bought the T-shirt. Or rather, cardigan.

It's in the corduroy hats and the mis-patched jackets, cuffs so ink-marked they might have come second-hand from a squid. It bleeds through the calloused typing fingers and caffeine-blurred gaze. For all the coffee though, the eyes penetrate hard. Even from behind Professor Yaffle spectacles she sees more than she should. It comes from a life of criticism, I suppose. Digging into sentences since sentience first formed, appalled at a stray subjunctive in *Mother Goose*.

I'm being wicked. Because the eyes strip me back and show me my weakness. Faults I've always been aware of. I'm as expert as anyone in hiding from the truth, but if I've ninety-nine problems, lack of self-awareness ain't one. I know I make play to distract, to divert from the depths.

Humour is a hiding place, but a comfortable one, and I like it there.

My tutor wants me to get out more. Although that's not the half of it. Apparently I'm also solipsistic, prone to commentary, self-commentary, and exposition.

She takes no joy in this, of course, in staining her sleeves red with her critical pen. It's all designed to raise me up to her level. A hand up, not a grinding boot aimed to keep me down where I belong.

We have these conversations in pleasant tones during class, surrounded by earnest future Hemingways and plain-Jane ostentatious costume-drama fans.

Like everyone else I sit and listen politely as my pages are pondered and picked apart. She leans so close we can watch our words dance in the lenses of her glasses, until she flicks them off and sucks an arm in thought, or flings them out in gesticulations of ardour. We nod and promise to change. Mend our ways. But we're just people, and we never really do.

The old badger certainly does seem to care, I'll give her that. So this time I'll really try, I'll have a proper stab at her advice. Rein in the flippancy, explore my relationships with solemnity, and not overwork the playful charade. I've got to give her that much.

'Of course, if you're really presenting this as autobiography,' she chuckles, roving an eye across the classroom to emphasise a coming jest, 'you need include the influential, talented writing tutor as a character.' She all but winks.

I smile, more in relief than anything. She can see through me, it seems, but not inside me.

'I'll do my best. Anything else?'

'Try to use dialogue for something other than setting up stupid jokes. Show me pathos.'

Frankly, that seemed unrealistic. But bring on the pathos. Bring on all the musketeers. I'm not actually against a bit of emoting. The actual problem, the real reason I don't do it, is because I'm so apt to utterly lose control, go wholly overblown, and leave those without a heart of stone bursting with laughter.

But enough excuses. Let's enter the bleak house.

No man, it transpires, is a puddle. There is drainage. Seepage. Even a life of active avoidance cannot canopy a desert. Rain will fall even on the superficial plain, and percolate by drip and trickle to drown you all the same.

I feel. Feel deeply.

Still, I am what I am, and like a raindrop in the thrall of gravity I'm falling into pathetic fallacy. It is the easy option I suppose, and I can hardly deny I'm all for easy options on the whole. Darkness, sadness, raining, tears, I admit that would be where I'd go for a funeral, given half a chance. But for once I've no heart for invention. The truth is a natural fit for twisting, if that helps tricks tick along, but right now I can only deal in what was real. Sometimes nothing less will do.

Some things even I can't lie about.

It wasn't wet, and it wasn't winter, though it was cold. Crisp. The sun, low-slung, hung like a sliced potato in a salt-white sky. The spire alone rose up, jutting into pigeon territory, a perch and a target, a toilet for Columbiformes. Everything else huddled, grounded. Uneven paving gathered thin pockets of wet dirt, slate grey as the chilled stones of the church.

Narrow streets and lean houses idled by, close and curious. Cutting off escape. I won't say I'm so paranoid that I need my exit points planned, but when I'm somewhere uncomfortable, somewhere I don't want to be, then yes, I do prefer a kinder panoramic view.

Am I being unfair – unkind? Fond memories do blow through, from time to time, when I think on past haunts. The time I did there, some of it could have been worse. It doesn't really seem right, to lash out. It isn't the fault of a land, if you don't fit in there, or don't find your feet.

To be clear then, it wasn't Whitby itself I was hemmed in and trapped by, although the specific point on the edge of the map didn't help. It was the connotation, the association. I was in a churchyard for a reason.

Nobody attends their mother's funeral expecting a good time. Even the types of sick insects and arachnids that eat their own parents are probably not throwing parties about it. I can't claim I was sadder than average when my turn came to mourn.

Although, sod it, why can't I?

I didn't know who Mum had kept in touch with. She might have been careful, for my sake or my dad's, but God knows she'd been a soul of her own too. I never got the feeling she truly hid herself. All that she went through, she might have shared. Not the full story maybe, not the disorder and the devilry, but parts.

There must have been people who mattered to her.

Funnily enough (ha fucking ha) the funereal scene itself was not my biggest problem. Sure, I had lived in Whitby, and Mum had stayed here, years. But I wasn't dead in town. The people who might remember me wouldn't be confused to see me upright.

But what if others came, from far away?

Many of our ports were fleeting, many partings conceivably complete and painless, yet there were straits where we dropped anchor, too.

All those days by a hospital bed, watching me fade out. Where did she go with that? Surely Mum's need for relief must have passed my dad's capacity to absorb or support. It's beyond imagination that she had no friend to help her through. Or that she found nobody who needed her, who could benefit from her experience, tea and empathy. A bond forged in that cruel crucible could easily last a lifetime. Could I count on her not having kept in touch?

And what of Oxfordshire? We played happy families there for four years. There must have been neighbours, networks. Mums on the school run, chance meets in the streets. I remember my own friends from that time with a vivid colour that defies the time lapse. Mum's chums are more distant figures to me, glimpsed through the eclipse of a distant grown-up world, the places she went when the babysitter came. That doesn't mean they weren't important to her. Did she throw them all away when we ran out of town?

Or was there a homeland, where extended family and their friends proliferated? Grandma Ava territory, where my mum had roots?

I didn't know. Mum left with my dad, and I died elsewhere.

Still there could be some who would remember me, if by no more than a death, and a name I no longer used. The chances of being recognised by any resemblance to my toddler-self ought to have been remote, but the semblance of Mum in my face might have been enough. While more recent acquaintances, those who had known a later version of me, could hardly be relied upon to have entirely forgotten.

So maybe I can claim to have been sadder than the mean: I couldn't stand up at the front and let my grief flow. I had to attend in disguise.

Disguise is a strong word. I wasn't wearing a weird playdough nose or borrowed beard. Just a big black coat and hat, loaned from the one man I knew who routinely dressed like that. Dark jacket and dark glasses. In terms of tropes, it may have been the most vampiric I've ever looked. Except for the tan.

My only protection was to spot history before it spotted me. I arrived early, undercover, and lurked. Red-eyes open.

I began to pick them out. Potential churchgoers. Like vultures they came, in ones and twos, drab and dribbling, croaking platitudes of time, the great healer. I followed them, keeping a distance as they crossed the graveyard, a wrecked tangle of weed-ridden grass, home to mouldering, crumbling gravestones. Monuments to so many men long-dead, now mud.

Clad in elderly finery these storm crows stalked into

the church, nested in the rear rows. Watching through thin veils they hunched and murmured, feeling closer to the dead since they were closer to death.

All strangers.

Nevertheless, I kept my dark glasses and hat. For five years I'd sported them by routine, to shade my eyes from a Mediterranean blaze. Now they served to hide swollen lids, and the trace of my father people used to say they could see in happier times.

Twin lenses to cast the world in suitable darkness. Suitable for hell. Because it isn't all brimstone and burning souls, you know. Hell is bleak, and black. It's torment after torment, unlimited to your own mistakes. It's other people. It's parents. My lost mum and my unburied dad. His ghost.

His spectral shadow, haunting me. I swear it's his fault I hate being enclosed. Vaults, crypts, dungeons. It probably doesn't take a psychology class to work that one out.

The oak door shut me into the back of the church, and the dead coiled around. An underhand history pressed down. Images I'd worked hard to bury flamed in torches along the long-lost corridors of my mind.

Unable to escape the flashbacks, I tried to make them work for me, trawled my past for vicious visions to take the edge off the present. Self-harming in search of perspective, I sought the sick peak of cancer treatment, the black press of a mud-plugged windpipe, a crowbar exploding my nose.

All in vain. There was no crueller plain, no harder pain. The worst place in the world was that church. That time.

Physical beatings can't compete with emotional ones. Nothing can empty you like loss can, strip you so bare.

Though empty isn't the word, and naked doesn't cut it. Nothing else can so violently wrench away all you have. Shake your understanding and force you to flounder in your own fragility. A shattered vessel, exploded beyond repair, you spill out and burn away, turn to less than dust.

I'd take any death over that. I'd be eaten alive again. Even if I wasn't me.

But there's no bargain you can make.

Numb and dumb, forced to listen to the lonely vicar. Left adrift at his lectern he chuntered words that faded to nothing before they reached deaf ears. A broad sermon gave short shrift to a singular life, one I should have done more to make special.

Slumping down in my pew I crushed my eyes with closed fists. The chapel in Greece swam in my mind. Had I brought all this on, somehow? I'd taken the bird as a sign, that I'd be back at this church, with my mother, with her and yet without her. And here I was. Bereft of parents.

I wished myself elsewhere. Free. In the open air.

Another memory.

Another hard bench, a warmer day, a green day, a park fulsome with the sweet scent of sticky sap. An ice cream melting in its cone, running in sugary streams down my hand, tempting flies to hover drone-like ever closer. She sat with me, face protected behind insectoid shades, shoulders exposed and pinking. I turned and with my little finger traced the words inscribed on a brass plaque between us.

'Who is this?' I asked reading the name aloud.

She glanced down, scanned the plate and platitude, deadpanned, 'Someone who loved this view.'

I didn't really get it. 'But why is their name here?'

She paused. I licked ice cream off my fingers, and some from the cone. A line of crystallised raspberry ripple stung my tongue.

'It's a kind of tribute, to someone who – who died. A way for someone who loved them to show they cared. A way to remember them.'

I digested this, with my ice.

'Did you get me a bench, when I died?'

I wasn't supposed to talk about it and she threw a sharp look back. But there was nobody around, only insects humming. An indulgent smile spread across her mouth, like the sunrise. 'We didn't need to, darling. We still have you.' She gave my arm a pinch.

'Because I came back.'

'Yes.' She said it with the full stop. Rested back and closed her eyes.

A fly landed on my sandal, crept down onto my toe, releasing itching twitches out of all proportion to its trifling feet. I watched it, meditatively circling my tongue, sculpting ice cream into a frosted peak. I looked up at Mum, peaceful, bathing in the English summer, arms relaxed and flopping, knees shining with lotion.

'Most people don't come back.'

'No.'

'Will you?'

She turned and in a continuous, sinuous movement crumpled me into a hug. I was still holding my cone and I had to thrust it out at an awkward angle. My arm began to ache as the seconds edged by, but I made no move to pull back. The fly was still clambering, I wiggled my toes to chase it away, heard the angry whine as it thrummed overhead. Eventually she sat back, took my face in her warm, smooth hands, traced the flush of my cheek with her thumbs.

'I won't leave you,' she whispered hotly, wet eyes joined with my mind.

I blinked. She was gone. I was left.

Looking away, drifting in daydream, or daymare, searching the church with unseeing eyes, I lit upon light. Hope? The faraway gold of candlelight. Further memories fluttered. Ideas flickered. An ache took me, to complete a circle. My hand even went to my pocket, and my heart froze to find it empty. I should have brought pictures.

Now closure was on my mind, time slowed. Brief history became slow eons. The gaggle were hissing along to the Lord's Prayer in judgemental undertones. My toes tapped in irritation. Impatient I waited, willing the mockery to end. Imagining real comfort. A personal touch. Reviving tradition.

At last the chords of the final dance struck up, and I lowered my hat, distracted, stepping back to let the mourning tourists move with crippled, sluggish steps towards the light.

At last alone in emptiness I approached the flames. Planning, as I picked my way back along the long ago, to find a photo and come back. No, two pictures. One of her, and one of a finch. Unless – I stopped, and my heart stopped – what if they were still there? I imagined them aged, turned up at the corners, fusty with dust and time, but keeping that link alive, tying that line into the past. I hurried on, reached out—

Disillusion. Of course. They were gone. Of course. Years before no doubt, swept away by zealous hands. I'd known they would be, really. That was okay, I told myself, I could live with that.

But the lights had been extinguished too. Wax and wick were in memoriam, the eternal flames were out. In their place sat small, cheap plastic bulbs, programmed to wink in a pale imitation of life.

It all surged back. The hopeless sickness, the damage and cost. The transience of hope, gone in a hummingbird's heartbeat.

And, in contrast, the irrevocable loneliness of forever.

Even a gesture of remembrance exposed as shallow and fake. No escape. Just a mirror, pointing back at me.

I left.

Stumbling away, directionless, the sunlight did nothing to warm me. I couldn't face the wake, the fate of ignoring the walking dead as they cawed mawkish sentiment, clawed at cold meats and pallid quiche. Sickness descended. It was clear I shouldn't have come, and the only course of action was to go.

Lurching, pulling my coat closer, I faltered forward. Anxious only to get away, avoid unwanted encounters. Lurking around the first corner, a dark-suited shape with the sun behind. Hissing a curse, I rubbed a cheek in gruff futility. A mix of salt and light had me blind. Sunglasses won't do much to hide torn eyes when tears are streaming.

They would at least, I thanked my lucky stars, prevent any chance of my being recognised.

'Hello, Jay,' he said. And I remembered. I never had any lucky stars.

Like a Bat out of Hull

We stalked along the river, slouched shoulders, pocketed hands. Far too much family resemblance on display. The brown current plodded thickly beside us; after the Med it seemed mere moving mud, a mockery of water. At points it narrowed to a trickle and the sludge rose up to meet us, rippled with tidemarks and pocked with the prints of waders, gulls and sandpipers. Here at the banks it found itself fenced in, half-rotten wooden joists criss-crossing, an abstract shipwreck, moss-mottled, alive with lichen. Prison bars raised from the deep.

The boats that did float were squat to the water, flat and industrial, weighed down by greasy cranes and giant spools of steel rope, manned by faraway men, mummified in orange skins and woollen hats, gritted and girded against the weather, the ever-cold of the river.

Not a jolly scene, not the Yorkshire coast through

white rose-tinted spectacles, but what do you want? If ever a city was designed to be written about with blunt realism, it's Kingston upon Hull. It's a proud place and should have no truck for patronising filters. Again, not to knock it, you could paint a heck of a picture, and I'm sure plenty have. Just expect Turner, in a stormy mood, and not Manet.

That said, I could have been in Venice, and still not been in the mood for light.

He had not worn well, there was that much to cheer me up. Though there is little pleasure in spite, and less still at the expense of a dystopian mirror. The possibility that I was looking at myself in twenty, thirty years was not one to be revelled in.

His clothes were well cut, if I may employ a tailoring term which I am not entirely sure of. I mean, I suppose, they looked expensive. A tightly contoured coat hung from his shoulders, reached down to his knees and his shiny-trousered shins. His shoes scooped out to sharp tips, elaborate patterns stitched into their sides. I don't know. You can probably tell haute couture isn't my thing. Truth be told, I'm not even sure what it means, I've never been terribly au fait with foreign phrases.

Point is, he was dressed up. But however much lamb was in his authentically-woollen scarf, he was mutton. He looked what he was. A man who had died too many times.

I'm not sure who could have painted him. Lucian Freud, at a pinch.

He appraised me just as fairly.

'You've got scars, Son. What's the matter? Not burnt in a while? Too scared?'

144

I felt around my temple, a fading white lumpen line. Remembering old pain. What hurt more was him having the cheek to call me his son. I didn't correct him, didn't answer at all.

We trudged on down, close to the estuary before he spoke again.

'Risky, turning up like that. At the funeral.'

'For you?'

He nodded. 'For both of us.'

More dirty water under the bridge.

'I had to come,' he said at last. 'Business.'

I could have swung for him, maybe should have. All those years, whole childhoods ruined by him, his selfish nature and greedy love. I got as far as twisting my fingers into a fist, but I knew I'd never do it. However bad he was, however wrong, I couldn't hit him. It wasn't respect, not even fear, really. It was regression. However big a part of me wanted to shove him into the slime and watch him sink, it was impossible. Beside him I was just a child, and powerless.

He seemed to sense something, however, and pulled back.

'How did you even know?' he asked. 'No one could have told you.'

'A feeling.'

He allowed me the corner of his eye.

'I was in Greece; there was a goldfinch. Do you remember how she loved them?'

I saw the beginning of a sneer, thought about giving up, fought up the courage to wipe it off his face with my boot. Lost, and lost again.

'I don't know what to tell you, I just felt it. The guy I was with, travelling with. I told him, and he made some calls for me. And it came true.' I gazed up at the heavens, or at least, at the wide-open sky. 'I don't know how, but it came true.'

He snorted. My muscles twitched.

'Getting spiritual in your old age?' he scoffed.

I shrugged. 'I don't think so, Da—' I stopped. 'I don't think so.'

We walked on. Out on the mud flats a small dark bird explored, delved with a fishhook beak. I felt compelled to add something. 'There's more to heaven and earth though, we both know that much.'

'You think your dreams come true?'

'Dreams?' I looked at him with all the hate and hurt my heart could muster, hurled a look at him, flung it, lashed right in his face. He never flinched.

I choked, but whether on a laugh or a sob even I couldn't tell.

'Dreams, I'll tell you a dream: back there in Whitby after the church, I was wishing for a parent. If my dreams do come true, I wish they'd stop.'

I wanted to say it harder, to shout and swear. And I still wanted to smack him. But I was a child. Words were the best I could do, and even they took it out of me.

He shoved me, mock-friendly, on the shoulder. Rocked me back, then clasped me with two hands, one on either arm. Holding me in my place.

'Don't get carried away, Son.' Proprietorial, tough-guy. 'You're nothing special. There's no such thing as prophecies, let alone self-fulfilling ones. Whatever power you or I ever had over death, we never brought it on anyone else just by thinking about it. We both know if wishes came true we wouldn't be here right now, so just man up, and no more bullshit, okay?'

He slapped me again, high up, close to the neck, and walked away.

I counted to ten, and then followed.

I spent a fair number of hours trailing after my parents. Fair or unfair. Most kids do, I would expect. With my mum it was high streets and hospitals. Somewhere in between my first couple of expirations she developed a bit of an unhealthy attitude to medical check-ups. No sneeze or wheeze could pass without me being prodded or probed by some concerned authoritarian with power over a stethoscope and an empty wooden lollypop stick. I was dragged down any number of bleach-white corridors, quite often very much against my own free will, and even at times despite my fingertips clinging to door frames. She had my interests at heart, albeit alongside her own. Is that harsh? Is it selfish to over-care? Thing is, if I paint her as too perfect, present her as my saint and saviour, you'll stop believing in me. So maybe it's time to drip in a little reality. Yes, she built me. She was my foundation, and my scaffolding. But she was also the annoyingly petty planning inspector with a clipboard and a health and safety fetish.

She was human, she had faults.

Like shopping. God, I hated shopping with her. The amount of times I ended up turtling on a supermarket floor, screaming for sweeties while she hung onto a rein and took deep breaths... actually that story doesn't reflect badly on her, so much as me. Oh well, perhaps you can't force these things.

Following after my dad, you'll never guess, dredges up harsher memories. Cold, dark, grainy, bitter. The last sip from a long-ignored cup, tasted by someone who never liked the flavour in the first place.

He only seemed to lead where I had no desire to follow. On missions I had no interest in. It was never the toyshop or the fayre, always to see one of his associates on some grim errand.

'This is the boy,' he would nod down at me as we walked in. I'd be tight around his legs, holding on even though neither of us really wanted me to.

Some disinterested crook would take me in with less than a glance, mutter something about hoping I could keep my gob shut, and then forget me forever, except perhaps as a name on a doctored document, or an airbrushed passport photograph.

Invariably then I would be left, and it would always be somewhere seedy. The backroom of a pub, someplace like that, and I would be too short for the darts board and too bewildered to play the fruit machines. Abandoned with nothing to do but kick my heels on a stool and eat crisps, I'd pass wearisome hours wondering why he bothered buying me a football for Christmas, when he never took me to the park.

'Are we going home now?' I'd ask when he got back at last. He'd be packing a folder into a rucksack, shady acquaintance in his shadow, thumb-counting notes, on guard for wet ink.

'He's a barrel of laughs, isn't he?' one muttered one

time, shooting me a look that suggested I'd spent the last two hours crapping on his carpet, rather than just knocking pool balls idly back and forth along the baize, making up rules of a game I didn't understand.

Another dad might have chuckled, ruffled my hair, said I was alright, a good lad. Maybe even stood up for me. Given it a bit of "what kid wants to spend his Saturday in your crap hole of a bar, bud?"

He could have put his arm around me on the way home, told me not to worry. Told me he was sorry if I'd been bored, suggested we go and see a match next weekend instead.

He could just have ignored it.

He could have broken a pool cue over my head, and stabbed me with the shattered end. That would have hurt less, and healed quicker.

But he wasn't any of those dads.

'You try living with him,' said my dad, and walked out.

Leaving me to follow.

Through my twenties, more than before or after, I was a migrant. A vagrant at that. Call it curiosity, necessity, whatever, I kept moving. But my dad never lifted a toe unless compelled to. I should have known he'd brought me to Hull for a reason. To the river. We weren't really wandering. We were heading somewhere.

The port loomed slowly as we approached, creeping with deceptively aimless steps. Hull's a flat place. That's not a metaphor, I'm not talking about a lack of party vibes. I'm just saying it's on the level. If the Grand Old Duke of York had marched forty or so miles east-ish, he'd have struggled to have much of a rhyme written about him. Nothing is very tall, the skyline is what it is, and things sort of just drift up into your eyeline as you near them. In our case, it was the ferry boats. Floating leisure complexes, hotel, casino, breakfast bar and car park stacked up in front of a stern and behind a bow, looking about as seaworthy as any other shopping mall.

They are boats nonetheless. Means to an end. Hull, like Whitby, like all harbours, is a place you can get away from.

A woman shifted her way up to us as we approached. Dark suit, dark glasses, forgettable face. She was pulling a case on wheels, except one of the wheels was broken, and it scored an abrasive, shrieking line in the asphalt, loud enough to draw attention. The woman stopped, embarrassed. My dad shook his head at her, drawing a grimace.

'Going somewhere?' Perhaps it wasn't the question I wanted to ask, but it was the only one I felt comfortable with. Or the only one I didn't fear the answer to. If he had a replacement for my mum here, now, well, I couldn't contemplate it.

'No,' he said, handing me a folder. 'You are.'

I looked at him, no doubt, dumbly. The folder was familiar, although I'd never seen it before.

'What is this?' I asked.

'Your mum did well by us.' He spoke quietly, firmly, as though these were words he took no pleasure in, but which needed saying.

'She'd paid off the house, she had some savings. Life insurance, the NHS pension has paid out.'

'And?' I was trembling.

'She left it all to me.'

I could hear my heartbeat, blood throbbing in my ears.

'To you? You weren't even there. You left her. You left us.'

'And you stayed, did you?' His voice turned strident. I saw his spit hit the air as he rasped, 'No. You had your cake, Son, and your little foreign holiday.'

He leered as I reeled. 'Yeah, I've still got my sources. I know you've been about. Don't forget who got you those passports.'

I hid from his look, glanced down at the folder instead. 'What's this?'

He actually smiled. 'This is me being generous.'

I fumbled it, half opening it, half intending to fling it in his face.

'Not here,' he snapped. 'Jesus, grow up. It's everything you need. Condition is, you don't come back. Not ever. *Capisce*?'

And that was it. He was speaking cod-Italian and disowning his only child. Transition to pathetic little gangster complete.

That would have been the time to swear, or punch his teeth in. I just stood, silent.

He waved to the woman, standing by, shuffling from foot to foot.

'Your stuff is in the case.'

At last, I found my voice. 'Am I supposed to thank you?'

'All you're supposed to do,' calm, calculated, liquid nitrogen cold, 'is disappear.'

The woman moved in and I took the case from her.

Felt its weight, or rather, its lightness. The depressing emptiness of my life.

Suddenly finding momentum, I felt reckless.

'I'm his son,' I said, 'did he tell you that?'

Blankness looked back.

'Did he tell you it was my mother's funeral yesterday?' I could hear hysteria hovering in my own voice. I got nothing. A bland void.

'Do you even know what he is?' I blurted.

She nodded, meekly, and I realised, hell, she really did. Even as her eyes responded my dad shouldered between us, pushing her away and me onward, seaward.

I tried one last time. 'Did Mum really leave it to you?' What I was trying, I don't quite know, but it did something. He stiffened, just ever so slightly. His hand tightened on my arm, just another nasty vice.

'She could hardly leave it to her dead son now, could she?'

'What?'

'You're dead. Every you there ever was. All gone, as far as anyone will ever know. Happily enough, some of you had some life insurance too. Enough for one last life.'

He tapped the folder.

'Now run along. Leave me with mine. You've got your Goth.' Once again, he enjoyed my reaction, my shock. 'He's already stowed in your cabin. Like I said, I've got my sources.'

He harried me on, away, out of his picture.

'Off you go, Son.'

'I'm not your son.' Finally, it fell out.

I don't know what I was hoping for. Shock. Tears. Agreement? Not what I got.

He stopped.

For a long time, nothing happened. I don't know why I didn't walk away. Perhaps because I didn't have the benefit of hindsight. Really, though, a memory should have been enough. Still, I stayed.

'I did love her, you know,' he shivered, stared out across the Humber, eyes on the other side.

'You should at least know that. Your mum was special.'

A snort seemed the only appropriate response. I gave it.

He nodded back the way we had come.

'She's not.' The woman. 'She's just blood.'

There didn't seem to be anything to say.

'I loved your mum,' he said again, to the sky. The clouds, the sun. The invisible moon.

'And you,' he looked at me, dull-eyes beneath a retreating hairline, skin somehow pallid, worn beneath a grimy tan. Almost pitiable.

'And me?'

He sighed, then turned it into an exasperated little grunt.

'You were something too.'

I could almost have laughed. He saw it. Gave the crooked smile I've seen in so many reflections.

'We've never been any good at this.'

Thing is, I hadn't been laughing because it was funny.

'What is this?' I might just have been asking the wind. 'What are we doing?'

'I just mean, it's different, for the likes of us.' He shook his head. 'I'm not the same man I was. Literally.'

He turned, faced inward. Towards the city, the old town. Built up, knocked down, remade, burnt, bombed out, cobbled together again. Is that laying it on a bit thick? He looked inside.

'The man who loved your mum, he died. I'm not him anymore, Jay.'

'I'm not Jay.'

'My point.'

'So, I'm not your son?'

He gave a vain guffaw. Was there ever a conversation recorded with such a distorted humour-to-laughter ratio?

'It ripped us apart. You died and it killed our family.' He saw my face. 'No, I'm not even blaming you. It would have been over either way. But I shouldn't have done it. I should have known, you can never go back.'

'Sorry for existing, *Dad*.' Ironically, probably the most father-son moment we ever had, as, searching for emotion, I cast myself into whiny teen petulance.

'I'm sorry too,' he said, voice teetering with genuine regret. 'I should have left you dead.'

I turned away from him then. We turned away from each other.

Folder awkwardly in one hand, grip of the case in the other, there didn't seem much else to do but leave.

He didn't follow me.

Part 3

We Don't Disintegrate
in Sunlight

Bad Blood

There you go. There I went, rather. Transported off as punishment for existing.

Those events, being outwitted, sold out, I actually considered relocating them to Whitby. Taking advantage of that artistic licence we've spoken of before. Could have made a lot of sense, kept some continuity, avoided another new place to describe.

More than that, Whitby's a port. Not just any port, the port that succoured Dracula, schooled Cook. What better place for the undead to embark for Australia?

From a technical point of view, you could argue against the sense of it. You can't really sail anywhere from Whitby these days, except up the coast and back in a replica *Endeavour*. But then, it's not like we headed round the Cape from Hull, either. We took a ferry to Amsterdam, and flew from Schiphol.

In the end I left it as it was. Not from any firm commitment to the truth, nor entirely from lazy imagination. More to save the images of regrowth. The city fitted the narrative. Also, I'm a sucker for a pun in a chapter title.

The only lasting regret is that lost transition, footprints on Sandsend beach shifting to Bondi, or looking back at Robin Hood's Bay, forward to Botany.

But wait, you say, just do it anyway. Stick in one of those little first-person interludes we love so much. They're all Whitby-based, and you can segue on later to your heart's content. Well, thank you. Don't mind if I do.

By three a.m. I'm heading north, more or less. Tired. The wide salt-washed street is decked in nothing but guesthouses, all white and homely. All safely locked. Floral curtains hiding visitors from the sea view. Probably a hundred neatly turned-down eiderdowns within crashing distance, but no pillow for my head. There's a metaphor in there somewhere. Water, water, everywhere...

... and the sea remains a constant. Vast and flat, beyond the beach, far beneath.

Another hundred yards and the town peters out around me, dwindling into a final housing estate and the dying spiral of a road to nowhere. The main thoroughfare breaks away to run up the coast, arcs inland to give the golf club room to breathe.

A treeless space, green. Unnatural, somehow doubly so in the dark. Soft landscape contours parody the ocean. Unwild and strange. I'm tempted to hop a fence and cut across the fairways. It might save time and my legs are faint and unsteady, my mind frail, unstable.

But I don't. I don't know the way. Over-cautious, perhaps, to worry over losing my path through a wide-open plot, but there's no light. A ravine lies out there, a footbridge I might not find. These are real concerns, not metaphors.

The road is long. Safe though.

At the last moment my mind buffets on a puff of salt air, my track changes. The highway's too far, the Links isn't my way. There's a third way, where the course is clear.

Stumbling down steep steps, scrambling fast as an egg. Down the cliff path, down, shale-gravel skating, down metres, fingers trailing through wet sweet-stems of tussock grass, down to the sands.

A sweep of cinder-black, slowly sloping away from the shadow of the crags to a sea that is heard but not seen. The brine is gliding away, leaving ridges and pools. Trotting along, my socks are soon soaked and feet get gritty, but every step is now in the right direction.

At low tide you can walk the shoreline from Whitby to Sandsend. Or run. Or stagger. And with that as an option, why wouldn't you? There have been other beaches in my life, but you'd have to fly a fair way to find a panorama so picturesque. If the North Yorkshire coast had Med weather, you'd never have heard of Mallorca. Over my shoulder lies the postcard view. Landmarks, lighthouses. The Abbey headland. A golden mile.

Of course, it's dark, and I can't see any of it. But that's not the point. It's quicker.

And ahead lies my destination. Vlad's new lodgings. Seward's asylum.

Truth is, truth is stranger than fiction. At least say those who've never read H. P. Lovecraft. Or Richard Scarry. But then, I don't think anthropomorphic worms, with or without lederhosen, are the point. It's more the coincidences, isn't it? The quirks of fortune. It's okay if your protagonist is a squid-faced monster, but don't stretch credulity by having her walk into the one gin joint in all the world where her ex's mate is tinkling the ivories with his tentacles.

Now, clearly Ingrid Bergman is nobody's idea of a monstrosity, and *Casablanca* isn't usually used as an example of bad writing. Also, if I'm honest, I've never read any Lovecraft, and although I am familiar with Lowly Worm, we all know that none of that is the point.

This is just an exceedingly clever way of working in the topic of chance, and chancers.

Beaches, sons of beaches, fathers. All roads lead forever back to the same places, faces. Disgraces.

Another advantage of crowbarring the last chapter into Whitby would have been to easily merge Vlad with my dad, set them together in the scene, talk up the similarities, down the differences. That's gone now, and this paragraph will serve only to presage a real crowbar instead.

Probably for the best. They aren't alike, don't look it, don't act it.

The only thing that connects them is me, knocking an impossible peg out of a square hole, trying to wedge an equally unsuitable one in.

But life isn't linear. The past guides the present. I am where I am because of who I am. And they made me.

He is always inside me, my dad. In my worst traits, in my fears. I figure it's his fault I don't mix well in an underclass. Because that was who he mixed with. And they beat him, bought him, fought and forged him. Until he became them. I never wanted to be that.

And I don't like being underground. Because I saw him burn himself to death in a cellar. So, yeah.

Yet somehow, back during the Greek blunder years, on one memorable occasion which I'd rather forget, I let Vlad convince me to meet a seller in a cellar.

You could probably divide the people of earth into two taxonomic tribes: those who say love makes the world go round, and those who sing the same of money. Then there'd be some space scientists and such, who'd grumble something about gravitational pull. But even they might lean one way or another, be drawn into a secondary sphere in this Venn diagram, depending on whether they got into physics for, well, for love or money.

What I'm circling around to is that I've had to get about a bit. Around the world in fact, if that's not too heavy-handed. And it costs money. However you travel, there's no such thing as a free launch.

Vlad sponsored me in more ways than one. What cash he had, he flashed. I wonder if the subtle expansion of our semi-symbiotic bond was a common occurrence for my kind. We find someone we're content to rely on, a blood donor, and end up attached for darker reasons. Might have been my parents' story. I'll never know now.

What held me to Vlad? I don't even think I'd put our blood-bond at the top of the list. It was neat to have a safety net, but my hedonism was never whole-hearted. I never thought I'd really need him.

No, it was both deeper than that, and shallower. I needed, even if I might not like to be frank about it, openness. A safe place, as in somewhere to be honest. What stopped me from being human for half my life was not so much that I wasn't actually human, but that I had nowhere to be me. Vlad was in many ways the world's worst listener, and the truths I told him were often not those he wanted to hear. But a friend who happens to be an emotionally tone-deaf narcissist who once cut your throat can still be a friend. Even a father figure. I really baulk at describing Vlad as either, to be honest, as mate or pater. But beggars, famously, have no choice. My friends are those that can tolerate or support me. I am their cross. And in any case, father figure is hardly a compliment where I come from.

As for the shallows, well, we're back to keeping in the black. I stayed with Vlad, as much as anything, because he paid my way.

He was always a little tight-lipped about how much he had stashed. Not working more than a few honest days in his life, he lived, had lived, off his inheritance well into middle-age. His various and nefarious schemes and dreams supplemented drips and drops here and there, but I can't imagine vampire tourism was exactly lucrative. It wouldn't have you scratching around for golden geese analogies. I can only imagine his family fortune must have amounted to a fair bit in the bank, under the mattress or bubbling away in magic bean stock.

Whatever investments he had or hadn't, he probably saved more through frugality. Far be it from me to indulge in stereotyping Yorkshire folk, but he pegged out his teabags to dry. No, he wasn't that bad, not even to poke figurative fun at, but nor did he have lavish habits. His fancy pants outfitting came often from charity shopping. Indulgence was only ever an affectation.

His pipe smouldered on with minimal fuel. A small glass of absinthe, tasted with teasing temperance, could last him all night. He cultivated the image of a gourmand, but was rarely expansive at any expense.

We could afford then, even if barely, to travel on his ticket for a while.

Sometimes I suppose I felt bad about it, and attempted to contribute. Or at least, to cost less.

Which explains, somewhat, why we're about to circle back to that crowbar.

By the nature of drug deals I suppose they're subterranean. At least, mine were. There must be a certain percentage perpetrated by Man from Del Monte types on luxury yachts. I've always existed lower down the crude chain, bungs for bongs in bunkers and back alleys.

This deal went down beneath a cheap Italian restaurant, and regret had kicked in with my first step on the stairs, when the parched basement-must rose up to my sinuses and the low ceiling closed me deep into a memory of claustrophobic dimness, catching me in a vibe of dust-dry decay. Flies dying slowly in webs.

The hopeful outlook was that the stains ingrained on the hardwood floor were bolognese or Barbera. A fool's hope. The dealer was a Sicilian of very low-level family connections, yet to graduate to the sharp Armani. A

163

brute, six-six in his socks and sandals, sweat-heated bristles surrounding a thick, bald skull. Hefty, glowering forehead casting a black curtain down his face. He needed no English; his body language was fluent enough for me to know he wasn't happy. Fair enough, you might say. His prices, unlike his herbs and compounds, were not to be sniffed at. No salesman is going to be chuffed to meet a punter who has no means to pay.

Although a greengrocer or chemist probably won't come after you with a steel bar.

I'm not daft, I knew I needed to back out long before that. I knew before I set out. Even in the hot light of day, Vlad's clucking bromides should have carried little weight:

'What can he actually do to you? No lasting damage. Worst case scenario: you die. Well, we have a cure for that.'

It was all part of the adventure you see, breaking the crust to dive into life's rich and creamy tiramisu. Vlad wanted me to experience everything. Every thrilling spill and physical buzz, every ruck and rollicking. I don't think he actually wanted me to be hurt. I don't think he did. It was more the idea of putting me in a place of danger, letting me feel the pulse pump, the adrenaline and/or endorphins plink, plink, fizz. So I turned up to a drug deal with no money. Met a thug in a hole to offer him nothing for his trouble. Stupid plan. Stupendously so.

And I can't even tell you why I went with it. Peer pressure? Ennui?

Practicalities?

'Because after all, money doesn't grow on trees, you know.'

The cut-price cutthroat caught me by the neck and imbedded me into the dry brick wall with one hand. Halitosis spittle flecked my lips as he spat at me in a tongue I didn't need to understand. A swarthy thumb and index finger rubbed together in the universal gesture, before joining the rest of his fist in ploughing into my face. He let me go and I dropped like a stoner, flopped to the floor and searched for loose teeth with my tongue. He circled away, arms out like wings, shouting operatically. I was allowed a moment to revel in the idea that I'd got off lightly, before he picked up the crowbar, and I gave up all attempt at imagining the floor's red blemishes had ever been sauce…

'It's ironic,' Vlad ruminated later, laconic as ever. He gave no impression he was spectating anything spectacular, though blood was still spraying from my split nose, an exploding tomato throbbing on my face.

'You may actually have less tolerance for pain than a normal person.'

I bunched up my shirt and mopped at the spill, watching the red spread and flower. I'm no fan of my own blood, but it was better than looking at his smug face.

'Do you think the knowledge that you could make it all go away actually makes it harder to deal with?' he mused.

'Do you think the knowledge that it's your fault I just got battered in the face with a wrench should make you want to shut your mouth?' I would have said, if I wasn't all smushed up in a wad of saturated cotton, potential comeback muffled.

Or maybe I wouldn't have said that anyway, I wasn't exactly thinking straight. It was such a senseless plan before

165

I went with it, and the bust face was my comeuppance for compliance.

But I needed money. And I needed a father, of some kind at least. And where else was I going to find that?

Padding along the beach beneath the bluff, reeling in the last mile between myself and Vlad, it was hard not to think of him in that box. Where else do you go, when you're in so much trouble that the rest of the world won't touch you? Back home, back to family. Even if you hate them, there's other stuff tangled up there too: Obligation. Residual responsibility.

Sure, Vlad wasn't a blood-relative, not technically. You work with what you've got though, don't you? I mean, it's a vampire trope anyway: you live long enough, you leave everyone behind. Think of that movie interview, the miserable unlife, unhappy ever afters, a lost clan and a burned girl.

Like the Pointe du Lacs, my birth family has been and gone. Louis was two-hundred years old though. I'm scarcely a fifth of that.

Maybe Vlad was a better option than Lestat. Although I'm not sure I really want to get into that. Comparing my ersatz dad with the vulgar fictions of a demented American. All I'll say is it felt innate. Almost as if he were my natural father, and I was a little bastard.

Which I was. I've spent enough time sticking it to my mad, bad proxy dad, probably fair to accept my share of the faults. Certainly gave him enough to complain about. But, that's the right way around, isn't it? You take, take, take when you're the young one. Worse than that. You wind up, you aggravate, and you punish.

Is that part of it?

Part of me, as I cut the corner below the golf course, smarts with a stinging inner shame. On the surface, my search could be perfectly well explained as a quest for aid. Almost noble, not to overplay it. Alienated from the family I've forged, there is nothing I won't do to rekindle a spark.

And meanwhile fate, or chance, has brought me back so close to him, close enough to hear the chords, as time goes by...

Of course I'm going to him, to ask him to play again.

But does it add a frisson, after his antics, the metaphorical torture, the leaching, the literal facilitation of my beating? Is there payback here, too?

Am I just going for help, or am I on my way to steal the lifeblood from a sick old man, as relish for a dish served cold?

It changes nothing. I have to go on. I run on, fear and fatigue working together to smear my back, stick my shirt.

I feel the weight of guilt. But it's almost a comfort, a hint my soul is not as dead to light as the inky sand, even with the sun on the other side of the world.

But enough of that. I'm nearly there. Time for that segue.

Coasting

I could feel the weight of the sun. Souls seared on scalding sand. Sweat shone on my face, painted thick gloss across my scalp.

I was never a sun-worshipper, but I took a certain pleasure in cooking on those Aussie beaches. Enjoying being back in shorts and loose cotton, hiding below a hat and shades. I liked the way my hair lightened. On my arms it curled pale against my skin, glowing healthy and platinum. I liked how the sunshine made me smile.

For his part, Vlad suffered in the heat. Blotching and rashed, he limped from shade to shade, complaining. I didn't see that as a downside. It gave me space, a place he wouldn't follow. He came as far as the sands, but the waves were mine alone.

What did I say about Whitby beach? Something to the tune of it would be the best in the world, but for a caveat over climate. Sure, you can swim there, if you don't mind being blue-cold in grey waves, battling hypothermic rigor-mortis by keeping in constant motion. Pushing back up to the sea wall on numb feet to be blistered dry by a gritted towel. Hoping not to be shat on by seagulls, or have your chips nicked.

This was different, opposite, opulent. A bright, soothing spectrum to luxuriate in or under. Bathing water you could bottle and sell, or simply float in, relaxing, exfoliating in liquid solace. Buoyed by lazy, sporadic flicks, I could contemplate a continent. And feel content.

Back on dry land the stressors were greater. Pricey ices, poor quality sand-castling land, tanned goods distracting from a good chance to read… okay, it's hard to sell as hell. Threadbare towels to cover pillows of gold, no billows to hide the hot-blue sky… an unshakeable suspicion of spiders jumping in every shadow. That was about as hard as it got.

Except for the trouble I'd brought with me. Vlad took it upon himself to be affronted on my behalf, irked by my deportation.

'We're wasting time here,' he grunted, watching from the discomfort of his self-imposed black prison. Or clothes, as I suppose you could call them.

There was no point denying it, my diary was not full. Wasting time was exactly what I was doing, and I was entirely okay with it. Still, as basking seemed preferable to proffering this reply, I kept half an ear on the sea-shell sounds of home, and left him to continue.

'You don't seem to care.' Whether that was the real reason for his irritation, or whether the weather had him hot and bothered, he was right. I didn't care.

'There are worse places to be banished to, all in all.'

Slapping another layer of sunblock onto his forehead, before settling his hat down over it, he shook his head, and simmered.

Maybe because of the heat, the outdoorsy culture, I rolled into a soothing sort of vibe in Oz. It's nothing magical, all very much under the rainbow, but everything seemed a little less serious. To me at least. I think one of the reasons Vlad never saw eye to eye with life over there was that he couldn't quite scratch beneath that veneer. I was okay while it lasted, skating on top of it. He always needed to be deeper.

The tourist traps troubled him. The dirty white, broken eggshell towers of the Opera House fell below expectations. No twentieth-century structure quite enchanted him, yet Vlad might have discovered appeal in an edifice so inwardly and outwardly dramatic. A player ever in search of a stage, he might have liked to have seen a way in. He remained well-dressed for such an occasion, turned out in hat and shirt, silk cravat. I believe he owned opera glasses. But he didn't like the music, and we still couldn't afford to do anything just to be seen. We mooched around outside a bit, feigned a phantom interest, tried to feel awe or whatever. Took a couple of pictures that would never get printed, and wandered on.

The Harbour Bridge was spectacular enough, albeit after a few minutes of staring, we couldn't quite shake the thought that we were basically just looking at a really big bridge.

'Be a heck of a troll to live under that.'

Vlad ignored me, sensing a mythical creature teasing. Lucky really, I had nowhere to go with it. Not so much as a goat pun.

Walking back to the hotel along a wide promenade, he dragged his feet. Stopping for a swig of water, I let him catch up.

'You didn't have to come with me.' I wiped the bottle top, offered it.

'I wanted to see it.' He stopped, stooped. Hands in pockets. 'I'm the tour guide, remember. Culture is my meat. Sightseeing my drink.'

I shook the bottle at him, he ignored it.

'I meant, you didn't have to come here at all.' My gaze took in the path, the palm trees, the passers-by. The skyscape, the vista. 'Australia. You could have stayed.'

He looked uncomfortable. 'Surely, you know you need me more now than ever?' He sounded uncomfortable, waited for a pocket of tourists to file through. 'With your mother gone, there is nobody else who knows the true you.'

That hadn't occurred to me. Perhaps I hadn't let it. There had always been doors to the past I'd tried to keep closed, now there were possible futures to ignore too. Portals leading to avenues of loneliness, dead-ends and one-way streets.

'Still—' I began, but he brushed by.

'I gave my word,' his lips were tight as he wobbled away, 'to be close should you need me. Your path is mine, wherever it should lead.'

'It's okay, though,' I called after him. 'It's not what you thought. I'm not what you thought. I wouldn't blame you.'

A group of teens came between us, boys and girls heading to the beach, all surfboards and swimwear, laid-back vibes and tied-back hair. Absorbed in a better world they mostly paid us zero heed. One or two flicked a glance before flitting on by.

What did we look like, to them? Still a curious couple? Vlad looked odd in Oz anyway, of course. Not that Goths are a rarity there exactly, but greatcoats in summer are unusual. I was out of place as ever. And not twenty-two anymore. Easy to ignore.

'We don't have to stay together,' I murmured, as they passed.

His frustration burst out in a hiss.

'That isn't the problem. The issue is you are wasting—' He ran out of words, and simply pointed at me. 'This.'

'You want me to take more risks?' This wasn't a new argument. 'Is this Greece all over again?'

'There has to be more to being a vampire than sunbathing.'

I laughed, he could still bring that out of me.

'You're still upset I don't turn to dust, aren't you?'

He smiled, a little smile diluted by disappointment, and repeated, 'There is more to who you are.'

Next morning we did things a little differently, in that I did the same, and he left me to it. Wiling away the sunshiny hours on the sand, staring out over flat, wet emptiness, it was sweet to think of nothing at all. As the day grew hotter the sea gave a cool welcome, a place to chill and bob without a care. It felt good to ease off, to pointedly not learn how to surf.

When evening came I hiked back to our cheap-rate hotel, and didn't ask Vlad how his day had been.

He told me anyway.

'I've been to the library,' he grinned, before I had chance to close the door, 'to learn about the local *wildlife.*'

Still searching for citadels in the sky, he lived to unearth folklore and his soul solace on those scalding days was that Australia has as many ridiculous stories as anywhere. Bush ballads of bunyips lurking in the billabongs, dreamtime under the eye of the rainbow serpent. Squizzy Taylor, Simpson and his donkey, Banjo Patterson and Bob the Railway Dog, all waltzing, Matilda-like, beneath the min-min light. And, of course…

'Yara-ma-yha-who.'

'Who?'

'Exactly.'

Vlad tapped a page, swept away an imaginary cobweb from his borrowed book.

'Colourfully named critter, isn't he?'

'Who?'

'Yara-ma-yha-who. Legend tells it that he lives in the fig trees. A little red man with an outsized head,' he paused, pretending to check, 'and a wide mouth stretching ear to ear in a toothless grin. He has suckers on the ends of his fingers and toes. He somewhat resembles a frog.'

Unpacking my wet towel and drooping it over the back of a chair, I tried to picture all that in my mind, came up short.

'Yara-ma-yha-who does not leave his leafy loft to hunt for food, but lurks aloft in the branches.'

'You're out of your tree.' It was an autopilot response, glibly made and studiously ignored.

'He waits for a wanderer, too weary to be wary, who will pause on his walkabout to think of a snooze. Not giving a fig for anything, this unsuspecting soul settles down for a rest in the shade.'

'Lucky bugger.' It was evening, but it was still too hot. Shade appealed.

'Not so, no,' Vlad continued. 'Our toady friend then drops from his perch and attaches his suckers to the slumbering traveller. He drains their blood.'

Well, of course. Where else could this have been going? Vlad gave a little lick of his lips, perhaps the hint of a thirsty slurp.

'This is where it gets good. Little red puts his big mouth to use, and swallows his prey. Swallows him whole. Then he drinks some water and takes a nap.'

I have to admit I enjoyed that little detail. The postprandial siesta.

'Afterwards the traveller is regurgitated. The victim comes out a little shorter than before, and his skin has a reddish tinge. When Yara-ma-yha-who gets peckish again, the process is repeated. The unfortunate shade-seeker grows incrementally smaller and redder, until eventually transformed into a froggy little vampire himself,' Vlad gave a knowing look, 'because even a purist would accept we're talking about vampirism here.'

I sank onto an unmade bed.

'Aren't we always?'

My interjection was irrelevant. That was a feature of our conversations generally. I've probably mentioned it. Even if not, you may have noticed. Still, breaks up the monologue, doesn't it? Vlad was still talking.

'Clearly there are one or two differences to the classic European legend. For example, the antipodean amphibian is active in daylight, and indeed only in daylight. The advice given to avoid him, if you're ever considering napping under an outback fruit tree, is to play dead until sunset.'

'Still sounds like a bit of a gamble to me.' I rolled over tenderly, turning like a sausage on a barbie. 'Might be safer just to avoid orchards altogether.'

Vlad shrugged. Like I say, as an audience I was unimportant. The story was just his way of finding his feet. Something to sink his teeth into. Or get his suckers on. It gave him a grounding in Australia. Set him on a path.

A different path. After Sydney we ought to have headed inland, looked for further legends around Uluru or somewhere. We should have left the edge of the charts. Instead we avoided the void.

It's interesting, perhaps, that if you took a map of Australia and heat-spotted the populated parts, you'd get a great, slim ring with an empty space at the heart.

Vlad came to find Australia hollow. That's not a stick to beat the country with. You chuck a stick at Australia and it'll boomerang right back to smack you round the face. Not worth the aggro, on the whole.

If he'd hounded down an aboriginal shaman and got the inside scoop on you-know-ha-who, the madman could have been happy as a kangaroo with a didgeridoo. Or something that makes sense.

But he found nothing else. Never sought it. He became distracted.

We headed up the Gold Coast, directionless. I dabbled a bit in danger, without getting in too deep. Until I did. But we'll get to that.

It was little more than a rerun of the Ulysses years really. Only shorter, and less... less interesting? Is that the right word? Less something. Less everything.

Extreme sports. Watery adventures. Cigarettes and alcohol. None of it really hit the spot any more, if it ever had.

That's what I discovered in Australia.

It's why people travel, isn't it? To find themselves. I found I was slightly boring.

You can't force yourself to be something you're not. That's the bottom line. I was never going to be an adrenaline junkie.

Or any other kind.

Vlad seemed to follow, preoccupied. For all he was nominally watching over me, there were lengthy periods when his eye ranged elsewhere. I suppose I knew he had his own agenda, gently guiding. But he didn't seem to push me into anything, or drop suggestions.

Only when we reached a tiny headland township, halfway between nothing and nowhere, did his weirdness become manifest. With little to see and less to do, I'd happily have been on the first bus out. Vlad had us stay for a week.

A week where we watched the grass grow. Saw it dry, and die.

Not that I'm against a lonesome coastal locale, but there wasn't even much of a beach. In fact, there was little more than a truck stop, a soulless caravan park and a hypermarket. A place to pick up spare tyres, snake repellent and sad stories. A place to leave behind, and then forget.

Sparsely occupied, we somehow spent less and less time together. Vlad read the book or two he had to hand. I stared out of windows, into a future filled with more of the same. A day or so in and even our conversations faded out.

Long days wasted away, walking rocky outcrops, grey shale and dashed pebbles. Searching for a place to dip a toe, or even skim a stone. Looking at nothing. Wondering if a floating mass was a jellyfish or a plastic bag. The poisonous or the poisoning.

Later laying on a lumpy mattress, cold beans on fire-burned toast, pondering the lack of largesse my inheritance could afford. Knowing I should at least be writing something down, following those old *On the Road* dreams. Instead reading cereal packets cover to cover.

Meandering empty shopping mall aisles, exploring acres of strip-lit shelving just for something to do, somewhere to go. Wondering at the foreign use of a common language. Vegemite. Tim Tams. Golden Gaytime.

One night I filled a basket with pre-packed tuna sandwiches and a screw-cap bottle of red wine. A peace offering. It wasn't that I'd missed our chats, as such, but we were lost in the world together, and I didn't fancy spending eternity alone on the edge of a cliff, searching for shrikes to strike up a natter with.

Walking back to the site of our un-stately home, I mocked up a sort-of plan in my head. A suggestion of something new. Somewhere to go, to get us back on track. The Great Barrier Reef seemed like a thing we should see, close as we were. I rehearsed a couple of ways of introducing the topic. Ways of saying anything at all.

What it needed, I thought, was a hook.

'Hey, Vlad. Fancy seeing some cool fish?'

Sea creatures weren't much his thing though, not real ones anyway.

'Ahoy there, Vladimir, could I interest you in a kraken?'

Probably too far.

'Hi, Precua, I've got a lead on a Vampire Squid...'

Too obvious?

'Alright, Vlad,' I actually said, opening the door, 'want to see if we can see a dugong?'

But instead I saw, saw that much like a victim of Yara-ma-yha-who, I'd been suckered all along.

Down, Under

For six nights we'd been haunting that pokey rented caravan. The static type, stuck some time in a previous century. Rusted shutters and lax roach-proofing, every surface yellowing, except the ones that had started out yellow.

I'd been sleeping on a pull-down bed, one which could never quite be persuaded to the horizontal. Nights had been restless. Now it appeared I had no bed at all. Vlad had repurposed it, as a desk.

A number of lined pads lay open, showcasing tidy notes. The handwriting could have been called spidery, I suppose, by anyone willing to oblige the cliché. Personally, I doubt the penmanship of the average arachnid, but certainly it was the work of some cold-hearted beast.

Where my pillow should have been lay old-school files, a strewing of thumb-worn letters on unfolded foolscap, and photocopies of pages from some supernatural library, all fluorescent with highlighted passages and questioning marks.

Such litter should really have been pinned to the wall, connected with tacks and twine. That's how a proper lunatic conspiracy theorist would have done it.

'I can't believe you've been lugging all that around with you,' I started to say, before realising he hadn't been. A number of broken-down brown boxes, courier stamped and labelled, were stacked on the floor.

'This is your postal address now?' I said instead.

'I've been thinking about the exhumed Romanian,' Vlad fairly chirruped, ignoring my questions, 'poor old Arnold Paole.'

Realising it was going to be one of those nights, I opened the wine.

'That occurrence had all the hallmarks of vampirism,' he went on, 'but since I've come to accept you for what you are, I now realise there might be other potential explanations.'

I threw a sarnie at him.

'Big of you.'

He shot me a look, held it for as long as he could bare to pause.

'I have always suspected there were more secrets to uncover. Even before I found you. For years I searched through tales and tellings, through letters and contacts that led to networks and fellow-seekers.'

'Right. You had pen pals?'

My cattiness was greeted with a sorrowful shake of the head. I clearly didn't understand. Well, no change there.

He sighed again, blowing out his cheeks. I emptied and refilled my glass before he spoke again.

'I am part of a… collective. A friend was good enough to forward these, at my request,' he waved at the boxes. 'You see, we really had to wait here, tied to these admittedly less than salubrious surroundings. Having given the post office as my address, we had no choice. But it was important. I was close to a truth.'

'What kind of collective? What kind of truth?'

'We share knowledge on the peculiar and the occult.' He patted some of his papers. 'Keep records of that which cannot be explained. Things like yourself.'

'Charming.'

Over more poor wine, he relayed a tale. Heard first as whispered by a little bird, a legend of an empty white corpse, bloodless but otherwise unspoilt, discovered in a ditch by a sideroad, a Maine artery.

It wasn't a story that could be substantiated. But in Vlad-world that was just fuel for a fire. It meant press suppression, hush-hush cover-ups. Those on the supernatural grapevine were free to make their own judgements: the X-Filer's interpreted aliens, demonologists insisted on imps. Vlad's faction voted vampire. A subset played a local horror connection for copycat murderers, they were loudly shouted down as being far too prosaic.

Like all such rumours it faded away, replaced by the next dead thing. Vlad filed it in his mind with a hundred other mysteries, to be disinterred when required. Which apparently was now.

'Back in Sydney, reading about Yara-ma-yha-who, it struck me we were going in the wrong direction in every sense. True, that was a charming tale, but it was too far from the facts. I knew I needed to think again about the realities. The actual cases.'

'Actual. Facts?'

'Yes.' He pretended to pout. 'While you have been sunning yourself I have been busy, keeping up with my correspondence.'

He shuffled some sheets of paper around his makeshift workspace. I surveyed the scene, wondering more than anything when I'd be able to get to the actual sheets beneath.

'And I think I've made a breakthrough.' He was serious. 'The Cumberland County case has been on my mind for some time, but until today I have been unable to reason why.' He lowered his voice to heighten the tension. 'I looked again, comparing with Paole, searching for similarities.'

'Okay?'

'There were none.'

Nodding, I pretended to follow him.

'Paole rose from the dead. He walked, he bled. The body in the field was just that. A body.'

Turning away I looked out of the propped open pillbox that passed for a window. Even so late the heat pressed down. It rippled in waves you could see, see as clearly as those that punched up the nearby rocky shore.

All around us, the earth absorbed it. The ground ate it, pushed it out in bush and desert flowers, fodder for marsupial grazers. Pollen and nectar for the twilight buzz of bugs.

In surrounding vans sweat pores fed on it. Across a continent of open spaces, skin shone with it, flashing it back in angry pink or rawhide brown. Five million people took its energy and ran with it, sporting, racing, loving, hating.

Even here, nowhere, anything less than alive seemed impossible.

'What's your point?' I asked, trying to get a read on wherever he was headed.

'Well, it's obvious, isn't it?' Like all the best passive-aggressive debaters, Vlad said obvious when he meant opaque. 'One was the creature, the other the victim.'

'Arnie was responsible for the body in the field?'

'No. Arnold Paole has been dead for centuries. But someone like him was responsible. Someone like you.'

The last orange slice of sun slithered beyond the horizon, sinking down on her way to warm the distant north. The left-behind sky held the light from the town beneath, a starless space-blue, painted over in brushstrokes of yellow and purple. Through the open shutter came an arid air, the only hope of fresh relief, laced with the risk of fever and mosquitoes.

Windows, eh? Outside lay the whole world. Wide world, small world, dark world. Mad world.

Inside, only Vlad.

'Now, isn't that a curious thought?' He toyed with his beard, a go-to move to display thoughtful wisdom.

'You think Paole was like me?' I asked.

'I believe it to be very likely.' Tone all knowing, and worldly.

'Based on what? A hunch?'

He screwed up his face in pantomime anguish.

'Look around!' He plucked a fountain pen from the bed and stabbed, 'Here!' jabbing at a notepad, an ancient family tree, branches of conjecture.

'Here!' at a typed letter, torn and taped, a series of clues sewn together as much by hope as judgment.

'Here!' at a smudge grey photocopy of who knew what.

'The evidence is…' he prattled, rattled, '… evident!'

I read it. Can't say I took much in. He probably counted on that, the volume putting me off.

'Alright, alright, Professor Research-Librarian.' Not my sharpest retort, perhaps, but the cheapest wine can dull a tongue. 'So, what do you plan on doing with this wealth of knowledge?'

Vlad scratched his lip with a thumbnail, giving my sarcasm the scarcely deserved credit of his full consideration.

'We should go to the source.' He stood decisively, as if he meant to march straight out of the room that moment.

'The source? Romania?'

'Cumberland County, Maine.' We looked at each other. 'USA,' he clarified.

'Thank you, Doctor Geography.' It seemed only fair to give that failed line of attack a second chance. It was quietly dropped thereafter.

Vlad began to stack and pack away, transferring his argument from mattress, to folders, to his suitcase.

It dawned on me, he thought he had won.

'I'm not going to America, Vlad.'

He stopped.

'Why not?'

I moved to take a sip of fortitude, found we'd killed the bottle. Vlad went on instead.

'We're accomplishing nothing here, our pact was for you to live, to experience. To taste the spice of life.' Moving around, he made our confined surroundings his cramped stage. 'The only risk you're exposing yourself to here is skin cancer.'

His acting was so far over the top it was dancing in no man's land, but that was just Vlad. He could no more help that than I could stop mocking him for it. That his emotion was genuine was clear from the glister in his eye, if not the bluster of his motion.

It didn't help him.

'This is working for me, Vlad. This fits. We tried following the undead around Europe and we found the sum total of diddly and squat. You hated it, and I wound up dead.'

He opened his mouth but I wasn't finished.

'And don't talk to me about any deal we had, because we tried that too. And I'm not ending up with a crowbar wrapped round my head again just so you can pretend your life has some purpose.'

The hurt he showed me was a mask. It hid real shock.

'You were serious,' he said, after a moment, 'when you said I shouldn't have come.'

'Yes. No. Maybe. I don't know.'

We stared at each other for a while. When no further words came, we went to bed.

At breakfast the tang of alcohol hung on the back of my tongue. I sat on the step, watching not very much of the world go by. Vlad lingered inside, brooding. Trying, it turned out, to come up with a new low blow.

'Good morning, Judas.' He appeared behind me, formless in the dark interior.

'Jesus! Do you have to creep up on me?'

'Not much choice when you sit in the doorway.' He hovered in the gloom. 'I'm trapped, in here.'

'Okay, okay. Very subtle.' I shuffled out of his way. He stayed where he was. I stood, stretched, strained something, winced.

'I honestly believed you would be more interested.' He eyed me, over a sip of tea.

'Do we have to do this again?'

'I just thought you wanted to be different to your father?'

'How does this make me like my father?' I hadn't brought a hat out. My head was hot.

'He sent you here, he's paying for you to be here. You're on his path.'

This was grade A swill, of course, calculated to push my buttons. Idling away, running my fingers through my hair, I worked to keep cool.

Even without looking I could see his face, imagine it twitching away, manic Machiavellian devilry dancing in his eyes. Internal cogs all turning, figuring what he could say to bend my will, or break it. His mind was already a million miles away, or ten-thousand. However far America was.

'You've got a nerve, you know,' I said, falsely-bright, still not turning.

He begged my pardon, albeit in an unbeggarly tone.

'Sulking, that I said you didn't have to come—'

'That's not why—'

'Or that I'm not some puppet on a string.'

'And I am not sulking.'

He stomped out into my eyeline.

'You're not here,' I told him, 'for my benefit, or as part of any pact.' I paused, pushing down pent-up passions. 'You're only in Australia to get me out.'

He flapped in frustration, a bird in a net.

'Yes!' Spluttering. 'I need to get you out! At long last, you're starting to see sense.'

My mouth opened and closed. Nobody could be this obtuse. Not without considerable dedication.

'I like it here,' I said, firmly, hopefully finally.

'There is nothing here!' he exclaimed, whirling around to illustrate three-hundred-and-sixty degrees of proof.

'Well, not right here…'

'Not anywhere. Look, I'm at fault here too.' That was a first, but the perception in his next comment floored me. 'Listen, it's time to face facts. You are not cut out to enjoy yourself.'

I was never one, according to Mum, for putting myself out there, joining in. Children face-plant when they lean too far. Is that a lack of fear, or a failure of equilibrium?

I didn't really partake in a whole lot of playgroup, nursery shenanigans. Partly because I was slithering through death's door, but also to an extent because getting involved was just never my jam. I've said before, I'm not here to stick my oar in on any nurture versus nature

187

debates, just throwing out the possibilities. I've no solid memories as to why the edge of the circle appealed. While the other tots toddled and tambourined along to ring-a-ring-o'-roses, it made more sense to me to watch. Never liked singing out. Being singled out seemed appalling.

Things didn't change all that much after I died and went to school. My hand never went up when the teacher asked a question. Granted, I might not have known the answer, but that wasn't all that held me back. Being noticed never worked for me.

No man is an island though, Antipodean or otherwise, and the effort required to live like one necessarily influences other facets of existence. Pulling up a drawbridge keeps out friend and foe alike. It keeps you locked in. Not trying one thing means you're less likely to try another. A kid who won't sit on a horse is never going to ride a rodeo. I didn't talk to people, I didn't get involved. Didn't really didn't do anything.

You can't be socially cowed and not be a coward. At least, I couldn't. I was never a natural daredevil. Long story short: I just wasn't cut out to enjoy myself.

'What's your point?' I repeated, this time knowing the answer full well.

'The time has come to cut our losses. I promised to follow, to allow you to live your full life. Yet here we are idling in an outback wasteland with nothing more to amuse us than rust, and dust, and, and—'

He faltered to a halt, a planned speech gone wrong. Either agitation was on top of him, or something else was starting. The stirring of a first symptom? Perhaps.

'Come on!' Exasperated, I took the chance to jump in. 'We're here because you chose for us to be, waiting for Postman Pat. I've been ready to get out for days. We're in Australia, man, on top of the world—'

'Buy a globe, you ignoramus!' he shouted, upset with himself for fudging his lines. 'In America we could—'

'Metaphorically,' I spluttered back fast, not wanting to regift him the momentum. 'Metaphorically. This is our new world. I want to see it, this country. Walk these beaches, sail the reef. Swim with the dolphins.'

I didn't, particularly. But more than anything, I didn't want to be twisted into chasing his crazy dreams.

'The search for truth means nothing to you?' he said, sadly.

Was he right? Should I have chosen purpose over porpoise? Perhaps. But then, how would I have worked in that terrible joke?

'I'm not leaving.' I set my jaw, which was something I had read about in comic books. Captain Resolution, here to stay.

'Well then,' Vlad murmured, beating a sorrowful retreat to the camping stove, and his teapot. 'Okay.'

'Okay,' I echoed, suspicious of this victory.

'I will honour our fait accompli, if you won't be reasonable.'

'What's that supposed to mean?'

'I'll stay with you, I'll watch you swim.'

Only, when the time came. He wasn't there to see.

Once Bitten

And so we went on, up the coast and back down again. And out of defiance, or boredom, I did what I'd always done. Tried to. Dared myself to be the devil I wasn't.

There was a bungee jump, all sense of up and down was lost. Water rafting, black or white, I can't remember. Everything blurred to shades of grey. I may have jet-skied. I think we went to Nimbin, but I doubt anybody comes out of that haze with any clarity of mind. The Big Prawn at Ballina could have been a hallucination.

Stupid thing after stupid thing, just to prove Vlad wrong. And, sick to admit, to keep him with me. Each of us waiting for an accident to happen, hating it more than ever.

I'd always known, deep in the psyche, that falling into the depths could break me. Not being happy in playgroup, not being all up in Jack and Jill, or Humpty Dumpty, that may have had some impact on my disinclination to tumble. I'd lay a bet that actually hurting myself has had more.

I've bruised myself plenty. Immortality is not pain free, inside or out, I would hope I've made that clear. Alright, I haven't got the scars, not the external ones, they heal themselves with each new iteration of me, but I've lived the experience. Lived and died.

So, here's the thing: removing fear of death does not remove the fear of dying. You can still slip from a height or sink from a boat, slide with gathering pace and unravelling grace. You can still crack and fracture, sever flesh and shred tissue. You'll still scream.

And I didn't want to.

I get that I could get limited sympathy here, the guy who can't die whining about physical safety, but I just didn't enjoy pain, or even the risk of it.

Which might raise the question of what the hell I was even doing. Bottom line, thrill-seeking was simply something, anything, to do next. Only, as it happened I was more mouse than man, and as is oft the case with an ill-laid scheme, it ended gang a-gley.

Decadence I could surf on board with, more often than not. But forced fun bored me more and more.

Maybe it was impossible to truly enjoy the libertine lifestyle without sufficient comeuppance. And what, for me, could come up?

I know I could still feel frightened.

The whirlwind freefall, the hot rush of embracing gravity with my legs strapped to a giant elastic band still mucked with my mental consistency. Messing about on a river, a mere veneer of rubber as an anti-drowning prophylactic still left me up a creek, paddle or no. Imbibing herbs stoked my paranoia, or so the voices in my head told me.

But in the end I had to wonder, was my safety net the issue? Could jeopardy divert me when all the while Vlad was watching from the shadows, warm flask at the ready? I could have bungeed without the cord. Careered a canoe down a crocodile's craw. OD'd on any substance smokable, drinkable, inhalable or ingestible. All without any cost, save for a transitory agony.

It's more nuanced than that though. I can be brought back, have been brought back. But the dice don't have to roll that way. For a kick-off my body has to be found. Pretty much impossible to cremate me without it.

Bit of a problem if, say, I got eaten by a shark.

Jaws is nonsense. Let's get that out there straight away. No offence to Benchley, no slur on Spielberg. Good book, great movie. But nonsense. Sharks are not bastards. Sharks are the stars of the aquarium. Sea turtles are lovely, tropical fish are splendid. A school of jellyfish is a living lava lamp, and watching them float and fall is a fantastically chilled out way to spend a hungover Wednesday morning. But sharks are the bomb. Sweeping through the deep, tail a leisurely scythe, a shark is a beautiful creature, full of grace. A cold, dead-eyed dreadnought, sure; but not in the way pop-culture would have it. Not out to get us. Not learning a taste for human flesh, not zeroing in on our kin.

You're more likely to be killed by a coconut than a shark. Or a falling icicle. Champagne corks are deadlier.

Of course you're going to be thinking you spend more time under palm trees and icy rooves than you do in the sea, so the odds are bound to stack that way, but honestly, the shark isn't hunting you down any more than the bottle of bubbly is.

Even if we stick to animals, cows kill a herd-load of people every year. Daisy won't eat you, but a shark doesn't want to, either. You don't provide the necessary nutrients. Dogs on the other hand will chow you down as soon as look at you. Man's best friend my gnawed-on foot. Again, you'll likely state that unwary farmhands and tasty pet-owners are just more numerous than surfers and swimmers, which would account no doubt for the lack of horror movies set in barnyards. But how do you explain hippopotami? Hippos off about three thousand people a year, worldwide. That's about a thousand times more than sharks. But they get a cutie-pie hungry, hungry board game, and sharks get labelled as the animal kingdom equivalent of Freddie Krueger. Someone's lost their marbles there.

No, whichever way you slice it, sharks are not the villains we've made them out to be. People eat more sharks than sharks eat people. That's the gimlet-hearted fact. They're really nothing to be scared of.

Unless, of course, you're not in the aquarium. You're off the coast of New South Wales. A little too far out. It's quiet. Dusk is filtering the light, and the lapping waves slapping your shoulders are dyed blood-red by a cloudless crimson sky. There might be sand beneath your toes, but it's a couple of feet below and you're treading water in that splashy, clumsy human way that ripples away for sonic miles. It's pleasantly cool as the dry forty-degree heat leaks sluggishly away, but cool turns to ice cold when that thin fin cuts through the water towards you.

Jaws is nonsense. I stand by that. Sharks don't deliberately bite people, and the chances of being eaten are as close to being nil as you can get. There's a mere severed handful of fatalities in any year. Scant comfort, of course, if you're one of them.

I don't know why I keep saying you. I'm talking about me.

And I never saw the dorsal fin, because this wasn't a film. Not so much as a tip's wake troubled the surface. It's hard in hindsight to be sure, but I think I did sort of sense it, the tumultuous tumbling of water making way for a hundred-and-fifty stone of fish closing in at close on thirty miles an hour.

On the first pass it swept on, grazing my dangling shin and spinning back into the night, leaving me splashing in a tight eddy of nightmarish disturbance. Taut and edgy, feeling rather than seeing my assailant reeling away in a wide orbit. Keeping me guessing, was it coming back? Had it even been there at all? It might almost have been imagined, but for the lingering pain.

I kicked for shore. A forlorn hope, a full-on act of self-delusion. Not that I knew, at the time, this is what they do. Circle, bump. And bite.

The second attack came from behind and below. The first I knew of it was a sharp tug under, as teeth wrapped around my thigh, serrated, searing, tearing. I shook and struck out instinctively, flailing unseeing, still somehow hoping I wouldn't hit anything, weirdly squeamish to touch this creature, even to dissuade it from eating my leg. I didn't want to look.

Pain, delayed by shock, came rushing in hot and raw, and with it fear. Real, brutal terror. Heart drilling into my chest, blood flooding my ears and drumming. I doubt my experience was special. This is probably how anyone would feel, being mauled. Out of my depth, out of my element. Up a creek, no paddle, no boat. No hope. I screamed.

I lost my grip on fresh air and sank, yanked down too fast to close my crying mouth. Saltwater gagged my throat and plugged my nose, plunging my distress into deeper hysteria. I battered down in a frantic tantrum, knuckles scraping and bleeding on relentless flesh. The jaws never loosened, only grated, my thigh still held in a vice.

Yet the momentum, the driving violence of the attack had thrust us back, further up and further in. There was no room for manoeuvre so close to the beach. Not quite in open water, the hunter twisted and writhed for its purchase, buffeting up a billow of sand as it crashed against the seabed. The clear black water blurred with debris, and with blood. Even I never knew I had so much blood.

At the moment when I knew I could take no more, something snapped.

The shark let go.

The release of pressure brought a harder surge of pain. I shouted again, still underwater, drowning myself. Blood filled my mouth, from inside or outside I couldn't tell. In a final maelstrom of lashing tail the shark was gone. Back into its circuit, lining up a new and final blitzkrieg.

Not daring to dream this was over, I surfaced more by luck than strength. Saw ahead the safety of the harbour lights, grainy pixelated points. They were showing me the way. Even as I was choking and spitting and spilling I felt the current carry me back, saw the brightness of life recede. The sea drew me back inexorably into its net. Trying to kick brought only a fresh wash of hurt, vigorous and juicy. New blood appeared in front of me and I tasted it with salt amidst my brackish sobs. My leg felt wrong. I knew it wasn't all there.

Held in the tide I drifted. And at that final moment, knowing it for what it was, I reached rock bottom.

I felt nothing. Thought of nothing. Not of family, not of those who made me and broke me, those I had lived with and had lost; hated and loved. Certainly not of Vlad, waking up the next morning in a quiet guesthouse, wandering the town, the beach. Perhaps even looking out over the water, wondering what might have become of me. Never knowing he could finally have found his purpose, if only he could have found my carcass.

I didn't think on all the things that I had done. Not the places I had been, the sights I had seen. Not the women I had idolised and idealised and left behind. Not the drugs I had taken, the risks I had ridden, the mad rushes I had sought and fought for.

No. After years of searching, when the time truly came for my life to flash before my eyes I saw only the present. The horror of my impending visceral slaughter, and the realisation that this would be my true end. There could be no rebirth from this.

And when it came again, it was no release, no welcome catharsis. It was grim and bawling and horrible. It was teeth and death and agony.

I fainted.

It was still dark, but I was burning. Heat was in everything I touched. I felt the earth beneath me, still turning. Grit sanded my raw flesh. Saline stung in my eyes, teased out tears. Slowly my fingers burrowed into the damp ground, grasping after clarity, reality. I threw up, hard. Water and bile. Oxygen bubbled in my lungs. I was alive.

A long time I lay. Night ebbed, dreams flowed. Dreams I have forgotten. I felt the first creep of dawn down my naked back. Slowly, blinking the stars from my eyes, spitting the sand and sick from my mouth I reached out with my senses, searched the space around me. The salt breeze lifted the hairs on my neck. Through a broiling fever came whispering the creeping chill of lucidity. My face was an inch from the beach. My own little sour rock pool stared up at me. Hello, dry land. I gave a last dry heave and rolled away.

Turning myself on my elbows, I gazed into the heart of the ocean, now dancing glitter-auburn with the dawn. I had met true dread, out there, in the midst of the fight.

All washed up on the shore, half-drowned, half-eaten, dulled mind and blur-blind, suddenly I saw with crystal clarity. The sea and her servant had spared me, spewed me back onto the beach. But I wasn't grateful. I didn't care. I was still crying, a stump weeping. No pain though, no fear anymore. Just a single stark realisation.

It wouldn't have mattered if I'd died. Like properly, not-coming-back died. If I'd been a fish's supper, or maimed and drowned and washed out to sea, too far and deep to be found. Beyond the reach of Vlad and blood and reclamation.

None of it would have amounted to a hill of might-have-beens.

Death wouldn't matter, couldn't matter. Because I had no life.

Part 4

We Can Cross Water

Falling

Sandsend. Journey's end.

The fence isn't too high. Not to climb at least. A little high to comfortably fall off. Half a minute of less than dignified scrambling brings me to the top yard, which then wavers wildly under my weight. Shifting, lithe as a sloth, I'm dumped inside the grounds. Way to go, action hero.

Time for a breather. Not as young as I was, not as limber. Rubbing the knee I've just skinned, I stop, take stock.

The site is prime ocean-view location. Large, dignified, white and pragmatic. It wasn't hard to find, looming, quiescent in the moonlight. Possibly a converted guesthouse, some Georgian mainstay of a time when salt air and bathing cured all ills. Or at least the ones that didn't kill you. From three sides, wide windows look out on an excess of sky, a greyscale of sea. The fourth, the half-acre or so of land at the back where I'm standing, holds a sparse copse, an allotment, and a slumbering rose garden.

So twee. Vlad must hate it here.

A home-cum-hospital. They moved him in after his stroke. They? Some faceless them. That's who you really want to be scared of. Not fiends who go bump in the night, but bureau-fat-cat-crats, stealing your autonomy when you get too wobbly to wipe your own dribble. Drool-Nazis.

Vlad was a biggish fish, a sort of homely dark carp in a small pond. It had been his habit to swim and feed between the same reeds and weeds for many years, give or take a decade or so of mysterious disappearance. He was a character. A piece of the furniture. His descent was remarked upon, and in a slow news week his retirement hit the local press. A town institution being moved into one, the small loss of an eccentric legend-in-his-own-locale. His infirmity made page seven, beneath an article on a stolen toothbrush.

Sophie saw his picture, and remarked, 'Wasn't that your old friend? The one you were travelling with?'

Sophie. Can I just drip a name in like that? The first drop from a blue sky, the herald of an unexpected storm?

Well. I just have.

She pointed at his face on the page. If ever a man was easy to recognise in black and white it was him. Still, I grunted, noncommittal.

'You should visit him.'

'He probably wouldn't want to see me.'

There was more, behind the little shake of her head, but she didn't push it. Tucking a strand of hair behind an ear she left the room, an indulgent smile lingering, cat-like, behind her.

After a minute I picked up the paper. Made a mental note.

Now his new home hangs over me. All night I've known where to find him. Inside. I've known all along.

Shivers shudder through me. A rumour of breeze makes wind-chimes of fir cones and leaves, sways the trees in rhythmic imitations of the nearby breakers. Beyond, a black-green sea waves, carrying currents of Norwegian brine, undercut by the peaty scent of compost from the flowerbeds.

Inhaling deeply, I seek some inner calm, even succeed in pushing away a few feebler feelings. Forget the trespass, and the smarting patella.

The dark is my time. What better mask for what we do, than the shadows?

Normally.

A final check of my phone shows no more calls. No new messages. Maybe there never will be, ever again.

There is no comfort for me now, not there, not in darkness. Not anywhere. Swallowing the sea air from an ocean planet wouldn't break the strain sawing through my brain. There's not enough sodium and chloride in the galaxy.

Moving towards the building with slow, spacewalk steps, any clutched-at sense of serenity drifts away. A wafting illusion, a lost scent of incense. If there was any tranquillity left in my world, I wouldn't be here.

Reality bites, rends and tears. Composure trickles away like blood from a wound.

Fact is, I could be stealing through Elysium right now, and still be antsy, anxious. A casual observer, an owl perhaps, might have had me down as quiet, swift, purposeful. Inside, I am creased, crushed and crippled. Crawling, hauling myself forward. A parched and broken legionnaire in the desert, drinking sand with every laboured shuffle. No stomach, no guts. Only lonely pain.

A knowledge flogs me: that nothing can ever be right again. Happiness is lost. I'm hapless. Functioning is impossible. My chest is exposed and a phantom heart throbs inside, known only by the nerve endings left bare. A hole left open inside me, one I can never fill.

Sick to my stomach, I'm ill and empty, gnawed by a nauseating hunger that has no sating. Knowing that the best of me has dried to dust and drifted away.

No. Not dust. Ash.

And in ash lies hope.

I need Vlad. That much is clear. And he's near. Which is why I'm here.

Well, that and the random hand of fate.

Is this a good time to stop and talk about love?

Maybe, maybe not. But on the whole, I think the moment has probably come. It had to crop up eventually, didn't it? How can you write a book without romance? Unless it's like a car manual or something. Internal combustion for dummies. And this isn't that. It's a chronicle, a life. And though some lives are without love, some of mine even, surely we all adore adulation? You know, the sort of sensations songs are sung for, to the accompaniment of plucked heartstrings and beating pulses. These are universal feelings I imagine each of us can understand, whether we revel in them, hope for them, dream of them, or fear them. You can run, I suppose I'm saying, but you can't hide.

So, no more running.

Partly because I'm tired. Emotionally, you know? Thoughts are fighting forcefully to the forefront of my mind, recent actions won't stay buried, and ghosts demand attention. Under the circumstances anywhere has to be better than the present.

The past is a foreign country. One I've often felt xenophobic about. But there are islands. Isolated, friendlier climes. Pleasanter stories. Backstories, coincidentally, that will help make sense of my current state and situation: breaking into a Whitby nursing home to steal blood.

But anyway. Love.

It started in the New World.

'You'd move to England? For me?' Her eyelashes fluttered, flirted. A mock-serious mien, as if her face alone was launching my ship to follow her across the Atlantic. She only asked the question because she knew my mind was made up. I was made up, that she would even consider inviting me.

'I can't wait.' I couldn't.

'You won't mind the cold?'

For technical reasons, she may have thought I was Australian.

'I'd move to the North Pole for you. I'd live in an igloo. I'd arm-wrestle a narwhal.'

Her giggle made my insides skippy, she held me in place with a hug.

'You're sweet.'

'I know.'

'But I don't think there will be any narwhals.' On her tiptoes her mouth came level with mine. We locked in. Beauty may be in the eye of the beholder, but that's not to say it can't be in the eye of the beholden too, and her eyes... dark irises, golden brown rings of power, enticed, enchanted, gazed back at me, studying intently. Her lips twitched.

'Not in Essex.'

'They'd have to be pretty lost,' I admitted.

'We'll have to find some other way for you to prove your... love.' She rolled the last word over her tongue. It was still new to us, so powerful.

'Name it.'

'I mean, does it have to be beating up animals? There isn't much in Thurrock.'

Had I been Vlad, the name would have triggered an instant connection, no doubt. Which only shows how little his knowledge had rubbed off on me.

I pretended to think, which is usually the best I can manage anyway. 'Probably wouldn't expect dragons.' I don't know why I riffed off in a mythical direction, maybe it's how I'm hardwired. 'Or a unicorn.'

She laughed.

'Why would you fight a unicorn? Unicorns are nice.'

'Maybe I'm a bad boy?'

She laughed harder.

'There's Carfax, I guess.'

Still I didn't get it.

'What's a car fax?'

'Dracula's house. Don't you read?'

If I had been in an igloo, at the North Pole, with a narwhal wrapped around my face, I could still hardly have frozen further, faster.

'What's the matter?' Her eyes crinkled, locked me down. 'Scared of vampires? We'd better never visit my mum.'

My grip on her loosened instinctively. My mind swam as I fought for footing in the conversation, knowing I was jumping to wrong conclusions. Coveting equilibrium I blurted something, anything…

'Bit of a bloodsucker, is she?'

A playful slap on my arm, a dig in the ribs made me arch back into our embrace.

'She lives up near Whitby. Place is full of them. Infested.'

Pulling her in closer, tighter, I rested my chin on her shoulder. She could no longer see my eyes.

'Small world.'

For a long time, it didn't seem to matter. Whitby was avoidable. Until it wasn't. I can't say I wanted to come back, but life rattles along, situations are rarely static.

I have lived a frightened fighter, ducking, weaving. Artful dodges often too slow to evade impact. I get knocked down, I get dredged up again. Bowed but unbloody, living from round to round, bell to bell. Always going forward, trying at the very least to avoid repeating the same misdemeanours. Not so much in a changing, growing way, more with a practical bent. As I found out twice before I was ten, you can't stay in a place when you're dead there.

Still here I am. The boy is back in town. I guess maybe some places you just can't walk away from. Maybe ley lines run through our souls, or certain spots are the centre of spiritual whirlpools. Emotional vortexes, forever dragging us in.

Vlad proposed his own thoughts once, on a bus ride through the White Mountain Forest.

'I do wonder if a town can become infused with special meaning, as if locations draw in rumours and reality, nurturing, even creating mythic energies and environments,' he had mused, somewhere in the foothills of Maine.

'Just look at Whitby. Something drew you there. Stoker was inspired there. Who knows how many others have felt something?'

I hadn't heeded him at the time. Sure, there's such a thing as too much coincidence, but there's still only a certain amount of credence you can give to Vlad, him being mad and all.

For example, to put this all into context, we had been on our way to Salem's Lot, to find a god. You could be forgiven for thinking I'm being totally scattergun here, but honestly, I'm not. Not totally. Because sometimes when you go looking for something, you discover something else. In this case, not to put too melodramatic a point on it, a goddess.

But I'm getting ahead of myself.

Messing with chronology is one thing, but you can go too far, I think. All very well peeking behind a curtain, piquing an interest, but talking about coming home from America before telling you how I got there, that's verging on confusing, isn't it?

It's just that I'm trying to explain, even if only to myself, that everything happens for a reason. We're not talking about predestination, flies and wanton boys. I don't think. It's more about action, and reactions. Only, less scientific than that.

Contemplating forced entry to a care home, it's natural for me to think back to a parallel exit. Breaking out of a sanitorium, or somewhere similar. Something I once did, jumping out of a window... you see, this is getting out of sync again. But that was when I met her. And she, through a circuitous series of events, brought me back here, to Whitby.

Right where I needed to be, just when I needed to be there.

Although thinking about it, there would never have been a need, if I'd not met her?

This seems to be straying way into existential territory. I need to shake it off. The time for procrastination has passed. Now for action.

Stretching out, rotating a crick out of my neck, flexing, checking my newly knocked-up knee. Taking off at a steady walk, breaking into a broken gait. An old nag about to hurdle the knackers yard fence, remembering express pony days. Jog, trot, limp, trot. A skip and a jump, fingers on a window frame. Hauling up, scraping skin and tasting mortar. Grunting, exhorting exertion, barely holding on. Pausing for a gasp.

All night, all through the town, all along the cliff top the tension has been screwing me to a rack. Cuttable with a knife. No amount of reminiscence can change that. Only one thing can. Cutting with a knife.

Pulling myself up, I slide inside.

My Lot

I didn't want to like New York.

I wouldn't have gone, but it was somewhere to land. The end of the world is rarely served by decent transport links.

America you kind of love or hate before you've even been, based on pop culture, and your tolerance for bigness, brashness, badass bravado and bolshiness. The Big Apple is a microcosm of that.

'I doubt calling them Bolsheviks will win you any friends,' Vlad retorted, when I relayed my theory to him. I hadn't, but I didn't bother arguing. There had never been much point debating with Vlad. He was verbally slippery. It's not that he'd say that black was white, it's that he'd claim everything you'd said was green.

We'd already got into it once, high above the blue planet. Packed tight, itchy sweat starting to stick me to my seat, the shared air sour in my mouth and on my skin, nothing to do but search for Rorschach patterns in the crazed symmetry of the furshishings in front, I'd made the mistake of peering past him to the window. The plane banked and the ocean tipped into view.

'It's one of the weirder ones, isn't it? Vampires can't cross water.'

I regretted the thought before I'd finished expressing it. Whatever his new goal, Vlad remained touchy on old tropes. Something about me destabilising his entire belief system.

He was silent for a while, and I hoped he hadn't heard. But after a pause he mused, amused, that he didn't see why.

'Well, they can't cross running water. Except using a bridge. Or a boat. Well, that's just anyone, isn't it? You might as well just say they aren't strong swimmers. My mate Ali nearly drowned once, but no one was accusing him of feasting on the blood of virgins.'

Vlad, who was travelling in the lightest and sunniest elements of his wardrobe, and who still looked like a steampunk Batman, gave a supercilious shake of the head.

'As usual, you discount centuries of storytelling. You assume that myth is plucked from nowhere, when it is the smoke of long-glowing embers, from every fireside commune since man learned to fear the night.'

I don't know if that sort of thing genuinely just popped into his head, or whether he spent the midnight hours aching over epigrams, then waited impatiently through daylight for the opportunity to wheel them out.

'Sometimes there's smoke without fire,' I countered,

shifting in my seat, searching for an extra millimetre of legroom.

'You also assume,' Vlad blithely continued, 'that humans cannot share occasional traits with vampires. Simply because I can do some things a vampire can, does not make me one. That I cannot do some things they cannot, no less so.'

I pretty much gave up, and began trying to remember if losing all feeling down one side of the body was a symptom of early onset deep vein thrombosis. Concentration had long gone out the window. No parachute.

Vlad continued merrily by himself.

'For example, a man may be skilled in hypnosis, or harbour a hatred of garlic, but still be human.' He treated me to a condescending smirk. I knew him well enough by this time to realise that he only acted so pompously when he was actually at his least self-assured, so I was relatively sure his strand of logic was frayed. At least, I started off sure. As the seconds drew out, and I couldn't work out why, and the only punctuation to the silence was his patronising snigger, my certainty evaporated.

'I'm lost,' I confessed.

'You always are,' he said, complacent self-satisfaction capering in his eyes.

You might as well wrestle a soapy goat. I pretended to be asleep instead.

'Of course,' he cogitated, as we idled through the wilds of JFK some two hours later, 'it isn't really about the physical obstacle posed by a body of water, any more than the same is true of a rose thicket or a line of salt. The barrier is often purely symbolic…'

213

See why I never argue with him?

New York, New York, so nice they wrote about ten million songs about it. That's about one each for everybody who lives there. If you count the rats.

Don't get me wrong, I've got nothing personal against the city. There's plenty of places I never liked. Any place where there's too many people. Where there's no obvious line of escape.

We hit the subway at commuter o'clock. Above ground it was barely bearable, beneath, in the tunnels, it was bat-crap mental.

Feel it: there's a person so close behind you that their breath is down your neck, and that's all the ill-wind your sails need to tread on the heel of the person in front. You can't go left or right because there are people there, in fact any point of the compass you care to mention is needling another person. Even the gaps between people are filled with people. You're probably trampling a carpet of them too, but it'd be impossible to stop and check, you're up to your neck in the rip tide. It's just a human stew, packed so close you can smell what they had for breakfast, practically taste it. A stream of humankind being flushed down the sewer. Except it isn't, because they've lost all humanity. It's unnatural to the point of absurdity. Seriously, fist-fight to force your way into a shoebox with sixty strangers, embed your nose in an armpit and lose a toe to a stiletto. Get shoved, get "accidentally" felt-up, take a sneeze in your ear, and you'll get the basic idea. There's nothing human in it. Not anything natural. You wouldn't catch a zebra all up in that, would you? You wouldn't catch anything with the power of movement and brain enough to use it. No matter how many wildebeest galumph across the Serengeti, however many salmon slalom paddle-less up a creek, you'd never get personal space invasion on the scale you do under Times Square on a Tuesday teatime.

But no, I don't hate New York. How can you hate a city of three hundred cultures, and each with its own takeaway? I don't hate it, I'd just rather have my privacy.

I suppose if – gun to my head – I'm going to be serious for a second, I never stayed anywhere long enough to hate it. That's the upside of vagrancy. You can always just get up and get out.

Like a pair of pathetic moths, furthest from the flame, we found our way to a bedsit halfway to Hackensack. I couldn't help feeling that maybe I'd abandoned hedonism too soon after all.

'Why didn't we at least go somewhere warm?'

'You had your warmth, swanning around Australia, now it's my choice.'

Again. No point in opposing.

Vlad had framed it as though I owed him one, coming here, as if I'd dragged him Down Under. In any case, after almost dying, like dying-dying, no-coming-back dying, I'd begun to understand that I needed to shake it up a shade. Do life differently. Be useful. Maybe follow in the footsteps of Orwell and Hemingway as a mercenary fighting for truth and justice. Or become a doctor, heal the sick and make the blind see. Only problem being, I didn't know how to fire a gun, or cure so much as a headache.

Plan C had been to go along with Vlad.

We were clasping drinks again, coffee from a jar, granules settling in a tooth mug and the top of a flask respectively, dis-respectably. Vlad wore fingerless cotton gloves, and his breath chuffed out in steamy clouds. I was feeling sick again. The flight. The lack of sleep. Life.

'What's next, then?' I muttered. Since our spat in the outback, we hadn't really talked about anything serious. Or anything ludicrous, like his plan.

Occupying the single chair, Vlad nudged my legs off the bunk and unfurled a voluminous map of the northern states. Stain-worn and shredding along the creases, it had seen better days. Well, hadn't we all?

Yet as he traced the routes and highways with his finger, my cynicism retreated, at least a mote. There might be a different America here, one I could get behind. He drew a line with a sharp, black nail, through Green Mountains, White Mountains, up between splatters of lake and forest. Circling foreign words that would trip your tongue: Natick, Nipmuck, Narragansett. Crossing over more familiar names, borrowed names for stolen lands: Manchester, Portsmouth, Dover. Montpelier. That wasn't the attraction. There's no romance in cultural genocide. It was the width, the breadth, the depth. The promise of space, and an excess of it at that. How many England's would fit in New England? How many Windermeres under Moose Head? How much Scafellding to Katahdin? How much more spare air was there to breathe, to share only with bears?

Far towards a torn corner, the painted finger stopped and tapped. 'Here.'

'What?'

Small, slightly smudged words identified a little settlement. North-west somewhere. Or north-west nowhere. I peered closer.

'Piscataquis,' I read. That sounded like I felt.

'Salem's Lot.'

Slurping grainy dregs from my cup, I resisted the urge to spit.

'Another story?'

He looked at me cryptically. Like if a scrambled Rubik's cube had a face. Although all the colours would be black, obviously.

'A story. Or the story behind the stories.'

'Helpful. Thanks.'

We left next morning and followed the fingernail trail, leaving outlet malls and urban sprawl behind. It was autumn, or should I say fall? The sun never fully rose but stayed behind the treeline, settling the colour of off milk. Empty branches clawed at the haze. The leaves that clung on strung along like hot painted bunting. Fireside red and orange, every yellow from dandelion to medallion. Dripping from maple or spiralling in lazy sycamore pirouettes, those that fell matted the ground in deep drifts, dry and crackling in places, wet mulch elsewhere.

The road ran on, ever on, a drab, grey line between the scenery. From time to time a church, or a billboard, or a squashed fox hove into view. But mainly it was trees. And more trees. The monotony might have been quite relaxing, if every step hadn't brought us a moment closer to our destination. By a succession of Greyhounds, hitches and bad motels, we climbed the map.

'You have to agree,' Vlad asserted, on our third or fourth bus, 'the idea we will be travelling through the setting of *Salem's Lot* is intriguing.'

There was a rash up the back of my neck, either an eczema sort of thing, or a reaction to some foreign flora. It wavered on that itchy line between pain and irritation, daring me to touch and explore, despite the knowledge that scratching would just make it worse. I didn't reply to Vlad, which left him free to spout that crack, alluded to earlier, about towns becoming magnets for myths.

'Can a town become infused with special meaning…' blah blah blah. You don't need me to type it out again.

The skin at my hairline burned slowly as his mock off-the-cuff soliloquy turned in my mind. I sat on my hands. Having put myself in his claws, I was going to have to find out eventually what he had in store. It just felt better not to know until I had to.

'… Whitby… you… Stoker… how many others?' he sat back, self-satisfied.

A hand crept out. My fingernail teased around damaged skin, sparking frisson of pleasure-pain.

'Maybe none.'

'Always so cynical!' he chortled. 'But what about here? Another famous vampire novel, another – whatever you are – drawn together.'

I'd say I had a premonition of impending doom, but let's be honest, it was way past the time for premonitions. We were looking at doom in the rear-view mirror.

'You know, now, I have long made a study of the abnormal and unexplained,' Vlad continued, entering full-on Gandalf mode, 'of the thought-provoking and Fortean.

I have considered it a matter of professional pride to keep informed.'

'Or you just read a lot of vampire books?'

His sigh was the usual theatrical event.

'I'm telling you, it is more complicated than that. And you still can't explain away the connection, between real life and fantasy. The ley lines we are drawn along.'

'Could be a self-fulfilling prophecy? Us seeking them. I've been to Transylvania, I'm on my way to Salem's Lot. We're all searching for clues, searching for one another?'

'Possibly.'

I massaged my neck with my fingers, it felt coarse and somehow delicate, thick-skin and thin simultaneously.

Vlad tilted back his well-worn travelling hat, peered at me through filmy eyes as though revealing a mystic secret of the universe.

'We have always known that there are more,' he affirmed. 'Your father, for one. Paole, we assume, for another.'

The desire to dig with my nails was becoming intolerable. How easy it would be to give in.

'That's it, then? That's what we're out here for. You've found someone else. Another "whatever I am"?'

Vlad smirked.

Unique to my kind, I suspect, is the feeling you don't really have to put up with discomfort. Where something is too tender, there is always a solution, albeit an extreme one.

Not wanting to kill myself over an itch, I waited.

On the bus rolled through wood-clad hill passes. Wheels went round and round, wipers swish-swished, horns peeped. Children sang nursery rhymes, writers used artistic freedom.

The Goth king turned in his seat and took a look down the aisle. There was nobody particularly near us, but he spoke in a hoarse hush.

'I have found another.'

My God

The bus stopped, somewhere. Another small town in a big country. We got down, searching for food.

The restaurant we found was a cheap one. Restaurant might be overstating it. Formica tables stuck to a linoleum floor, glued by congealed food. Sauce the source of the stains on the walls. Plastic cutlery. Everything rang just slightly false. Certainly my lurid yellow milkshake had never had anything to do with a banana.

'The Goddess Kali,' Vlad began, as if that was the most normal conversation starter in the world, 'is associated with time, death, and doomsday.'

'And I need to know this because…?'

'Because we are going to meet her.'

I slurped my shake, imbibed my E-numbers.

'Well, that makes sense. Chances of me bumping into the goddess of rainbows and lollypops were never high, were they? I don't have that sort of luck.'

Vlad was hunched over the table, continuing his global tour of disappointing teas. Slopping out milk from a finicky mini-carton, shaking white fingers muddling with sugar packets, he looked utterly out of place in the human world. Watching him as he sweetened his brew and sweated beneath his feathered hat, flustering to keep his lace sleeves dry of dairy, I had to ask.

'We're not really meeting a god, are we?'

'Oh! Dear me no!' he giggled, delighted. 'A god? Of course not. No such thing.'

'Well, no.'

'Her followers only *think* she is a god.'

It's already been mentioned I'm sceptical when it comes to religion. Partly because the concept of an afterlife doesn't really apply to me, mostly because holiness is so obviously a construct. It's not that I'm an atheist, exactly. I'm not sure enough about anything to commit to nothing. But if there is more to heaven and earth, our ideas of what that might be are nothing other than dreams.

Long ago we created gods in our own image, and I'm not prepared to jump through the logical loops required to believe in any of them now. I don't want to single out the Judeo-Christian model here. I'll make an example of him though, as he's the one I think I know least-least about.

He may be up there, stroking his beard, enjoying harp music. But he isn't interested in any of what goes on down here. Not because he lets children die, or allows priestly hands to wander unpunished, or permits good men to go bald. But because so few of us actually follow him. Here, now; then, ever. Across the course of human history, the number of people who have actively worshipped this all-powerful being barely amounts to a hill of beings. It'd be a slither on a pie chart. For thousands of years humankind bumbled along, living in caves, trodden underfoot by mammoths, before any sort of serious civilisation got under way. When the species eventually got its act together, invented the toga, the amphora, the deity, they still didn't take to the idea of a singular god for literal ages. When they finally did, nobody in Africa, Australia or the Americas was allowed in on the secret.

1492, C. C. sailed the sea, sea, sea, to see what he could see, see, see. Another three hundred years and Cook found Australia, just lying around where its owners had left it. At a conservative estimate, more than a millennium had passed since the death of Jesus, and he was about as globally famous as someone off of an Israeli soap opera might be today. Does that sound like omnipotence?

Even when and where God is known, millions on millions of folks choose other faiths. Or none at all. The only conclusion you can draw, ultimately, is that he just hasn't been all that convincing.

Here's my thinking on the matter: if he exists, he's either not all powerful, or he's really not bothered about being obeyed.

Which is fine, whatever. I'm not judging. If I was given godlike power over ants I wouldn't expect them to devote every Sunday to boosting my self-esteem.

Anyway, that's my thesis. Obviously you're free to believe what you want. Personally, if I had to go down a theist route, I'd probably go Buddhist. But that's maybe just because I've been there and worn the second-hand T-shirt. Other pantheons are available. Choose one, or all or none.

But if I were you, I'd steer clear of Kali.

'So, who is this god? Carli?'

Vlad looked to the heavens. 'I wish you would read once in a while.'

He petted his book, which had appeared beside him at the table. Yes, the book was back. Perhaps it had never been away. It had simply been secreted in his luggage, lurking under cover of darkness, and under murky underpants, waiting to reveal itself and shed its secrets. Like most of what he owned it was a prop. Large and weathered and mauve-leather bound, it was meant to be judged by its cover. Presumably the same edition was available in paperback, but where would be the cache in that? Lucky for Vlad our travels pre-dated the e-reader. His pronouncements on quaint and curious forgotten lore would really have struggled for gravitas if he'd had to download them first.

'*Kali* has been much mentioned in Western culture,' Vlad continued, carefully stirring his mug of brownish discharge with a wooden pick, 'though mostly misinterpreted and misappropriated. In fiction, supposed worshippers have included one cult at the heart of an Indiana Jones movie, and another who tried to sacrifice Ringo Starr in *Help!*'

'Are you trying to tell me *Temple of Doom* is made up?'

'As ever, educating you is a challenge. I'm trying to tell you that it is loosely, very loosely, based in the mythos. Kali did have a blood cult following: the Thuggee.'

'I haven't the thuggee-ist what you're on about.'

He closed his eyes and whispered a quiet prayer for patience. I smiled. It was always nice to win a round.

A waiter called our number, and I signalled him across. His white shirt was an impressionist landscape of contaminants. He came laden with two plates of what could loosely be described as food. How many of the five senses would have agreed with that account would rather depend on the individual, their sensitivity, discernment, and species.

An unfussy warthog might have been chuffed with it.

I digress. Vlad was still talking.

'According to colonials...' he infused the word with the same evident distaste I had for the food, distancing himself in his mind from empire and establishment, '... these Thuggee believed that human sacrifice was necessary in order to preserve mankind. Without it, Kali would drown the world in a tsunami of blood.'

I looked down at my plate.

'That's quite an image.'

'I added the tsunami,' Vlad confessed, 'for colour.'

Hefting my cutlery, working up the courage to take the plunge, I nodded. 'Sure, sure.'

'Blood is the food of Kali. Her sustenance, her right. Bloodshed is her *rite*.'

He looked at me across the dirty table, head bobbing encouragingly, incorrigibly.

'The second rite as in r-i-t-e,' he intoned.

'I got it, *thanks*.' I hit the gratitude hard, to show it was insincere. Not sure it came across.

'I'm talking about blood sacrifice,' he clarified, absolutely unnecessarily.

'Can you stop saying blood for a minute? I'm trying to eat.'

I prodded at my primordial sludge with a spoon, gently, in case it tried to fight back. Vlad pecked at his portion with a similar lack of enthusiasm. In all honesty I was glad when he dabbed his face with a silk kerchief and interrupted again.

'From the British perspective, the Thuggee were no more than murderers, the ritualistic Kali-worship simply a ruse to justify thievery and brigandage.'

'Brigandage?'

'It's a word.'

'Thought it might just have been more colour.'

He showed me his shut-up-and-listen face, otherwise known as his resting expression.

'In any event, critics have discredited the colonial view as inconsistent and exaggerated. I suppose a demon cult is easy to demonise,' he sighed.

'Poor cults.'

Vlad raised an eyebrow. I raised him back, almost did myself an injury trying to keep a straight face.

'Some say the Thuggee were a mere invention, an excuse to visit brutality upon the Indians. The stories were designed to fashion a strange and alarming adversary. To amplify the otherness of the enemy. To create a bogyman, if you will.' He paused to stroke his beard. 'Talk of Kali was no more than spurious and deliberate cant.'

I bit my tongue. It was that or more of the food.

'Although of course, this too is inaccurate. They most

certainly existed as highway robbers, hence the etymology of "thug".

Vacuuming up the lumpy remnants of my shake I ruminated on where we were up to, which as usual with Vlad appeared to be somewhere completely different to everybody else.

'So, we're talking more Dick Turpin than a Wicker Man fan club? They were just thugs?'

'Oh no. They were a blood cult.'

I would have banged my head on the table, but I was genuinely concerned about cholera.

'One more time from the top?' I pleaded.

'It's quite simple really.' Vlad leant back with smug satisfaction. 'The Thuggee were a criminal fraternity, robbers, stranglers, thieves.'

'So far so good.'

'Rumours, religion. A Goddess of Death. The raw ingredients were all there for the British to invent a mythology around them. And they managed this so successfully that the stories have never gone away.'

'Ringo, and Indy,' I nodded.

'Quite so.'

The waiter, now displaying parts of the menu down his trousers, returned to clear our picked-at plates. We didn't order dessert.

'But what's the truth?' I asked, when he had gone.

'The truth, as ever, lies somewhere between two extremes.' Vlad pointedly closed his book.

'This isn't in the book?'

'Only if I write the next chapter myself.' He picked it up and carefully stowed it back into its velvet travelling sleeve.

'What? That book is your bible. What are you basing this on?' Genuine puzzlement began to evolve into exasperation. 'Vlad, we've trekked halfway across America. Tell me this is not a hunch?'

'No, no. No, not at all.'

'Good.'

'I've deduced it thoroughly.'

'Oh Jesus.'

'You deserve quite a bit of the credit too, actually.'

'I really don't feel like I do.'

The diner, clearly suffering from a well-deserved reputation, was quiet. Save for three or four other suckers we were alone.

'Consider,' said Vlad, glowing in the microwaved humidity, 'the common belief in vampires.'

'I don't think anyone really believes—'

'The common myth, then,' he interrupted. 'On one end of the spectrum, a monster, at the other end, scepticism. Non-belief.'

'Sane people,' I muttered.

'Then take the Thuggee. The rumour, the gossip, the dark fantasy on the one hand, the pragmatic facts on the other.' He stopped talking. The waiter lurked by, grey cloth ready to re-spread some germs if we abandoned our table. Vlad waited for him to lose interest and wheel away to hit on a waitress.

Then he leant in.

'What do the two tales have in common?' He was uncomfortably close. I could smell him.

'I don't—'

'You,' he said. 'You in the middle. Your kind.'

God Opens a Door

Some days New England felt aptly named, when the higher peaks were lost in skeins of cloud. When smeary pewter skies slated down on stony lakes to cast a sheen of steel on still waters, and even rainbow trout swam like shades of smog and shadow. When forests seemed sketched in charcoal and every tree grew grey as ash, then starlings and blackbirds huddled in the branches, and twitching English hearts turned to the heartlands. For a Whitby lad, what could have felt homelier? Perhaps only gulls. Screaming harbingers of the coast, and hidden depths. For half our travels the sea had shone unceasingly by our side. But blue, and otherworldly. Here we stayed inland, yet on familiar ground. Though the miles between ourselves and our port only lengthened, Vlad's comfort grew in proportion to the thickening of the weather. It may have had something to do with the mission, a proximity to destiny, but I suspect he just felt at home.

The bus was late, maybe that helped too. After dark, we crawled on higher. Longer, slower.

Almost into dreamland.

'You like it here?' I broke the spell.

Vlad blinked. He'd been lost in the midnight stillness, staring at his reflection in a dim window. Forests slid by beyond. A collage of green-baize trees, stained black, and pasted onto a night canvas.

'It's fine.'

He lapsed into silence, but there was no sleep to be found on that rolling road, and it was one of those rare times when I actually needed some conversation. Normal conversation, not demon cults.

'Just fine?' I prodded. 'No better than Oz? No worse?'

He arched his back. 'I'm a man of the world.' His voice came across as a careless breath.

He was seeing what he wanted to, I suppose, in that black glass. Seeing the man he thought he'd be, when he was a boy.

'Is this what you imagined,' I wondered, 'when you said you wanted to see the world?'

He grimaced, rolled in his seat, sighed. 'I may have envisaged greater comfort. Fewer inane questions.'

Turning away, my neck rolling with a chorus of clicks, I rowed back on my desire to talk. Boredom was preferable. Discomfort and insomnia could be my friends. But you can't put a lid on a can of worms.

'It isn't as though this is my first time,' he muttered. 'I have travelled, you know.'

He told a story, some trip he had taken in his youth. Turkey, or Torquay. I can't really remember. There was an anecdote about a lemur stealing his camera, if that narrows it down. I did try to listen. I wanted to. We'd never talked a lot about his past adventures. He'd never ventured, I'd never expected. I was curious enough. But for all I tried to stay in tune, my focus slipped, shimmered in and out like his face in that darkling pane. The whole tale was just too… too *Vlad*. Too fluent, pattering along, all smooth edges and lathe-honed phrases.

'We saw him the next day, scampering along the promenade bold as a brass band, clutching a handbag in one tiny paw…'

Fluff like that, the emphasis on *clutch*, pursing his lips as he made a little joke. You can see why it would drive me mad.

He could talk all day, all your life, and he wouldn't really say anything. Little wonder my mind wandered. Trying to remember whether a lemur was a monkey or more of a rodent. Smoke in the chalky sky…

'… I went to run after him, but before I could take two steps I was heels over head in a heap. A small boy had crept under my feet without my noticing, and was busily polishing my boots.'

That new element tripped my attention. A memory came of the Med, a seafront, trying to walk while some poor kid crawled between my legs, smearing shoe polish on my flip flops until I dropped some loose change and he let me go.

'He'd certainly chosen his target. I was surely the only properly shod gentleman for many a mile. And he seemed to have been doing a good job, working away with a leather cloth and a greased elbow.'

It wasn't a memory I wanted. I didn't feel I came out of it well. Still don't. But what can you do? I've never been able to manage my own petty problems, let alone global poverty. And for God's sake, flip flops don't even need polishing. Still I knew it was there, even with his voice filling my head, a wave of words drowning out concentration.

'Of course, by this time the pilfering primate was long gone. I just let the lad finish. Afterwards he tried to move onto my friend, but she was wearing sandals, and didn't welcome the attention.'

He gave a chuckling flourish, a virtual nudge to let me know it was time to smile. But with his silence my synapses dried, and sparked.

'Companion? That was me. That was us?'

He looked at me, for the briefest moment uncertain, before rearranging his features into jocular order.

'Dear boy, you may have been many things, but never a lady, as my companion on that memorable day most assuredly was.'

I laughed, nervous, not amused.

'I remember the boy, he polished your wellies for ages, and then after you paid him, he wouldn't leave me alone. Followed me right along the beach. It was on Samos, or one of those islands. I'm sure, because I honestly thought about buying some wipes and earning a few Euro.'

'No,' he said. 'This was Marmaris, and before we ever met.'

My head swam again. It was in there, it was real, I was sure it was. But he was talking again.

'Oh yes, you aren't the only one who has dallied, young friend. Alette was French, from Champagne

232

would you believe? She certainly had the proverbial *je ne sais quoi.*

Words, wine, intoxicating. Not stimulating but stupefying. Verbal moonshine, every sentence washing out sense and sentience. The more he said the less I heard, the more uncertain my own times, my own mind became. Who was real? The boot boy? The French girl? What was imaginary? The Med? Me? Whose memory was it anyway? Had I imbibed it, with blood? Was part of him inside me? Or had one of us just heard it before, in the mists of history, and forgotten, and found it again in the fog?

It was my turn to stare through the window, that unlooking glass. Nothing stared back. Blankness, blackness. Not even that. The grey haze hid the night, and dawn would be grey too.

Even here, as close to home as it was possible to be while half a world away, nothing was illuminated.

Vlad's final, hurried explanations certainly didn't uncross any tease. Walking from the bus station, navigating identikit avenues of white picket fences, he recited:

'In skin of tiger and necklace of skulls, Kali issued forth. Eyes red, maw gaping, armed with both sword and noose.'

The soft words seemed out of step in suburbia. There was no place for a goddess of war between those tended lawns, by those stop signs and mail boxes.

'She fell upon the demon army of Raktabija and devoured them.'

Vlad looked expectant, as if I was supposed to know what he was on about. Which didn't add up, because

I never did. A pregnant pause gestated, with painful complications, until he finally delivered a petulant, harrumphing snort, and waved me on my way.

'Was that supposed to be…? What?' We separated, a couple of steps before it dawned. 'You wrote it?'

He flapped around, an unreadable gesture. I knew I was right. It didn't help.

'Very nice. It still doesn't help.'

With bejewelled thumb and forefinger, he massaged the tension into his eyes.

'The Thuggee believe, or were said to believe, that Kali subsisted on blood. The more the better. She drank the blood of those she slaughtered in battle.'

'It's not terribly Hindu-y, is it?'

'It's downright blasphemous.' He gave a sacrilegious chuckle. 'But since we're both godless heathens I don't imagine that's an issue?'

'Well…' Somehow, a mild moral pang did pass through me. I note it only for its rarity value.

We waited at an intersection, crossed behind a yellow school bus. Passed into an elm-lined boulevard.

'In any case, we know it's nonsense.'

'We do?'

'Keep up.' His off-white teeth showed in a smile. 'She isn't really Kali.'

'Right.' My brain shifted up a gear, albeit clunkily. 'She's like me?'

'That's the theory. In which case her acolytes feed her blood in a purely ceremonial sense, after each death, to sustain her immortality.'

'Well, that's alright then.'

We arrived.

From the outside there was nothing remarkable about the place. It was a building with windows and doors, the bricks were red and the mortar grey. A lawn was laid out in front, neatly mown, divided by a paving drive. Either side, two trees stood tall. Stage left, an X-ray spray of bark-wrapped bone, a multiplicity of stark, stark-naked limbs, reaching into stick extremities and twig fingers. Unclothed already for winter, to all appearances dead, and yet alive. The other was lower, squarer, less the traditional almond in shape, more a mass, a mess of ill-green fronds of frosted fir. Brown around the edges, grown beyond its means, it seemed to suffer beneath its weight. Before that tree stood a bench, but it was empty.

To see even this however, you had to be beyond the wall. Perhaps I should have started there. Eight-foot high and sharded with glass, it sent a message, and not a subtle one. The only gate was closed, and had no window. No handle.

Vlad took out his mobile phone, and tapped at it with old man hands.

His call was answered three rings in. Conversation was perfunctory:

'Hello?... Precua.... Yes, we're outside, now... Praise be to Kali.'

He hung up.

Digging my hands into my pockets, I stifled an imaginary yawn.

'Wrong number, was it?'

'They'll call us when she is ready.'

Outside we remained, looking in. Story of my life. His too, of course, in a way. Always the wrong side of some fence or other.

Out of place on earth, my gaze drifted, absent, to the grey haze above. There was a big picture, up there. A galaxy, a universe of stars. Not that I could see any of them. Only the vast, obscuring cloudscape.

'How long have they been doing this, do you think?'

'There is no way of knowing for sure,' Vlad pondered, studying the gate as if for mystic runes. 'The body in the field was the first clue.'

The clouds didn't budge. There was no wind up there. Nothing but mist and peace. Was there anything else, invisible, unknowable?

'That was, what now?' His eyes glazed. 'What year did the pub get refurbished? Before we met, in any case.'

'Not so long,' my lips murmured, 'in the grand scheme.'

'I have investigated since, of course.' He tipped imaginary spectacles down his nose, so that he could peer earnestly over them. Perhaps it made him feel properly studious. 'Tracking the movements of the Thuggee, to trace the connection. The earliest I can unearth of them in New England is '89.'

Numbers sailed absently through my mind. Years.

'I'd died twice myself by then.'

Vlad grinned, impishly gleeful as he only was when putting me right about something.

'My dear boy. *1889.*'

Well, that made a difference.

His phone rang.

'They're ready for you.'

The wind, missing from the sky, found its way into my chest. Filled me with breath I couldn't expel. Another of my kind. The first I'd ever heard of, not to count my dad, not wanting to. Was this my chance to fit in, to belong? I looked again at the sky.

If not here, then where? Grounded, with Vlad? Planet Earth wasn't exactly his home territory.

I stepped up. 'Come on then.'

'Just you.' Vlad stood down. 'Just you.'

My head shook, of its own volition. I couldn't quite figure. We'd come so far. He'd led me.

'But, this is your—' I began, and faltered. 'I mean, it's not me that wants to—' The gale inside grew, and thundered.

Vlad's eyes were wet, jaw set. 'Just you.'

Still hesitating. 'If it's only one of us. It should be you.'

'It should,' he said. 'It should, but they do not see it that way. They have...' he reached for a word, '... rules. Age limits.'

'What do they know about me?' It occurred to me, too late, to ask.

'Not what you are,' he said, quickly, 'just that you are young. Healthy.' He all but whistled insouciance.

I looked up at the gate.

'Why am I here?'

'To see a goddess. To meet your kind.'

Any other time, I'd have picked him up on all but calling me a god. But there was a bigger question.

'Why do *they* think I'm here?'

This time, he had the words prepared: 'For the needs of your kind.'

He'd screwed me. A sacrifice. Memories of a cellar, of blood spilled like wine.

'But I can't do that.' He'd screwed them too. 'I'm not human.'

He tugged his collar around his ears. 'Then they cannot hurt you,' he said.

Perhaps that was the chance to go, to get away, from him, them. Everybody. But then again, maybe it was already too late.

'It's up to you,' he said.

Of its own accord, the gate clicked open. Alone, and without looking back, I walked into the light.

Telling Stories

When I was very small, and very ill, my ward carried a stock of books. Mongrel-eared, thumbed and torn. Donated, or left behind. Inscribed under the covers by hopeful hands: *to Peter on his 4th birthday, 15th April, 1954; Get well soon Christine, love Mummy and Daddy; to Bobby, with best wishes from Uncle Jeremy.*

All well read, well loved. Peered and pored over by Peter or Christine or Bobby, or others. A hundred sticky hands, countless sickly children. Heads nodding, eyes glazing, dull or drugged as parents told and retold the tales inside, watching and yearning for better times.

Who knows how many had their wish? How many patients got to grow up, go on, and forget. How many didn't.

The story I most remember was Aladdin. Or a form of it. It struck me, stuck with me, and not just because it's the only time I recall my dad reading to me.

I'd say it resonated, but it couldn't have done, not then.

Very different to the *Disney* version, which I only saw much later, this was older, screwier, scarier. I've tried to track it down since, but I don't know who wrote it, or published it, or when. There's a possibility, I suppose, that my dad made it up. It's hard to imagine him pulling a children's story out of his hat. That doesn't seem like his style… although, one that's still messing with my head a lifetime later? Yeah. That's possible.

I'll have a little go at recreating some of it here, but don't go getting het up if it does happen to be real, and a cherished favourite of yours. I'm no Scheherazade.

There's some pre-amble, and then:

Aladdin landed with a bump on his rump, and for a moment the breath was knocked right out of his body.

'Well, this is a fine pickle!' he muttered to himself, looking around. Not that looking around was any use whatsoever, because the cave was deep and dark and he could not see further than the end of his nose.

Clearly written by someone who had never left Hampshire, but hey, Ray Bradbury never went to Mars, did he?

Al bumbles around a bit after that, stumbles into various objects collecting bumps. Fumbles upon the lamp and brings on the magic:

With wisps of gold and silver smoke a genie appeared.

The cave is lit, and gaudy treasures come alive. You'd think at this point the lad would be preoccupied with the big smoky fella in the fez, but turns out he's more concerned in locating all the objects he tumbled over in the dark. What he took to be a jagged rock, a branch, and a bucket of nuts and bolts become a crown, a sceptre, and a casket of rings and gemstones. The last thing he jammed into was…

… not a creaky old scarecrow but a man, ancient and withered, his white beard fell down to his ankles, and though his head was as bald as a billiard ball his eyebrows sprouted like garden weeds.

Comedy, I suppose. It didn't make me laugh. Aged no more than four, I'm sure I still felt something darker at work.

His bony finger shook and his voice trembled 'Beware the Genie of the Lamp, beware his gift of wishes three!'

Here we find the crux. Genie stands, combustible and impassive, as the fogie relates how his own hubris led him to demand the earth, and everything in it.

'My first wish was for a palace, and every room was to be filled with treasure. A room of pearls, a room of emeralds, a room or rubies. When the wish was granted I found there was no room for my

wife, or children, or friends. No room for servants, or food, or drink. I could not talk to pearls, or eat emeralds, or drink rubies. Wealth brought no joy.

'My second wish I thought long about. Believing I was wise, I sought to outwit the genie. Knowing I still had a third wish in reserve, I bade him show me happiness, thinking I could then claim this for myself.

'He showed me my life as I had been before. My wife, my children, my friends. All the things I had given up for cold metal and lifeless jewellery. Knowing that all I had held dear had been brought to ruin, I was driven to madness and despair. Casting the lamp deep into the darkest dungeon of my palace, I threw off my finery and wandered the world as a beggar.'

I think we can all agree that was a strange choice. Although I imagine that using the final wish just to get right back where you started would be a bit of a downer. Could send you on a bit of a spiral. Still seems better than the solution he eventually comes up with after a classic desert epiphany:

'I determined that never again should the genie plague another life as he had mine. And so, recovering the lamp, I made my third wish. That I should become the guardian of the lamp. That I should stay with it always. That nobody should hear the genie speak without first hearing my story.'

That's his choice, his last desire. A sort of eternal purgatory. Aging and withering but never quite dying, enduring endless darkness alone, only as a warning to others.

From there it gets less interesting, sort of segues back to regular Aladdin, making good choices. That's what it's supposed to add, I guess, a bit of backstory to explain how he sidesteps avarice and embraces humble nobility.

Arguably it doesn't do a whole lot for the story. It's an unnecessary sort of prelude, additional atmosphere, if you like that kind of thing, but at the expense of the flow. Slowing it all down, fooling around. Maybe the writer was being paid by the word, or he liked the sound of his own inner voice. My theory is he never wanted to write for children. He was in a trap himself, having set off on an epic quest to be Homer, or Milton, or Dante, only to fall, or find he wasn't who he thought he was, or at least nobody else believed him, or believed in him, leaving him lost and alone in a cave of his own, a prison of his own devising.

But, you know, I could be overthinking it. Chances are it's not even a memory. Not a real one. Who would trust the senses of a child? A dying child. A blot of custard or a crumb of cheesecake could have cheated them. Or being hooked up to enough drugs to feed a festival. It doesn't seem that real, that realistic, if you think about it. A little kid listening to chat, soaking it in. The idea of my dad being there, doing a dad thing. Those details.

That's what bugs me, the details. If it isn't real, did I dream them? Those fragments of prose, odd plot holes. There's a layer too many, I think. And my dreams don't usually last so long.

One thing is for sure, I didn't just make it up off the top of my head as a sort of weird prologue to introducing the oldest woman in the world. That would be crazy.

Then again, there's no non-crazy way of introducing that topic.

I don't know why they're always white, these dying places. Black might be the shade of death itself, depending on which culture you choose to die a part of, but you can't beat white for the preamble: hospitals, hospices, clinics and care homes. They're always so stark and bleak. Dulux probably have a special colour chart catalogue: bleached coral, dinosaur bone, polar bear rug. All just variations on a paper-thin theme. I suppose if nothing else it's clean. I mean, any dirt should be clearly seen. But actual germs, they'd be microscopic anyway. No chance of spying the little monsters, whatever colour you daub your sanctuary.

The nurse, or familiar, or whoever she was, wore white as she brusquely engaged with an intravenous drip. Even I wore white. Downstairs, before they led me through cooled corridors and into a sterile elevator, they'd given me a gown, and a cap, and a pair of those ridiculous plastic overshoes. I don't know why that's the part I've chosen to identify as ridiculous. Like there's a line of preposterousness, which hadn't been crossed by trekking four-and-a-half odd thousand miles to take part in this freak show, but somehow wearing plaggy bags over my trainers tipped me over the edge. I suppose as I slipped them on I do remember wondering why the hell I was there.

I had to know more though, I think that much at least is understandable. The rumours and whispers that led us to that hermetically sealed hermitage could hardly be ignored. Even if I ninety-nine per cent knew the end result would be disappointment, disgust, depression. And even though somehow it succeeded in surpassing all that, leaving me witness to damnation.

Why are "d" words all so deleterious? Dull, doleful, delay; dire, disgust, dismay; dying, dead, decay. It's enough to make you disown your dictionary. Damn, what a dreadful digression. But what other words can I use? Discouraging, disheartening, dismal?

Everything about that room was dreary. White, yes, but dark. There was no natural light, only what modern technology and ancient custom combined to afford. Low-watt halogen bulbs, heavily shaded, cast a glow designed not to stress even the most sensitive eye. The carefully crafted lambent ambience was otherwise punctuated only by the fairy-light blinking of the monitors, checking and re-checking for breath and pulse; and by the incense burners, which in any case cancelled out their own contribution with eclipsing wisps of sage-scented smoke.

Some Aladdin's Cave, hey? You know better by now than to get me started on hospitals, but nothing screams "not having a good time" like medical miscellany. This room had it all.

The bed was on wheels and had handles to help the invalid sit. The visitors' chairs were so uncomfortable as to be chiro-impractical. They'd sprayed me with about a boys' boarding school dormitory's worth of disinfectant before I came in, but still there was a soap dispenser in case I wasn't clean enough. The windows and doors were double-glazed and double-sealed, and all hidden away behind the kind of thick PVC flaps that always put me in mind of the shower curtains at an internment camp. In short, it was a room designed to keep out death, but which in doing so had neglected to let in any life.

Unless the thing in the bed could be said to be alive.

She looked dead.

She? It.

It looked dead. Less than dead. Never alive, not even a corpse. A waxwork. A thing that belonged beneath cold glass, locked in a museum.

Did you ever have a school trip to a museum, where you saw something so old you could never imagine it new? A coin that couldn't have been round? A treasure that could never have shone?

This visage was a mere mask, a mummified disguise. A replica relic of rotted nature. An ancient accident, exposed to too much, for far too long. A liquefying candle. A prop from partway through a face-melting movie scene.

Except nothing like that.

Like worn brown paper, the old-fashioned kind used to wrap parcels. Too much paper for too little gift, left ripped and wrinkled when torn away. Discarded somewhere slimy, wet. Oiled to a thin translucent state. Dried, flat-ironed, taped together. Disgusting, and yet… almost asking to be touched… you can feel how it would yield, sort of smooth and dry beneath your fingers, but with folds and creases still there in the memory, visible beneath a skin-deep veneer.

Except, not like that either.

But something horrid.

A worm's face, stupor-slow, man-sized, flat and earthy, blind.

No.

A walnut shell, left in the dark, putrid, cold and mouldering, and yet, with the smallest gleam of a Promethean gift somewhere, lost but everlasting, hid inside…

Worst of the lot.

Forget the face then. The body, dead body, the shape beneath the sheets. Nothing but a rag doll, straw and kindling. Ribcage a tissue of fragility, to be crushed by any but the lightest thread-count of Egyptian cotton. Hollow chest unable to rise or fall of its own accord, trachea all but visible through the exposed throat, forced to suckle air from a bag.

A creaky old scarecrow… ancient and withered…

A monster then.

Yes, a monster. And the me I might live to be.

Falling Hard

It might be a hard sell, fifty-or-so-thousand words into a book all about myself, to suggest I'm no narcissist. Well, what the hell. Hospital beds remind me of me, sick people don't so much inspire sympathy as unhealthy recollections and unhelpful reflections.

In that cold prison, eyes fixed to the goddess of blood, that might actually have made sense.

She was me. The me of my nightmares.

Not actual nightmares, those tend to be silly things, trivial and laughable. A recurring terror that awoke me in my youngster-years was an angry purple octopus eating my mum. I think I'd have trouble shredding any sincere fear out of readers for that, by the light of day.

Daylight in that room, artificial as it was, shone on actual horror. If I haven't described it well enough above, if the blithering analogies didn't paint it right, well, bloody hell, it isn't exactly easy. Try it for yourself. I'm serious. Picture your own personal worst-case scenario. The foulest projection of your fate. How would it feel to be faced with it? Forced to see it made flesh, made to dwell on hell, then describe it? Put yourself in my overshoes. Imagine being confronted by the ghost of your own future.

Repulsive, isn't it?

So forgive the inbuilt introspection, pardon my selfish meditation on my own lack of death.

Only, you don't actually need to. That whole paragraph was as red as an inside-out herring. Standing there, dressed in white, eyes desperate to find something to catch them and tear them away from the angel of death, willing even to contemplate a sick past rather than face a sickening present, I wasn't thinking about myself. The one time I justifiably could have been.

I was thinking about my dad.

Well, my dad and me.

Alright, me, in hospital, but with him. Or him with me. The wrong way around, either way. As the younger generation, I should have been the visitor. I should have been the one hovering, shuffling around at the foot of the bed. Checking my watch. I should have been avoiding his eye, as he laid on the bed, weighed down by sweat and lethargy, inert, bloodless. Air ebbing away through a tube. I should have been allowed to watch him age before my eyes. It should have been his deathbed.

A dark train of thought. Though train implies logical progression, and I can't claim that, or admit to it. I can't imagine having a mind that works that way. You know, linearly. As if thinking could be constrained by rails. If my thoughts moved like a vehicle, it would be the DeLorean from *Back to the Future*, post-lightning strike, bouncing around space and time guided by nothing more than luck or fate. Or a wild-eyed old eccentric.

Maybe even, if mad inventors are in play, something like Wonka's Great Glass Elevator. Every wall a window, every direction a possibility.

But there will always be weightier thoughts, deeper, murkier. Some paths are more worn, trodden into ruts and furrows. Dragging attention back their way, again and again. Like how when rain falls, it will find a channel. And what is a channel, really, if not a rail?

Shows what I know.

Anyway, that's what I thought about, in that white room, cold room. Emotionally cold room. The actual temperature was controlled to a perverse degree, but passions were maintained, dry and tempered. Even mine, as if coldness were catching. It was the only thing that could have been, with every breath trapped by a mask, every gasp measured and weighed, recorded on a graph. Science and superstition in unholy matrimony, as a god, or a demon, or something in between, died and lived and died again, over and over. Never really living a day.

I thought about my dad, watching me age and die. Staring at me on that bed, as old as I had ever been. Older at four than I ever would be again. Because that was my real life, my only human life.

And I knew then. I'd always known, but that's when it crystallised. I knew what I'd felt since those lonely Whitby days. I knew what I'd suspected in Greece, chasing dreams and waitresses and finding only emptiness. Knew the truth behind the pain-induced hallucinations I'd suffered while part of me drifted away across the Tasman Sea in a shark's gut.

Every encounter with my dad, every incident from Aladdin onward had stacked another layer of evidence on the scales, but it took a mockery of a dead woman to make me see it.

I couldn't be him, and I couldn't be her.

That was the push I needed.

Better dead than undead. I jumped out of the window.

Similar to the shark thing, films give us a particular view of jumping through a window. Rarely does an action blockbuster go by without some testosterone-toned titan tanking his way pain-free through a pane, often tumbling several stories after, only to pick himself up, dust himself down, and star all over again.

There's a couple of possibilities if you try this at home, without the benefit of CGI, a stunt double, or sugar glass. The first is you just bounce back into the room with a headache and a bruised ego. The second is you crack it, which is much worse. Anything going through a smashed sheet of glass is going to get sliced up pretty bad.

Apologies, then, for a bubble-bursting let down. The laws of physics are stronger than I am, and so is a thirty-mil window pane. Usually better not to get cut in half if you can get away with it, I always think. Sure, I jumped through the window. But I opened it first.

It had been a while. A hinge is a simple mechanism

(unless you're asking me to build one) but this specimen was stiff with time and paint. Given the environmental stasis Kali's sick acolytes surrounded her with, I don't suppose they made a habit of throwing open a welcome to the outside world. And she herself couldn't have mobilised a muscle to find fresh air. Not if her life depended on it.

Even for a relatively healthy monstrosity like myself, my forearm burned with the effort of throwing the handle, and it took the force of my shoulder to knock it wide.

'Where are you going? What are you doing?' A paper-suited nun, crisp behind a mask, gave voice to a pair of vacuous questions, before seemingly working out the answers for herself. The clue was me being perched on a window sill, I suppose.

'Your blood!' she cried. 'The ritual! The sustenance of Kali!'

'My blood's no good.' I tried to sound rueful. 'Sorry.'

'Nobody can leave having seen the goddess!' she may or may not have shouted, I can't be sure. The wind was already whistling through the coolest exit I've ever made, even accounting for the lack of splintering shards to accompany my flight to the pavement. Which I never quite reached.

Because I landed in heaven.

Fell into heaven, right out of hell. Falling into poetry, thinking about it. Because of that beautiful girl.

It was hard not to write "that girl of my dreams" right then. A terrible cliché. There are only so many words though. Little wonder some become favourites.

She wasn't my dream, though. That wasn't what I was

seeking. If I'd found a magic lamp and rubbed out free wishes, I'd have asked for answers, not a girlfriend. Deep, universal truths. Is there anybody out there? Where do we come from? Why is the sky black?

Not that I'm complaining. Life skipped lemons and just gave me aid. Not the lover of my dreams but the meaning behind my waking days. Does that sound overblown? See, this is my problem, the real reason I balked at the cliché, it's not the factual inaccuracy, it's the hyperbole. Love is like death, apparently. Impossible to write about without going overboard. Also, on that basis, something like walking the plank. Or like making a stupid joke. Ill advised, impossible to resist…

Can I get a little leeway, though? Sophie didn't just change my life, she gave me life. She made me human. As good an excuse as any, surely, for bursting lilac fireworks of purple prose?

What were the chances, I wonder, of that action-hero escape turning, mid-flight, into a romcom entrance? Well, let's just say you couldn't make it up.

Ridiculous, really, to have met on that mundane Maine street. We should have had our epic encounter in an exotic nirvana. India ideally, that would have made way more sense. Not just because I was on the trail of subcontinental death cult, but for the dramatic licence it might have afforded.

It could so easily have happened that way too. Sophie's steps could have led her to Gap Yah central. Not that she needed a spiritual journey to find herself; if anyone seemed pretty certain where all their jazz was located it was Soph.

She just loved to travel, and the trekkers heartland would have suited her roving eye.

If only I'd been searching for Hindu separatists in the right hemisphere, I might have fallen for her there. She'd have rocked the look, no question: shades on her forehead, hair hippified up in a kabbalah bandana. Sleeveless shirt to show off henna tattoos of Hindi words for "love" and "peace" and "happiness", or "gullible tourist", if the artist had a sense of humour.

It's an easy picture to paint, because that's how it should have been. Sophie dancing down to bathe in the cappuccino-brown foam of the Ganges, ignoring what the chocolate sprinkles really were. Wallowing and playing at worship with a hundred others, a thousand others, all caked in powdered patterns of exploded rainbow, like they'd lost really badly at paintball. Pirouetting clouds of sun-gold dust, billowing pink pollen residue, flowering sprays of every blue you ever knew, even the river running infinite red and ultimate violet, and yet still her face would have been more alive than every other movement, every colour, every scream and shout of ecstasy, every spiced and scented flavour in the air. And when all else shone with zest and seasoned brightness, who would she have seen but me, shipwrecked in perpetual night?

Yes, that's really what ought to have happened. Maybe I'll say it did. What price truth, anyway? Who cares? It happened. It was fate.

In the end that's what I have to hold on to. It happened, and it would have happened whenever, wherever, however. On which basis it doesn't really matter why it was Maine.

It's still crazy to think though, that in all the years that followed, there were some things we never truly talked about. Like how Sophie never told me why she was in New England, other than because she got free air miles working for a travel agent, and her best mate from college had moved out there to marry an apple farmer, and Soph was godmother to their daughter. And it was the Christening... spurious stuff. Meanwhile, I never told her I'm an undead, soulless monstrosity. Everyone has their secrets, I suppose.

Anyway, she was in town for her ritual, and I was there for mine. Fate.

So why not let it be the classic Hollywood meet-cute? In my mind I tumbled out of a window and landed on top of a beautiful woman. I may misremember slightly. I did, after all, suffer a blunt trauma to the back of the head. Also, I'm kind of wedded to the India thing now, so at least half of this may be wishful thinking.

My first sight of her was flash-lit with stunning brightness. A sudden surging splurge of colour, so far removed from the blind, pallid crypt I'd escaped from. Not Kolkata colour, perhaps, but close enough in contrast. I'd come from death, you see.

Launching myself from that white room, that place I've tried so hard to banish, I was escaping suspended animation, leaping back to reality. Little wonder if the world had never seemed so real. Everything existed in technicolour. A humdrum all-American sidewalk became Bollywood incarnate. The north-eastern gusts, chasing away frosted air con, hit me with the shock of an Indian summer, hit me like a punch. A hot fruit punch straight from the pan, full on mango and mint, mulled and sweetened to a boiling shot, slapping the sweat out of my pores before I hit the floor. Or at least, hit that girl who cushioned my fall, colliding into what should have been a tangle of sari and black plaits, sliding against almond cream skin and bruising my cheek on hers, breaking a basket, scattering lemons and squashing melons as parades danced by.

No, it didn't go down like that. My landing pad wasn't Princess Jasmine in the market place, but a Piscataquis housewife, spilling frozen tikka masala from a Walmart grocery bag.

As if that's in any way relevant. What mattered was Sophie, across the street. Stopped in her tracks by the spectacle, like everyone else. A face in a crowd, and yet different. Apart. Special. For a lifetime of a second our eyes met before a surge of regular folks bustled in and broke the spell.

In a heartbeat I was on my knees, only to catch the turn of a perfect neck, a sculptured shoulder as she looked away, leaving her likeness burnt behind my eyes, like a sun I'd stared into too long, longingly. She left.

Compulsion had me up and fumbling to follow but I fell and couldn't rise again. Sensory overload, perhaps, delirium, waves of ginger-burning heat. Maybe blood loss, as the flattened shopper's husband shattered a jar of coconut oil on the back of my skull. All I know is that even as I lay in that puddle of blood, sweat and spilt-milky goodness, I was already desperate to see that girl again.

A Breath of Fresh Air

Following my flight and lost fight with a pavement, I was limping, trending towards circles if I didn't focus to correct myself. There was a lump on the back of my head approximately the size of my actual head, far too tender to touch.

I'd lost sight of the girl, and that was another layer of pain. You can believe that or not, depending on your own cynicism, that a fleeting glance had been enough to know I'd lost something. Perhaps I am exaggerating, or hindsight is tinting my recollections, turning a small-town street into a rose garden. It's real now, anyway, even if it wasn't then. I ache if I imagine not finding her again.

True, there were other imperatives driving me too. The need to sit down. The feeling it might be a fine idea to get out of sight, to elude the potential pursuit of white-suited blood-thirsty pacifists.

Whether I was searching for a girl, a hideaway, a soft place to fall over, or nothing at all, the door to the coffee shop appeared in the right place at the right time. Intercepting my stagger, leaning open to invite me in.

The roasted caffeine troposphere pinned my eyes open and pinioned my brain to the back of my skull. Wheeling in a parabola of parody-drunkenness, I slopped into a vacant chair, which sank and squished beneath me, sucking me in like a honeytrap.

'Do you always fall over a lot, or are you just having a bad day?'

I looked up. Sophie was smiling at me. Fate was smiling on. Inside, I've hardly stopped smiling since.

'What were you doing jumping out of a window?'

She had brought me tea. It came in a glass. Vlad would have hated it.

'Long story. Or should that be tall story?'

She had also brought napkins, for the blood. That's life partner material, right there.

'Was that a joke?'

'Yes, but the way you ask that doesn't make me feel good about it.'

For a man who has spent most of his adult years wearing shorts and sunglasses, I'm not actually that chilled. Rapport doesn't come easy. Going along with a casual chatter is no laughing matter. Being breezy, no walk in the park.

Very few people have I ever formed an instant bond with. Perhaps as few as two.

Yet within minutes of meeting Sophie, I was artfully

dodging personal questions. That might not seem like a connection. Granted, it's not a normal one. Thing is though, I was making the effort. That meant I wanted to keep the conversation going.

'So?' She looked at me, over an oversized coffee.

'You wouldn't believe me if I told you.' From the start, I only ever wanted to make her happy. To unpick all the ways to make her laugh. Unpack her admiration.

'Try me?'

Deception wasn't ever what I set out to do, words just slithered off my forked tongue, like lying was second nature to me. Except that it always came first.

'You know how some people find God?' I began, eyes down, afraid to gauge her reaction. 'Well, I kind of did. And I didn't like it, so I ran away.'

That was about as close as I could circle to the truth. Of course, it made her laugh hysterically.

We didn't stay much longer after that. She had a perfectly plausible excuse about meeting someone she actually knew, and I needed to get undercover and have my head examined.

There was just enough time for me to discover where she was headed next. Not in a stalking way, you understand. Just so that I could follow. Keep an eye on her. Make sure she was okay, that kind of thing.

Which might actually be what it says in the stalker's handbook.

To get my excuses in early, what else was I going to do? Vlad seemed to think there was a chance the cult would still be out for my blood, if only to shut me up. In his usual hyperbolic way he recommended the avoidance of all major roads and airports. Anywhere that could be watched.

'They saw you fall from a window, so I should be able to persuade them you're dead. And we gave them one of your old names. If they go hunting for a backstory they'll discover you were never actually alive at all.'

'I'm not sure that's comforting.'

'Better safe than sorry.'

'What about you? Aren't they mad?'

He waved that off. 'I was only ever the facilitator. A contact. You were the… er…' he had the semi-decency to look almost embarrassed, '… the true… um…'

The only other time I ever saw him bashful was after he'd stabbed me to death, so I had to appreciate the effort.

'Victim?' I tried to help out. 'Human sacrifice? Martyr?'

'Don't exaggerate,' he huffed. 'You were never in any danger.'

'I literally jumped out of a window.'

'And you're fine.' Having ridden out his bout of guilt, he went back on the offensive. 'Not that there was any need for such histrionics. You really need to act more responsibly. I wonder if your abilities have negated in some way the need to act like a grown-up?'

'What?'

'Well, you can afford not to be prudent, so you never are.'

'I thought you agreed I was being sensible? Planning to trek the trails, get lost in the woods. Take the long way around.'

Vlad snorted. 'It might be the right thing to do, but that's not why you're doing it.'

Of all the arguments with Vlad that I never won, that may be the one about which I have least complaint.

Sophie was on her travels, knapsack on her back. Not the type to hop halfway around the world only to sit in a Starbucks, she was always going to take a gander about. Chase some wild geese. With her party in the USA all petered out, she had rifled through a *National Geographic* to see what she should see, and was about to set out and search for it. So she told me in the coffee shop.

She even happened to mention some specific sites and sights. Baxter Peak being one. Which was a coincidence, because I wanted to see that to. Or at least, see her atop a gigantic natural pedestal. Some people climb mountains because they're there, I guess. Some because there's a woman they really fancy at the top.

This isn't sounding any better, vis-à-vis stalking, is it?

Stalking is a facile way of putting it, though. Glib. There was, I'll admit, a certain amount of pursuing. But she had told me where she was going. And it's not like I shot straight there... although partly that was because the great outdoors is just so bloody big. Even when I knew where she was headed, it took almost a week to find her on the road. That would be the nature of wide-open spaces, I suppose. It's not easy just to bump into somebody. Particularly if you want to make it seem sort of random.

I saw her before she saw me. Well, that wasn't surprising. She had been everywhere with me, ever since that first sighting, every time I closed my eyes. The image of her was etched inside, easy to recall in any waking dream. And honestly, my psyche didn't seek to make any enhancements. I mean, she was perfect, so there was that, but it wasn't idolised, idealised perfection. My imagination never tarnished her with an airbrush, or even a hairbrush. Maybe symmetry is over-rated, but I never found her nose needed straightening. When I saw her again, accidentally one-hundred per cent on purpose, I knew her in an instant.

I was behind her, which, come to think of it, may have been another reason I saw her first. Saw the concave curve of her back, and her hair ruffled up in a bunch above her neck, exposing a mole I could never have seen before, but still somehow recognised. I'd planned for the moment, of course, having had that handful of panicky, searching days to picture running into her. I'd planned hard. The plan was to think of something witty and suave on the spur of the moment.

Like, "Of all the coffee shops in all the world" if we happened to be in another coffee shop, for example. Something like that, but better.

As it happened, we were in a camping supply store. Lot of opportunity for wit there.

'Fancy skiing you here! Hope I'm not crampon on your style?' You know, nothing too in tents.

Thankfully, the actual sight of her tied my tongue far too tight to attempt such tiny talk, so when Sophie turned around, in slow motion, soft-focus, she wasn't subjected to such dribble, just my opening and closing mouth, and daft, fixated gaze.

Luckier still she was holding a harness, the kind designed to stop mountaineers tumbling to rocky ends, holding it and giggling with the salesman. Perfect.

'I could have done with that,' I chuckled, 'last time we met!'

Her smile rolled away, her face a beautiful blank. She had no idea who I was.

She smiled again later, after I'd overcome that soul-crushing setback and levered my way back into conversation with her. After the salesman had slunk away, taking his harness with him. Taking his hopes of a sale, maybe hopes of something else.

I assume he was trying to flirt with her, because, well, why wouldn't he? I was. Sweaty though I was, horrible though it felt.

I've always been a terrible flirt. Terrible as in abysmal, rather than incorrigible. You could put it down to lack of practice, lack of intent perhaps. Lack of opportunity. Whatever, it rarely felt right. I never knew where to look, where to put my hands. I could feel my face, sense how wrong the words felt, stumbling out.

It's silly really, to be afraid of words. Albeit ones that can change the course of your life, and someone else's.

Especially since, if I flatter myself, I often thought I could scribble at least a little bit. It may be arrogance. A residual drip drained down from my dad's gene pool, maybe a bit of an ego comes with the superhuman territory. Whatever, I always felt I knew how to put one word in front of another. With a pen, anyway.

It's harder off your cuff. Out of the mouth I never truly progressed beyond that fidgety fourteen-year-old sort of embarrassed debasement. Sometimes even the simplest question can leave you wishing pulling pigtails was a socially acceptable alternative to answering.

'What brings you out here, then?' she asked, fingers trailing along a row of mittens. 'The call of the wild?'

Smiling, pretending to inspect some futuristic-fibre glove, I ran a gauntlet in my mind. Again, I didn't want to fib. It wasn't so much, so soon, that I was worried about implications. I didn't exactly think anything I said would come back to haunt me, or be held in evidence. But the lies you lay are always foundations, and I suppose I hoped, just hoped, that something was building.

Still, the truth was not an option, couldn't be used to explain where I was, generally or specifically. Or psychologically, but let's not overcomplicate it.

I was there because ever since I'd bumped into her I couldn't stop thinking about her. And even if the bumping had occurred in a normal context, rather than in the midst of fleeing some semi-immortal demon, I didn't know how to say that without sounding creepy.

It had to be a lie then. A backstory for my presence in the backwoods. But something small. Believable. My eyes roamed off from handwear, passed snoods and gilets, and over to a small, unassuming shelf of books. Rough Guides, Lonely Planets. Maybe a lost Douglas Adams.

'I'm a travel writer.'

Okay, I could have gone smaller. Thing is though, there was an undercurrent of truth. You see, I did always write. However lightly I might have packed for a trip, I'd always squirrelled away a notebook, made time to fill it with descriptions, found room for a view. It's hard to say why exactly, except that it's something I started doing, and then never stopped. I guess old habits die almost as hard as I do. It's not that I thought I'd ever be Theroux or Kerouac. If I've managed to pronounce their names right, it's as close as I could get to them. There was always a feeling though, that I should be making a record.

'Oh?' I'd caught her interest. Exhilarating. 'Who do you write for?' and terrifying.

She'd told me before she worked in travel, lived it in her spare time. She would know the scene.

'I'm more what you'd call aspiring, at the moment.' No doubt I was blushing. Probably giggling. Is that gendered enough to make me sound like a schoolgirl? This is what I mean by flirting. It's just the worst. If there had been an option, I'd have passed Soph a note. Words.

She moved on through the store, down the bear-repellent aisle into hunting and fishing, taking it all in with the idlest of curiosity.

'I could read something you've written, if you wanted?'

Following behind, I caught the tinge of pink in the turn of her cheek before her eyes darted away, reflecting along a row of bowie knives.

'I mean, I could show you some stuff, if you wanted.' I spread my palms, as if this were somehow a generous offer. She drifted slowly off, languorous rather than ponderous, like cream pouring over dessert.

'I'd like to see what you've got.' She slipped a smile over her shoulder. My mind reeled among the fishing rods. Was she – could she be – flirting back?

I suppose I'd seen stranger things.

The Fall and Rise of the Roaming Vampire

The sky is a magical place. Space, and what lies beneath. The cloudy wreaths and mountainous reefs that sparkle in sunlight or rain alike. Streams of air, squalls and sounds of singing winds, stillness and silence too, in their turn. Scents carried from afar, salt from seven seas, lingering messages, spices from four corners of the world, a map of the continents in condiments, hints of journeys to take, or take again. Colours, literal rainbows from red dawns to dark-violet nights, and all the whites in the world, so plentiful the Eskimo alone can name them.

I've dwelt here before. Perhaps I envy the birds who dwell there themselves. Wings spanning currents and change, riding updrafts and drifting, loftily looking down on ice-tipped peaks and wandering, earth-bound souls.

I wonder how they feel? Do they grow light-headed, so elevated? Do their tiny hearts sing? Do thrush get a rush?

For myself, I never felt higher than under blue skies, on top of the world. I won't talk about gods again, but some might have felt their presence, up there. And after all, hadn't everything seemed to progress by design? Not mine, but one more intelligent. Since Sophie asked, I showed her some writing, and the quality of my descriptive prose notwithstanding, we sort of ended up travelling on together. Together.

And even if I'm not a believer in destiny, I do think it was inevitable that we ended up touching the sky. In prosaic terms, that's because we climbed a mountain. But it's weirdly awkward to admit how quickly I fell. Love at first sight? It's painful to type, it's so twee. I certainly couldn't say it directly, not so soon. Even approaching it from an obtuse angle seemed to make her laugh.

'This is heaven.'

She laughed. That was okay. I got to see her laugh.

'You're an idiot,' she giggled.

'No, honestly.' My smile broke out. It always did, around her. 'Well, I mean, yes. Sure, I am an idiot, but this is my idea of heaven. I mean it.'

We were up a mountain. I just need to reiterate that. We were high. It was the wrong time of year, cold enough to be uncomfortable. Possibly dangerous, if you didn't have the right gear. Which despite our sojourn in the camping store, we obviously didn't. My trainers leaked, and if the dew-drained grass around my seat was anything to go by, my trousers had been woven from sponge. My hat was a good one, but Sophie hadn't brought one, so I'd lent it to her, and pulled a scarf around my head, to resemble a very lost T. E. Lawrence.

As well as my hat, she was in enough fleece to fill three bags full, including a spare pair of socks over her gloves.

'What's the matter?' I watched her face glisten. The air blew crisp, specked with a hardness that might have been ice and it made our eyes water. 'Tell me what isn't perfect about this?'

'Frostbite?' she beamed, like sunlight.

'What are a few toes compared to this view?'

I got another chuckle. Cold hands, warm heart.

Heaven.

Those of us who've been to paradise though, we know it is easily lost.

'It's nice enough, I guess,' she wrinkled her nose, 'as far as views go.'

'Better from where I'm sitting.' Sure, it was cheesier than Welsh rarebit without the toast, but that's where I was at. There was no possible way, at that place, in that time, for me to exaggerate how I felt about her.

I'd have gone blind, to stare at that face. I'd sooner have read a look from her than lifted a finger to save all or any poetry from eternal deletion. A word from her was more to my ear than any composer could compete with.

'I wish today would never end.' That's how crumby I was. I should have been toast.

All too soon the day did begin to end, as every day does. That's the problem with days. With anything. And the problem with mountain tops is that the only way is down. Happiness is ever on a fine line.

In this case, that fine line was a mile-long, mile-high skyway lofted in the Appalachian clouds. The Knife Edge, it is called, and aptly so. A tricky track that bridges the gap between Baxter and Pamola peaks, her skirts are steep granite gradients, swooping down from either edge. Spectacular rock-monsters line the way, crags with features and faces, centuries-old sun-killed trolls swept into piles of rubble, trials and trouble. Hard and grey in most places, green and unpleasant in others, the blade is outwardly handsome and inwardly hostile. Gorges can be gorgeous on the pages of geographic magazines, they're less pleasant when you're in danger of falling into them.

Such danger is real, surreal and present, the path is a mere metre wide in places. In favourable weather a misplaced foot can send an unwary hiker hurtling from the mountain shoulder, a thousand pitching, crunching rolls, breaking bones on brutal boulders, into the valley of the shudder of death. In wet weather, icy, slippery cold, finger-numbing weather, you'd have to be some mad thrill-seeker to even think about being up there.

I've spoken before about the daredevil stuff. In that I'm not one. I was up that stupid overgrown hummock because Sophie had wanted to go, and I'd have followed her up any other summit just as willingly. Everest. A restless Vesuvius. Any of Tolkien's goblin-infested eyries, you name it.

Baxter was no breeze, even by those comparators. A place for the insane alone. Or the indestructible.

I was both, of course. But Sophie wasn't. Beyond our beaming mouths a gloom was deepening, breeding frost.

'I'm getting cold.'

I looked at her, face falling into darkness, blending with the shadows. She reached, clasped my hand.

'We should go.' I struggled to stand as she clung on. Something passed from her to me. I felt it, froze with it. Fear.

'I won't let you go.' My breath was steam.

'Promise?' There was a brittle twitch to the corner of her mouth. Her fingers tightened, squeezing, breaking through layers of synthetic insulation, searching for something real.

Our eyes locked.

'I promise.'

Hand in hand we wandered along that mountain track in what had suddenly descended into the bleakest of midwinters. Every careful footstep was made onto a slick veneer, with only the questionable grip of a cut-price trainer to save us from grim, cold pain. And believe me, it is cold in the Maine mountains in winter. Worthy of italics *cold*. The only reason the whole state isn't iced over is because it's already under a metre of snow. And we were high, lung-achingly high, so extremities deadened and grew dull, and each exhalation stung the lips, chugging out in hard-fought vapours to join a frozen mist writhing in wraithlike agonies. If it counts as mist at that height. It might just have been cloud.

Cloud. The light, so bright at its peak, was shrinking. Shroud-dark, the sun lost in sensible hibernation. The distant beauty of the neighbourhood crests faded in the gloom, which basically negated the only half-worthwhile reason for being up there in the first place. Sightseeing was right out. Survival was suddenly the only game in town.

Our scarves were frozen to our faces by the time we shouldered open the cabin door to escape the icy slopes. Inside we found an open fire cracking logs and thundering, kindly kindled to please the host of happy après-hikers who crowded close, all sweating knitwear, beards and beer steins. They parted with jovial toasts, encouraged us to press between them and succour frosted fingers.

Flames bellowed and rolled in bright contrast to the white night outside, gobbling black wood into blisters and ash, feeding out currents of bright billowing heat, waves you could all but see, throbbing, shimmering, drawing you in. It was perfect.

'Let's go somewhere else,' said Sophie, bracing my snow hat tighter around her face.

There was nowhere else, not for miles, not on that mountain. It was sub-zero and falling, and darkling forests all around probably howled with peckish packs of wolves.

We'd booked rooms, we had to stay.

'What is it?'

A look told me.

'It's the fire?'

I knew I was right, but that didn't help.

'Sophie?'

She was frozen.

Eventually we skirted the room and hunched as far from the fireplace as possible. Throughout a thrown-back meal of mutton peddled as lamb she kept an eye upon the storm of sparkling embers, as if afraid they'd coalesce and come for us, like some marvellous supervillain. We were gone sooner than was comfortable, up wooden stairs to rustic quarters. Twin beds, and heating that had, thankfully, progressed beyond flint and tinder, though only so far as hissing apparatus that stank of oil and steam.

Alone, Sophie showered herself back to life. I lay on a bed and pondered.

When she emerged I could see the bathroom behind her, a grand term for a sink and shower crammed into a space approximately the same size as the plughole. Accommodation had not taken a notable upturn since ditching Vlad, although the company had. Hair damp and tousled, skin tickled pink, she was a girl-next-door worth crossing continents for. True, her nightwear was so marginally less bulky than her daywear that from the neck down she rather resembled a womble, but I was willing to place a long-term bet that whatever was underneath would be worth the wait.

'Not a fan of the bar then?' I asked. Not sure I should broach the topic at all, settling for skirting around it. Trying to sound blithe, 'It was a bit noisy, I guess.'

'Sorry.' She hid behind some small task, packing or unpacking further socks.

'It's cool.' Such temperate word choice might have missed the mark, after a chilly supper far from the hearth, but I suppose it could have been worse. 'Everyone has their stuff. Personally, I'm a hot mess around candles.'

Again, there have been smoother lines in the history of romance, but…

'Kiss me.'

The socks were gone and she was in my arms and everything else, the threadbare room, the toxic fumes of an ancient stove, the wind rattling down from the Arctic Circle to shudder the window panes, it all became out of focus and faraway. There was only softness, tightness, closeness. Only us. Only warmth.

Much later, in one bed, beneath two quilts, and wearing between us at least three sets of pyjamas, she unwound herself from me sufficiently to show her eyes.

'Sorry,' she whispered as if abashed, 'again.'

'For what?' I was being genuine, couldn't remember a before. There didn't seem to be a time in which that bed hadn't been our whole world.

'You know,' she wriggled, 'downstairs, earlier.'

It took me a moment to figure she wasn't speaking figuratively. Although nothing had happened there. I'm a gentleman.

'The fire.'

We lay, and I stroked her womble-hide. 'It's okay.'

'It's kind of a trigger for me. It probably seems silly.'

'It doesn't.'

'It's to do with my dad.' I tried to keep my face steady as she stared at me. 'He – I don't usually tell people this until...' she blushed, '... until I get to know them.'

'You don't have to tell me anything.'

'I want to.'

Under the blanket cave I tried to remain calm. Obviously I've never been open myself, and for that reason I've never really encouraged it in others. Even right then I'd probably have been content for her to have stopped, zipped it, kept her own secrets and left me with mine. Trouble being, from where I was, contentment was a giant

273

step back. I was staring joy and wonder in the face, and willing to risk it all to keep them.

How bad could it be, anyway? I mean, we've all got dad stories. Mere metaphorical monsters weren't going to impress me much. And even if he was inhuman, a yeti, say, and her fear of fire sprang from the torchlight of angry townspeople at the entrance to their mountain home, well, what right would I have to judge or criticise?

'Tell me about your dad,' I said.

'He always lied.' She was dark and hidden within our humid nest. 'We were used to that.'

I was glad she couldn't see me. It made it easier to mould my reactions to the moment. I replied with a squeeze.

'Even when I was little I knew. It was just silly things, mostly. He'd promise us presents, or a holiday, but we knew it was just words. One time, I must have been six or so, I held out because I had my heart set on something. A Christmas tree, is all it was. You know the fibre-optic kind? This was when they were new. I just wanted a small one, of my own, for my room. They came in pink.'

She paused, and I could picture her face flushing to the colour of that long-remembered knick-knack.

'He said I could; he would get it for me. At first, in time for Christmas. Then that changed to Christmas Day, because that would be "more special". Afterwards he said he'd get it in the January sales. He said it had been a rip-off. Who tells a six-year-old that? And I never did get it, by the way.'

She sighed, and I breathed it in. Beyond the sheets the

heater tolled and toiled ever more quietly, strangled by the deepening cold. Our sanctuary stayed warm.

'It was worse for Mum, I suppose.' She shifted to stir the hair from her eyes, releasing a scent of apple shampoo into the crisp air. 'He always had some scheme, or something, that was going to turn things around for us. A get-rich-quick thing, like smuggling booze across the Channel, or breeding greyhounds. Aromatherapy was one.' She gave a throaty, frosty little laugh. 'He spent a week filling little bottles with tap water and food colouring.'

If an involuntary grimace shuddered past my face, could you blame me? I'd swear my own dad had peddled actual snake oil in his time.

She exhaled her tale in a series of anecdotes. Missed birthdays, pawned possessions. Each little parcel of personal pain peeling away a layer between us. Each containing some nugget I could connect to.

And then the grand finale, to bring the house down.

'He burned the house down.'

I'd almost known it was coming. I had to pretend to start in shock.

'Mum and me got out and we watched it burn.'

Insurance fraud by numbers, sure, but nonetheless moving and shaping for her. The clarity of her recollection brought it right into the room, just as Pepys' diary affords a close encounter with infinity, or T. S. Eliot lets you feel the gentle fall of ash. Or, like, if you've seen the Turner, you've witnessed the Houses of Parliament burn. Though you know it's only oil and canvas, you still blink as the red-stained smoke stings your eyes, blanche from the heat in that blistering molten yellow heart. These things singe the memory. Nobody could forget the predatory black-and-bronze chasing Shere Khan's tail. Or Jerry Lee Lewis's great balls.

In the same way, I saw Sophie's family home go up in smoke. I was there. Helped of course by my own peculiar frame of reference for burning fathers.

'The house was insured,' the words shivered, like ghosts from her mouth, 'and so was his life. He never came out. We just waited, watched the front door until it burned down to ashes. But he never came out. We thought at first he'd doubled up. Faked his own death and disappeared. There wasn't a body. But then the money came through, and he didn't.'

Silently I held her. Another level of silence, as if in our bubble we'd slipped beneath the sea, submariners in fathoms of empty space, only echoes and each other for company, but as far from lonely as I'd ever been.

'He tried to get away, out the back.' With every word she grew quieter. 'He managed to climb over the fence, but they think he'd already inhaled quite a lot of smoke.' So soft now, I was almost inferring meaning from gentle respirations. 'There was a slope, a ditch...' A slithering, a beck, a brook at most, a hurt in the fall. A sudden impact, a rock, or senses tired and dulled. A sliding out of consciousness, lungs too tired, a life too heavy. A slow, solitary leaving. A covering of autumn leaves.

'It was a long time before they found him.'

The outpour dwindled, into stillness. For a while we lay in each other's arms, in our own thoughts.

She settled against me, empty, fulfilled. I kept quiet. In a while her body rocked in gentle sleep. Some fire inside quenched, perhaps. Still I lay, thinking on flames of my own, catalysts and cataclysms. Funny how fire itself had never worried me, not like being underground. Everyone has their own burden, I suppose. Their own faulty wiring. But that wasn't what kept me awake.

I'd recognised the window of opportunity, of course I had. So soon after a real window had opened to let me into her life, here was another, symbolic one, to let her into mine. To tell her who I really was. Yet I'd said nothing.

Was it fear? It might be the ultimate in risk taking, after all, letting someone inside you. And like I said, I don't dare, and I'm not a devil. You have to have some indulgences in life though, I think. You don't live longer by eschewing sex and drugs and rocky roads, just feels like you do.

Well, sometimes I've lived longer, and sometimes not, and along with the obvious advantage that gives me, here's a quirkier little thing: I get to compare lives, and deaths. Situations. It's a funny game, not one everyone would have time for, sure, but you have to have a hobby. And there aren't many more obvious contrasts than the bleached sands of an oceanic beach and the snowy peaks of a North American mountain. There's whiteness in both, beauty, if you're able to look for it, but it's mainly differences.

The sun and moon. Heat, cold. High, low. A world of opposites. To me though, remembering between lying, dying on the Gold Coast, and slipping, gripping to the silver slither of the Knife Edge, the difference was all inside.

That day, on the slope, I cared. Simple as that.

Instead of sliding through grains of sand, feeling a natural hourglass feed away pointless seconds, I had been holding onto something. Instead of red eyelids, shutting out a blood sea and setting a mirror to myself, I was looking outward, to a face I wanted to see. Instead of nothing, there was something.

That was why, crossing that crevasse five thousand feet above any sensible step, it had crossed my mind to crap myself.

All I had been able to think of, with every timorous, tremulous step of our descent, was that I couldn't die. Even if, by some miracle, Vlad found me and thawed me, there'd be no point coming back. Because Sophie would still have believed I was dead. In which case, I might as well have been.

That was the realisation that hit me, in the cold, failing, light of day. I wanted to live. No, more important than that. I had a reason to live.

And under those blankets, holding that reason tight, I wasn't going to risk letting it go for anything as rational as the truth.

Part 5

You Don't Have to Invite Us In

Bedside Manners

Espionage has never really been my thing. Yeah, there are a few picked pockets in my past, a forced entry or two. Maybe worse, if we're going full-on confessional. But that doesn't mean I have to enjoy it. It's just that a body has to live, you know? And when you don't officially exist, it's not always possible to play by the rules.

The corridor echoed as I padded down. There was nothing I could do about the sound. The lights were the kind that trickle on when you walk underneath them. There wasn't a lot I could do to stop that, either. Just hope that nobody paid me any attention.

There's a skill to that, though. Nothing is so suspicious as getting up like a ninja and slithering through shadows. You have to hide in plain sight. I used to take precautions, have a little kit. A high visibility vest and name tag. True, the latter was from a vacuum flask trade convention from

1992, and the name tagged was Mrs Heidi Choo, but chances were against anyone reading it.

My writing tutor once asserted that "God really is in the detail". I'd always heard the same about the Devil, but perhaps it's a matter of perspective.

In the absence of any other props, I jangled a bunch of keys, and whistled. Theme tune to *Crimewatch*.

I didn't meet anybody.

Lounging on our luggage back in JFK, seats constructed from packs and cases, I had strained to explain it to him.

Listening was never Vlad's forte.

'I just know I need to do this.'

He was his runaway truculent self. 'I simply can't understand why you would give up now.'

'How am I giving up, Vlad? I saw it. I know what I am.' I massaged the bridge of my nose, rubbing concourse sweat and grime in deeper. 'We got the answer we were looking for. We did it.'

His voice rose an octave in complaint. 'You did it. I wasn't allowed in.'

'I've told you everything.'

People swirled around us, pushing trolleys, pulling children, stepping over and around and on top of each other, parting around us, for the most part. The occasional shoe or wheel would scuff our nest, jolt us, causing Vlad to tightly grip his cardboard cup of rip-off tea. Nobody really saw us though, nobody listened or cared.

They whirled around us, easy to ignore. For me at least. Nobody was anybody. I'd always liked it that way. Told myself I liked it. Roots are all very well, if you're a tree. But a person needs to be free. So I'd always thought. Recent events might have swayed me to consider there were different ways. Maybe ways to grow.

'It was a monster, Vlad. That's what we found.' Even saying the words let in a demon. It juddered down my spine, knuckles under my skin, ice on my vertebrae.

'I can't let myself become that, Vlad. But that's where I'm heading if I keep doing this.'

'Can you run away from who you are?' His voice wobbled. I think he knew that what he was asking wasn't right.

'I have to try. I can't keep coming back. It doesn't...' I couldn't find the words. 'Look at that... that thing. Not just that, look at my dad. I don't want to end up there.'

His jaw tightened, trembled. He didn't want to let me in. Couldn't show me himself, not even then, at the end of everything. We began looking around, everywhere but at each other. Craning our necks to ridiculous angles to avoid accusing eyes, pity and feeling.

All human life was near, from pushchair to wheelchair. Toddler to towering hulk, rake to waddling glutton. Brown eyes, green eyes, blue, blurry; every skin shade on a spectrum from albino to ebony. Straight hair, wavy, spiralling ringlets, bald through time or worry. Cheeks smooth, wrinkled, stubbled, bearded. Crinkled with joy, wet with tears. Tongues wagging or lips listless. Minds racing, meandering, meditating. Bodies still as statues, ambulating, jog-trotting, rushing, running. All racing, one way or another, along with eight billion others, towards the grave.

All human. All bar one.

'I want to be human.' It was such an obvious statement, and sentiment. Although I'm not sure I'd ever articulated it before, even inside.

Maybe I had always needed the motivation. An actual life to chase. I wasn't even sure, then, what I'd found. I only knew that every second I'd spent in my new world made me want more. My smile felt like some wild, happy monster in my head, bursting to be seen. Of course I was scared, I had no idea what I was doing. But then, when did I ever?

'Maybe it's just one more thing I have to try.' And I meant really try. No safety net.

It hit me then, weirdly, that this was *the talk*. We were breaking up. The most it's-not-you-it's-me moment ever. Summoning up the courage to look at him again, I caught him cold-eyed. Wagging his beard as he talked to himself in silence. It would be nice to believe there was some turmoil going on in there, that he actually considered not saying what he said.

'After all this time, searching for yourself, hunting, digging deeper. After everything, you're running away because you didn't like what you found?'

'Don't…' I began, without really knowing where I was going. Don't lash out, I meant to say, or something like that. Don't say something you'll regret.

'Don't make it difficult,' came out. 'You always wanted me to try everything. Maybe love is the drug?'

Vlad shrugged.

Then came the lash. The reason why I should have said something.

Although I probably couldn't have stopped it in any case.

'You will never be human.'

There was a lot I could have said to that, and yet nothing.

'I have to try.'

The airport held us hostage hours longer after that. But that was the essence of our warped goodbye.

Or *au revoir*, as it turned out.

His room was in darkness. Opening the door to a distinct lack of any ominous squeak, I found him lying in the bed. Immobile, barely breathing. Barely recognisable. At first I thought they'd shaved him. I'd never seem him without that grizzly little beard. Never would have guessed losing it would have made him look worse. Older. It was a while before it registered that it wasn't just the beard that was gone. He was hairless. Skeletal and naked.

Thanks again to that tutor, I'm very aware of avoiding cliché: sallow cheeks, hollow eyes, waxy complexion. You know the deal. But what else is left to say? He was skinnier than I remembered. Skin a shade greyer. Truth is, he looked dead already. And I'm not just saying that to make myself feel better.

Taking a step closer, lifting his bald forearm, I felt the fragile pulse. Checked the plastic wristband. Read his real name. I'm not sure I'd ever known it. I could see why he'd gone down a different path. Who would listen to macabre tales from grey old Fred Neil? It could never have suited him. Until now.

Double-checking, I found his age and blood group.

Yeah, it was him alright.

'What are you doing here?'

Dropping his hand like a hot potato I flat-packed myself up against the wall faster than a rat up a drainpipe. Jesus, now I can only think in cliché. But what's the alternative? Scalding root vegetables and a rodent racing up a sewage conduit? Hardly Proust is it? But maybe you get the picture. His arm did happen to be the hue and grain of an over-boiled tuber, so that one kind of works. As for the rat, well, matter of opinion, I suppose.

Pressed against the wall I hugged it while my breathing slowed. Inhaling composure, exhaling shock, until finally ready to fake a smile, and talk.

'They let the wrong one in,' I grinned. Figured he'd appreciate that. He'd have liked it more if I'd dressed in evening wear and worn a cape, but that might have taken the whole hide in plain sight plan that one step too far. Anyway, I like to think he tried to smile.

'What do you want?'

'You know what I want.'

'I thought you didn't do that anymore?'

Moving back to the bed I took his hand again. Clasped it. Stared into eyes filmed with sickness and infirmity. Inhaled composure, exhaled compassion.

'It's not for me.'

Reborn

The new life my father had bought for me was designed to keep me out of his. I was fine with that. The problem was it kept me out of the country altogether, as anything other than a tourist. He had made me Australian, clearly as a way of thrusting me as far away as geographically possible, and while Aussie passport holders can enter the UK without a visa, that only lasts as long as a six-month holiday. Returning, via America, I became a traveller in my own land.

For the first week or so it worked out pretty well. We landed on the assumption I was here to be near her, and so I wasn't expected to have any other life carved out, to have anything to do or anywhere to go.

I emptied my backpack into Sophie's flat, and we were together. Sort of. She had a few days before she needed to go back to work, but she wasn't free. It quickly became clear that even as my worldly goods fitted into a single shelf in her spare room, so my existence would have to compress into whatever leftover moments fell my way.

Like a gas, her social life expanded to fill the space it was in. A pleasant gas, obviously, nitrous maybe, but still. Trying to wedge myself into her life was like trying to find room in Bethlehem at Christmas.

Braying loudly above a clap-along soundtrack, eight faces glowed under pink lights. Cheeks glistened as the food grew hotter and the wine ran away with scalding tongues. Sixteen hands capered between forks and glasses, back patting and napkin dabbing, pointing and picking and pouring. The white tablecloth splashed korma-yellow, orange, red.

'Top grub, ay, mate?' I've always steered clear of accents and impressions, because in general they are very hard to do well, much harder than most people think. Sophie's friend, a sort of cocky, stocky broker, hairy wrist wrapped in a Rolex, Versace shirt puffed up around a peacock chest, had no such qualms.

'Stoked you could make it anyway, cobber. Any mate of Soph's is a mate of mine.'

'Thanks,' I nodded, with an overly tight polite smile.

There were eight of us, seated around a circular table in an Indian restaurant. The evening had begun in a flurry of happy-teary hugs, bellowed hellos and screeching greetings. And that was just the stockbroker. This was Sophie's uni reunion, convened to welcome her home from travelling, and I had been plus-one'd along to meet the crew. Three couples and a couple of singles, ebullient faces, hooting along in harmony at shared histories and you-had-to-be-there memories.

Seating had happened randomly and I felt far away from her, trapped in small talk with big mouths. I'm used to being the odd one out. I have been really, since finding out what I am. For once, that night, watching Sophie's lively eyes animate those around her as she skipped through recollections, I felt that it mattered. I didn't want to be one of them, but I wanted to be someone. Someone she could care about, and not just for a night.

'What part of the outback you from then, Bruce?' To be fair to the jolly, jowly moneyman with his duff Ocker accent, he was at least trying, and I probably didn't make it easy for him. Nudging a wine glass around in circles on the table between us, I found myself casting longing glances at the exit. But Sophie was between me and the door. I needed to stay.

'Gold Coast, most recently.' I decided to stick with the truth as far as I could. This was going to be draining enough without engaging the imagination.

'You don't sound very Aussie,' the broker frowned. He may have been a banker.

'Well, neither do you, frankly.'

Soph shot a warning, mouthing, 'Be nice.'

It was alright for her, ensconced in the bosom of familiarity. I'd been itching to leave since sixty seconds in. I stuck it out for her.

'I went to school in Oxfordshire,' I grimaced, portioning out another crumb of fact.

The lady next to me swept around in a cloud of fragrance, a beam plastered on her plain face.

'Oh really? How fascinating. Have you met Marcus? He was at Bloxham.'

'I think perhaps I missed him.'

'Oh, you must know Marcus! Everybody knows Marcus!'

I winced internally. Sophie was distracted, her head turned to listen to a tale she'd heard a hundred times before. For the rest of them, long years had melted into seconds, the old in-jokes and anecdotes had turned the table into a time machine. From the moment we'd walked in she had been enveloped by these people, all friendly, all overflowing with milk and honeyed words. All hard for me to bear.

The genteel interrogation continued.

'Soph says you're interested in writing?'

I scratched my head. 'That hasn't really taken off yet.'

'What did you do back in Oz, then?' the broker yapped, unwilling or unable to leave his source of amusement untapped. 'Crocodile hunter, yeah?'

'Ah, nothing quite so exotic.' I squeezed out a rueful chuckle, turned to find someone else to talk to, only to find I was central to attention.

'Seriously, though. If you're looking, Gavin's in recruitment.'

'Gavin…?'

'Marcus's brother.'

'Of course.'

'He might be able to find you something, if you're staying?' The emphasis was startling in its lack of subtlety. From around the table, eyes enquired. I began to realise

I was being interviewed. Sophie was oblivious, laughing, living. I took a too-large gulp of wine, and tried to think of actual jobs.

Lying is never as simple as some people like to pretend it is. In fact, if anyone tells you they find it easy, chances are you can already see that their pants are on fire. You can't just say any old thing, that's the issue. Sure, I could have reeled off any number of professions, from fisherman to filmmaker, but the chances of being caught out would have been sky high. Pretty much anything you claim in these scenarios leaves you wide open to awkward follow-up questions:

Example one:
    'What do you do?'
    'I'm a fisherman.'
    'Oh fascinating, what kind of fish do you catch?'
    'Er...'
    'How big is your boat?'
    'Ah...'
    'How fast can it go?'
    'Well...'
    'My Uncle Gideon drafted the fisheries management regulation zone byelaws 1999 clause 17, boat size directive 2b, and I put it to you, you're talking codswallop.'

Example two:
    'What do you do?'
    'I make films.'
    'Really, how amazing. What was your last one about?'

'Erm. Fishing.'

See Example one.

Basically, either you need to be incredibly well primed, or spectacularly vague, or just head for somewhere so out-there that nobody can question your destination. Whichever furrow you choose to plough, you need to stay lucky.

To have a fighting chance of knowing more than the people I was lying to, I needed a job I knew something about. Having never really had one myself, I plumped for the vocation laid claim to by the only person I'd spent any real time with in the past decade.

'I was a tour guide.'

Sophie crinkled an eyebrow.

The broker topped up my glass. 'In the bush?'

I smiled in his chubby, charmless face. 'More around the sort of cultural side of things really. Myths and legends, that kind of thing.'

He sighed and slowly shook his head.

'I don't think Gavin would have much use for that.'

'What was that about?' We were in the taxi back to her place. She didn't sound angry, she was smiling. A perplexed sort of smile, as if confused by a conjuring trick. Her eyes searched for a coin that had vanished into thin air. I didn't feel like a magician. I didn't even feel completely in control of my own head. Thoughts fumbled, fell thick and sticky.

'How do you mean?'

'You were a tour guide?'

'I dabbled.'

Out of the cab, her silver dress rippled as we fell into the welcome fresh air. I tried to gather myself while she paid the driver.

Into the building, stumbling upstairs. It was a first-floor flat, and the narrow, shuddering lift was not tempting.

'How come you never told me before?'

We were clutching at the handrail and each other. We'd been apart all night, still in that phase where physical contact felt fresh and exhilarating. Sophie's heel skidded on a step, and we fell together, grasping, giggling. Kissing.

'Let's talk about it in the morning?'

She clambered up, my knees and shoulders were rungs on a ladder, 'til she held out her hand to haul me after. We reached her front door and she groped at the lock. I watched her, wasted time I could have spent thinking. I could have come up with a story. Instead I just watched her.

Bundling through the door she lobbed her bag in the general direction of the sofa, picked off her shoes one at a time, an inelegant flamingo. Even her awkwardness entranced me. Made my head spin. Spin faster.

There's a cinematic trope, the Manic Pixie Dream Girl. MPDG for short. The quirky, kooky kinda hippie chick who skips into some disillusioned boy's life and shows him how everything could really just *be*, if only he embraced life, or learned to love himself, or wrote and directed a movie, or something.

An MPDG's a cutie, obviously, cheeky and chirpy. Eyes like a Disney princess and body designed to look amazing in anything, even the sort of jumble-sale jumpers and homemade jewellery she regularly wears. A little bit crazy, she's terrible at everything: painting, pottery, karaoke; but she does it all anyway. She has a propensity to skinny-dip, and probably cuts her own hair.

But like a Wild West film set, she's flat. A cardboard cut-out painted to resemble something tangible. The MPDG has no backstory, and, with no goals of her own, no future. She is the coin you find in the gutter, but then spend. The magic ticket, but not the event itself.

And there's the difference. Sophie wasn't immune to mania, and she was cuter than a toadstool full of pixies. My dream girl. But everything she was, everything she had, existed before me. And could exist after.

She headed into the kitchen.

'Do you want water?' her voice echoed from the other room, still sounding like music.

'Please.'

Returning, she placed mismatched glasses on the coffee table between us. Then she came to me, lifting onto her toes to kiss me again. Water on her lips. I leant down to take her in, she ducked and skipped away.

'Tell me something.'

'What?' I licked my lips.

She shrugged off her coat and dropped it. 'Anything.'

It was an open-plan flat, doors off the living space into kitchen, bathroom, and bedrooms. She walked to the bedroom, pushed the door open, paused, turned and looked back.

'I don't really know anything about you.'

I started to step towards her, stalled at a look. Hovering,

I turned the movement into kneeling down, taking off my own shoes. Working on the laces to cover my silence.

'You met my friends tonight,' she said, wrists crossing in front of her chest. 'You know where I grew up, what my mum does, where she lives.'

The smile was still there, a degree less certain, perhaps.

'You know where I work.' She unclasped an arm to wave around the flat, taking in the streaky-peach painted walls, wonky self-assembled shelves, stacks of second-hand books, strings of darkling fairy lights. 'You know where I live. You know who I am.'

All of this was her. The labyrinth behind the saloon facade. And none of it needed me. Which was terrifying.

'You know about my dad.'

Rocking on my haunches I stared at my shoe, as if I might look right through and see the sole, and then allow that to stand as a clumsy metaphor.

Sophie stayed, half in the bedroom, half out, perched with the toes of one bare foot wriggling over those of the other. Still missing something.

I was on my knees wishing there was something of myself I could give away. More than that, knowing that there had to be, otherwise this was over before it had begun.

'Hon, we haven't...' I scrambled to my feet, caught between needing to say something and not letting the wine talk for me. 'I mean, it's been, what, a month?'

'I had eighteen years of it.' She seemed suddenly solemn, unusually subdued.

'What?' Tipsiness tripped me on the trail of her thread.

'My dad…' You could see the words behind her eyes, but she couldn't find a way to get them out. 'He was never… he didn't…' She wanted to stop, but how could she, in the middle of calling me out for not being open?

'He wasn't present,' she fumbled to a conclusion.

'I get that.' I really did. 'My dad was…' I realised I didn't have words either. At least we had something in common.

'I just need to know who you are.' She looked at me, open-eyed, open-hearted. 'God, how hard can it be?' The last vestiges of her patience washed away. 'Just show me you're human.'

Rewind

Somewhere beneath the lush undulations of the Cotswold Hills, a spring rises. Through rills and channels it rolls, green and brown through grass and soil, grey and blue below billowing skies. Ancient oak and beech and birch, silent and stately, watching sedately while waters seep and spread, over root and under branch, channelling, tunnelling, sometimes slithering, often running, leaving Gloucestershire behind. Wending in to sheep-clad fields, winding o'er meadows strewn with wild flower clouds. By dry stone wall and wooden fence and stile, village inn and church and spire. Cackling, chuckling, hosting bobbing ducklings, dancing flies and water boatmen. Rod and line, hook and sunken floats, laying bait for grayling, perch and chub. Crossing fords and stepping stones, inspiring bridges, arched and rising, brick and rock now married to moss. Into Oxon, and onto the Thames…

Don't get me wrong, there's value to the anonymous bustle of a big city. No place to get lost like a thriving metropolis. And there's something of the coast in my heart. But as a boy I was part of the English countryside, the wild, the hinterland, the heartland of heathland.

Oh, this England! This royal throne of kings, this scepter'd isle, this green and pleasant land; this home of Auden and Austen, Newton and Nelson, Nutkin and Twinkleberry. The thwack of willow on leather, the tang of warm beer, the call of the corncrake, and the haunting strains of nationalist politicians talking bollocks wafting on a summer breeze…

Not that much of that matters if you're stuck inside with a couple of other seven-year-old castaways, playing Test Match Cricket on your Commodore 64.

Time, like a river, flows onward, ever and anon. But plots and narratives, like yachts and narrowboats, have some autonomy.

Even that's understating it. There's more than one way to spin a catchy yarn, to navigate the stream of a storyline.

Some novelists enjoy a barge. Straight lines, sedate, somewhat unwieldy. Each to their own, but a writer has miles more leeway, should they want it, than a mere ship's skip. I can hustle my vessel through space and time, through any dimension in any direction. All at the tap of a key, with nary a worry for the journey. Give me a keyboard, and I can fly a time-travelling helicopter.

All that matters as I move my craft, is that I move you with my craft.

If that entails circling back from circa 2000 to an ostensibly utopian 1984, so be it. If it also encompasses picking myself up from the aftermath of an Essex curry house to splash down in a parody pastoral idyll, that's life.

Some parts of this story are harder to hear than others, I know that, because they are harder to write too. Worse to live through. I've been putting this off since basically chapter two, but now I need to get it out there. I need to tell you about the second time I died.

I could write a book about that day. That hour. That minute. You could get every detail, gory or otherwise, everything I remember with utmost clarity. Or believe I remember. It could spoil the flow though. Spending too much time in the flood would mess with my narrative arc. That's my dilemma. How much is too much, or, how little is too little? Is it worth getting started on character development, for boys who never crop up again beyond this chapter? Is it expedient to get in deep on the geography and geology, the map of the town, the history and the meteorology? Should I talk about the weather? It sounds a daft question, but the context might be handy.

It could up the ante in the drama, build a bit of theatre and a sense of spectacle. Help create some tension, and play on expectations. Setting the scene is all part of the plotting, the pacing. If I was doing this properly, I'd want to do just enough to form a feeling that something grave is coming, dilute it with sufficient hope to shape a suspicion that it might still turn out alright, and then deliver the killer blow with a cruel bit of timing that strikes like the twist of a knife.

Or can I just cut to the chase? Will that work, in the scheme of things? Can I still ask people to care about a character I haven't had the time or inclination to introduce? I could roll out the bare bones: say that he was seven, and a bit of a nerd, but overall decent. I could tell you he was kind to small animals and never to my knowledge fried a spider with a magnifying glass. Would that get you invested? You wouldn't want that boy to die. Is that enough?

Maybe if I really lean into the melodrama right from this moment, create and paint a diorama, bloody and visceral, built from guts and skin and sinew, smeared in lieu of gloss with sweat and tears. The boy trapped in that black cataract, slight and frail against the dirty wash of heavy clawing water. Legs swept out, kicking for purchase, mouth open and crying, eyes white and screaming. Fingers tearing, scoring claw marks along his friend's arm as they try to hold on. The friend bawling too, two scared little boys betrayed by lack of thought or foresight, negligence, stupidity, or just by acting their age…

I'm psyching myself up, I know I can do it, if I can just find a way to get started, without prevaricating with riddles about rivers. When I spoke to my creative writing tutor she suggested reading other novels. Not sure I get the point myself, searching for influence or inspiration. She's adamantine in her belief it will help. Then again, she still thinks I'm just making all this stuff up.

Personally, I just think I need to get on with it. I don't think other books have any real impact on me at all.

It was the best of times, it was the worst of times... wait, does that sound familiar?

Cards on the table, that's just a fairly silly joke. And a set-up for a sillier one coming soon. 1984 was neither the best nor worst, particularly. Bit of a mixed bag, sure. The ups and downs you'd expect from any normal childhood spent living on a very steep hill. Bit more blood maybe. Still, highs have flown higher, lows have tunnelled lower. No Dickensian poverty, or guillotined heads to report. That would all come later. Still.

It was the best of Times, it was the worst of Times. That didn't bother me, because I read the *Beano*. Because I was seven.

The best thing about being seven, if we're going to keep going with the best/worst thing, and I feel I'm wedged pretty far down that particular bunny hole right now, the best thing was that I had friends. True friends, I think, for the first and last time.

Before that, I just got the ones my parents picked for me. That's if you don't count nurses, or soft toys. And unless I want to wind up back in the care of nurses, in a room with soft walls, I think I probably shouldn't.

Others might have had it different, those who went to playgroup instead of intensive care. But I'd still guess seven might be around the age you get enough independence to decide for yourself who you knock about with. To a point.

And after seven, well, what was the point?

When I was seven I spent the whole summer with Ali Sajid Khan and Raisin Dave. I seem to remember that one of those wasn't a real name. Ali and Raisin were seven too, or close enough. They both lived round our way. If this were a novel we'd have spent that summer building a treehouse; patching up, painting and learning to sail an old Topper; switching identities with a wanted member of the French aristocracy. Something like that. In reality, we just sort of kicked about.

Ali, let's be honest, would have stood out in any of those potential plots. Hard to imagine a sorer thumb than an Asian kid in Arthur Ransome or Enid Blyton. Albeit this was thirty years after the fifties, multiculturalism hadn't really made it down the Windrush to West Oxfordshire yet. Dark Ali people used to call him. People are arseholes, of course; were, are and will be. I'm not picking on a particular place here. I've been around the world, from the Costa Blanca to the Gold Coast to the Côte d'Ivoire, and, speaking as an outsider to your bastard species, I'll never understand the way you ostracise each other based on arbitrary pigmentation. Seriously, you're no better than reindeer. Apologies for getting on a soapbox tall enough to stable a high horse in, but why did Raisin never get any comparable stick for being the palest kid in class?

Ali was a good lad. Quiet, articulate, timidly warm, into the same shenanigans we all were: Star Wars, Indiana Jones. Ghostbusters. But the kids just used to laugh and call him names, never let him join in any games.

So the poor bugger was stuck with me and Raisin.

Raisin was just a bit off the wall. Nowadays, he would likely have some kind of diagnosis. Back then, we just thought he was funny. He made incessant bulging eye contact and couldn't modulate the volume of his voice. He had a habit of taking off his clothes. His mum didn't let him eat chocolate. For snacks he had nuts and raisins by the fistful. Why the heck we didn't call him Nutty Dave I have absolutely zip idea. Raisin must have seemed funnier at the time.

It should be obvious without me spelling it o-u-t, but we weren't exactly the cool kids. Just the leftovers. The damaged goods. Makes me feel a bit sad looking back, how well I fitted in.

I was the new boy, all funny accent and face that didn't fit. Ali had the western drawl down way better than I did. Of course he did, he was born in the county. That wasn't my main problem, though. My issue was my mum wouldn't have let me up a treehouse, in case I fell out of it. She wouldn't have allowed me in a boat for the same reason. Hard to imagine what she'd have made of me entangling myself in the revolutionary Terror. Don't suppose she would have been a fan.

She was happy then, for me to run with the out-crowd. The others who actively avoided fresh air, who revelled in the suffocating cloy of being wrapped in cotton wool. Like Raisin, for example. All uncoordinated limbs and spare funny bones. Gappy teeth and sticking plasters, specs held together with tape. Any actual adventure would have ended in guaranteed fallout for Raisin. Even just staying in playing Star Wars, which is what we mostly ended up doing, landed him with stiches once, when Ali threw a Chewbacca at his head. The kid could cut himself with playdough.

We were home birds, basically, all three of us. And more so when it was wet out. Until that day, that one day when the river we crossed every day suddenly became central to our lives.

Like many a settlement, here, there and elsewhere, the water came first and the town grew up around it. That's an old story. Easy to forget the part liquid plays in our lives, when we can turn on a tap or twist open a bottle of sparkly strawberry flavour, and have a ready supply at our tongue tips. Once, where water was meant something more.

The river brought the people, and people brought the industry. In this town that meant blankets. I'm not a historian, if you want the details someone else has probably written that book, but somehow getting wool from a sheep's back to your bedcovers meant working with the rushing muscle of the current. Harnessing nature with wheels and cogs.

And then the world turned, and that ended, or all but ended, thanks to sweatshops or synthetics or some such, and the town moved on, as much as a town can. The mills became museums, the gears fell to rust and the blades ran dry.

Machines went, Cotswold stone stayed. Buildings and walls were harder to move, less susceptible to trends. People stayed; habits and homes are stronger than currents and tides. The town stayed, straddling the river, for long seasons after the reason for its founding had faded. The river became little more than a water feature in local joints, a pretty focal point. Even crossing it twice a day on an old stone bridge, you could almost forget it was there.

Periodically it put forth a reminder, and that year the famed English rain fell in long spells. Late winter spats seeped into April showers and ran on into the customary May Bank Holiday downpour. When the uplands had accepted every drop they could and the earth was thick and full, then the torrents gathered on saturated fields and funnelled to swell channels and streams. The river grew, and raced on, fuller, hungrier. Brown and strong, carrying branches and broken umbrellas, running high and eroding, cannibalising banks and shorelines, taking in mud and sand, and water, always more water.

And then bursting.

Seemingly seeking the centre of town, before breaking free and spreading a dirty great reminder of its presence and power, spewing across streets and gardens, filling drains and drowning flowerbeds. Dispensing flotsam and dispersing jetsam, remaking the world in its own image of reflections and ripples.

People fought back with sandbags and stoicism, but the liquid march stole on. Under doors and over floors, shorting plugs and bleeding over carpets. Drinking up insurance claims.

Schools and businesses closed as the town sank into a shallow lake. Grown-ups grumbled as the levels rose over their wellies, while the irreverent and boisterous element canoed down the roads past shipwrecked cars.

Oh, the kids were delighted. No rain could dampen an unexpected school holiday, and the adventure was accentuated by the strange new world that had descended upon our cosy wold. Our playing fields were paddling pools, knee-deep undertows and squelchy under toes. In the playground the swings seemed to rise, half-formed out of the depths. The see-saw was submerged, and the slide became a flume.

To the children, out was the new in. It wasn't even cold, which clinched it. Even for Raisin, Ali and myself, fresh air became irresistible.

We met at Ali's house, and pondered what to do in our new pond life.

Raisin had heard a rumour there were ducks swimming in the high street.

'Let's go and throw stones at them,' he suggested.

Ali and I looked at one another, sharing one of our moments of fear that Raisin might not be joking, that rather than being funny he was a little bit unstable. He looked back at us, hood up on his Paddington Bear duffel coat, casting a shadow over manic, blinking eyes.

'Or, we could take them some bread?' suggested Ali, diffidently.

Raisin dismissed that as baby games, and the proposal petered out.

Ali lived near the bottom of the hill. The closest to the scenes of distraction. We were sitting on the front porch, raised above the flood by a short flight of stone steps, flicking pebbles into the water and watching them ripple and sink. Time began to dawdle.

'Some kids are sailing rubber dinghies up on Church Green,' I mooted, though none of us had a dinghy.

Ali backed me up anyway. 'Shall we just go and watch?' he said.

Off we went, splashing down the high street. The famous three? Not even in our own heads. More four short of a Loser's Club, about to find out it doesn't take a malevolent inter-dimensional spider-clown to make a sewer drain dangerous.

Raisin was in wellies, comically ungainly. Like most of his clothes they seemed to have been intended for someone else. Or something else. I swear he had a woolly jumper that had been knitted for an octopus. The water slopped into his boots with every step, and periodically one would wang down the lane in front of us, leaving him hopping after it in soggy off-key cords and a saturated sock.

Ali was better turned out, hard not to be, wading in waterproof trousers and boots that stayed on. A neatly pressed polo shirt gave him the dapper air of a rural heir, running the rule over the family estate.

I was dressed for summer.

'Where are you going?' Mum asked me that morning. It was Monday, or Friday, or someday in between, and I would have been school bound, if not for the deluge.

'Dave's,' I answered, without missing a beat. It wasn't premeditated, just a natural, instinctive fib. Raisin lived up the hill, out of harm's way.

'What will you be doing?' she persisted anyway. 'I don't think I want you playing outside in this.'

'In what?' I shrugged. A glance out of the window showed a pallid sky, not blue but high and dry. Not warm but wrung out. In town the unusual pools were gently evaporating into haze. But up on the high ground it hardly looked a bad day. Not that bad is always visible.

'You know what I mean.' She gave an uncharacteristically waspish turn.

'We're going on the computer.' I gestured down at myself, standing in the hallway in shorts and a loose blue T-shirt. Barefoot, indicating I wasn't dressed for out-of-doors. My mac hung on a hook and my boots stood underneath. I looked everywhere but at them, as if putting them on had been the furthest thing from my mind. I chose a pair of flip flops instead.

'Can't you play here?' Mum eyed my skinny bare limbs in concern as I skirted around her attempted eye-contact.

'Dave's got a new football game. We need to play it at his because he's got two joysticks.' I trotted out the lie and trotted out the door.

'At least take a cardigan.' Mum followed me out. I led her on down the garden path.

'I won't need it, we'll be inside,' I smiled through the goosebumps.

'Don't be late, then.'

With a cursory wave I was away, up the hill, already plotting a circuitous route back down to Ali's place. I can't say I didn't feel a pang of guilt, though not so much for the lie itself. I just never liked upsetting people. The few I cared for, anyway.

Dave had started laughing when he saw me, his wild eyes distorted and distended behind thick, bully-bait glasses. But as it turned out, sandals weren't a bad choice for paddling, once you embraced the wetness. I could feel the slow movement of cool water squirting up through my toes with each step, displacing belches and bubbles of thin mud or thick water. It was certainly better than having wet socks. My shorts, eighties-style, ended high up the thigh, and escaped with droplets and muck spots and little more.

The main thoroughfare was still busy with waddling, sombre adults, making ineffective movements with mops and hoping the levels would fall and let them back into their comfortable lives. I badgered my friends into turning off, heading around the back roads, away from enquiring eyes and awkward questions later.

'Mummy's boy,' jeered Raisin, kicking the water to splash at me. His left wellington escaped and drifted over my head in a lazy parabola, but I remained largely dry.

'I don't want grounding,' I countered. 'Just be cool.'

Did I talk like that when I was seven? Yes, pretty much. Only, probably with more direct Harrison Ford quotes.

'It's not much further round anyway,' Ali chimed, leading the way. We normally sided with each other, mitigating Raisin's wilder moments. Might have been better for both of us, that day, if it hadn't gone down that way. That's life, though, isn't it? Wrong turns look right at the time, or we'd never take them. We left the town centre to follow a newfound stream, explorers in a different world.

We found the meadows behind the backstreets now a peaceful marsh. Nobody else had come this way, and even the sparrows and crows seemed to have taken against the fields. The town was clearly visible, mere metres away, but it seemed to face inward, away from us. We were truly outside, and free. Happy as we'd ever be.

Drained

'What happened next?'

This wasn't a Freudian couch, just the sofa in Sophie's front room.

'You can tell me, baby.'

She was stroking my hair, hushing and lilting. Almost as if I had regressed, though not quite to babyhood.

For a long time, I didn't reply. A few seconds, or an hour. It was one of those nights when the clock starts to lose all meaning, just ticks and tocks, a minimalist background soundtrack, travelling in circles.

'There was a drain, a storm drain.'

It was black magic. All that water. It seemed impossible that the washed-out watercolour sky could have given so much. The gushes, the clouds and the downpour, all the darkness torn down and swirled around beneath the ground.

'Like a plughole, like the town was a bathtub, full of mud. But emptying, fast.'

It drew us in, a conjuror's eye. Raisin first, of course, flopping his welly on ahead and following it, a puppy with a new toy.

'We ran after him, me and Ali. Laughing at him, with him.'

Laughing like you only can when you're wild and young and you don't care who is watching, so loud and careless, laughter that lasts long beyond any memory of a joke.

Swept along, bellowing out-of-character, Ali jiggled a foot in his Queen-green boot, waggled it off and launched it high. How we screamed – we could hardly breathe.

'The water caught it, it was so flat and placid everywhere else. Just paddy fields really. But not around that drain.'

My head shook. Her hands were still there, cradling, comforting. The room was growing orange, translucent curtains unable to hold back the dawn, unstable fragments of a new day showing through in chinks and patches, glowing in complex patterns on the wall.

'Do you want to keep going?'

Of course I didn't, but I had about as much choice as that boot, caught in the current.

'I've never told anyone any of this.' Not that I used to tell anyone anything, but she didn't necessarily know that.

The shadows shortened on the wall, blurred and fading. If you tried you might find pictures there, like the shifting shapes made by clouds. They didn't show me a way out. And I needed something, because I'd run out of truth.

'I went in after it – it was stupid. It was a boot.'

I'd been on my back too long. The sofa wasn't soft enough anymore. All I wanted was to sink inside, let it swallow me. Lying again made me sick. But what choice was there?

'It was moving fast, but I thought I could get it back. I don't know why it mattered. I guess I thought we'd get caught. If he went home without a boot, the story would come out somehow. I'd be in trouble.'

No, I didn't think any of that, because I wasn't in the water. Ali was.

'This stupid boot was going around and around, and I just thought if I headed straight for the drain, maybe I could cut it off.'

Maybe that was what Ali was thinking, I've never been able to ask him, but why else would he suddenly have headed straight into the mouth of that thing?

What I do remember clearly is that he was suddenly screaming.

'Ali came in after me. He must have thought he was a stronger swimmer or something.'

My mum had made me get all my swimming badges. She thought it would make me safer, I suppose. Anyway, I got to him.

'He got to me.'

Sophie was like stone against me, her fingers still woven into my hair, almost gripping, frozen. The room had caught our chill. Spiders stopped mid-spin. Dust was held in suspense. Outside, birds fell dumb.

'Somehow he got under me.'

Somehow, I was under him.

'After that, it's all a blur.'

That last was true. Water does that, being underwater. The murk, the muck, green and grime. It gets in your eyes, your ears, your mouth. The bitter taste in the back of your throat, your sinuses. The deafening weight of it turning the world above into hollow faraway echoes.

It doesn't take a shark. It's all about loss of control. A frightened foot in your face as a kid kicks for his life. I know he never meant to, to break my nose, to keep himself up by pushing me under.

Everything ached, everywhere hurt. There, then. Under Sophie's tender hand. Even the most natural position starts to burn, when held for too long.

'I just feel so guilty,' understatement, 'so *guilty.*'

True again. Can you imagine feeling responsible for somebody else's death? I can. That's why I could never be an actual vampire. One of the reasons. The actual act of killing someone, deliberately, accidentally, by whatever compulsion or circumstance, that has to change you, and not for the better.

Poor little Ali. That's how I still think of him, since that was the last I saw of him. A scared child, screaming and crying. The last I ever heard and felt, his panic, his flustered, frothing thrashing. Two feet, one still booted, the other shod in a sodden sock, cycling, treading, pounding me as the blood and water beat in my ears and my eyes filled and my throat overflowed and my larynx closed to cut off the water. And the air. My body floated down, sinking, slurping into filth and becoming slime. With eyes closed or useless I can't say I saw him, still weeping and writhing, unless my soul rose up as the rest of me bogged down, and I don't believe that. Nevertheless, I have the memory, an invented one I suppose, of a forlorn boy, in bursting tears, sobbing and choking my name even as Raisin's shrieking hysteria finally brought help running, reaching with longer arms from higher ground.

'I've had to live with it.' I couldn't remember closing my eyes, but I opened them then to look up at her.

'I'm sorry,' her voice was little more than a breath, 'so sorry.'

What I'd had to live with I didn't exactly say. The implication was the death of a boy. But Ali didn't die. He grew up and became a civil engineer, he got married and had a kid of his own. Played golf on weekends.

That's a guess, I've never looked him up. Always been scared to. Because what I do know for certain is that he has carried me around with him ever since that day. Thinking he killed me. And I could never set him straight.

'It wasn't your fault.' A whisper in the morning stillness.

But it was.

'Do you feel better, for telling someone. For getting it out?'

Weirdly, wrongly, I kind of did. Is a lie still a lie, if it's the most honest you've ever been?

Somewhere, in a world beyond the window, a lawnmower revved and reverberated. Starlings took startled flight. Inside, a fly beat against the glass. Reaching across I flicked off the lamp. The world stayed bright. It would not grow any lighter.

'Thank you.'

'For?'

'For sharing yourself. Being real.'

A kiss.

Not the most romantic of my life, over the memory of a dead boy. Not the longest. Not hungry with sex or desire. Just a touch of lips, fleeting, fluttering. A butterfly's wing, with immeasurable meaning, begetting a hurricane.

It was cement, it was glue. It was me and her, touching, entwining. It was a gesture. Acceptance and anticipation of a future together. It was a gift.

It was a boy, for the first time in many lifetimes, brought to life.

How to Become Immortal

Frank McCourt, a man who knew his way around a memoir, had the idea that only the wretched times are worth writing about. I'm paraphrasing of course, or perhaps just outright misquoting. But I haven't got his book to hand, and I find if I stop and search for this sort of stuff too frequently it breaks me out of my flow, you know?

Of course, I'm not frank, in any way. Partial though I may be to a bit of blarney, and a paragraph or so of pretty poetic prose, in none of my identities have I ever been Irish. Still less a Catholic, thank God. As for poverty, that I avoided by the grace of Vlad.

I'd still say I've had my share of misery and misfortune though, if that isn't the world's worst ever brag. And I think there is something in it, from a literary slant. Could Count Tolstoy have penned twelve hundred pages about calm and peace? Would *A Tale of Two Cities* have shipped so many copies if it had only been the best of times? How many people would have taken that caterpillar to heart, if he hadn't been very hungry?

Dark times bring drama. There is no tension in sunlight. The best years of my life are the hardest to write about.

It wasn't a decade of smooth seas, I'm not saying that. There were complications. An A-Z of them. Affording rent, buying a flat, changing jobs, decorating, electricity bills, feeling trapped. Going on holiday, hiding my past. Ill winds, jury duty, kitchen-sink drama, losing the keys. Money worries, never going out, old flames, parking fines, queues at the supermarket. Red lines, spilt milk, taking out the trash, uppity neighbours. Visa compliance. Where to spend Christmas... Xmas... yuletide. Zombie nightmares.

The last one may seem a bit crowbarred in, but there were still uncertainties. Had Vlad's measures to protect my identity been successful? Or was I still supposed to be on the run from a bloody cult? There was no way to be sure, and even if I had been, there might still have been dark nights, cold-sweat awakenings with that vile memory blistering bright and bloody in my mind. That long-dead, flaccid witch, ruined by worship, laid out on her slate in a sick mockery of a sated goddess... you see, I could put down pages about that. Chapters full of invention and imagery to bring that stark white fright to life, if life can ever be the right word for that skin-and-bone monster, that vacant, passive, lost-eyed disaster... there I go again. Proving my own point. Horror stories, blood-draining demons, they write themselves. Real life is harder.

Little niggles, everyday anxieties, how do I engage you in that?

'Don't give up so easily.' This is my conscience speaking, or something. An inner-ear murmur more used to reminding me I'm not all that wise, that I know naff-all about books, writing, or anything much at all beyond how it feels to be me.

'It may be easier than you think.' It's also my tutor, casting my notebook back onto the desk, my hard-wrought lines heavily annotated in her own personal code. I'm all for believing that those who can, teach. But they don't seem to be able to write legibly to save their lives.

'This is the easy part, the chance to give your character some depth.' She gave an encouraging little nod. The classes were held in a sixth-form college, and however hard we all tried, it was always a little bit like being at school.

'Which is easier for people to relate to: a made-up monster, or a real human being with a life, emotions, and things to do, milk in the fridge?'

'You want me to write about whether it was blue-top or green?'

'Anything, little details.' She pursed her cracked lips and blinked. 'What do the rest of you think? Could you do with some help relating to the character?'

A couple of the others mumbled hesitant agreement. Part of the experience was supposed to be peer learning, critiquing one another, growing through sharing. Which was a bit odd. If I'm trying to study something, do I really want the opinions of a load of other amateurs? I don't suppose it would happen in dentistry.

'I do find the character a bit unbelievable sometimes.' This from a bloke who looked like a warlock, and whose central protagonist was an ice dragon.

'Thanks, that's helpful.' I clicked my tongue, and made a note. Include more blue scaly wings.

'Have you ever thought about giving him a family?' continued the D&D escapee.

'That might help,' a cardigan'd old Scotswoman agreed. She had pictures in her wallet of her grandchildren. I knew because she showed me every time we met. She also wrote more powerfully than anyone else there, if that's interesting. 'That would help me get to know him,' she said, kindness burrowing into me.

I squirmed. 'I'll think about it.'

But I already knew they were right. Perhaps there was something in peer review after all.

So I'll skip on a bit. Maybe that makes sense, anyway. There's so much left to say, and so little time in which to say it.

What's the quickest way to get there? Just out and say it, I suppose. But so soon after ruminating on writing class, I surely have to be a little more creative.

There might have been a restaurant, a couple of years into living together. A Date Night, keeping the magic up. Although that makes it sound like there were deeper issues than I think there were. We were happy. Conversation was still breezy, luminous and untroubled. Some work, all play. Bills, but not hell to pay. Easy street.

Then the first intercepted look. Her eyes over my shoulder as she told me about her day. Glancing back, without even really noticing I was doing it. There was another couple. Younger than us, maybe not looking it. Between them a boy in a highchair, red-faced, blowing raspberries and sputtering fruit puree down his chin. I pulled a face. Not at the boy, turning back to Sophie, I gave an exaggerated wince. She flushed a little, and chattered on. And that was that, for a while.

That was the ski-lift though, to the peak of a slippery slope. More of these moon-faced goons arose. Always in the grip of some feverish emotion, ever splattered in something. Children were everywhere. Subtly, stolen glances in shops, parks, became common. One day she stopped, walking through a department store, and fingered a pair of tiny shoes, asked me to agree they were the cutest thing I had ever seen. I couldn't. Then her friends started dropping sprogs and it was basically all over. Pictures appeared, first shared almost shyly, then pinned to the fridge. The ski slope was a nursery run, we were near the foot of it, and minute booties were an inevitability. I didn't know what to do.

I should say here, I didn't not want a kid. I wasn't against the idea, not altogether. Is there a way I could say that with more negatives? Maybe not, but you get the picture. I knew I loved Sophie. I can't overstate that. But love is complex.

And writing about it, we've already established that's a challenge. For the first time here, I'm regretting the first person narrative. How much easier would it be to describe myself as the greatest romantic hero since Heathcliff, if I could pretend I was talking about somebody else? As it is, I'm stuck with me, my voice, and the natural inclination when talking about Heathcliff to make a stupid joke about a cartoon cat. Yet I genuinely believe what we had was special. Literature-worthy. Those feelings I had, have had, have: they would compare with the greats.

Had she been a Capulet, no duelling Tybalt or thumb-biting servant could have swayed me to entrust our tryst to some half-baked friar. If Queen of Egypt, I'd have taken her asp.

Should her face have launched a thousand ships, I'd have given them all the slip. Not Arthur and half the Round Table could have kept us apart.

Next to us, Elizabeth and Darcy were platonic pals, Jack and Ennis quitters, Scarlett and Rhett blown away.

Just to hold her, to feel the warmth of her thaw me, the murmur of her breath on my neck. Don't get me wrong, I fancied the pants out of her, every little thing she did was an aphrodisiac. But more, she was my balm, a painkiller too. I could tell you of a thousand specific times when a hug alone was enough to heal me. Often the thought of her was all it took. I know, dear tutor, I know, show don't tell. But how can I, when I can't even count the ways?

I could take the night, I suppose, when the long-alluded-to question finally fell out into the open. It wasn't planned, not something she led up to, certainly no carefully laid snare. Just the point where the future intruded and became the present.

We were in bed, when she told me she wanted a baby. Not in flagrante. In pyjamas. Bodies easily entangled, fingers entwined, veins throbbing pleasantly with alcohol. In short, in bliss.

'Do you think we should have a baby?'

It didn't shock me, too much. Though I didn't reply for a while. As I say, I wasn't against a family of my own, but there were complications. Legally, in that I still existed as someone I wasn't. Genetically, more pressingly. Morally.

And yet, I loved her.

If I say I didn't want to deny her, it sounds like I was backed into a corner. It wasn't that. I loved her.

I wanted to give her everything, every part of me. I wanted us to go on, to live forever. To live on how people are meant to live on. To defeat the parody of immortality, to reproduce ourselves.

So there, in our bed, tumbled and twisted together, tousled and tangled, we deepened our pact. And I lay that out as my proof: that I loved her, as truly, madly, delightedly as any lover ever, invented or otherwise.

Who, really, has had such an obstacle to overcome? Of the examples above, you'd have to say a spot of pride and prejudice doesn't really come close to being undead. Being gay in the sixties was probably more problematic, sadly.

I'm not saying finding the one, keeping it together, has to be a struggle, or should need a test. I actually think love should be a victory march. Just, if there are trials, and, let's face it, there are, then they can be overcome. For the right people, adversity should be a forge. A crucible can have positive connotations too, and change, transformation even, is not always bad.

See, it's not even about compromise, or sacrifice. Because if you're two halves of a whole, you're not actually giving anything up. Your happiness is locked together. It's not so much like being hobbled in a three-legged race, as merging together. Bringing a leg each to the party. That's how I look at it, anyway.

Then it doesn't really matter what befalls, up to and including crossed stars or civil wars, because whatever doesn't destroy us can make us stronger. Having been eaten up from the inside by cancer, and from the outside by a shark, I've always had that phrase down as absolute drivel, if I'm honest. But you know what I mean. You grow together, stick together. Become stronger together. If you belong together.

Sophie was my right person. Wanting to make her happy made me happy, kept us happy. If that's not contradicting myself. Which it might be. Explaining love is hard.

I'm probably better at death. Then again, I've died more times than I've been in love.

And we'll be back talking about that again soon enough.

But first, life.

Generations

The move up to Whitby had been Sophie's call. I'd say her choice, but, well, you know. There's such a thing as being a little too pat.

When we found out we were expecting, she was drawn back to her mother. A tractor beam, bringing her home to some kind of ship. There were causes for me not to be keen. Reasons to be cheerless. One, two, three.

One, the old stomping ground. For me, for my dad. For Vlad. Plenty of people better avoided. The two just named didn't even top the list, bothersome or burdensome as such encounters would likely be. They would at least understand, and not call the police. Or the Ghostbusters. My dad had killed me off before he had me transported, a paperwork death, to obtain a certificate. It was hard to say how newsworthy that might have been. He would probably have kept it low-key. Steered clear of combine harvester accidents and what-not. But still. Small towns talk. It's never a good look to go back, and I'd managed to avoid it. Since the funeral.

Two. Memories. We'd lived there long enough, me and Mum. Long enough that each street held a trace of her, a place where her face drifted through the shadows. Her reflection glinted in the window of the café where we had talked about A level options in a futile attempt to be real. An echo of her voice rang outside a shoe shop, where a gull had shat on her coat, and I'd laughed and she'd called me a dickhead, and it was the only time I ever heard her swear. Her footprints still led through the worn pathways of the park, she was in the rain that drizzled on the bridge on a grey day, and in the taste of salt on the pier. The song of the seabirds was her lament.

Three, if you need some closure on that blockheaded Ian Dury bit I was doing: I didn't really want to live near Cora, my not-quite-mother-in-law. Though there's probably nothing unique in that.

Not that she was anything other than lovely. Neat and fluttery, with small, birdlike features, she flitted into our lives a few times a year, to gently remind Sophie that she wasn't getting any younger, and wonder why nobody took holidays on the Yorkshire coast anymore.

Luckily there was always a good reason. Until there wasn't. Sophie had a lot of the world to see beyond her mum's adopted home, and never really needed persuading that other destinations were available. Until an embryo changed everything.

Suddenly she had compelling motivation to settle due north. Not least, she'd tethered herself to a feckless clown, and probably figured she'd need real help raising a kid.

'And,' she said, cradling a bump that hadn't yet grown visible, 'work can sort me out a transfer, no problem. There's a branch in Whitby.'

No objection made any sense. They could never even be voiced, not without going down a one-way runway to full-on disclosure territory.

'Sorry, I can't live near Whitby, I'm dead there. And in several other places you should know about.'

It just couldn't be said.

'I don't want to live anywhere near your mother,' couldn't be said either, from a rather more prosaic point of view.

The next best option was compromise. A house outside of town, close enough, but far enough away. Simple economics meant it made more sense for me to try and work further out anyway, York or Scarborough, somewhere there might actually be the odd job.

Theoretically, setting foot in town could be a rarity.

Life finds a way though, doesn't it?

Unpacking into the new place felt oddly grown-up. As if reality had finally caught up with me. True, Sophie and I had been under a shared roof for a good while, and I'd been the same person all that time... but arguably that person had still been imaginary. There had always been something make-believe about our life together. Home might as well have been a Wendy house.

Here there was a garage for a potential car, an attic to hoard obsolete electronics in. Space on the walls for pictures, not posters. Our names were in the phonebook.

Things felt real.

Cora was there to help us with the move. Making herself useful, pointing out what needed carrying, sweeping up mess I was in the middle of making, bringing out unwanted trinkets and heirlooms, things that "might come in useful", but never would.

She cornered me in a bare box room, picture hooks hanging empty, naked bulb drooping from the ceiling as I stood on a spindly stool, draping curtains over the outside world.

'I like those. Sophie always loved ponies when she was a little girl.'

The pattern was unicorns, but I didn't bring that up.

'Shouldn't you have painted the walls first, though?'

'White goes with anything.' I twisted a screw that didn't need tightening. The rail creaked.

'Oh, but a splash of colour would be nice for a nursery, don't you think?'

I looked out of the window. A fenced-in garden big enough for two wheelie bins and a plant pot. Red rust on the railings, a trail of mauve catkins blown in from next door. The oily rainbow-grey of a foraging pigeon. Green shoots between the paving stones.

'What colour, though?'

'You can't go wrong with pink for a girl, can you?'

'She might like black.' I wouldn't have said it if Soph had been in the room. Needless needling, the kind of thing I'd kept out of my life since the exit of a certain faux-parental figure.

'Oh no.' Cora wrinkled her nose, and just for a moment

Sophie's face was transposed upon her own. 'Not like one of those horrible Goths!'

For the first time I think I felt genuinely close to her.

'I'll pick up some pink tomorrow.'

'I'm concerned,' she confided in me, later that evening. Sophie had gone to bed, pleading exhaustion. Cora had only a short drive back into town, but was briskly rearranging a kitchen cupboard Soph had already sorted, seemingly bent on building a precedent for familiarity with our space.

'I suppose it's only natural.' I hunted through the fridge for a beer, came out with a green bottle of bubbly water.

'What is?' Cora turned, tucking a wavy length of hair behind one ear.

'Concern?' I twisted the cap off the hissing bottle, confused.

She thought about it. 'Well, yes. I worried so much for Sophie, you know. With her father.'

So that was it. Family-specific rather than common anxiety. That could have been an easier topic to offer reassurance on, given my own issues. Could have been.

'I had the same. I mean, my dad, he wasn't…' I stopped and sucked the froth off my water, '… he wasn't really around.'

Cora stopped bustling and stared at me. Incomprehension writ large in her eyes, the way most people look when faced with the instruction manual for a self-assembly closet. The type that's been translated from Swedish into Japanese and back again by an online app with a sense of humour.

'We don't talk about that,' she said shortly.

'Now I'm lost,' I confessed.

Cora flushed red, a cricket ball barrelling over a boundary.

'I'm sorry.' She tracked back to her cupboard. 'I thought you knew.'

Glancing wistfully at the fridge I remembered back to a time when the biggest mystery in my life was where the beer had gone. I mean the biggest mystery that I wasn't the cause of, obviously.

'Knew what?' I had to ask.

'If Sophie hasn't said… I'm not sure it's my place.'

What a time to discover tact. Leaving the last tins unstacked, she closed the cupboard door. 'I should go.'

I didn't correct her, just sipped my drink as she gathered herself. At the front door she paused, met my eye with artificially assembled brightness.

'I'll see you in the morning.'

'You're coming back in the morning?'

It was the wrong thing to say, of course. But then, it had been that kind of evening. My turn to try and rewind.

'Of course you are, I'm sorry, I'm tired. Thank you.'

Her face remained brittle, but she nodded.

'Shall I pick up the paint first?'

'Paint?'

'Pink. For the baby's room?' Shadows lengthened between us. 'It doesn't matter, I'll call Sophie before I set off.'

She closed the door behind her.

I'm not actually prone to introspection, autobiographies aside. At least, I've never really regretted my mistakes.

Things I've done deliberately, that's a different matter. Clambering the stairs, attempting to keep my weary tread light, I wondered for the first time in a while whether I'd done the right thing.

Since setting eyes on Soph I'd been swept up, swept along. It had been a wild trip, and I'd tended to imagine I'd had no more control than a rider on a rollercoaster, a water boatman on a log flume. I'd told myself I was at the mercy of higher powers, never stooping to remind myself I didn't believe in any.

Abandoning Vlad, coming back to England, letting myself into another person's life. Up to a point it had all been defensible, if never sensible. Now it had spiralled. The pregnancy. The move back close to Whitby. Any chance I'd had to get a grip seemed to have slipped away.

In the upstairs hallway the floorboards creaked under my feet, and I was uncomfortably aware of shaky foundations. Passing into the wannabe nursery, I stared at the unicorns, the immaterial undulating over pleated material. I'd assumed Sophie's skeletons were all out of the closet, dancing in plain sight. But what right did I have to trust that? Or to judge?

Picking up my screwdriver and mounting my makeshift ladder, I set about unwinding the last thing I'd done.

'What are you doing, love?' Sophie stood in the doorway, draped in an old shirt, hands cradling.

I stepped down. 'Worrying.'

Moving into the room Sophie spread her arms and we melted together. And we stayed, melded, for so long.

'Is that a screwdriver in your pocket, or...?'

We laughed and broke apart.

'I need to take them down.' I nodded at the curtains. 'Your mum wants me to paint the room.'

'That'll be nice.' Her smile broke through me like moonlight through half-mast curtains. 'Is that all you were worrying about?'

'That was it.' After all there were worse fates, I thought, than this. Whatever this was.

'Let's go to bed.'

Later, as we settled under the covers, I dared to dream I'd never need to know. If she could settle for me, I could settle for ignorance.

You're never the captain of your own ship though, not really. There are tides, and winds. Maybe even mutiny.

Another hint at hidden threat came when I tentatively touched on a home birth. Not that I really wanted to sit around a paddling pool in the living room, listening to whale music:

'Just, you know, I have this thing about hospitals...'

But it turned out we couldn't. Our natal care was what they call consultant-led, doctors in charge and not midwives. Not knowing much, I didn't really question why.

Still wanting to steer clear of the town if possible, I pretended to do a little research on the relative merits of larger wards.

'I'm not driving to Scarborough with a baby hanging out of me,' Sophie was firm, 'and anyway, my medical records are in Whitby now. I've met the doctors. Why are you being weird about this?'

331

I felt like a rat in a garbage compactor. Walls were closing in. Of all the hospitals in all the world, I really wanted to avoid that one. Mum had literally worked there. There was a genuine risk of recognition.

I began to grow a beard.

My appearance has never bothered me. Maybe never had to. The vampire thing, the not-a-vampire-thing, I guess I've done that to death by now. You know I age, but – and I don't know if this is down to regeneration, though I guess it probably is – I don't do too badly. The few photos that survive from way back when illustrate a similar man. His hair might be a grade thicker, a shade less grizzly; his waist an inch thinner, eyes a little shorter on mileage, teeth not so long. But all in all he's still the same collection of bones. I know it doesn't last forever, I've seen that in all its gory, but it would be churlish to complain.

Well, guess what? I'm a churl. Add it to my growing list of faults. I wanted to look different, needed to. To some it would probably be second nature. To the dieters, the hair-dyers, the contact-lens wearers, collagen injectors, the tattoo targets. Those willing to go under a knife. The gym-goers or the dedicated followers of fashion. But I've never been much for self-enhancement. More because I'm careless than because I'm vain, although if I actually wanted to make myself a better person I tend to think I'd stand a better chance with books than with Botox.

I'm not even sure it would have stuck. Would a nose job survive regeneration? Would an ink dragon up my arm? Besides, hide in plain sight. Nothing ostentatious.

The beard felt a safe enough bet.

At tests and appointments it felt itchy and uncomfortable, which to be honest so did the rest of me. The truth, had I been tuned into it, was beginning to trickle out. Even our presence in clinics and consulting rooms should have been a clue. But I didn't know enough, or didn't question enough. Didn't want to pick a scab and have my own gaping wounds exposed.

We're back to that ship-captain analogy, though. Even roping myself to the tiller wouldn't have kept the course I wanted. Ultimately, whether I liked it or not, there would be a collision.

The final days ticked by, and the house lay ready. Cot assembled, pram road-tested, overnight bag packed in the hall. The nursery, blushing over its fresh flamingo finish, awaited in silent anticipation of infant wails.

The three of us, three being the new two, were downstairs, drinking raspberry leaf tea and staring at the remnants of a takeaway. I willed the mess to clear itself away, knowing Cora would volunteer any minute, and make me feel bad. Unfortunately, power over inert objects isn't in my gift. Maybe if I'd been an actual vampire I could have summoned some wolves or something. Though I doubt lupine waitstaff would ever really catch on. My lack of telekinesis was at least balanced out by my stunning prescience.

'I suppose I'll tidy this up then, will I?' Cora stood and stretched her short frame.

'No, no. You're the guest.' Balancing foil and cutlery I escaped to the kitchen. It was hardly an onerous task after all. Washing three forks, rinsing packages and sorting them into a variety of colour-coded kitchen bins. Still, there was no rush to rejoin the room. I put some music on and made a meal of it, disposing of the final prawn crackers by stuffing them into my mouth. A bit of extra weight would strengthen my disguise. You can never be too careful.

Having wiped a few surfaces to my own unexacting standards, I filled the kettle and wondered back to see if I could tempt either of them with a top-up.

The music from the kitchen must have drowned my entrance, because neither Sophie nor Cora glanced up from the couch.

'Is that what it looks like?'

They were crouched together, poring over what appeared to be old photographs.

Cora nodded. 'Yes, that was the time it flared up badly. After your uncle hit him.'

'I wish you hadn't shown me. I feel sick enough anyway after the takeaway.'

'I just want you to be forewarned.'

As Sophie slid away I caught a glimpse of the picture exposed. A body, stomach exposed to display a stain. A poison-boysenberry blot, spreading up from the hip, blooming like an ugly orchid, of the skin yet out of place, tattered litter polluting a white river.

Okay, I saw a blur of meaty flesh and looked away, but sometimes a writer needs to give a little more colour, and you know I can't resist luxuriating in overly-elaborate, ultra-violet floridity. Particularly when leading into a dramatic revelation.

'Most grandparents would bring a cuddly teddy. Not pictures of what haemophilia looks like.'

On autopilot I pedalled slowly backwards out of sight. Not out of earshot. Was it wrong to keep listening? Perhaps I had a right to. So easy to cough and interrupt though, or to turn up the music, turn the other cheek.

I all but pressed my cheek to the door.

'You need to know the signs, Sophie.'

A sigh came in reply.

'What's the matter?'

'I'm fine.'

'Fine?'

'Fine.'

Fine, fine. They were both fine. Except that nobody was. Their quiet voices screamed with subtext.

'What about the baby?' Cora persisted.

'I never got it, did I?' Soph resisted. 'Dad never passed it on to me.'

'It's still hereditary, Sophie,' Cora insisted. 'It can skip a generation.'

The music had developed an incongruous beat, a thumping drum out of sync with the bassline. It took me a minute to realise it was my heart.

'I had the test, you know I did.'

'And it was inconclusive...'

My mind's eye saw Soph cover her eyes, hiding her exasperation. An expression I'd seen a hundred times.

'What else can I do?' I almost heard the set of her jaw. 'I'd have the baby anyway.'

'I know, love.'

There was a minute or two of silence, then shuffling. Could have been a conciliatory hug. Could have been photographs being hidden away. They could have been playing Boggle for all I know. The door was closed.

I moved away to reboil the kettle before I opened it.

'Anyone for tea?' I announced loudly, telegraphing intrusion.

They looked up, a bag between them. Source, no doubt, of the shuffling. It drew my gaze, although I tried not to let it.

'It's a cuddly cat,' Sophie smiled, 'from Mum. I'll show you later.'

But later never came, and I didn't ask.

Regenerations

The clock above the bed was dead. No more steady laps for those hands, a day of labour had broken them and they hung, waiting. It was just after 10 p.m., twelve hours in, and time was standing still.

The clock was the cheap, plastic kind. The bed crisply white-sheeted. The room was more commodious than I had expected, accommodating a wide row of almost-comfortable seats, en suite facilities, and enough floor space for all of our luggage.

I'd had to go back for the luggage; we weren't initially sure when we would need it with us.

'There's quite a bit,' I explained apologetically.

'That's alright, there usually is!'

The "usually" was comforting.

'At least one of us has done this before,' I joked, weakly.

Later, with the luggage open and strewn, nothing was anything like comfortable. On the bed Sophie was writhing in sickening twists of pulsing pain, the slender whiteness of her wrist marred red with four failed attempts to hook up a drip. The fifth effort connected her to a tube, to a bag, to the clear liquid that had been pumping into her system all day, and which was now causing her to clench and tighten in grunting, knuckle-whitening, nail-into-palm pain. Pads on her swollen stomach were wired to a monitor, lurking in the shadows like a baleful lizard, counting a heart rate that spiked into the 190s.

The nurse had gone, seeking an errant anaesthetist, and in that moment there was just the two of us, as there was at the beginning, locked together.

Sophie looked up at me as another wave rocked through her pale and fragile form. Her hand searched through my shoulder for my collarbone as her fingers sought a purchase, leverage to somehow push back against the hurt. But it was her eyes which stung harder, searing with unknowable experience. Discomfort seems too weak a word, though it covers distress, uneasiness, anxiety. There was more there too: desperation, pleading, agony… and something horribly akin to hatred. Her deep brown eyes made a cauldron of it all, while mine, as if to dampen the hurtful flame, brought forth tears.

Maybe this is where I should have begun, way back on page one, trying to define pain. Not because expelling an alien body is ghastlier than being consumed by one, but because watching is the worst. Physically, this wasn't my fight. As much as I tried to be there, Sophie was alone in her body. And I had to watch. And there's no greater suffering than seeing a loved one struggle, being utterly useless beside them.

No. Of course I didn't just say that childbirth is more painful to watch than to live through. That would be ridiculous. Although, I am in the habit of saying some pretty ridiculous things... hear me out...

If the blood, the screaming, had been shark induced, if it had been teeth that were tearing, then would I have swapped places? I believe I would. In fact, though a far, far better thing than I have ever done, I'm sure of it. Not because I'm brave. I'm a stone-cold coward. But because I could. Because my rest could be made only temporary.

When I gave my second life up for Ali, that was a mistake. Don't get me wrong, I wouldn't undo it. But I was a kid, I wasn't being noble. I didn't realise I was risking my life, didn't even know I had lives to spare.

But having eaten the rotten apple of knowledge, then yes, I'm certain I'd take that bullet for Sophie. That literal bullet, even.

But I couldn't.

I could only watch. And being, as I say, a coward, I couldn't even do that for long. Twelve hours and counting had passed and there was no retreat, nowhere to run or hide. All I could do was close my eyes and take refuge in my thoughts. A stupid place to search for solace at the best of times, doubly so in the shivering heat of that feverish moment.

The only escape from fear was into panic. If that thing ever came out of her, what then? Would I be a good dad? How could I even measure that? I never had one myself.

Here we go again, you think. Thumping that old drum. Well, okay, I won't. You've got enough evidence by now to decide for yourself whether I ever had a positive male role model. Oh alright, one last tiny anecdote, if you insist:

We were in Spain, shortly after the drain drowning incident. My dad preferred England, as a rule. It made the form-filling easier, and he never had to learn any languages. But my picture had made a couple of papers, and he thought we ought to lie a little lower than usual. Worm-like lowness, essentially. If I was making this up, we'd have been in the Netherlands. But I'd never stoop that low.

We were walking to get fruit, for breakfast. Sound sublime? We trudged three miles from an undecorated shanty shack, into a faceless town for supermarket-wrapped bananas. I've had better mornings.

Though still early, heat beat down from above, radiated up from below. There was no pavement, and we slogged along in the dust and scrub. Traffic was scarce, but I trailed along in his wake, beating rhythm with a whitened stick.

'It's hot,' I sulked. That or something equally innocuous.

He turned, and without speaking, without warning, kicked a cloud of sandy soil up into my face. Grit hit my cheeks and mouth. Brown powder settled on my tongue, stung my nose. I stood in dirty shock. He spat on the earth and walked away. I was eight years old.

A low bar, then. Comparing myself to him, not actively inciting hatred would be a win. I wanted to do better than that.

Opening my eyes to refocus I found the world a more savage place than I remembered. Sophie had stalled. Her hands, the colour of frost, felt brittle and could move only to grip and trap. Her distended stomach arched in broken animation, moving no faster than that stopped clock, wrong 86,398 times a day. She had halted, shattered, frozen. Life begins, as it ends, in fear and torment.

Her life flashed before my eyes, and I saw a future of Arctic bleakness.

Then her eyes blazed.

'I can do this.'

I don't know if she was telling me, or the world, or herself, but that was the turning point.

Her face was red and wringing. We held hands. 'Yes.'

The screams didn't die, the pain didn't stop, but time, at last, rebooted.

Nora came into the world with a whimper, and to a shriek from her mother. Delicate but plump, pale and purple. Impossibly small, yet somehow longer than I expected, dark hair in matted wisps and eyes tight shut, pistachio slits. She was beautiful.

I couldn't get near her. There was cleaning and weighing, clipboards clacking and medical chatter. A cluster of scrubs pushed me to the back of the room, attending mother and child, mopping up the holy triumvirate of bodily fluids, sweat and blood and tear-induced tears.

My thoughts for the moment remained with Sophie, drained, empty, unbowed. She babbled through the haze, concerned for her new world and all around her, no time for herself amidst the aftermath of a brutal, taxing operation.

I took a step towards her, tried to hold her hand. A midwife bustled us apart.

'You'll want the baby.'

I did, still it seemed an eon before she was delivered into my arms, so light, inconsequential, and yet, everything. At least, that was what I told myself. In reality, I felt strangely blank. Whatever the clock said, my body knew it was at least twelve hours later. Jet-lagged and giddy, it might have been enervation, but my baby was already a ghost in my arms, detached.

Walking to the window together, we looked out over the town. She couldn't have seen it, I know, her eyes too fresh to focus. I held her in unsure arms, scared to squeeze or let slip, and from that eerie eyrie surveyed our new world laid out like a map below.

The shadow of the park, the harbour lights, the ghost of the abbey on the headland. Mostly space. Sea and sky. A damping mist, muffling the night-time noises, wind and waves and closing time at the pubs. Room to breathe, to grow, to escape.

I looked down at my baby.

'This is your home then, I guess.'

A cloud of wings wheeled by, gulls in the night – or bats? I stepped back, and in my arms Nora flexed and squawked.

With my little finger I tickled her palm, felt her hand curl around in a tight reflex. Only then did something grip me. The room swam, floor and ceiling, midwives and machines, even Sophie seemed far away in a fog, dissolving into darkness. We were alone.

The bustle, the energy of the room was extinguished, the surrounding town went out like a lamp. Maybe the whole world stood poised on its axis, there was no way to know for sure. For me, for us, this was all of existence.

Each other. A whole new tsunami of exhaustion drove me back, left me weak and incapable. My spine liquified, reversing evolution to render me jelly. Hips and legs shook and surrendered, and with what mind I had left I fought to keep my cradling arms from failing.

The universe shoved me backwards into a seat, jolting Nora into a wild-eyed shriek that realigned the planets, let in the light and parted a causeway across the room to Sophie, wild-eyed in fretful fatigue.

'What's the matter? Is she okay?'

She cried. With her whole face, her whole heart. Her mouth, little gummy bow, so pink and perfect, erupted into a chasm that split her head down the middle and exposed a yawning vulnerability within. White peach-soft cheeks raged purple, and sugar-sweet eyes pled and beseeched and drilled holes deep inside me. The sculpted arc of her back stretched and contorted with a strength beyond her weight. Tiny, creamy arms gave abandon to frantic hands, spreading, closing, haywire flytraps bunching and blooming and grasping for invisible gnats of meaning. She shook, with her whole being in a rictus of shock. She screamed. Full-throated, full-throttle. Piercing, demanding, entreating, imploring, with every gasp of her breath until choked hoarse and silent into juddering, wracking silent sobs.

I looked, beyond all that.

'She's perfect.'

'No... no bruises, blood?'

'Perfect.'

She was. But I wasn't. Nora's hot little fingers encased mine, an unbreakable reminder that, suddenly, I was accountable. Nothing would ever be the same again.

Degeneration

Sophie changed my life in every way but one. Settling down hadn't stopped me putting miles on the clock.

We were accidental soul mates, in a sense. The wandering bug that had bitten me in my twenties had given me an itch, a rash urge to travel. It's hard to say whether that was an actual interest in sights and seeing though, or just the artistry of escapism. After a while it became necessity; there was always something to be sought after, even if just another exit. In the end, I wasn't in New England for new views. But then, does anyone ever find what they're really looking for?

Sophie, more or less my age, was still in the heart of needing to go, wanting to know. She climbed every mountain in her path, or detoured thousands of miles just to find one. And I had to pretend that was my jam too, providing a plausible reason for being up there with her, other than because she was my heroine. Or heroin. Although that's about the one thing I never tried.

'It's so nice,' she said softly to me once, to a sunset, to the orange tide rolling up a beach just for us.

'So nice,' I murmured back, not knowing quite what I was agreeing with, but one hundred per cent certain of my acquiescence.

Her curls rested on my shoulder. Zephyrs ruffled them, fanned us with scents of ice cream and sunscreen.

'So nice we have this…' again I nodded, sure that it was, whatever it was, '…this connection.'

'Yes.'

'I guess, because travelling brought us together, these trips reinforce us, somehow?'

When I didn't reply straightaway she shuffled, almost shy, moved to catch my eye. Two pairs of sunglasses, reflecting each other, and a dying sun.

'Or is that silly?'

'No,' I kissed her. 'No.'

She kissed me too.

'It's perfect.'

It was left to Nora, then, to tie us down.

Nobody will admit having a baby cramps their style. Except me, here, now. Because it totally does. Sure, you see families refusing to accept that. At the airport, there's always some harassed dad, lugging luggage, carrier under one arm, baby under another, hopping to kick a pram along with a spare foot. All for the pleasure of hiding in poolside shade, stressing over heatstroke, spoiled milk and malaria.

We downgraded our expectations, left the squashed plane cabins and beach envy to others. There are plenty of places in England to visit, after all, exciting even for those who've made a habit of global adventure.

For us, a mile up the road then home for bed was fine. Convenience, quality of life. The call of the gulls. Trips to the shops, the seaside. The park.

Like everywhere in town it reminded me of Mum. Whatever else had changed in two decades, the park hadn't. Oh sure, surface features had evolved. The old aviary was gone, and the playground now met some safety standards. Caged birds and bloodied children being all very last century. The undulating swathes of green remained. Pockets of trees, tousled with leaves, nests and drays snarled in branches. Pathways of pine needles and fir cones, forest litter. Floral patterns, poppies, pansies. Roses of red. Other flowers of blue. Strays, too. Wood-sorrel and Shepherd's Purse.

We went there as a family, and though the past was often on my mind I wouldn't speak of her. Better to snap new shots on smartphones than dwell on the sepia prints of memory.

Sometimes we would go to the swings, when Nora was old enough to sit in one and smile. More often we'd just perambulate in circles while she napped in the stroller, a prelude to her main night-time slumber. Unlike those fools in the airport we could travel light, a knapsack of supplies to last an hour or so: bottles and blankets, emergency nappies. The kitchen sink.

On this night we walked beneath the trees, their eaves a natural umbrella to the elements, and there was silence.

Silence save the cacophony we carried along in her pram, and soon she too was still, hushed by nature. And we could relax, a five-minute holiday from a hectic home.

For a minute or two we ambled on. The twilight had grown chilly, but we had coats and closeness to keep us warm. And reminiscence. The knowledge that after the Knife Edge we'd never truly be cold again. At a bench we paused, seated in companionable quietude. Thinking.

'I've been thinking,' I said.

She made some obligatory joke, surprised I was capable of thought, before asking, 'What about?'

'What I might do?'

For a while it had been vaguely beginning to occur that with parenthood, with a life together, came responsibility. And with great responsibility comes… well, not nothing.

I needed to do something.

'You should write,' said Soph.

That made me stop, as much as you can stop doing nothing.

'Write? Write what?'

'About the world, I think.'

If Nora brought me down to earth in a literal sense, knocking off air travel, she gave flight to more figurative fancies. It was for her that I told stories.

She cried, you see. Babies cry. Not always. A good girl, a happy girl. Untroubled and lucky, in an Eden without pain. No serious pain at least, that I knew of. Pink and bouncing, you could have used her to advertise anything, even parenthood. If there were post-natal tests, further investigations into faulty blood, I never heard about them.

Without fully articulating it, even in my head, I suppose I assumed an all clear.

Still. All babies cry. When they're hungry, thirsty, tired, bored. Also when the opposite of all those things. And you can ask them all you want, they'll never tell you why. Sometimes it feels for all the world like a wind-up. Sometimes it's wind.

The trick then is to fix it, without a clue as to how.

For that, what you need is a gambit. Mine was stories. Not original, I grant, but there's no prizes for that in childcare. It's whatever gives comfort, and Nora seemed to draw solace from my voice. Her blue eyes would clear and focus at the sound of a yarn.

It began with books, but she didn't have many. Only the sort you can safely chew, or run through the washing machine. So soon the game became to select something from our shelves, flick through a Rough Guide, or a Bill Bryson, and surmise or summarise a story, bowdlerise out a theme here, insert a dragon there, where plausibility allowed. A waste of time, to be sure. She never understood a word. Only rhythm and cadence, and the bond created.

After a time the books went by the wayside, it being easier just to hold Nora in both arms and forage words from the backwoods of my head. Tales I shouldn't have told her, rambling roads for me alone. Home truths.

'I'm sorry you'll never know her.' My little girl rested on my chest, rising and falling in sync with my heart, her own little butterfly flutterments thrumming back at me.

'I don't remember my grandma, but at least I met her.'

Nora may have been asleep; face down in my T-shirt her eyes were invisible. Chances were I was talking to myself. Even if she was quietly awake, unlikely, and my words were falling into her delicate ear, there was nothing she could compute, or remember.

Unless...

Are there residual threads? Traces of ghosts, forgotten pools... driftwood... pieces of an abandoned puzzle? My guess is we can't even begin to know what we don't know.

'Your grandma was...' It was the first time I'd called my mum that, too late for her ever to know, and it stopped me short, lumpen-throated. For a while, space took all my attention. Staring around a room I knew so well, looking past pictures, ornaments, objects, art. Seeing only a void.

Deep breath.

'Your grandma would have loved you.' I stroked her hair, where her hair would be, a tufting little crest. 'You're beautiful. Like her.'

My eyes mapped a trail across the ceiling. Then had to swim their way back. Underwater. Not enough air.

A trembling against me let me believe she understood.

I held her tiny hand, and told a silly story about Vlad instead.

I was talking to the darkness when Sophie came home, so I sensed her before I saw her. She shot me a tired look from the doorway. But I didn't know how long she'd been there. I stopped talking.

'Is she asleep?' She slumped on a chair opposite, tugging off her boots.

At her mother's voice Nora stirred.

'Just about. A walk should do it. Do you want to go to the park?'

The park, again. A chuckle, heart as light as it had ever been, ever would be. 'Just the world? Not much then.'

'I heard the story you were telling Nora. You and Vlad, in Australia.'

My face flushed.

'Sorry,' she giggled a little, 'was that supposed to be private?'

Closing my eyes, I tried to remember the paths my tongue had wandered. It had just been so haphazard, not even events as such, just… impressions. Nothing incriminating. That I remembered.

'They were just thoughts.'

They weren't really anything.

'I liked them.'

She leant her head on my shoulder, weightless.

Did I mention it was summer? Nominally. Green leaves and wild flowers, to go with clouds and mud. Birds, who enjoy an old chestnut, tweeted in their nests. Possibilities shimmered, like gossamer in evening dew.

'You told me you were a travel writer, remember?'

The sunset passed over my face. 'Ah, I'd have said anything…'

'But you said that. And I know you kept notes.'

They were in the attic, a jumble of pads full of impressions. Probably mildewed and certainly illegible.

'That was just like a hobby, not a job. It'd be like paying Nora to sleep. Or your mum to nag me to finish painting her room.'

Sophie smiled and slapped my arm.

'Seriously though, have I done anything that

interesting? I'm not exactly boldly going, am I? Pushing a pram around a park.'

'But before—'

'Still wasn't *Gulliver's Travels*, was it? What have I got that's new?'

So what? she might have said. Who would ever do anything, on that basis? We'd all be Salieri, spending more time poisoning than composing, perpetuating nonsense to discredit each other.

The problem was, that wasn't the problem.

It was disingenuous, to even bring up my Lilliputian relationship to the literati. So much more held me back. Even if I'd been the best at something, demonstrably, measurably talented, how could I have shown it?

At school, at one of my schools, I ran a bit of cross country. It's an easy enough sport in which to edge towards the front of the pack. Just have to be quicker than the asthmatics, the fatties and the skivers lighting up in the bushes. I won a race or two, maybe a medal. Then I gave up. However far I ran, I wasn't going to get anywhere.

Look, I'm not pretending I was ever Mo Farah, or even fit enough to lace his spikes. Just, if I had been, well, it wouldn't have mattered. You can't run in the Olympics without a name on your back.

And nothing had changed. When you have more than one history, you have less than the sum of your pasts. Nothing adds up, and you're never quite real.

Turning to watch Nora snoring, humming in harmony with a hidden insect chorus, my thoughts travelled back to my own dad. Watching me, perhaps resenting me, because while making crime pay for one is hard, for a family it's savage.

Not that it was like that. Like father, like son. I didn't like him, never wanted to be him or even be near him. Never believed the ends justified being mean.

You don't always get your first-choice career though, right? Otherwise we'd all be intergalactic cowboys or something. My wander-years had pushed me away from anything nine-to-five, while at the same time giving me a set of tools useful only on the deadbeat side of the tracks. My dad fancied himself more the Godfather than a good father and under him I'd been apprenticed in talking to the right wrong-kind-of-people. Thanks to Vlad making a game of my life I'd only gone further down that road. Gypsy, tramp, thief. Not much else I could do with my particular set of skills.

The ink was still wet on all my qualifications, and any references were signed by my own hand. In short, the most useful skill on my CV was petty forgery, and that doesn't get asked for as often as you'd think.

Since meeting Sophie, the thought of losing her had kept me straight, though the path was narrow. My best bet was always borderline stuff, zero-hour gigs and favours for friends of friends. But I wanted better than that. For my daughter.

My daughter, whose mother held my hand, held all of me, in her palm.

'Just a blog or something for starters? But I know the travel business. And Marcus's brother is at Reuters now, I'm sure he could help.'

There is power in faith.

'I believe in you.'

That was my opening, it's clear now. Clear as moonlight. That's when I should have told her. Together, in the quiet and the comfort of that time, alone but for Nora's baby animal snuffle. Hid from the world, in green and darkness, with the stars and planets all in kilter.

'This could be your time,' she might have whispered, 'to be more than you are, to show us who you can be.' It might have been her, or the breath of the breeze, the night echoes of the trees. Either way, I hear it now, read it clearly.

We were in love. Life was just us. She was happy to give me all that she could wish.

I could at least have told her who I was.

Maybe that's the problem with living a life of second chances. You stop noticing when the real opportunities come around.

Still, love gave me one spur. I did write. The belief expressed in the park slowly translated into something tangible. Into this, in a way. Heavily redacted then, of course. The moment of truth had passed. Still, bits and bobs have made it this far, descriptive passages. Transylvania, Whitby. The lot. My story, without me in it.

These were the days of the writing classes, the kindly critiques, the constructive dismantling of anything I could produce. Don't get me wrong, there was right advice to be had. Hopefully I've even enacted some of it: use an active voice. Don't say "lambent" twice in the same chapter. Always think of three examples of things. And you do get better at writing once you know the rules, even if your whole life has conditioned you to break them.

Pros and cons then, for whatever the objective of subjective analysis, it really slowed me down.

Some nights Sophie would come home to find words awaiting. She read them by the light of a baby monitor, and gave encouraging smiles. If she seemed nonplussed I can hardly complain. It must have been like reading *Dracula* without the vampire, or *The Invisible Man* without whoever was in that.

At least she never complained that progress could be measured only painfully.

A bit of typing here, a scratching pen there. More sitting, pontificating. Someone once told me writer's block is a kinder name for laziness. I can't wholly agree, because I've lived with both and can see a distinction. Some days the page stayed white while I lay in the sun. Other times I swear I sat and tapped at that keyboard, but only as somewhere to drum my fingers.

In the beginning there was the word. And it was solitary...

The reality was, even if both energetic and unclogged, I didn't really know where I was going. There's no endeavour, other than art, where you just set off without a map. No other role in life where staring out of the window is in the job description. I tried not to procrastinate but...

Hang on, I just saw a Goldcrest.

Back.

Honesty, then. Umpteen invisible spills were wiped. Innumerable hands of patience dealt. Anything to avoid aimlessness. And the biggest time sink was simply watching Nora.

My idyll is to be idol. Ideally, there is nothing quite like doing nothing. Not so much floating in a vacuum, although I suppose that might have some womb-like appeal, but relaxing in comfort. Each sensory organ coddled to Goldilocks' standards of just right. You'll have your own thoughts on how that might be, of course. Cradled by the Red Sea with a long, cool mocktail. Ensconced in the snug of a real ale pub with a well-worn copy of Wodehouse. Butt naked in a sauna. Provide your own dream scenario. It's also up to you whether you're alone, revelling in tranquillity, headphones channelling the techno; or whether you're not.

For me, for most of my life, I would have been. Between my mother and Sophie there was only the curious co-dependence with the paranormal world's answer to the parasitic flea that could be characterised as a relationship. And there was nothing soothing about Vlad's presence. He was just so incessant with his grating chatter and fictitious factoids. He was needy and narcissistic and much too similar to me to be bearable.

Sophie, my soul mate, was delicious to unwind with, never to be superseded in companionship. But she was a doer. A mover, a shaker, an adventurous adventuress.

For busily doing nothing, Nora reigned supreme. Her form, when dozing, moulded seamlessly into mine. My shoulder pillowed her crown, downy tresses feathering my neck and snagging in the Velcro of my stubble in an intimate hook that tugged at my being. Pressed to my chest, her face compressed, one cheek flattened into her mouth and pushed her lips into a cherry pout. Even so distorted she was divine.

Her face was beauty itself. The loveliness of her mother was mirrored, so flawlessly captured in miniature, only with added freshness, new innocence, and just enough of a hint of myself to remind me she was mine. When she smiled the sun came out. Her laugh could banish winter.

So we lay. When Sophie was out working, and I should have been working in.

Swaddled in pyjamas her body curled in contentment, feet tucked above my pelvis, my shirt rucked up where her pinching fingers toyed with it. The only movement the gentle rocking as my heartbeat lifted her up and down. The only sound the gentle purr of her baby breaths.

Laidback on the couch, myself as her divan, that was the best nothing I ever had. The telly, on mute, could have been showing the worst film ever made. It wouldn't matter. Together in the shadow of drawn curtains, the world beyond could have been sinking beneath a lake of fire. It wouldn't have mattered. Nothing could hurt us in our bubble.

Only thing about bubbles is, they're hardly famous for lasting.

It seems cruel that such distilled contentment should give way to nightmare. But such is life.

The bubble burst.

Nora shook, a tremor ran through her and I think I became aware of sudden heat. A spasm thrust her skull up into my jaw, I bit my tongue and she retched. Not milk-spit but true, copious vomit. Our clothes were stuck with it, the reek thrust inside me, up to the junction between my nose and eyes. The weight of her sick lay heavy on my torso as I lifted her clear and she screamed.

Sophie wouldn't be back for hours. Cora, the one time she would have been more than welcome, was out of town. We were alone. Rocking and cooing I bore Nora through to the bathroom, setting her down on the mat to un-pop her filth-ridden jammies. She shrieked and I sang to her, stripping her down to her nappy. As I stopped to pull my shirt over my head she was sick again, slicking her skin from navel to chin, gagging and choking on the remnant. I hooked my finger into her mouth, fishing for chunks, before lifting her onto my shoulder, holding her as she coughed and wheezed, unable now even to cry.

Carrying my daughter in one arm, I reached across to turn on the shower. I'm not pretending I was thinking clearly, I just hoped to clean her and calm her and start again. Testing the temperature, I felt her go rigid against me, and a third flood sprayed down my neck and back. A rancid odour told me she had voided her bowel.

Whispering soft fragments of rhyme I told her everything would be okay. Tried to believe myself. Then I glimpsed our forms in the mirror, naked and shaking, and saw the bile down my back was laced with blood.

Life ends as it begins. In fear and torment.

Part 6

We Don't Live Forever

A Matter of Life and Death

'I didn't know who else to ask.'

There was no chair. I crouched on thin carpet looking anywhere but at him. Not that there was much to see. A simple bed, plainly made, a wardrobe from a chain store. Wall-art one step down from a hotel lobby, and watercolour flowers wilting in a vase. It was a space for transition. Nothing of permanence, least of all the occupants. In grander times the salt air had brought visitors still hoping to recuperate. Now it was a room with a view only to the afterlife.

You could have spread the atmosphere with a butter knife.

Oppressed by it all, and by time, I sought to broach the matter bluntly.

'I didn't even mean to come here tonight. I thought I could do it without you. But I can't.'

The last thing I felt capable of was making some sick sales pitch, but stories were Vlad's thing so I guessed he'd expect the details. Perhaps I was projecting. He lay, listening, listless, as I laid it on the line. Laboured out as much as I could. His eyes closed when I finished talking. Was there a translucency through his lids? Scientifically impossible, I suppose. Still, it almost felt as if I could see inside him.

And there was only darkness. Glancing back at the name on the chart I suddenly plummeted through a void. Was this no longer Vlad at all? Just Fred. Just another living dead body on a hospital bed? Rock bottom hit me. I saw this was no time for sales. I was here to buy. Or beg, or steal. The currency was his humanity, and I would be taking all of it. All that was left.

'Please.'

How often do you hear that word? It crops up so often, any interaction. Asking for a bus ticket or a packet of chips. Just basic civility. We say it so frequently that in repetition it loses some meaning. Becomes just a sibilant syllable.

'Please.' This was pleading in the purest sense.

The dead man opened his eyes.

'I don't…' his words were choked off in infirmity, and my innards froze waiting for his fit to subside. Seconds stretched out on a rack. I reached out again.

'Please?'

'I don't think I'll get through it.'

'What?'

I didn't understand, or didn't want to.

'What are you saying?'

He said nothing, although he seemed to be trying.

'Vlad?'

'I think…' more breathless pausing, '… I think it would kill me.'

My own eyes closed, and there was only the void.

'But then,' he paused again, to cough, or for drama, 'perhaps it's time.'

'Time?' I kept my eyes closed, hiding in my personal darkness.

'To walk into the light.'

And there was light.

What's the most you ever invested in anything? The most of yourself? How much have you ever paid out, or put on the line?

A life? Or a way of life?

Everything I had was hanging by a threadbare hope. And it's the hope that kills you. That or cancer. Or a knife.

My dad took me when I was four. He can't have had any clue it would work. How did he handle the hope? Did he care? He must have, enough to try.

For me, missing Nora was missing my own insides. Everything I had bound myself up in, all that made me anybody. For him I feel like it was a roll of the die. If it came up snake eyes, my old man could have washed his hands, rolled on home.

There was no path that way for me, just a chasm, and a bridge no more than cinders. If this didn't work then it was the end of the line.

A hundred unanswered messages on my phone hinted that maybe it was over anyway.

Pushing that thought off the cliff at the back of my mind I tried to focus on the murder at hand.

'I'm scared,' I admitted. They're hard words to say, but it was finally time for honesty. I owed him that much.

'It will work,' he smiled benignly. With new purpose, he seemed now to glow with a beneficent air. I found it annoying.

'You don't know that,' pacing again, the ghosts of a thousand fruitless arguments jostling between my ears, 'you can't.'

'Your father had this power. You have it.' He watched me to and fro, eyes ticking like a metronome. 'Your daughter has it.'

I still found his absurd, ignorance-masking self-assurance infuriating. But I wanted to believe him so badly.

'Jesus, Vlad.' I looked away, blinking. 'How do we know how it gets passed down? What do you and me know about genetics? A retired Goth and a failed drifter? We don't know jack, don't know the odds. We don't know if it's dominant, recessive… what any of those words mean.'

Vlad waved, impatiently.

'This is magic, my friend. Not science. Not reason.'

'This is madness.'

'This is who you are.'

Perhaps we were both right.

There was a functional sink fixed in one corner. I fetched the limp bouquet from the windowsill and tipped out the flowers, sluiced the vase clean. It looked about the right size. Vlad watched me. I stared at the wilted petals on wet porcelain.

'I didn't bring a knife.' I'd left in a hurry.

'Bring my cane.' A finger quivered to the corner of the room. 'The wardrobe.'

The cheap square unit was screwed to the wall, a pale pine veneer and two sliding drawers. A key dangled from a flimsy lock, but the doors rolled open at a touch. Inside, folded on low shelves and hanging from a single plastic rail, was Vlad's life. Pay no attention to the man behind the bed curtain, that was just a body. His heart beat in this cupboard across the room. It drummed in the heavy mock-military greatcoat, in the shirts of lace and webbing. Cavalier boots and Monopoly Man hat. A pile of socks sat neatly folded. All black. Somehow that caught me, in the throat, stayed my breath in my chest.

It took a moment to compose myself and locate the cane, laid across the lowest shelf, behind a tray of accoutrements. Jet and silver rings, the spider brooch. Reading glasses and a drawstring purse.

An ebony tube tipped with pewter and topped with a wolf's head handle, it balanced with a pleasing heft. Handy in a tight spot, certainly. A thumping good blunt instrument, but not what you'd call for to cut a steak with, say. Or an artery.

Vlad beckoned, and I wondered briefly if he planned on overpowering me. I figured I'd take my chances against skin and bone. He took the cane and twisted the lupine head. The wooden casing slid away and a slim rapier slipped into view.

'Should have guessed.' For the first time in many days, I came close to smiling.

Vlad chortled, dissolved into throaty, phlegmy spasms. I waited, reached for water, held it helplessly as he convulsed. If someone came running I wouldn't even hear them approach over the sound of rattling death.

After an age he shuddered still. Wordlessly we made an exchange, a glass of water for the sword. It felt cold and horrible in my hand.

He drank slowly, unsteadily. Dribbled down his smooth chin. His eyes watched me over the rim of the beaker. I looked away.

'When you're ready.' My voice shook and fell, trying to sound insouciant.

'Help me get dressed,' he said.

'What?'

'I want to do this properly.'

'Properly? Someone could come in. Vlad, I can't get caught.'

His head quaked, shaking.

'It has to be done right. There's power in the ritual.'

There wasn't. I didn't need symbols, chanting, pentangles or a wizard costume. But I did need his blood. I was still stuck under his control.

'Help me,' he repeated.

I fetched his clothes. Dressed him, like you would a baby. Rolled his socks over calloused toes, enveloped him into velvet pantaloons, buttoned his shirt over a stark, white rack of ribs. His rings squeezed over distended knuckles, then hung loose around thinned fingers. He chose the earring he wanted, winced as it pricked through a closing hole and begat a single watery droplet of blood. Licking nervous lips I wished that was enough. The spider, clipped to his lapel, judged me with eight lapis lazuli eyes. A silken scarf bound around his neck, his boots encased him to the knee. I handed him his hat, and he positioned it carefully over his naked scalp.

The coat stayed on its hanger. His sleeve rolled up and his wrist bared.

'Do you want a mirror?' I asked.

'No, no thank you, old chap.'

It was just as well. His finery hung around him, a pallid grey moth with wings too big for its haggard needle-body.

'I'm ready.' His forearm wavered as he held it to me. I stood by him, vase ready. Sword, not so much. My arm wouldn't shift. It hung flaccid by my side. My mind was frozen. I couldn't work out how to move. It was all I could do to talk.

'I can't.' It came out no more than a mumble.

My pulse beat in my eyes, vision impaired. Sweating and shining, my palm was greased around the sword handle. It suddenly felt heavy. A dead weight.

'Hold the vase.' The words seemed to echo in my head.

'Vlad, I'm sorry.'

He took the blade.

'I'm sorry.'

He cut himself.

'I'm so fucking sorry.'

He began to bleed.

I held his hand, even if I couldn't hold his eye. Clasping him under the elbow I felt his wrist throb as he turned a whiter shade of pale. His face became a skull.

The vase was full. We fell back.

'Pass... pass me...' he waved weakly. I found a spare shirt, began to wrap him in it, staunching.

'My coat,' he coughed. 'Complete the look.'

'You don't have time,' I whispered, harsh. 'I don't have time.'

He stared me out. The spell was still at work. I draped his coat around him. His arm wouldn't fit. The sleeve couldn't cover the rudimentary blood-soaked bandage.

Vlad relaxed onto his sheets, satiated.

'Give me a minute, then call for help, yes?' I held the vase as steadily as I could. His warm blood still spilled and ran. I covered the top with my hand.

He didn't answer.

'Jesus, Vlad.'

There was a button by his bed, red and alarming. I jabbed it, and a bell sounded, far away.

Life Finds a Way

It felt like an outer-body experience, the worst déjà vu in the world. Another hospital, another sickbed. Another set of parents watching another dying child. Nora was younger than I had been. Smaller, not even worth a bed, more an elaborate plastic cot, like an open-topped container for an exotic pet, easy access to oxygen and fluids, life's essentials through a straw.

She seemed to shrink so quickly. To give in. Pudgy fingers became brittle little twigs, too fragile to hold. Sophie sat by her all the same, unmoving, all but unblinking. To be a better man than my father I shunned the shadows and the corners, stood by her. I wanted to hold her tight, to give and draw comfort. All too often what transpired was no more than a cursory trace, smoothing her hair, brushing her arm. A limp and lost caress. Whether I felt the electric shock of rejection, or whether I imagined it, it burned and I withdrew.

The room, small even before being cut in two by a cellophane curtain, could be crossed in six circuitous paces, avoiding Sophie and Nora in a rough semicircle. I sloped from wall to wall and back again with an aimless, monotonous tread. All the while watching the bed. Watching my daughter die. As at her birth, we were joined by a procession of gloved and masked professionals who knew better. Yet in a parody of her arrival she slipped further from her father every second. Sophie, reduced to a waiting role, lost her spiky fighting self, wilted and waned, unable to control or even comprehend.

I felt, or dreamt, or created, a barrier between us. A shroud of devastation, desolation. In the hours up to screaming and pushing Nora into the world, Sophie had occasionally fixed me with a stare, ripe with unspoken wrath and rage, an implication that I was making her do this. As another door opened, and Nora slithered towards it, I would have given all for such a gaze, for the knowledge that the passion and emotion was still there. That there was anything more than hopelessness.

This from the braggart who asserted, a chapter or so ago, that his relationship was unbreakable. Who even had the indecency to utter that whatever doesn't kill us makes us stronger. Relationships evolve, is the truth. Sometimes into families. And our family seemed to be perishing with Nora. That which does kill you, it transpires, makes you weaker.

It wasn't possible to accept that then, there in that room. If you prescribe to the stages of grief model, I never got beyond denial. Never at all, perhaps, but certainly not in those brief, brutal hours.

It happened so quickly. A cruel trick of time, that the number of minutes she took to expire so closely matched the time it took to labour her. How shocking then, that Sophie's endurance and physical toil seemed to last so much longer. That contractions seemed expanded, while a life ebbing away flowed so readily. Giving birth took a lifetime. Death came in a heartbeat.

Ultimately it must count as a mercy she didn't linger, I suppose. The memories I have, the pains that haunt me, come from being old enough to remember aging though disease, debilitating. Nora was under the age of understanding, unable to reason why, to do anything but die. The curse of lingering, long years of hopeless suffering, boredom, anxiety, hurt, was not her cross to be crushed beneath.

Small mercies.

It ended, without even much of a whimper.

Days passed. The lights had gone out all over the house. Sophie sat in the gloom, unwashed hair in a drape across her face.

I came tentatively close, dilute smile lost in the dark.

'Do you want anything to eat?'

'What's the point?' It was hard to argue with that, without showing my hand.

'You need to…'

In the shadows she twitched. Her shoulders heaved, a stretched-out shuddering throb. Two steps, slow steps would have taken me there. I couldn't make it. Everything was different now, in this extended night. It didn't help that the room we were haunting was the short-lived nursery.

The walls hung with a parti-coloured ABC built from animal shapes. Grinning lions and unicorn fish. The cot squatted, unchanged sheets good enough for the lonely bow-tied teddy. It didn't help, but perhaps it didn't matter much either. Sorrow will find you no matter where you lie.

The trembling took her suddenly.

'It's my fault.' Her wheezing became whimpers and then sobs. Gut-wrenchingly, she cried the way Nora used to. Silent and shaking.

'No.' I finally found myself next to her. She was curled on her knees, cuddling a patchwork pillow. I crouched beside her, beside myself, tried to dab at a sea of streaming tears I couldn't see.

'The doctor,' a minute of wracking, ragged breath, 'the doctor said it could have been complications…' She stopped again, voice lost in misery. '… from haemophilia.'

'No.' It was more complicated than that.

'My genes,' she wept. 'My fault.'

It was in the broken heart of the storm that she had first spoken the words, with a guilt-cut glance in my direction.

'She might have it, it runs in the family.'

The consultants assured her, in statements bald and cold, that they had all the relevant information. A nearby nurse gave a mollifying nod.

I suppose she knew they knew. So was it for my benefit, to clue me in? She'd have seen it must come out anyway. Perhaps it was a way of lifting a weight off. That would be a human thing to do, if I'm allowed to make that judgement. To want to live without secrets or lies, even lies of omission.

'I never wanted to worry you,' she told me, as we lay slumped beneath the shrine of Nora's cot.

Maybe that was true. Maybe I even had the same excuse. Never wanted to bother her unnecessarily with the tedious facts of my undeadness. Even if that wasn't it, even if she was hiding some more selfish instinct, I had no moral high ground. I was a moral mole, inhabiting a morass of hidden depths, dark and dirty.

Still, the dynamic had subtly shifted. I would never have doubted her before. Couldn't have cast an accusation high enough to top the pedestal I'd built. It felt like another inward sign, that the normality I'd woven was unravelling.

'You will never be human,' Vlad had said to me, and I'd told him I had to try. Well I had tried, and fallen. A door in my life was closing.

And another, a grim and neglected portal, was falling open.

You don't have to wear black to be in mourning. I might have mentioned, and plenty of cultures tell you anyway. It's enough to wear your loss on your face. Sophie's eyes were a trapdoor to her soul, though it was too far down to make out clearly. Her grief was a black hole. She had fallen into herself, and was floating around down there, somewhere. Untouchable, unreadable. I could sit close to her, right next to her, reaching for her. But she wasn't there.

She had been the practical one, a hand on the tiller and a vision of where we were going. I was more like a sort of amiable deckhand, confused by port and starboard, let alone the science of navigation, but happy to trust in her knowledge of the stars, and dream of new worlds and paradise islands.

Adrift and rudderless, now was my time to stick an oar in.

'Have you thought about what you want to do, you know, after?'

All I got back was a blank stare. In fact, not even that. Her unchanging expression was directed at nothing, and nowhere. Not me.

Of course, I had an unfair advantage. The opening door. Hope.

'Are we sure we even want a coffin?'

'What's that supposed to mean?'

'I mean, I don't know, do we bury her? There's other, I don't know, ways.'

Against the advice in her eyes I ploughed on.

'We could scatter—'

'No.'

Sophie could not countenance cremation. Fire at the best of times caused a physical reaction for her, left her cold. Another inheritance from a father we could have done without. But there is never any use wishing things were different. That would make us different people, and who can say whether an uncomplicated her and an unproblematic me would even have met, let alone made so much progress together?

There were years behind us, binding us two. Between us, too. Deceit deepens, doesn't it? Gaps become chasms.

"You never told me that," is fine, can be funny, for something small. What you did for a summer job when you were sixteen. Why you don't like marmalade.

'That's so weird! Because you love oranges, and jam. And Paddington Bear.' A giggle, a wrinkled nose, crinkling eyes. Move right along.

That's a crack in the pavement though. And I'm talking about the Grand Canyon.

'We didn't meet until our thirties,' Sophie reminded me once. 'It's okay to have a past.'

I didn't probe what she might be trying to excuse herself from. How could I, when I had pasts, plural? At least any skeletons she might have would be old dead bones, not reanimated zombie realities.

No, there was no way to tell her when the sun was shining on us. Still less after the sky fell in.

She knelt with a picture in her hand, the one that had hung above the bookshelf. Three of us smiling, Nora in the middle, wide-eyed and gummy, surrounded by us, held up, held onto. Her parents, knackered and dishevelled, but mouths made for laughing, kissing. Her parents. For six months that was how we had defined ourselves. Suddenly that role was gone.

A delicate finger traced that peach of cheek, remembered its softness. Sophie stared.

'So beautiful.'

Gently rescuing the photograph from her dripping tears, I returned it to the wall. A line ran through my mind, but I couldn't say it.

'She will always be beautiful,' I said instead.

'She'll never smile again.'

That line a second time. Swallowed down.

Sophie looked up at me, Nora's eyes inside her, bright with unhappiness.

'I don't think I will, either.'

'There's a chance…' I finally said it. Some of it. Not enough.

She shook her head.

There's a chance I could bring her back.

Had a fissure really grown so quickly between us? Or was it cowardice? Maybe I'm better than that. Couldn't bring myself to give hope, where it might be false. I didn't know, did I?

Didn't know the odds. Didn't know how to say, at the end of a life together, who I was.

Couldn't ask her to help. Or wouldn't. Couldn't ask her permission. Or shouldn't.

Sometimes a secret has to be your own, even if it means you have to go back to being alone. Forever.

My birth right was all I had left, and for the first time in a lifetime it felt like it might have been a bequest, not a burden. A chance to make our family whole again.

But first, I needed Nora's ashes. And given I still couldn't tell Sophie why, and given a pyre at the funeral was off the cards, what choice did I have, in the red light of day?

I had to steal our baby.

The Circle of Life

It should have been simple, you're thinking. Breaking and entering is hardly a challenge when you have the key. Still less when you're already in. Just leaving one room, passing into another. But when tension burns at every nerve then even your own home can become an obstacle course, cluttered with odd shoes and trailing lianas of wiring. A hallway becomes a minefield of creaking floorboards.

Sophie was always a soft sleeper. Holding my breath couldn't stop my heart from stampeding as I snuck out from the sheets. She lay between them, wrapped and rocking, unable to evade darkness even in dreams. Eyelids flicking, lips mouthing. Limbs sliding, searching for missing loves and lives.

Slipping into shorts and a shirt, I padded through an unlit world of soft-furnishings and sharp edges, skirting beside bedside tables, dodging doorframes, careful not to go through the looking glass. I found an old travelling knapsack wedged not too deeply in the cupboard under the stairs, brushed off a few hitchhiking spiders and began to fill it, almost at random.

It couldn't have been done any earlier in case Sophie found it. It wouldn't have been possible to explain. There was no list for the same reason. I'd almost started one, before I imagined her discovering it.

Blankets, milk, chewable book… It would have been explicable to that point as historical, but if she kept reading, …*cigarette lighter, sharp knife, flasks for blood and ash…* she might have had questions. Obviously I'm being facetious, but you see why I was cautious.

Also, I'm just bad at forward planning. I stuffed in a bottle of formula, hoping it hadn't expired, a stuffed toy, and a holey blanket that ought to have been retired but which Sophie had kept for the scent. The flask we used for camping was in a kitchen cupboard, while in a laundry basket lay Nora's most recent clothes. Pointless to tidy, impossible to abandon, they existed in a neatly-folded limbo. I grabbed a vest and sleepsuit and bundled them in with my swag.

Three or four other items followed. I knew there were things I'd forgotten, but clean thinking is for people who aren't about to abduct a dead child. Hopeful fumbling was the best I could manage.

I did remember these pages. Electronically. The tablet was light enough to lug along. That plan had formed alongside the more vital one, in the days between death and departure. Though unready or unable to unfold the untold story, it was obvious even to me that if this worked I wouldn't be able to put it off any longer.

And if it didn't… well, that wasn't an outcome I could dwell on, not without a leaden lump blocking my throat, pulling me down into circles even Dante had left unexplored. But I guessed I'd still owe her an explanation. Or an apology. Pushing that thought back into its metaphorical closet, I soft-socked back up the stairs. Back to the nursery, to our future.

We kept her in the house, the night before we were due to say our final farewell. It sounded horrible and macabre when Sophie first thought of it, but she insisted on having Nora close to her, for as long as could be.

'I don't want her in that place,' – the funeral parlour – 'all alone without us.'

Though as ever my instinct was to give her whatever I could, my worry was this would hurt her more than she could see. Not that it mattered, it would have taken more than I had to oppose her. I had to make my peace with the short-lived nursery becoming a short-term chapel of unrest.

Only when I thought of the theft did I see an upside. Kidnapping Nora from home had to be preferable to busting into a morgue.

Sophie had wanted to sleep in the same room, and while it would be anatomically incorrect to hint that I put my foot down, or developed any kind of spine, I did manage to wheedle her away from that.

'I just want to be with her.'

'But sweetheart, if she's in her room, it's like it was, maybe that's how it should be. Our last night as a family, remembering how it was. How it should be.'

Insubstantial waffle to be sure, but maybe she was tired enough, or careless enough, or just guessed I wanted what was best. Which I did. In my own monstrous way.

For someone so au fait with death, I've had very little to do with coffins. I suppose because they're ultimately a storage unit, one I never planned on needing. I never realised how horrible they really were. A box for a corpse to rot away in. No offence, undertakers, I know you're trying to do your best within some pretty grim parameters, but that's just the worst thing in the world, however you dress it up.

For Nora we gave a wide berth to pink, rainbows and butterflies. God knows I'm not judging anyone who makes their choice. You've got to get through that horror however you can, up to and including invoking a deity, if that's your jam. For me, making funeral arrangements for a baby was the final and irrevocable proof that there was no guiding hand, at least no loving one. But, as always, other opinions are available.

Same with the container. I get that it might be a comfort to some, to search for something their little one would have liked, wood they would be happy in. Something pretty, like you'd find in the creepiest doll's house ever. The sucker with Nora was that she hadn't even been old enough to know what she wanted. For all we knew she'd have grown to hate mermaids and fairies. We went plain, classy, white. Innocence and simplicity. And it wasn't what you'd call coffin shaped. More like a miniature chest, for a treasure or a keepsake. The gravest of family heirlooms.

The saddest thing of all was the size. I could lift it

myself. You don't need pall bearers when you're not even one.

The lid eased open. There were no nails, nothing but a fragile clasp. It's not like they were expecting anybody to try and get in. Or out.

She lay still, of course. White, soft, still pretty, not pallid. I've seen enough of death to last me a lifetime. Living death, dying, screaming for an afterlife. Nora didn't look like that. She looked calm.

She wore a yellow sundress, cream tights and tiny shoes with sunflower toes. I couldn't remember seeing them before. She had never needed them. Never walked.

Winnie-the-Pooh was embroidered, pondering on her pocket. Her own ted cuddled against her arm. So she would never be alone.

What hair she had was clipped neatly to her scalp. Rose-pink eyelids rested closed. Her mouth a line, turned up in the faintest smile, an internal, eternal dream.

None of the dead words applied. Not pasty, not waxy or wan. I know it was make-up, blusher not blood, but her face was firm and vital.

Peaceful.

I stole her.

There was no guilt, not at first. Only a sort of manic elation. She was in my arms again, the feel of her real against me, and the very weight of her filled me with a powerful sense of protective righteousness. Nothing could be wrong, if I was doing it for her. I was her father, holding her up.

My initial thought was to head for the park, the dark, the covering of shadow. A place familiar from our play, a comfort, but practical too. Fire needs fuel and kindling, and what better place for that than a landscape strewn with sticks and stalks?

The problem? That was four miles away. The decision to live outside of town was biting back, hard. Four miles, under physical duress. Seven thousand steps. Uneven country lanes, unpleasant gradients, and the ever-present fear of being found out.

And once again, I'd under planned. Leaving the pram had seemed like sense. Releasing it would have made a risky, rickety racket, and in any case, there was no way I could chance an encounter with it.

Sure, to the casual observer we'd have been a father and a sleeping child, out on some perfectly explicable late-night errand. Small towns talk though, and villages positively gabble. However hard I'd tried to keep myself and my family to myself, this was a road we'd trundled down a hundred times and more, before, when bound for town. Not a safe place.

I couldn't even carry her in a normal way. Had to hold her, awkward but less visible, in a blanketed bundle under my arm. Before I'd gone a quarter of the way my muscles were burning. It felt like a worthy pain, a nothing-worthwhile-is-easy pain. Still, I knew I'd never make it.

Only then did I see the madness of trying. Why seek a park for shelter and tinder? I was surrounded by both. No doubt Vlad would have had a theory. The magnetic magic of a place, perhaps. Personally, I'd guess the impact of stress and fear were bigger factors, but then, maybe I'm not clear-headed enough to judge, even now.

My gait slowed as I searched for sanctuary. Unlit by streetlights, the way ran along through hedgerow and farmland. It was still too open to stop. But I knew soon, approaching the outer reaches of the town, amid a clutterment of small shops and big houses, a chance would come to turn aside.

There's only really one road out of Whitby, or into it, in any given direction. But where I was going, I didn't need roads.

I crossed the river, hopped over a stile, and into the trees.

The copse between Ruswarp and Whitby actually contains a paved path, although the stones are worn and green enough to feel like something more natural. It's secluded at any time, and certainly at night. I didn't have to crawl far to feel concealed. Veiled from the footway I found an enclave among the holly bushes, protected by thickets of twigs and thorns, lush with the scent of damp and sap. The dry surface earth was undisturbed by any wind or squall, safe beneath eaves of leaves, a verdure tent. A good place for evil. With good intent.

Here, at the close, when it came down to the dirty work, I realised with a sick, sinking sensation that I didn't know what I was doing. I'd been so fixated on taking, escaping, I hadn't thought about what came after. I'd never been able to do this for myself, never been forced to do it for my father.

But I had seen him burn.

The first task was fire. Placing Nora down with infinite care, I shrugged off the backpack and rooted for the lighter. Sweating and shaking, my thumb rolled without traction across the flint wheel. Unbidden I heard Vlad again, pondering how long this had all been going on, how long my kind had been conjuring sparks to persist. Picturing cavemen smashing ignition from rocks, naked natives rubbing two together, I somehow summoned a successful flame and dipped it into a nest of grass and bracken.

In very little time the fire burned blistering hot. Since it certainly wasn't down to my skill, I could only guess someone was looking out for me. A common or guardian angel, perhaps with wings of flickering gold. That was fine with me, I needed all the help I could get.

There would be smoke, and stench, and no way to hide them, though privacy afforded some protection, and at least the Yorkshire skies would absorb the grisly fumes into accepting cloud.

It was time, and I knew it, but my fingers were stricken by the horror of what had to be done.

Gamely, all gritted teeth and girded loins, I forged on. Unwrapped the blanket, undressed my little girl, taking it minute by minute, movement by movement. Until it came to the final moment. The time to burn her. There my arms gave out, my will gave in, and I fell and lay still.

Enough with heroic language. Stopping meant giving up. Failure. Failing her.

It's bearable being poor, so long as you've never been rich. That's one school of thought, at least. Having never had much in the way of two bits to rub together, I'm no authority. But that's okay, because it was an analogy. Or maybe something even simpler than that. You can be rich in currencies other than cash, am I right?

Hope and momentum, adrenaline and a downhill path. Since slinking out of bed, all had combined to drive me on, even stimulate or simulate a frenzied buzz. But the glow had faded, and the low now rivalled the high in weight of impact.

Lying flat on my back, every breath was a ragged tremor. My eyes had closed, and there was no strength in me to reopen them.

'Help me,' I said aloud, to nobody, to the world around me. The trees, the fire, the wind, the skies. To Nora, to the stars, to my mum, to heaven.

But there was only me. Not even Sophie, now, and no going back to her.

The fire spat at me, singed the skin above my wrist. Reality slapped me in the face. If there was no going back, the only way was onward. In a desperate rush to regain the impetus of energy I wrapped my daughter up in my arms, kissed her, held her for the shortest time I could bare to, and then thrust her, her perfect form, shoved her, my darling princess, buried her into flame and fire.

The smell hit me. I had to turn, to be sick. Even as my retches heaved and hurt my chest, the sounds, the horrible sounds screamed a tuneless barrage into my ears. Curling in on myself I hid from my senses, tried to block out the living hell of what I had done.

For the longest time I buried myself there, made a cocoon of my body and hid. But I couldn't shut out the sizzles and spatters, or save my throat from the smoke, or my nostrils from the horrible, nauseating thought of cooking meat.

There was nothing to do but endure, to dream of waking, all the while knowing this wasn't a nightmare. Fighting against the horror, I pushed into the past. Searched for solace in remembered words and faces. It was fruitless. Somehow in Sophie, all I could picture was judgement. In Nora, nothing but innocence, melting away. Even in my mum the best I could find was a world-weary sadness.

Distraught, I rejected conscious thought. Held my breath and counted as high as I could, until light-headedness made me forgetful, then heaved down a lungful and began again. Drowning my mind in the only way I knew how.

But drowning, a world apart from fire, still brought me back to death. Bodies of water, bodies and water… so indissolubly linked. Ali and me, in the Windrush. Vlad's knife by the Black Sea. The big fish off the Gold Coast.

Thoughts that made me cough and gasp, and grope again for air and comfort. Thoughts that flickered with the flames, as they carried out their destructive tasks. Grim thoughts, but less painful than reality.

Somewhere in the midst of it all, Sophie must have woken. Somewhere in my pocket, my phone vibrated for the first time that night. I never even noticed it to ignore, so at least I was spared that layer of shame. It was the first time since we'd met that I was oblivious to her. But it was only later that I thought of that. Thought of her fear, panic, her impossible loneliness. Then I felt guilt. More guilt. More weight for my own weak shoulders. More darkness in a never-ending night.

Yet at last time passed, and the work was done, and there was only dust and ash. A couple of pounds of death, as some idiot once wrote, give or take a gram. Little enough to filter into a flask.

It ended, though my hands shook for a long time after, and my mind trembled too. It ended. The worst, I had to hope, was done. All I needed now was blood.

Again, I hadn't planned for it. But I knew, there must be a million ways to get blood.

Part 7

We Can Reflect

Twenty-eight Hours Later

Last night was a long night. Perhaps the longest. But today has been a longer day. Long and hot. Is that too much use of the L word? Can I brazen it out as style? I'm too tired to care anymore. Maybe it's time to drop the pretence that this is creative writing anyway.

It's been a hot day, hatefully hot. Not that I've seen much of it, buried beneath a church of all places. Unable to appear under the sun. Light has not existed in my narrow reality. Still the heat has penetrated. A stifling sensation growing in the darkness, breeding discomfort. No, not discomfort. That's not the right word at all. Is unravelling prose a suitable synonym for a life that's reached the end of its rope? Because this is more than discomfort. It's not that I'm hurting, hamstrung by hunger and claustrophobia. Not that I'm sick of slinking out of sight, a mournful black hound, padding around a cell, sweat prickling through a three-quarters-beard and unwashed clothes. It's that for too long I've been hanging by a frayed thread, and now there's nothing left for me to do about it but wait. Wait and hope.

And reflect.

Vampires are famously bad at that, of course. Reflection. Can't do it. A good life, in contrast, requires it. A good novel too, in all probability. Then again, I'm not a vampire. And I don't think I'd claim to have lived many good lives. As for a good book… well, like I said. The time has come to reveal another truth. This was never supposed to be that. It's just me. Who I am. Who I have been.

Son. Drifter. Waster. Partner. Friend. Seeker. Finder. Loser. Lover. Father.

Saviour.

Ha! Yes, what a hero.

Too frightened even to come home, though a strong part of me wants to. Or a weak part. It's natural to want to share my fears, isn't it? To halve them? I wanted to, you know. I wanted to right from the start.

Longed to be open with you, Sophie. To labour again together. To hold hands and take baby steps, to find a bowl, something plain and clean and shallow, a receptacle for blood and ash. An anti-grave from which to grow new hope.

So easy to picture, sharing semi-shy sidelong glances, ribbons of confidence rippling between us. To imagine drawing out snug blankets, feeling smugly prepared.

The reality, the weirdness, stolen corpses and borrowed blood, that has all come about through a monstrous life

392

of wrongdoing and wrong turnings. Returning to you, making a bed for our baby, that would be human.

But life isn't fiction.

It hasn't been possible to return. Not so soon. What if it went badly? If I reappeared telling tales of alchemy and reincarnation, only to mix an inert mess in our kitchen? You would have thought I was mad, had me locked away. And you would have lost everything, all over again.

And the same applies now. Talk of sharing troubles misses the point. Doling out a portion of this problem would simply be selfish. My fears must remain my own.

Mine alone.

And I'm sick of this now, to be honest. Writing it down, bringing it up again. What a way to spend my final hours. Poring over my old lives, my own mishaps and mistakes. True, there have been a lot of them, enough to fill the time. But the hours remain stretched and thin. Perhaps there's only a few who have really seen how weak and watered-down time can render you. If so, I'm one of them.

Maybe that's why I'm no good, any more, at being alone. Which is rough. I always assumed I was a loner, a recluse trapped in a series of social circumstances. It's no secret I never enjoyed living with my dad, but even with Mum, was I really there because I wanted to be? Christ, there's not much I wouldn't trade now, to have her back, even if only for a proper goodbye. But at the time I was just another kid, battling full-nest syndrome.

Then there was my friendship of convenience with Vlad, which often felt more like an obligation. He was supposed to be there to enable me to live. Somehow that seemed to get lost in the situation.

Perhaps I always hankered to be a pack-wolf. Possibly I evolved, or you made me grow up. Either way, time spent in my own company bears the pall of slow torture. Aside from a furtive hour rolling down a barrel, locating paraffin and paraphernalia, I've been trapped here all day. All day I have sat in silence save for the soft clacking of these keys as I type. Type and delete, one sentence forward, two words back, trying to set it all down right. Knowing the end of the final page is approaching. The end of it all. But I just want it done now, and to hell with pretty paragraphs.

A lot of it has simply been editing. Going over the manuscript I wrote before life fell apart. Inserting truths, chewing off sugar coating. That's been okay. This last part, the new part, has been the hardest.

Because I just don't want to talk about last night. How horrible it was. Sorry to the writing fraternity, I'm just not going there.

'You can't have a vampire novel without shedding some blood,' my writing tutor told me, once.

'You've got to show the horror.'

Well, obviously I've never shown her these passages. I'm a fugitive, wanted for body snatching and quite possibly for the murder of Vlad Precua. I can't exactly walk into a classroom and ask for feedback on my new chapter.

But I'm sure she'd say the same again. Show it.

Instead I reflect. Walk the town in my imagination, idle around memory lanes. The sea is so close, I can all but taste the salt. In my mind I meander down, past bare footprints and fallen sandcastles to the waves. Stare out over clear waters, into the east. Remember a cult I met in the west. Wonder if they searched for me? If this was a story they would have. They'd have been relentless, dogging my steps. Lurking behind shadows. They'd have found Vlad, too, maybe even slipped him something. A vile hand with a vial of powder could so easily have trickled a trick into his post-ghost walk tipple. Triggered whatever went wrong with his body or brain. An omniscient narrator would have known that, showed that... but I can't.

I can't even say what happened to my own dad. If I allow my mind to float along the sands to the harbour, I suppose I might see him there. That scene of passing ships, real and metaphorical, could be his spiritual departure lounge. If I waited for nightfall he might appear out of the darkness. His ghost might come, face set in scorn. How else would my mind conjure him, after all, but sneering? I doubt I would learn much from such an encounter. Not why he left us here, Mum and me. Not what finally broke his chokehold on us. Not where he went, or why. What he did, or where he is now, if he is anywhere at all. One day he'll run out of regenerations, or run out of acolytes. He and Kali both will. They might have already, or I might run out first. Maybe tonight. Either way, he said his goodbyes a long time ago, and I don't need a reprise.

Anyway, I'm not sure goodbyes are meant to be final. And even if they are, even if you knew in advance, that the last time would be the last time, would it make a dot of difference? I knew with Vlad, I'm sure I did. But it didn't feel any more under control.

I guess the siren didn't help. They never do, blaring, shocking shouts of sound. That's what jerked him upright from his deathbed. Coughing, spasming, sloughing makeshift bandages and slurring. In panic I ran for the window. Even as I touched it he fell back on white-red sheets, chuckling.

'You were right all along, you know.' Only Vlad could be so superior uttering such a sentence. 'You were never a vampire.'

I wasn't sure if that was an insult, or forgiveness. There was no time to unpick it.

Lifting the sash, I swung my leg out. The night air bit.

'It was the town. The place bred the myth, and I fed you into it. If you'd grown up in Haiti you'd have been called a zombie. Pop culture would style you as a superhero, clad you in spandex. The followers of Kali saw her through a filter of Hinduism.'

He paused, moistened his lips with his tongue.

'All wrong.'

Muffled noises came from the corridor. There was no time for philosophy, the clock had ticked. I had to go. Perched on the window ledge, I caught a last sight of the man I knew as Vladamir Precua.

'Give her a new name?'

I don't know why that came into my head. Maybe because he'd sort of be her godfather now, or bloodfather, or something. Maybe because he was good at fake names. Maybe because it was all I had left to offer.

Maybe because naming her would make her real again.

'It's obvious, isn't it?' he rasped, smug to the end.

Obviously it wasn't.

'It's what I've been trying to tell you,' he sighed. 'You're not a vampire, nor a zombie. Nor a god.'

'So, what?' I snapped, regret and curiosity entwined.

'Name her after a bird,' he said.

My grandmother fluttered in fields of gold behind my eyes.

The door handle turned.

'Call her Phoenix.'

I dropped out of sight.

And hit rock bottom. Recent life has had a steep trajectory. All precipitous. The hope has to be that this is the low point. Otherwise what's left to do but lay down and die? Well, maybe that's all there is anyway. But I still need to finish this.

Only, I can't. There is no momentum from my slippery slope. Time is pressing and deadlines approach, soon another door will open, and I'll have to be ready. But that gives me no impetus. It's too hard to relate any more. Too tiring. I long to stop.

The only outlet is a retreat to move forward. Resume my imaginary ghost walk, hope to find truth through a flight of fancy. A flight to the abbey perhaps? It's a natural vantage point. And a natural home for Gothic horror. Easy enough to allow my disembodied semi-sentience to ascend, to sit, albeit ethereally, where Stoker once sat. To hang like that monastic shadow over the land, seeking some way on. What better place, after all? A collage of rough-hewn rock and centuries-smoothed stone, seemingly designed to disintegrate, to become a seaside shell. A jagged, geometric silhouette squatting above all it regards. Dominating and inspiring, terrific and terrifying. Perfect inspiration for a mythical creature with no supporting myth.

It would have made sense, wouldn't it, to have gone there? Found a haven among the graves? Reckless to rush through, frantic to turn the purgatory of ignorance into knowledge, not caring whether that led to heaven or hell, I could have gone anywhere. I could have turned to the ruin.

It might even have added up. Like, if I'd believed in the example set by the lost followers of Kali. If I'd thought of this as religion.

Or if Vlad was right, and there were ceremonial niceties to placate. In that case the abbey, or the churchyard, would have been the proper place to honour his sacrifice. Once that's what he would have wanted.

Me on my knees amid the tumbledown tombstones, body a shield to keep the breeze at bay, wishing there was some way to fend off nerves the same way. Hands shaking so I could hardly hold a homemade urn, fingers buttery with dread and hope. Light-headed, heavy-hearted, tense and sweating in the cold air. Drawing my daughter from my pocket, uncorking her flask and pouring her out into a pyramid, finer than sand, darker than space.

Working quickly, edgily careful not to make haste, teeth denting my lower lip as Vlad's last gift dribbled onto the cone of cinders, thick, dark, red. The smell of it in my throat. Coating, mixing, gluing.

Then waiting, crouching in anticipation. Licking the salty tang from my lip where I'd bitten too hard. Waiting and watching.

Desperate to believe.

Desperate is the word. I can't sell it. Maybe the spirit of the truth is worth more than the letter, but if I'm going to lie my heart should be in it. And you know Vlad's paint-it-black-by-numbers playbook was never my thing. There was no supernatural incentive to be anywhere. And he couldn't even convince himself, by the end.

No, I never went near the abbey last night. Although it wasn't all about shunning scenic debris. There were practical reasons. Hoping to bring a baby back into the world, I needed somewhere safe and sheltered. Seldom do maternity wards allow the elements into the room. And however well you hide in gloomy ruins or behind tombstones, you always run the risk of prying electric eyes. Dracula never had to worry about CCTV, did he? Lucky beggar.

Whither now then? Back to reality. Back where it all must end. Back where it began, so many times before. In a cellar. Inside a church, which is ridiculous, blasphemer that I am.

Last night I found my way, stumbling in urgent need of somewhere to disappear. This portal loomed up at me in a moment of need, and what can I say? It seemed apt. In the dark and the silence it stood alone. Hidden in plain sight. After all, what other house was less likely to be occupied, in the witching hour, than a house of worship? Scouting around I found an annex, and a backdoor. Close to the shore, a wedge of sand had built up against it, so I could be sure it was not often opened. It was locked, but not sufficiently, and brushing aside a litter of spiders' webbing I pushed inside. The hallway carpet had been eaten by moths, old pictures on the walls were framed in rust and decay.

Moving inside, an innocuous door led down to an overlooked basement, a harbour for nothing but leaks, stairs cultivating mould. The only movement came from falling dust motes, making no sound, because nobody was there.

Neglect, if not abandonment, was apparent.

The ratio is wrong now, I guess. Not enough flock to sustain so many sheep pens. I'm not crowing about that; the rise and fall of Christianity is a little outside my sphere of influence, godless monster that I am. In the slow hours since, I've been grateful for the space nevertheless.

In I crept, like a crook in the night. Well, not like one, as one. Wormed my way in, to brew my elixir.

Vlad once told me the word elixir was derived from Arabic, or maybe Greek. I never really listened. A powder for drying wounds. Alchemists picked up the term as a catalyst for the Philosopher's Stone. A haste maker. They were kooks, obviously, chasing an immortality which doesn't exist. For me, though, the word seems fit.

Powder and wounds. Ash and dreams.

In a forgotten church, I mixed my compound, and prayed.

You read that right. For the first and last time in my lives, I prayed.

And since then… limbo.

Just me and my pen. Metaphorically. And like I say, long hours, so you'd think a hobby would have been a bonus. But writing isn't for pleasure, anymore. And it's sure not with hope of making a living, or getting me anywhere. Except maybe back to you.

There's no pretence any more that these words are for anyone else. You told me to write, Sophie, and I tried. I took those classes, I spewed out words. I didn't even know what it was I was working on, at the time. A creative non-fiction? A novel memoir? A confessional?

In the end, it is only for you.

At least with that mask off there's no pressure to show. No need for you to hear more than you need to know, about the blending of remains, the reversal of the natural order. The squirming, the thickening growth of raw matter into a throbbing chrysalis. The evolution of that bulbous, bloody cocoon, budding, bubbling in its soft nest of blankets. The creation of that red-rubber egg, firm but delicate, smooth and giving but uncomfortable, alien, not something to hold. The hatching...

I haven't got to write about that. I don't need to show the horror.

Because this actually isn't about horror, it's a love story.

I don't know if you want that, any more. I'd understand if you didn't. I'm awful and deceitful and literally inhuman. But I'm also selfish and wilfully blind enough to hope... and to know this is my only chance. To lay my life on the line, out in the open. Naked. A life of crime, grime. But mine. The only one I've got. If you could call it one life. Let's not go there again.

I've bared all. Now you can decide.

Because it worked, Sophie. Not prayer. At least, not to a degree that can be known, or proven. But something. Hope, or belief. Determination or determinism. Something worked. Magic worked.

Your daughter is yours again. Whole and well. And she is yours. Believe me. The same girl. Just like every identity I've ever had has still been me. However often I've had my slate smeared clean, I've always been myself. My personality, my psychology and complications. Like any animal I've grown up, shifted, changed. But unaltered in my soul. Deep down, I'm like any human, in all the ways that matter.

She's more you than me though. So much of you in her. The light inside, glittering through her eyes, her bubbling smile. The spring in her step, though yet she'll only crawl. The set of determination in her jaw, no nonsense furrows on her tiny brow when faced with a challenge. Her playfulness, and pleasure in small things. Her patience for my slowness, my sadness.

The internal warmth of her, laid against me, listening rapt to my rambling nonsense, rhyme without reason. Just like when you used to lie in my lap, your hair winding, wending through my fingers as I told you all the things I thought you wanted to hear.

She will look so much like you when she's older. Her own version of you. Bright with life. Self-possessed, stronger than me. Smarter.

But for all that, I've given her something. All that I could. A second chance.

A second life.

It's up to you now, whether she ever knows that. And whether she ever knows me.

Because this isn't a novel, it never was. Turns out it's an instruction manual. Well, that's the hopeful prognosis. But likely enough it's the world's longest suicide note.

That might seem extreme, but I just can't tell you any of this. Not to your face. I'm still certain it isn't fair to even try. So I've written it down. You'll get my side, if you can stomach it, with time to digest.

But I do want to hear your voice one last time. I threw my phone into the sea. Maybe I could just have turned it off, I don't know how they trace those things. I wasn't willing to chance it. There's a call box on the corner though, and when I reach the end, which is in plain sight, then I'll ring you. Ring you back, I mean. Better late, I hope, than never.

I know you'll try to ask questions, but I'll just tell you where to come, where to find us. And I know you'll come. Maybe with Cora, but I hope alone. You'll come to this strange, lonely place. A fitting place for hatching, and dispatching. You'll walk down those steps, or run down, scared, excited, agitated, but brave. And you'll find us.

Our little girl, bedded down in a makeshift manger of a cot. Sleeping off symptoms of a return to life. Beautiful as ever, an eternal flame. Our Phoenix.

She is yours, back for good. I know you'll love her, like you always did. Like I love her. Like I love you both.

You'll find me in a pile of ash. Safely contained in my drum, like father, like son. And if you want me back, for good or ill. Well, I suppose you will know what to do.

I love you.

Jay.

Acknowledgements

There are a number of people without whom this book would not exist (should you feel the need to blame anybody...)

My primary school teachers, for the seeds they planted. All of my teachers and tutors thereafter, particularly those who laughed.

Principally Ray French, whose belief in this project built mine.

My friends. The readers of *The Thurp Saga*. The Pub Lads. The Lads of Legend.

My MA cohort. Joe, for showing the way.

Everyone at work who allowed me the freedom to sneak off and be creative for three hours a week.

Griffin, for believing ideas are worth conceiving, or some such nonsense. Also, for some of the jokes.

In publishing, anyone who ever said 'yes' to anything I sent them; on which note:

Becoming Familiar was first published by Wild Pressed Books. Enormous, unquantifiable thanks to Tracey for the faith that she showed.

The team at the Book Guild.

Bram Stoker, for obvious reasons. The quote on p.69 is, of course, from *Dracula*.

Above all, my family.

My grandad, for so many stories.

My mum, my dad, my brothers. For showing me Narnia, and many other places. For building the Brill Box, and building my imagination. Mostly for the unconditional love, and the safe space to grow.

Stormm, for being the one.

My beautiful children are excused any of the blame alluded to above. After all, they did more than anyone to delay this. I thank them instead for showing me the true meaning of a legacy.